THE BOLTHOLE

Also by Peter Papathanasiou

The Stoning (2021)
The Invisible (2022)
The Pit (2023)

Son of Mine (Salt, 2019) – a memoir

PETER PAPATHANASIOU

THE BOLTHOLE

MACLEHOSE PRESS

QUERCUS · LONDON

First published in Great Britain in 2025 by

MacLehose Press
An imprint of Quercus Editions Limited
Carmelite House
50 Victoria Embankment
London EC4Y 0DZ

An Hachette UK company

The authorised representative in the EEA is Hachette Ireland,
8 Castlecourt Centre, Dublin 15, D15 XTP3, Ireland (email: info@hbgi.ie)

A CIP catalogue record for this book is available
from the British Library.

ISBN (TPB) 978 1 52944 307 3
ISBN (Ebook) 978 1 52944 308 0

1

Typeset by CC Book Production
Printed and bound in Great Britain by Clays Ltd, Elcograf S.p.A.

MIX
Paper | Supporting
responsible forestry
FSC® C104740

Papers used by MacLehose Press are from well-managed forests and other responsible sources.

For MS, who helped inspire this story

Chapter 1

Glancing into his rear-view mirror, Richard Marlowe adjusted his carbon-black aviator lenses, making sure they were spirit-level straight. Despite his middle age, Marlowe's face remained ruggedly handsome, his jaw angular, his hair thick and salty and peppery. A Botox smooth brow, neon white teeth. The collar on his designer polo shirt flapped recklessly in the sea breeze as he powered his sleek sports car to its horsepower maximum with a satisfied sneer. Checking the sapphire crystal face of his wristwatch, he tensed his calf muscles and pushed his boat-shoed foot to the floor.

The long sweep of coastal road stretched out before Marlowe like an infinite serpent snaking east and west. The late-autumn evening was warm, a tangerine sun sitting low over the turquoise sea and pristine white beaches. It was tourist brochure material but a closer inspection over the side of glowering limestone cliffs revealed an ocean that was saturnine and turbulent. The shark-infested Great Australian Bight bubbled with swirls and vortexes, with razor-toothed predators hunting and killing and feasting.

If the yin was the water, alive and buzzing, then the yang was the land, deadly still and blackened with the fresh scars of a megafire. It had swept through the bushland and national park at the height of summer and napalmed the landscape barren, sterilising it with thousand-degree heat. The fields were empty and ashen, dead trees rearing their gaunt and withered limbs. Flashing past like a tracer bullet, Marlowe's motor clattered a fire-blackened road sign hanging loose on its screws and seared clean of all information. Slung low to the road, the car had curves and slopes designed to minimise drag and optimise downforce, while every surface was crafted to manage airflow. In the near distance, what animals had survived the inferno moved slowly and gingerly among the skeleton trees, roos and wombats and goannas and dunnarts, their coats burnt, paws cauterised, bodies rattleboned. But amid the devastation, there were also signs of earthly regrowth, new sprouts on the trunks and branches of carbonised trees. The green shoots were normally dormant and a sign of vegetative recovery, but also deceptive epicormic buds that were toxic to starving wildlife.

Marlowe zoomed past the carnage – the skinny, dizzy creatures that wandered onto the roads and their resultant carcasses. He was seemingly oblivious to the natural world's destruction, his coruscating car catching the sun's rays to make a sharp contrast against the muted grey land. Once neat and well-trodden driveways now lay silent and led to only charred remains, to what used to be people's generational homes. Marlowe eased off when he passed a tiny, weather-beaten camper trailer parked by the roadside, but only for long enough to smash his car horn loudly and obnoxiously. In his wake, an old farmer emerged from the trailer to cough hoarsely and give a single-finger salute with each hand.

Further along the road, Marlowe's phone rang, which he answered hands-free.

"Good evening, Mister Marlowe," said a dry bureaucratic voice. "Sorry to call you so late in the day but the Minister has an extremely busy schedule."

"Of course," said Marlowe. "I understand."

"But there is good news – he's had a cancellation tomorrow morning so can meet with you at eleven."

"That's excellent, thank you. And please thank the Minister for being so accommodating. I'll be flying to the mainland in my helicopter and will be sure to arrive in good time."

"Thank you, Mister Marlowe," said the adviser. "We look forward to seeing you tomorrow."

Marlowe hung up and smiled to himself.

Arriving at his property, he drove slowly up his teardrop driveway. The landscape gardeners were still finishing up for the day and he gave them a cheery thank-you beep before accessing the secure underground garage with an electronic swipe. He ascended the half-turn staircase, his feet light on the floating floorboards, and accessed the bespoke wellness room. Taking a seat beneath the calming hues of the Himalayan salt wall, Marlowe closed his eyes and inhaled deeply, feeling its release of negative ions soothe both his allergies and stress levels.

It was a moment of pause. Of respite. Of mindfulness. Centring.

After five minutes of steady breathing, Marlowe opened his eyes listlessly and stood, his limbs a degree floppier. Perusing the wine racks, he chose a bottle of chilled rosé from the temperature-controlled cellar. The dogs had detected his presence by now and were yelping and scratching at the door.

"Evening, boys. Did you miss me? Where's Mummy?"

Banjo and Maple, his two purebred Samoyeds, greeted him exuberantly, leaping all over their owner and enticing him to roughhouse. Marlowe wrestled their sturdy frames until he was slightly breathless, the dogs still too youthful and energetic for his relative vintage. They scampered off, their soft paws slipping on the smooth walnut floors as they led the way to the rooftop balcony overlooking the Indian Ocean. They ran up to Holly and sat dutifully by her side. She was already enjoying her own glass of wine.

"Phew, just in time," she said, taking a sip. "You avoided a major catastrophe."

Marlowe pecked his wife on her flawless cheek. He opened the fresh bottle and topped up her glass before pouring his own. The wine cooled Marlowe's thoughts and warmed his toes.

"Look at that sunset," Holly said, gazing out over the water. She presented it as if trying to make a sale with commission. "Just look at it."

"You couldn't put a price on it," said Marlowe.

"Want some dinner?"

"No thank you, darling. I'm not hungry."

"You sound tired, baby. Didn't the salt help tonight? How was your day?"

"How was yours?"

She groaned. "More issues with Luigi and Juliette. I swear, they make life so difficult sometimes."

"I'll talk to them."

"I mean, we're paying *them*, right? They said the eastern wing would be finished a month ago."

"I know."

"Not to mention the budget." She gulped her wine, as if trying to put out a fire inside. "I'm sorry, darling. I must sound like a broken record every night. Tell me, how was your day?"

Marlowe sighed. "Not much better. Problems at the restaurant."

"Like what?"

"Just a bad review. Grayson blames it on me, as if I'm somehow cooking the food. And the usual financial headaches, the locals seem to be running out of patience . . ."

Holly gave him a tight hug. He inhaled her warmth and shampoo, infused with extracts of white tea and pure caviar.

"We'll work it out, baby," she said. "We always do. It's all been worth it, you know. Coming here. I could just stare at this view forever."

Marlowe finished his rosé. "Where are the kids?"

Holly stared back over the water. "Where else? Cooped up in their rooms, playing video games and scrolling aimlessly on their phones."

"They'd rather stare at a blue screen than a stunning sunset." Marlowe exhaled heavily. "What a shame. This big new house was supposed to bring us together, not drive us apart."

The dogs watched him shamble back inside.

The sleeping quarters were accessed via a long stretch of corridor that always made Marlowe feel like he was back at boarding school. Knocking gently on his son's bedroom door, Marlowe patiently awaited instructions. The room was silent, its throat dark. He was finally granted permission to enter and sit with Roland, trying to find a common frequency. Up against numerous forms of technological distraction and the raging hormones of a gloomy teenager, Marlowe was an old fogey who stood no chance. It was much the same with Allegra, two doors down, whose moods were even more prickly. Marlowe knew his twins loathed him remarrying after divorcing their mother, and were determined to remind him at every opportunity.

Dejected, disappointed, downtrodden, Marlowe returned to the living room. He poured himself a crystal snifter of aged scotch whisky on his epoxy resin bar. Designed to resemble the ocean, it was a flashy artistic feature that had shocked him at first but had since grown on him, like a bold new haircut. Taking his drink, he eased onto his Scandinavian-inspired, handcrafted sofa of hardwood and leather in the expansive living space to take in the ceaseless sea views in the hope they would fill the emptiness inside. Banjo and Maple joined him, as though for moral support. Marlowe worked a while on his laptop and phone, attempting to clear his inbox while sipping his whisky neat. The sound of waves crashing and ocean churning outside had a tranquillising effect after a long working day, causing Marlowe's eyelids to grow heavy.

The sun set in a eulogy of reds and purples, draping a shroud over the watery horizon. A dozy Marlowe found his wife and kissed her goodnight. She was in the kitchen steeping a mug of magnolia tea on the soft-green marble benchtop.

"The early bird gets the worm," he told her. "I'll make pancakes for breakfast tomorrow, maple syrup and local blueberries. And then I'm heading to the city for a meeting afterwards."

*

Marlowe woke just before dawn. Only the dogs noted his presence and preparations. Holly stirred but ultimately continued snoozing. Roland and Allegra were unlikely to rise before noon.

Changing silently into a black neoprene wetsuit and cushioned leather sandals and carrying his neon yellow surfboard, towel and phone, Marlowe headed down to the beach. It was deserted at that hour, which was precisely how he liked it. Marlowe stood a moment, taking in the liquidy colours of the new dawn sun as it cast its fledgling rays over the swashbuckling sea. There was a great calm as if Nature was in a profound repose. Marlowe breathed the fresh, salty air deep into his lungs and listened to the distant reverberations of the breaking surf washing in from the Antarctic. It was a ritual he repeated every day, and it never ceased to bring him peace, regardless of the tensions and worries raging in his busy life.

Checking the face of his black sports wristwatch, Marlowe wrapped his sandals and phone in his towel.

"What an absolutely incredible morning," he said to himself as he took to the water and vanished from sight.

Chapter 2

A range of mountains towered over the township of Cape Jervis at the western tip of the Fleurieu Peninsula. Detective Sergeant George Manolis and Senior Constable Andrew Smith watched them disappear into the distance.

"And how long's this ferry ride again, boss?" Sparrow asked.

"Nearly an hour," Manolis replied. "It's sixteen kilometres across the Backstairs Passage strait."

At dawn, the two policemen had travelled down from the state capital of Adelaide, a two-hour journey punctuated with a bland drive-thru breakfast. The wrappers remained on the floor of their sterile rental car.

"About to depart the island of Australia," Manolis had texted Emily as they boarded. "Hopefully there's no queue at customs! See you on the other side."

She hadn't replied. Manolis wondered if she understood his lame joke. She was probably just busy preparing herself for work and their son for school, drying her hair and packing a lunchbox.

Their unmarked sedan was now safely stowed in the ferry's lower decks for the crossing. The outer deck was packed with what appeared to be a mix of retiree tourists on ecotours and laid-back locals heading home. Sparrow eyed them dubiously, sizing them all up as suspects. Manolis blew on his kiosk coffee and adjusted his tinted sunglasses, taking in the big blue expanse, salt lining his nose and lungs. The channel was regularly subjected to strong currents and steep tidal swells.

"And this bloke is, what, missing? Dead?" Sparrow asked.

"He's missing," replied Manolis. "A local resident. Jesus, didn't you read the brief?"

The young Indigenous cop sighed. "Sorry, chief. I'm just distracted."

"By what?"

Sparrow didn't answer the question. "But why are *we* here for it?"

Manolis shrugged. "Porter," he said, referring to Detective Inspector Paul Bloody Porter, who had caught wind of the case Manolis had cracked undercover in Greece when he was supposed to be on holiday.

"Yair," Sparrow breathed. "This is what happens when you're too damn good at your job . . ."

"Why?" Manolis said. "What the hell did you get up to while I was away?"

Sparrow grinned cheekily. "I'll show you mine if you show me yours," he said.

"I couldn't help it," Manolis said. "A family friend was missing. He was imprisoned but I found him safe and sound."

Sparrow playfully slapped Manolis's woolly head. "Nice work, Sherlock! You only went and *found a missing man.* No wonder we're stuck on this raft bound for a rock, like a pair of exiled convicts."

Manolis was feeling a new sensation around his colleague, a conflict that stemmed from guilt. He had recently discovered what his late father, Constantinos, had done to Jimmy Dingo in their hometown of Cobb many years ago. Since then, he'd reached an uncomfortable but necessary peace with his father's memory, distancing himself from his murderous actions, and – while never condoning them – accepting that it was a different time with different motivations. What gnawed at him now was when to tell Sparrow. Or should he tell him at all . . .? The death of Dingo had been a defining moment in Cobb's history, particularly for its Indigenous community. Raising it, let alone admitting a personal connection, was not something to be done lightly.

At least Manolis now had a new cousin in his life, his late aunt's illegitimate child, half-Aboriginal, whom he had met only recently. It had been an encouraging if surreal experience, one that he was still processing.

"Right then, mate," Manolis said. "That's mine. Now you show me yours."

Sparrow admitted his "crime" while Manolis was away had been solving a cold case in outback Western Australia and locating a body buried decades ago. He had broken seemingly every investigative rule in the police handbook in the process, which is why he was so reluctant to discuss what happened.

Manolis cracked a smile, his crow's feet appearing. "Sounds like you solved a missing person's case, too."

"Ha. Then it's both our faults."

"And what did we learn, young Sparrow? Life is about learning, after all."

The constable screwed up his face as if doing advanced calculus. He finally scratched his chin and said: "I guess I learned that I've still got a lot to learn. And that life is short. What about you?"

"Much the same really . . ."

Manolis was thinking about his young son, Christos, now in primary school, wondering how long he would be away working on this latest case. Days, weeks, months . . .? This time, he also had his ex-wife, Emily, in mind.

"We're in the process of reconciling," he said.

It came after a long period of separation, which personally made him reluctant to travel on assignment for any extended period. Emily had always hated Manolis's devotion to his job and worried for his safety.

"That's pretty awesome news about your missus," said Sparrow. "I bet your little fella's stoked."

"Yeah, he's very happy to see his silly mum and dad trying to work it out."

The ill-tempered ocean rocked and pitched across the Backstairs

Passage. The ferry rolled with the punches, causing several passengers to put away their bags of nourishing trail mix and retreat inside. Manolis sipped hard on his sloshing cup of coffee; it was bitter but strong. Fish emerged from the water in leaps and spurts, which only attracted seabirds to circle above in the hope of a briny feed. Manolis found the display beguiling, even as the immense power of the vast ocean made him feel infinitesimal by comparison.

"So, what about this missing bloke, then?" Sparrow asked. "This new case?"

Manolis peered into the distance, searching for their final destination, the tiny land mass at the entrance of the Gulf St Vincent. The triangular inlet was one of two sharp incisor bites that had been ripped from the southern Australian coastline.

"Sarge . . .?"

"Huh?" Manolis said. "Sorry, wasn't listening."

"Now who's distracted? This bloke who's gone missing – who is he, what do you know about him?"

Manolis scratched the base of his neck, as if it would help him dredge up the details from the police brief.

"His name's Richard Marlowe. Early sixties, husband, father, businessman. Last seen going for an early morning swim at a beach near his home."

"Shark attack," Sparrow said instantly. "Did they really call us out here for that . . .? Jesus Christ. What are we supposed to do? Arrest the shark as guilty of being a shark and doing shark things?"

"How are your tracking skills in the water, mate?" Manolis asked.

"Laser sharp," Sparrow replied.

The young cop went quiet, his eyes fixed on the water, his gut emptied of its outburst. Manolis considered his colleague. Relative to Manolis, Sparrow was still new to the business. Manolis sat easy in his seat, his eyes and mouth relaxed with age and confidence, while Sparrow appeared jittery, his words impulsive, gaze uncertain, lips bitten raw with worry.

Hoping to change the subject, Manolis retrieved a tourist brochure from his back pocket that he'd collected from the departure terminal before boarding.

"Kangaroo Island was named by British navigator and cartographer Matthew Flinders," he read. "Commanding the HMS *Investigator* in 1802, he approached the island's eastern shore at Nepean Bay. As they rowed in towards the beach, they noticed a mob of about thirty kangaroos feeding in the thick scrub."

"Fucken roos," Sparrow grizzled. "Like cockroaches, they'll survive a nuclear blast."

Manolis ignored him, read on.

"Flinders and his party killed the kangaroos, shooting them with guns or knocking them on the head with clubs. He noted how incredibly tame the kangaroos were and compared their timidity to flocks of sheep or herds of wild deer, saying they looked him in the eye as he killed them."

Sparrow showed white teeth in a contented smile. "What a yarn," he said. "I love a happy ending."

"To the east of the Backstairs Passage there's a pair of rugged islets called the Pages," Manolis said. "Flinders thought they looked like pages guarding the strait."

Sparrow looked to his left, squinted. "Oh yeah," he said. "I think I see 'em."

"They're uninhabited," said Manolis. "Flinders was also struck by the absence of people on the island, which perhaps explained why the kangaroos were so tame. The sailors skinned and cleaned the carcasses and had a hearty feast of thick steaks and rich soups. Flinders was so grateful for the meal the kangaroos had provided he decided to name the island in their honour."

Manolis looked up at Sparrow, an expression of shock and disappointment on his face. "It's pretty grotesque when you think about it," the detective said. "To name an island after a mass slaughter."

Sparrow scoffed a laugh. "Mass slaughter of roos, eh," he said. "Yair, how tragic." His tone was insouciant.

"Mate . . ."

"Look, I know that sounds heartless," Sparrow said. "And sorry. But deep down, this is pretty much the last place on earth I want to be right now . . ."

With a deep exhalation, Sparrow finally began to explain his dark mood. He admitted that he had almost refused to accept the assignment because of the history of mistreatment of Indigenous Australians on the island. This included brutal abductions of women away from their families on the mainland and the island of Tasmania – Van Diemen's Land – during the early nineteenth century. At the time, stealing Aboriginal women wasn't considered a crime – it was considered a pastime.

"My aunty was one of those women," Sparrow said with an air of angry resignation. "They stole her body and then changed her name."

Sparrow described how one of his ancestors whom he called his "aunty" was stolen from mainland Australia to help the island's first arrivals from England learn how to survive in the harsh island environment.

"Those Pommy scumbags would've otherwise died of malnutrition or disease, forced to live off unidentifiable watery slop. Women like my aunty taught them bushcraft and hunting skills. They showed the men how to cure skins, set wallaby traps, and catch possums. They found mutton bird eggs, dived for crayfish, and built shelters. They could identify food sources in the dry and empty land, and not get lost in the thick scrub. The women were often traded for packs of dogs or gallons of rum or bags of flour. They were sometimes even stolen from other settlers, most of whom had multiple wives like some kind of harem owner."

The ferry swayed, buffeted by the relentless waves. Sparrow clasped a handrail tightly and began to recount stories of his ancestors attempting to escape the island, trying to swim back to their homes on the mainland across the Backstairs Passage.

"They were that fucking desperate," he said. "Some of them even carried children on their backs. Can you imagine, trying to swim in a violent ocean with another person clinging to your back . . .?"

"I can't, no," said Manolis.

"I can barely stay afloat in a kiddie pool with a swim vest," Sparrow said. "It's no surprise that most of the women drowned or were eaten by sharks. It was a death sentence, and it was the same when their husbands – my uncles – tried to swim to the island from the mainland to rescue them. So, you'll excuse me if I don't shed a tear when I hear that a rich whitefella went for a relaxing morning swim in the same body of water and was never seen again."

Sparrow was getting increasingly agitated and louder as he spoke. Overhearing his stories, the ferry's other passengers soon all went inside, seemingly uncomfortable with what he was describing.

"Mate," said Manolis. "Sorry, I had no idea."

"That's just blackfella history all over," Sparrow breathed. "Forgotten by the white man, erased. Not your fault, but here we bloody are."

Hearing Sparrow say that made Manolis recall his father and what happened to Jimmy Dingo. He'd need to tread very carefully.

"Did your aunty die trying to escape the island?" Manolis asked.

Unexpectedly, the lines on Sparrow's face softened. "She was lucky, she managed to escape by stowing away on a boat. Meanwhile, women who fell pregnant often killed the half-caste kids."

"Holy shit."

"My People believe they were only following orders, small children were a hindrance to hard work."

At other times, women who tried to escape were hung from trees and beaten with ropes. They then had the fatty flesh cut from their thighs, cheeks and buttocks with broad sealing knives. They had their ears cropped, which was a legal penalty in Christian England. Manolis struggled to process such medieval torture.

"To this day, my mob, and my People, haven't forgotten such treatment," Sparrow said.

"How could you forget it, even if you tried . . .?" Manolis was shocked but in no way surprised. "Look, I'm not defending what those men did, but those were wildly different times. It was a world unrecognisable today. And things are changing now."

"Are they? Are they really?" Sparrow was circumspect, guarded.

"Mate, to be honest, it's hard for me to apologise for what those heartless fuckers did to your People. I can relate more to you than to them – my migrant family were considered outsiders as well."

"That may be true, mate. But it was hardly the same. And you still benefitted from what happened to my ancestors."

Manolis returned his gaze to the choppy water. Of course, Sparrow was right. Personally, Manolis might not feel the same white guilt as many Anglo-Australians, but his parents had certainly enjoyed the opportunities that came from generations of Indigenous genocide. They arrived from Greece, bought a house, ran a business, gave their only son an education, and young Manolis had been oblivious to it all bubbling away in the background. The deaths of First Australians went without investigation, their social plight was ignored, their protests fell on deaf ears. And now, there was his father and the murder of Jimmy Dingo, which really did make things personal. Sparrow's perspective was confrontational, but also honest. Manolis vowed that his own son would grow up with a keen awareness of Australian history, though he still wasn't sure how he'd broach the subject of his *papou*'s criminal past.

"Anyway, long before all that happened, around four thousand years ago, my people disappeared from this fucking island altogether," Sparrow went on. "Just vanished like this Marlowe bloke apparently has. Don't you find that strange? When the colonisers finally turned up, the island was nothing more than a huge game reserve."

"Plenty of roos," said Manolis.

"But no blackfellas," said Sparrow. "That's why the mobs in this part of the country describe Kangaroo Island as the land of the dead. The spirits are led across the water to rest on the island. And when you combine that with what the British settlers did, it makes me feel like I'm visiting a mass grave."

Manolis wondered how his young colleague might fare on the investigation. Would Sparrow be in a frame of mind to fully focus on the case? Or would he be even more focused if he were somehow able to see and hear things in the fourth dimension that Manolis could not . . .? But what if those sensations only served to distract Sparrow if he continued to sense the island's sorrow and loss? It didn't fill Manolis with much confidence and brought about his own reluctance to set foot on the oncoming rock as well.

The island's headland was visible now and getting closer every second. But it was appearing and disappearing on the horizon in a rush as the waves bounced the ferry around. Racing across the water, the rolling waves smashed into each other like the boom of artillery, while the air howled with blasts of hot wind. The massive swells and mighty squalls were a world away from the hot and dry outback that most people recognised as quintessentially Australian. But theirs was also the island continent, vast and variable, wild and woolly, with tens of thousands of kilometres of rugged and precipitous coastline. Given the country's hostile terrain inland, it only made sense that its surrounding waters would be equally fierce and feverish.

Manolis looked across at his colleague – Sparrow's face suddenly appeared drained of all colour. He was no longer vocal, his head rolling to and fro with the motion of the waves. Now reclined limply to one side, he was seemingly nearer to death than life as they approached the island of the dead.

"Shall we go inside?" Manolis suggested. "The motion may be gentler in there."

"Fresh air is better," Sparrow insisted. "I'm a landlubber. That was another reason for not wanting to take this bloody case."

"I think you just need to harness your inner chicken," Manolis said.

Sparrow pulled a face. "What's that mean?" he asked.

"Ever seen a chicken run around . . .? Their bodies move like crazy, but their heads sit still, only bobbing lightly to stabilise their vision. Just try to move your body in sync with the boat, keep your head as still as you can."

The senior sergeant demonstrated, moving his torso and arms in an exaggerated, comical motion, with jerky movements back and forth, up and down. It came across as completely awkward, but was also an attempt to lighten the mood in the hope it buoyed the young cop's spirits.

"I may be a sparrow," Sparrow said. "But I'm no chicken."

"Then try to think of something more pleasant," Manolis said. "All these horrible stories from the past only make you feel worse right now."

Sparrow thought a moment. "There's apparently sandboarding on the island," he said weakly. "That'd be cool to try . . ."

"Mate, if it's any consolation, I don't really want to be here right now either," Manolis said. "I'd rather be home with Emily, things still aren't properly settled between us. So, let's try and wrap up this case ASAP for both our sakes."

The great wall of coastline continued to rise and fall with the ferry's undulations as if it were somehow sucking the vessel into its grasp. It was an inauspicious start to a new case with neither cop really wanting to be there, and one feeling sick to his stomach and traumatised in his mind.

The ferry finally docked at Penneshaw, a tiny seaside hamlet with modest cottages and beach shacks, a general shop and folk museum, and that staple of all Australian towns and life – a well-stocked pub. Stepping again onto dry, stable land, Manolis felt his feet tingle with a strange electricity, while Sparrow remained queasy and pale.

The detective checked his phone – he wanted to either text Emily and say he'd arrived safely or see if she'd replied. But there was no reception. An unpromising start alright.

A young man in a powder-blue shirt and black cargo shorts met the new arrivals warmly, extending firm handshakes. His hair was thick and black, his eyes and smile luminous.

"My name's Noah," he said. "Noah Volavola. Local constable and general dogsbody. Thanks for coming. Welcome to Kangaroo Island. I'm based out of Kingscote. You blokes hungry, thirsty?"

Before either could reply, he added:

"Let's go to the pub and debrief. My shout."

Chapter 3

The pub was heaving with a thirsty lunchtime crowd of locals and tourists. They sat at opposing ends in their various cliques, like rival fans in a football stadium. Instead of a handrail, Sparrow now clasped the cool waist of a schooner glass to calm his senses. Noah had his own cylinder of domestic ale to slake his thirst, while Manolis stuck to iced water, his glass catching the noonday light to glisten like quartz crystal.

"The police station is undergoing repairs," Noah explained. "The roof was badly damaged in the recent fires by falling trees and flying embers. There's builders on site today, hopefully completing the work. It took them ages to get around to us."

Manolis examined the drinks menu – it featured beer, spirits and aerated waters, but also cocktails like Fluffy Ducks, Gin Slings and Brandy Alexanders. He also admired the pub's odd combination of incongruous furniture, gaudy lighting, worn carpeting, and local sporting memorabilia plastered on the walls. But what was perhaps the most impressive feature was the four-metre-long fibreglass shark mounted above the front bar, jaws open.

"That's a replica, a reproduction mount," said Noah. "Traditional taxidermy apparently doesn't work for sharks because of the high water content in their tissue."

"Replica of what?" Manolis asked.

"A tiger shark once captured offshore," Noah said. "There was a hungry group feeding on a dead southern right whale. And that was the smallest one they caught."

The three police sat in a secluded corner, away from the throng, where they could talk with a modicum of privacy. Manolis felt slightly uncertain in this new environment but went along with Noah's small-town ease. Sparrow was simply grateful for a steady floor beneath his feet.

"I've worked Homicide a long time and my experience tells me the most likely suspects are those close to the victim," Manolis said. He wanted to get on the front foot early and propose a theory.

Noah wiped a speck of foam from his top lip. "Holly, his wife, remains a person of interest," he said. "So far, she's been cooperative with our enquiries."

"That's encouraging," Manolis said. "Have any of Marlowe's family or associates been in any recent trouble with the law?"

"Not to my knowledge," Noah replied.

Sparrow let rip a sly burp of approval. "I gotta ask though, mate," he said to Noah. "My colleague and I, well, we're both still not quite sure why we're even fucken here. Though I do rate the local drop."

Manolis nodded. "No body's been found, and from what I gather, there's no evidence of foul play."

"It's all got to do with Marlowe's background," Noah said. "He's got clout, influence, a profile—"

"Oh," Sparrow interrupted. "You mean he's loaded."

Noah chuckled. "Marlowe's flush, no question. But I imagine you being here is more for us local police, to avoid liability if it ends up being a murder and we're accused of not having investigated properly."

"So, we're an insurance policy," said Manolis, his tone flat.

"Or the fall guys," said Sparrow. "Perfect."

The mutton-chopped publican appeared behind Manolis's shoulder, which took him by surprise. Noah seemed unperturbed and introduced him simply as Nails.

"A nickname from his footy days," he explained. "Every time he played, he was hard as nails."

Nails grinned proudly at the mention of his sporting prowess. "Aw, don't let Noah fool you, he was a footy star, too," he said. "He once won a grand final with a goal on the siren. Instant local hero, free beer for life."

Husky in stature and sweaty in presentation, the humble publican was a twitchy chap with fur in his ears and bushy eyebrows. With a raspy cough into his hand, Nails admitted that he was from one of the oldest families on the island, tracing its lineage back to its very first settlement.

"Gimme any surname and I can ring up a five-generation genealogy lickety-split," Nails said cockily.

"Smith," said Sparrow.

"Very funny," said Nails.

"That's my name," Sparrow said.

Nails scrunched his red-veined nose, seemingly broken in several places.

"Volavola," said Manolis.

"Well, Noah's a more recent arrival," said Nails.

The local cop nodded. "My family's originally from Fiji, which influenced my parents' choice of Kangaroo Island as our new home – and reduced the culture shock. Mum always said that islands hold a certain charm."

"They certainly have character," said Manolis.

"But it was still hard when we first arrived because we weren't really accepted by the locals," said Noah. "Things slowly changed when people realised we were here to stay, that we were Islanders just like them. Becoming a cop also made a difference. I feel at home here now, a part of the community. And I must admit, the grand final win only helped."

Sparrow, whose overall colour was slowly returning, highlighted similarities in his own background. "And can you imagine how humiliating that would feel in *your own country* . . .?"

As if sensing the awkwardness, Nails's phone rang. He swiftly answered and wandered off, mumbling into its iridescent glow. Manolis's own phone now had reception but still no messages from Emily.

Watching the publican go, Noah explained that the Islanders had generally been very resistant to change and to the incursion of newcomers onto the fortress that was "their rock", as they put it.

"For generations, the Islanders have been self-sufficient and socially independent, viewing themselves and their society as different and distinct from mainlanders," he said. "It came from their history, from the penal colonies of Tasmania and New South Wales. They also developed separately from South Australia, which came later."

"Did they ever reach the point of wanting to secede?" Manolis asked speculatively.

"I reckon they were only ever a heartbeat away," Noah said. "It's not so much of an issue now but I know there's some Islanders who've *never* been to the mainland their entire lives."

"Well, securing a passport *is* a hassle," said Sparrow facetiously.

"Historically, there are two kinds of Islanders," said Noah. "The first are 'the locals' who live on the island, people like me who've only been here a relatively short time. And the second are 'the *local* locals' who have *always* lived on the island. People like Nails. The *local* locals are a more difficult nut to crack. They're intimidating. They speak a different language to the rest of us – the language of memory, from their collective experience of rituals, place names, families, and stories born from generations of owning land."

"Sounds more and more like Ye Olde England," said Sparrow.

"My wife and I now own a house, but we still feel like renters around here," Noah said. "When you cross the water, it's like you're getting away from it all. The island is a hidden secret, and frankly, the locals prefer it that way. They're free from the daily annoyances of the mainland – smog, traffic, crime, parking meters, bureaucracy."

"That might explain why the ferry fare was so pricey," Manolis said.

"Another thing the locals appreciate," said Noah. "A couple of hundred bucks for a return ticket keeps out the riff-raff, the young backpackers and tourists who couldn't afford the journey. The Backstairs Passage is apparently the most expensive ferry crossing per kilometre in the world."

"A higher class of sea sickness," said Sparrow. "Gold-plated vomit."

Manolis sipped his water reflectively. What he was hearing was certainly something he'd expect from a smaller, more cloistered settlement that didn't welcome the intrusion of outsiders. The island's isolation and geography intensified feelings of community, but it sounded more extreme than he'd anticipated.

"The island's history is dominated by only six or seven big families, land-owning families, who exclusively married other land-owning families," Noah said. "The same surnames were constantly recycled."

"Ye Olde England," Sparrow repeated.

"Land was everything," Noah said. "Still is. And on such a small island, there's only so much of it to go around. Of course, land has financial worth in and of itself. But more importantly, it allows you to marry into the right families, and maintain and grow wealth for future generations."

Noah described how everyday life on Kangaroo Island had been very stable and predictable for decades. In more recent times, the island enjoyed a thriving tourist industry and a brisk trade in specialist produce from both the land and sea. Local honey, cheese, wine and seafood. The mainlanders paid top dollar for the freshest, most organic and sustainable grub and grog.

"But all that started to change when some even newer arrivals came," Noah said gravely. "That took things up a notch."

"Even newer arrivals?" Sparrow asked. "Who's this . . .? Africans? Eskimos? Martians?"

The mention of outsiders and small communities stirred sour memories in Manolis of his birthplace of Cobb and how their immigration detention centre had changed the town – mainly for the worse – thanks to its draconian practices and unfettered incompetence. But the more Noah talked, the more Manolis realised the situation was actually very different.

"It all began innocently enough," the local cop said. "A small real estate ad in the local rag, and online as well. Followed by the sale of a large expanse of beachfront land on the island's southern coastline near Vivonne Bay that had been in one family for generations. *Local* locals, as I explained. The land was bought for a modest price by an affluent businessman from the mainland – the missing bloke, Richard Marlowe."

"Was the sale problematic?" Manolis asked.

"Not at all," Noah replied. "The asking price was fully paid, contracts exchanged, settlement reached, deal done."

"Does Marlowe have a criminal record?" Sparrow asked.

"I searched, he's clean," Noah said. "But he's a shrewd operator. He realised the land was undervalued, underdeveloped, and saw an opportunity for a big pay day. I won't quite say it was exploitative, but the vendor was pretty naive about property, having never sold anything before."

"Sounds like the deal the Indigenous people in America made when they sold Manhattan island for peanuts to the Dutch," Sparrow said. "But at least they got *something* for their land, they didn't just lose it for nix."

"On buying the land, Marlowe kept the largest and best portion for himself, elevated high on the cliffs above a stretch of deserted white beach," Noah said. "He then subdivided the rest, which he had since been selling on."

"For a whacking great profit, no doubt," Manolis said.

"Yep," Noah said. "Precise transaction details and sales prices have been kept confidential but many plots were bought sight unseen by people who hadn't even visited the island. Marlowe then poured millions into transforming his own plot of land. For starters, he built an outrageous designer mansion overlooking the ocean."

Noah was forced to use his fingers as he reeled off the new home's many modern features – cinema, library, bowling alley, billiards room, gym, eight-car basement garage, wine cellar, and solar panels.

"Meanwhile, the sprawling grounds have manicured gardens, an infinity pool, a diving pool, floodlit grass tennis court, American barn, fire pit, infrared sauna, 35-seater spa—"

"Helipad?" asked Sparrow.

"Naturally. And also biking trails, apiaries, a private koala sanctuary, and even a bushfire bunker buried deep into the side of a hill."

"Sounds like a real monstrosity," said Sparrow.

"Less like a residential home and more like a seven-star resort on steroids," said Noah. "I've no idea what it's worth but rumour has it they spent a million bucks on windows alone, all triple glazing imported from Germany."

"Bushfire bunker?" Manolis asked.

"Of course," said Noah. "A must-have feature these days."

"For those who can afford it," said Sparrow.

"I don't believe they're cheap, no," said Noah. "Concrete walls, reinforced flame-proof doors, and wine racks to pass the time. But they can also double as bank vaults. Those who have a bunker don't like to talk about them for fear of being overrun when disaster strikes."

"Complicated emotional territory," said Manolis.

"They intensify the feeling of haves and have-nots," said Noah. "But it doesn't stop there . . ."

Noah described how Marlowe's rich friends soon started flocking to the island, helicopters and private planes, buying up the other vacant lots to secure their breathtaking ocean views, undertaking major earthworks and construction, and ultimately trying to outdo each other for extravagance.

"Chest beating," said Sparrow. "Like gorillas in the wild."

"The least they could do was design their buildings so they were somehow tucked away out of sight," Noah said. "And that, understandably, was what began to really tick off the Islanders, both the locals and the *local* locals."

Instead of being welcomed, the influx of flashy newcomers created a tangible social divide within the tight-knit community. The new arrivals kept to themselves, didn't mix with the Islanders, and frequented their own select businesses. Marlowe even bought an island pub and transformed it into an upmarket restaurant with prestigious Chefs Hats.

"Nails won't even put a bloody sprig of parsley on his cheesy chicken parmigiana," said Noah. "The locals refuse to go to Marlowe's restaurant. They're angry because their island is changing, being cannibalised, its heart torn out. But their biggest fear, more than anything, is that they may one day be pushed out themselves if it becomes completely unaffordable."

Noah paused. "And I must admit, I'm a little worried about that too."

Manolis considered all he'd heard with another mouthful of cold water. "So why here?" the detective sergeant asked. "Why Kangaroo Island?"

"The only reason I can give you is that Marlowe grew up here," Noah replied. "But his parents left when he was young, went to the mainland, sent him to private school and university, and that's how he eventually made all his money."

Manolis rubbed his scratchy, two-day stubble. "Moving to the country, the idea of a sea change, has always been the dream of many people, especially during retirement," he said. "It's an escape from the pressures of daily life, a chance to leave it all behind. It was once like that for Marlowe's parents when they first came here, and it's clearly something that Marlowe wants as well."

Manolis took a moment to reflect on his own life. After the birth of Christos, Emily also yearned for a simpler and cleaner life, away from the polluted city and demands of their high-pressure jobs. And her job, as a solicitor in a corporate rat race, was asking more of her every day, oblivious to her transformation into a parent with a demanding newborn. The changes in Emily's body and shift in her outlook reflected her growth into a mother – life wasn't just about her now. But they also caused one of the early fractures in their marriage – their values were seemingly heading in different directions, one disconnected day at a time. And then, when things really deteriorated, Emily decided she no longer wanted the stubborn Manolis to be part of the changes that she wanted in her own life with her son. Manolis was recast as the outsider looking in. He regretted it at the time, and even more in hindsight. No matter how he looked at the world, what lens he viewed it through or logic he applied, his wife had an uncanny knack of always being bloody right.

Nails materialised, ghost-like again, this time with a tray of fresh drinks he presented like trophies, condensation still forming on the glasses.

"On the house," he said cheerily, and proceeded to suck on his own frothy schooner. The ratty, overgrown moustache crowding his mouth was soon dusted with froth. Having overheard their conversation, Nails added that "moving to the island is also an escape from people's pasts".

"See, I'm not so sure," Manolis said. "There was once an Australian writer, Charmian Clift, who lived on the Greek island of Hydra for many years with a bunch of other artists. They were all very brilliant but also jaded. She wrote about her isolation and lifestyle and said that on an island, eventually, you're bound to meet yourself. Islands are meant to be an escape, I get that. But in reality, they're not places of any escape because there's nowhere for people to run."

Nails nodded sagely. After a moment, Manolis added that Clift later returned home to Sydney and killed herself via an overdose of barbiturates.

Manolis's recollection seemed to suck the oxygen from the room. The table went quiet. Everyone took a big draught on their drinks.

"Look, island or not, we're a close community here, and we're hardened," Nails said. "These blow-ins shouldn't come around flashing their cash and making out like they're better than us. That's disrespectful. It's insulting."

"Insulting, eh?" said Manolis.

"There's more going on here than meets the eye," Nails said ominously. "All these quiet land purchases. Something's brewing."

"Like what?" Manolis asked.

"Dunno exactly," Nails replied. "If I knew, I'd probably be in on it myself. Maybe they're building some kind of new utopia. Reliable public transport, solar panels and fruit orchards as far as the fucking eye can see."

Manolis quietly thought that sounded quite appealing.

"Well, whatever they're building, it looks bloody hideous," Nails went on. "The houses are like festering sores, all bloated and inflamed. And they prevent access to some of the local beaches."

Without needing to be prompted, Nails said he was at the port to collect an early morning delivery the day Marlowe disappeared.

"I was with another business owner, a mate named Elvis Carter. You'll meet him soon enough. He runs a café. Top bloke and a footballer, too. And like me, he doesn't want our little island to become a bolthole for the filthy rich. All those newcomers who zip around the island in their fancy-shmancy electric cars and eat sustainable, organic everything – they try to make out like we all still club seals and abduct Aboriginal women."

It was now Sparrow who coughed deliberately into his hand.

"Shit, sorry mate," said Nails. "As if that's bloody true these days. Anyway, we just don't want to be made to feel like second-class citizens in our own home. So, as far as I reckon, it's good riddance to Marlowe and all those like him."

Chapter 4

With appetites satisfied and thirsts sated, Noah and the new arrivals headed off along rough unsealed roads ridged with towering eucalypts. Noah's sports utility vehicle was so grubby that it was hard to identify it as police. As it rattled across spine-shuddering corrugations and bludgeoned through puncture-inducing, axle-destroying potholes, Manolis wondered if the car had any functioning suspension.

"On Kangaroo Island, every single vehicle has some kind of defect," Noah said.

Being a lover of restored vehicles, Manolis was quietly disappointed. He'd thought he might see a few prime examples of cars from his childhood, Fords and Holdens and Chrysler Valiants, that had been lovingly brought back to their original glory. A small part of him had hoped Kangaroo Island might've even been like another island – Cuba – in the way its people valued their vintage cars.

"The salt air chews through metal in no time," Noah went on. "And the rough roads are brutal on the bodywork. Cars get flogged like nothing else."

The local cop described his own Korean vehicle as "expensive to run, unnecessarily heavy and hugely inefficient, but still uniquely suited to drive on the island's dirt roads".

"I always find it strange how many SUVs are sold in Australia," Manolis said. "They're marketed off the back of the vast distances and harsh outback terrain. But we're actually very urbanised – all the major cities are connected by multi-lane highways. And because of their higher bonnets, SUVs have limited vision, which makes them more dangerous to other drivers, pedestrians and cyclists."

"I blame tax perks and the lack of fuel emissions standards – it makes financial sense to drive super-sized vehicles," Noah said. "And I'm seeing more of these Yank tanks on the road, imported and converted to right-hand drive. Six metres long and with stonking great eight-cylinder diesel engines."

"Autobesity," said Manolis.

"Truckzillas," said Sparrow.

"Too right," Noah said. "It feels like an arms race."

"And for this, the environment is eternally grateful," Sparrow said, deadpan.

"Size is about protection, real or perceived," Manolis said. "It's about keeping the tribe safe."

Noah rolled his arms lazily from side to side as he swerved to dodge roadkill wallabies and feasting flocks of predatory birds.

"There's too many dead animals on the roads these days," he said. "They sit there for weeks on end, you get to know them like the potholes, which never get repaired. There's more accidents than ever before, some of them fatal."

"I can imagine," said Manolis, gripping his seat for the illusion of security.

"Fucken roos," Sparrow muttered from behind.

"We've got a local ranger but she's always flat out, especially since the fires," said Noah. "So many animals died, whole ecosystems that'll take generations to bounce back."

"I remember seeing it on the news," said Manolis. "Bloody awful."

"They came from lightning strikes, and nearly half the island was burned," said Noah. "Half. Almost the entire national park at the western end was destroyed."

He spoke of the island's geography, roughly 150 kilometres long east to west and 50 kilometres wide; about the size of Puerto Rico or Long Island. It was Australia's third-largest island after Tasmania in the south and Melville in the far north, and took about four hours to circumnavigate by car.

"There's eight distinct regions, which makes for some pretty intense football grudge matches," he said. "Tribalism is alive and well."

He said the local league had only five clubs, but the rivalry was all the more intense for it.

"That said, the league itself only exists thanks to the grit and grind of dedicated volunteers," Noah added. "Many blokes work all week on their farms and don't see another soul until game day Saturday."

"What's the local team like?" Sparrow asked.

"They're a nondescript mob in a forgettable competition," Noah replied. "The island's coastline is more spectacular than its football."

"And where's the sandboarding?"

"That's near Seal Bay on the south coast. It's just down the road from the stretch of secluded coastline where all the swanky new residential developments are underway. We call it Millionaires' Row."

Staring out the car window, Manolis's brown eyes scrutinised the landscape. Salty, flat and dry. Was Marlowe out there somewhere? Or was his body?

"There are no deep valleys here, no roaring rivers, no tall mountains or lush rainforests," Noah said. "At most, we have gullies, creeks, hills and scrub. But the coastline makes up for it, the beaches and cliffs, the views."

Passing the island's small airport, Noah floored it along a straight stretch of tree-lined track. Seeing a road sign shoot by, Manolis arched an eyebrow.

"Jews Highway?" he said. "Interesting name . . ."

Noah chuckled. "Sorry, not trying to poke fun. The road was given that name by a local legend, an Indigenous bloke named Tiger Simpson. He even served at Gallipoli. When the road was first cleared, he claimed the contractors were tight with money. So, the name stuck."

The island was replete with similarly colourful geographical names that reflected local history: Pigs Head Corner, Stink Corner, Staggerjuice Corner, Firewater Corner, Stomach Ache Corner.

"Felt Hat Corner always has a felt hat sitting on it," Noah said. "That was Tiger too, he always put his hat on a stick when he was walking about so he'd know the way back on his return, like leaving a trail of breadcrumbs. Today, Islanders continue the tradition. If the hat blows off in a storm, someone always puts it back on the sign."

Sparrow forced a laugh. "Great," he said. "A road sign and a grubby cap. What a way to honour a blackfella Anzac hero."

They drove on in tense silence, heading south and west, the road thrumming underneath the car's bald tyres.

"Did you know the island was once connected to the mainland, as Captain Flinders had initially believed?" said Noah.

"What happened?" Manolis asked.

"Rising sea levels," Noah replied. "They turned this place into an island in the same way they're currently swallowing up islands across the Pacific."

"That must've been what wiped my people out," said Sparrow. "Global warming, yair."

"The absence of Indigenous Aboriginal people was significant to the first settlers from Britain," Noah said. "It meant they could imagine the island as a true *terra nullius* and be free of the burden of white guilt that other colonial Australians might've carried."

Sparrow scoffed again. "Good to see they turned it into a positive," he said drily. "No blackfellas here, lads. Come on in, carry on!"

Manolis checked his phone, noticing the reception fluctuating. "What's phone coverage like here?"

"Drops in and out," Noah replied. "Better inland than on the coastline, but too far inland and it drops out again, there's black spots everywhere. The network here is different to the one on the mainland."

"That's not the only thing that's different," muttered Sparrow.

"I haven't seen any buses," said Manolis.

"There's no public transport," said Noah. "And no taxis either. You drive or walk. A few people cycle."

As they drove on, Manolis saw a mix of lush grassland, vast tracts of unspoiled bushland, steep ocean cliffs, and long white stretches of sandy beach. But the further west they went, the landscape changed dramatically from dense and green to bare and black. The raw fallout from the hellish summer bushfire that had destroyed properties and claimed the lives of hundreds of thousands of native animals – and even several people caught sheltering in their cars.

"I see what you mean about the fires," said Manolis in a defeated tone. "Such destruction."

"Believe it or not, it wasn't all bad," said Noah, swerving to avoid another animal carcass. "The fires brought us closer as a community. Most of the island are volunteers with the Country Fire Service, and people reached out to help one another."

"That tends to happen in a crisis," said Manolis. "I've seen it. Tough times, tragedies, bring out the best in people, in both families and communities."

Noah sucked on his teeth. "It started out well enough, everyone came together during the deadliest time to get through the fires. But the rebuilding process has been more individualistic and slow, and even divisive, with many people still waiting for their homes. There's been issues with development approvals and insurance shortfalls. There's now an accommodation crisis, which is why all these massive new houses are so galling. There's only so many builders to go around, and the rich pay more."

"So, the tradies follow the money," Sparrow said.

"Exactly," Noah replied. "And most of these new mansions are second and even third homes. People won't be living in them permanently, they'll sit vacant most of the year."

Almost as if on cue, a settlement of multicoloured tents by the roadside blurred past Manolis's window like a spinning parasol. A line of caravans was parked further down the road, and there were more drooping tents strung out on isolated beaches. Manolis saw Sparrow staring at them all intently with his big brown eyes.

"Those aren't holidaymakers," Noah said. "The housing crisis was a hammer blow coming after all the health and safety hazards – unstable trees, lingering smoke in the air, exposed asbestos."

"And I take it there's been no assistance on any of those fronts?" Manolis asked.

It was now Noah's turn to laugh.

"On top of that, there's all manner of mental health issues," he said. "People feel abandoned, left to cope among the ruins."

Bringing the conversation back to the case, Noah described how some of the Islanders organised a search party for Marlowe in the very first days after he went missing, zigzagging their way across the island in hi-vis jackets, backpacks and hats. It underscored the strong sense of community.

"Nails didn't take part, although he put on some free tucker at the pub," Noah said. "There was also a Facebook group created to help coordinate volunteer searches and pool information but it was deleted after it descended into personal attacks and infighting."

"Wonderful." Manolis sighed. "Ah social media."

"But not before we were treated to comments from some self-proclaimed psychic mediums who claimed to have spiritually connected with Marlowe," said Noah.

"Do they know the lottery numbers as well?" Sparrow asked. "Bloody online sleuths and armchair detectives!"

"Even now, there's a few Islanders who continue to look for Marlowe as they go about their everyday lives in case he suddenly turns up," said Noah.

"Alive or dead," added Sparrow.

The region known as Millionaires' Row soon appeared, rising from the earth like a series of hovering spacecraft. The houses were surrounded by publicly owned Crown land and reinforced by wild scrub, doubly solid, almost as if the area was gated to repel outsiders. The Marlowe property was fittingly impressive with high-security gates and the reassuring sight of multiple CCTV cameras located in elevated positions. The visitors were allowed inside after buzzing an intercom and being scrutinised by an electronic eye.

"Fancy shmancy," said Sparrow, his voice with an upward inflection.

Noah eased up along the teardrop driveway, parking the car at an awkward angle. The worn brakes unleashed a sustained, high-pitched squeal that assaulted Manolis's ears. Emerging from the vehicle, he felt the wind blast his face, as hot and fiery as a furnace. Sparrow cursed their devilishly dry country. All around, the grounds were bustling with gardeners and tradespeople in constant motion, cleaning, maintaining and perfecting.

"Organise a warrant to search the house and grounds," Manolis told Noah.

"Already in train," he replied.

"What about sending geo-targeted text messages?"

"I've reached out to mobile providers. But it's probably diminishing returns given the size of the island."

"Do it anyway."

"No worries . . ."

The house towered before them in monolithic slabs of smooth, curved concrete. The robust design was minimalist yet extravagant. From the exterior, it looked less like a home and more like a grand auditorium.

"I heard that it required 4,000 tonnes of concrete, 50 tonnes of steel, and 35 kilometres of electric cabling," Noah said, tone low. "It's not just a house – it's an engineering marvel."

Climbing a series of wide, sprawling steps, they approached the glassed entrance. As Sparrow rang the bell, he was audited by a second computer eyeball. Manolis quietly reiterated that "the partner's always the prime suspect in such cases".

The doorbell sounded with a deep, operatic tone, reverberating for several seconds in the cavernous space behind the double oak front doors. When the echo faded, they were met with a prolonged silence. Sparrow went to ring the bell a second time but stopped when they heard soft, calculated footsteps on the parquetry flooring. He instead took a conscious step backwards.

The door opened, a voice: "Ah, gentlemen, welcome."

It wasn't quite who Manolis was expecting – a middle-aged man, tanned complexion, silvery coiffure, with the kind of countenance that suggested he was getting better-looking with age.

"James Lavender." He smiled. "Please, come in."

Lavender wore an unbuttoned golf shirt, light cotton pants, and navy canvas sneakers that looked fresh out the box. He shook hands with a firm grip and fixed each guest with a steady, lingering gaze.

Noah introduced his colleagues. Manolis appeared relaxed in his own skin while Sparrow looked edgy, uncomfortable in the opulent surrounds. He kept looking around the brightly lit antechamber, his face betraying a combination of astonishment and circumspection. Sparrow's eyes caught glimpses of strange and unfamiliar things, of glowing plaster and cold marble.

"Right this way," said Lavender.

The soaring void made an immediate impact in the grand foyer. Lavender led them under a crystal chandelier and up a sinuous open staircase crafted from cloudy marble. A pair of cylindrical glass pendants illuminated the way. The muted hum and cooled air of ducted air-conditioning gently chilled Manolis's dry sweat to a comfortable sheen. Sparrow dragged his feet along the protracted corridor, his jaw gaping, his eyes everywhere but where he was actually walking.

"I'm not sure how much Constable Volavola has told you about me," Lavender said. "I've known Richard for years – decades, actually. We're old mates and long-term business partners, and now island neighbours. We're all still in shock he's missing. I'm so glad you've come to help locate him."

"I can imagine," said Manolis. "Can I ask where you and Marlowe first met?"

"At university," said Lavender. "I won't pretend otherwise – both Richard and I have been fortunate in life. We became rich together."

"And what's your profession, Mister Lavender?"

"Please, call me James. My background is in mining and exploration, but these days, I have a diverse portfolio of investments including property, shares and superannuation." His voice exuded quiet power.

A vast space bathed in natural ocean light opened up ahead. It was a living area with high vaulted ceilings, a floating fireplace, and a cosy arrangement of designer lounges. A dining-room table the size of a lap pool was nearby – timber combined with high gloss polyester, bronze steel, and marble in an object that was more of a gallery piece than practical item of furniture. A half dozen sculptural light fittings hung from above a millimetre-perfect row. More marble was to be found nearby in the kitchen – it formed benchtops, a monstrous splashback, and a sweeping, plinth-like island bench that resembled the crest of a breaking wave. Meanwhile, the Indian Ocean poured in through the longest single stretch of window that Manolis had ever seen.

"Fuck me," stammered Sparrow to himself. He sounded winded.

The house was unlike any other he'd ever seen. Concrete on the northern side and glass where it overlooked the water. It had an almost ethereal beauty to it, blurring the line between internal and external living. The interior space balanced views and softness, and seemed to reflect the ocean no matter where you stood. Manolis felt like he was walking on air.

"Can I offer you gentlemen a drink?" Lavender asked. "We have organic coffee, steeped herbal tea, craft beer, chilled wine, freshly squeezed juice, water—"

"Three waters," said Manolis quickly. "Please."

"Of course. Sparkling or still?"

"Still. Sparkling. Either one."

"Local or imported?"

"Either."

"Ice? Shaved, cubes?"

"No thanks."

"Lemon? Cucumber? Mint?"

"Again no."

Lavender disappeared into the graphite stainless-steel refrigerator with double doors and ice-maker and was soon heard lightly clinking glass. Manolis considered a framed, abstract artwork on the wall that he reasoned was likely valued in the millions and insured to the hilt. Sparrow ran his fingers along the island bench like he was somehow drawing on its energy. Lavender soon emerged with three glass bottles that he uncapped and presented to his visitors like a sommelier. Manolis took a sip – it tasted incredible, refreshing, crisp and clean, as if just chiselled from an Icelandic glacier. He placed the bottle on the bench, which was "worth an average yearly salary", as Lavender put in casually.

"Richard and I have always enjoyed a relationship of healthy competition, whether it's our sports teams or bank accounts or number of ex-wives."

"Who's winning?" Sparrow asked.

Lavender laughed. "Me, I think – I'm onto my third wife while Richard's only his second. Speaking of which, right this way . . ."

Chapter 5

Lavender led the police up a final polished staircase and onto the rooftop balcony. Holly Marlowe greeted them with an afternoon glass of cold Prosecco and floating strawberry held between manicured fingers. A pair of snow-white dogs lay obediently by her red-painted toes.

"Thank you, James," she said airily. "I don't know what I'd do without your support during this dreadful time."

Manolis guessed Holly was in her early forties, although his assessment was complicated by the cosmetic enhancement. She wore a light summer dress with tropical floral pattern, a wide-brim straw hat, a sapphire pendant, and wedge buckle sandals. Much of her face was concealed by a pair of shiny pink metal sunglasses that asserted her status and demanded privacy. Manolis thought she came across as elegant and dazzling.

Introductions were made, extending to the Samoyeds, whom Holly introduced formally as if they were humans with first and second names. Maple Marlowe and Banjo Marlowe tilted their heads quizzically and sniffed the new arrivals. Satisfied that their purpose was benign, the dogs sat back down, and it was straight to business.

"Constable Volavola has already briefed me on your husband's disappearance," Manolis said. "But if you wouldn't mind answering some of my questions as well, Missus Marlowe . . ."

"Certainly, Detective," said Holly, sipping from her glass. "Please, have a seat, and call me Holly. It's good to see James has already offered you a cold beverage but there's also some delicious wine if you need something stronger."

The commanding ocean views in Manolis's peripheral vision seemed to smack him in the face; they were a good deal more distracting than the windowless, featureless interview rooms he was used to, and it took an effort not to give them his full attention. Sparrow was weaker – he appeared more interested in the almost unnaturally blue vista than the line of interrogation, even though Manolis had underscored the importance of Holly as a potential prime suspect. He frowned at the young cop, who proceeded to ignore him and casually sip his effervescent water.

Unfurling his notebook and clicking his biro, Manolis proceeded to press Holly for details. She answered his questions as expected and without fluster – her husband had left the house to go for his regular morning swim and surf, and not been seen since.

"I'm always asleep when Richard goes out, like most people at dawn, and sometimes even when he comes back, depending on my level of fatigue," she said languidly. "So, I wasn't too alarmed when I woke and he wasn't home."

"I see," said Manolis. "And then what happened?"

"I had a shower, made coffee, checked the children," Holly replied. "But by mid-morning when he hadn't returned, I sensed something was wrong. Heading down to the beach, I looked around but only found Richard's sandals, phone and towel on the sand, there was no sign of him. I asked the handful of people I encountered but they hadn't seen him either. The dogs had a sniff around but they couldn't find a scent and they know their owner better than anyone."

"And your husband always went to the beach alone?"

"To my knowledge, yes."

"And to mine also," Lavender interrupted. "Richard often said he enjoyed the peace and solitude, it was something he very much treasured about this island. When your jobs are as demanding as ours, moments like these are worth more than fourth quarter bullion."

Manolis acknowledged the interjection with a light nod; he got the picture.

"The beach is just so life-affirming and amazing, the water almost unfathomably clear," Holly went on. "We see fish and manta rays in the water every day. Bottlenose dolphins and orcas and whales often go lancing across the waves just a little way out."

The mention of sea creatures in their natural environment piqued Manolis's interest. He was distracted, momentarily inspired by the wild animals, but he quickly refocused.

"I understand what you mean, yes," he said. "And where are the items you found on the beach?"

"They're all here with me in the house. The phone remains locked, I don't have access."

Manolis looked across at Noah. "We should be able to source the call data records, the CDRs, through the service provider," he told the local cop.

"I'm on it," Noah said. "These things take a while."

Manolis turned back to Holly. "Have you any idea what your husband was wearing the day he went missing?"

"Well, I was asleep so I didn't see him, but I imagine it was his black wetsuit, which he always wears to the beach, and his wristwatch. Both are now missing, too."

"You said he went for a surf. Did he take a board?"

"His yellow surfboard. Also missing."

"And that's all he does at the beach – swim and surf?"

"Yes. Sometimes also exercise on the sand, and perhaps even some yoga . . ."

She explained how she first met Marlowe at a yoga class: "It was his way of unwinding, of destressing, along with swimming and surfing. The water brought him peace."

Holly taught a class once a week. The house boasted a private yoga studio with yet more unobstructed ocean views.

"Does that mean strangers have weekly access to the house?" Manolis asked.

"I guess it does," Holly replied. "Why, what are you suggesting? All my students have beautiful auras."

"I'm just trying to define the pool of suspects."

"Then you'll have to include the dozens of tradespeople, gardeners, architects and designers we've had here recently. They've all had access to the house and grounds, and in some way or another, moved in our orbit."

Sparrow choked an uncontrollable laugh. Even Manolis had to pause at Holly's choice of words.

"I guess the obvious question is whether your husband might've drowned," Manolis said. "I've only been here a short while, and while the water is crystal clear, the surf and waves don't appear to be for light-weights."

"Couldn't agree more," muttered Sparrow.

Holly shook her porcelain face in dismissal. "Richard was a champion swimmer at school and even represented the state in competitions. I've seen his pennants and medals. And as a surfer, he's not too bad either, and getting better every day since we moved to the island."

Manolis wasn't so sure – even the strongest swimmers could get caught in a rip current or knocked unconscious by a massive dumping wave and dragged out to sea. At least Marlowe's surfboard was a distinctive colour and sounded identifiable from a distance.

"Holly. Where's my charger?"

The voice from behind them was demanding and tinged with anger. Manolis turned to see a teenage girl in a crop top and tiny shorts, her taut midriff and thighs exposed, nut-brown hair cascading to her waist. She looked like she'd just woken up but appeared nonetheless achingly cool. Her septum piercing sparkled like a rare diamond, which it could very well have been. The latest generation phone in her hand was the size of a paperback novel.

"Sorry, Allegra, I don't know," Holly replied. "Probably in your room. Did you check there?"

"First place, obvs."

"Then maybe check the rest of the house?"

"The house? The house will take all week. I'll need a fucking search party."

Her bare feet stomped away. Holly appeared embarrassed by the intrusion.

"Kids," said Noah. "I've got two myself."

"Richard's daughter," Holly said. "From his first marriage. Which makes me the wicked stepmother."

She drained her drink with a swift, dismissive glug. Lavender was quick to refill her glass.

"I sacrificed the chance to have my own children when I married Richard," she sighed. "It was a practical decision, choosing money and security and hoping instead to serve as a de facto mum to his twins. But it hasn't worked out that way. As teenagers, they're distant, absorbed in their own tiny but oh-so significant worlds. It's got to the point they even seem wholly unfazed by their own father's disappearance."

Manolis wasn't sure what to make of such insights. As an investigator, it came across as questionable, conspicuous behaviour. But as the father of an already self-absorbed pre-schooler, it seemed like a terrifying window onto his future.

"It's so hard with kids these days," said Manolis. "The way they grow up, the pressures, the electronic devices. Such a traumatic event probably feels unreal to them, like a movie or TV show."

"Roland's holed up in his room," Holly said. "It's where he lives, where he comes alive. The twins are normally at a private boarding school on the mainland. And they genuinely hate each other."

Reaching down, she patted the two fluffy Samoyeds with loving intensity. "These are my fur babies instead. Aren't you, babies?"

The dogs affectionately rubbed their big heads against her hand and licked her polished, pink fingernails. They seemed to smile, the corners of their mouths curiously upturned.

Activating her phone, Holly showed Manolis a recent photo of a wet, smiling Marlowe on the beach with his board, gear and dogs.

"Richard adores the pups even more than I do," Holly said.

Manolis asked for a copy of the photo, which she shared. She also played a recent voicemail that Marlowe had left her:

"Hello, darling. I hope you had a good day. Work has piled up so I'll be late coming home. Please have dinner without me and I promise I'll make it up to you this weekend. Love you."

Manolis thought that Marlowe sounded refined, almost to the point that his performance seemed rehearsed, his articulation and tone perfect in every way. It was such a mundane, everyday message, the kind that any partner would leave for their significant other, yet felt so extraordinary in its delivery, its oration. But perhaps that simply reflected the world that Marlowe inhabited – one of means, refinement and exquisite attention to detail.

"Richard hates having to work late, he considered those days of hard grind and long hours behind him," Holly said. "But sometimes, I guess it's unavoidable."

Holly appeared to love and adore her husband and seemed genuinely worried by his disappearance, but she also didn't come across as overly distraught. Manolis wondered why and whether it was simply due to her demeanour, her refinement and restraint, at least in front of strangers. Perhaps it was something that affected the entire household, a symptom of its collective affluenza.

Manolis found himself questioning his own parenting, what kind of future he could provide for young Christos in an ever-more-expensive world. He and Emily had stable jobs – and well-paid too, especially hers – but they were far from "wealthy", as he saw it. And yet he knew that privileges came with their own cross to bear, with psychological issues that manifested as narcissism, as fear of weakness and failure, and an inability to connect and empathise with others.

The detective sat forward. "And how was your husband's overall health?"

The query seemed to catch Holly off-guard. Her cheeks flushed shocking pink, or perhaps it was the Prosecco. Manolis sounded like a doctor armed with blood tests poised to deliver grave news.

"F-fine . . ." she stuttered. "At least, to my knowledge."

"Of course, what I mean is, just in case he had some kind of catastrophic medical episode in the water. He may be fit and active, which is admirable. But he's also no longer a man in his twenties."

"That kind of thing also happens to men in their twenties," Holly said.

Raising a steadying finger to a well-worn temple, Manolis decided to change tack.

"What about the state of your relationship? And also, the state of your finances?"

Holly waved a dismissive hand. "This line of questioning, is it really relevant?"

"Hmm, I tend to agree," said Lavender. "This is bordering on intrusive."

"The detective is merely trying to define the pool of suspects," Noah said, repeating Manolis's earlier pronouncement.

"I also had the idea of offering a sum of money in reward for information," Manolis said. "That's not uncommon in cases of missing persons."

Holly looked at the detective a while, carefully considering her words.

"How much of a sum?" she finally asked, sipping her wine.

"Well, there's no fixed amount but here. But I imagine something in the ballpark of a few hundred thousand would be appropriate."

Holly momentarily choked on her mouthful.

"Excuse me," she said, dabbing her wet chin with a serviette. "I'm so sorry, that's just more than I expected."

"That's extortion!" Lavender said.

"People often need a firm incentive to come forward," Manolis said.

"Look, as the wife, I know I'm probably the number one suspect," Holly said. "So, what can I say exactly? Again, to my knowledge, our marriage is good, there's love and affection. And of course, we bicker from time to time, but all couples do that. We spend quality time together with shared interests like yoga and cooking and French cinema and Australian literature. This house was something we built together, a joint project. At times, we argued over the details, but look how it's turned out."

Sparrow looked around the luxurious room. "It's alright," he said. "I mean, I guess . . ."

"What did you argue about?" Manolis asked.

"A house so extensive, there were thousands of individual decisions to be made," Holly replied. "We couldn't possibly agree on them all. But more than anything, the budget blew out. Also unsurprising, perhaps. Construction costs, materials, global markets and so on. Conflict breaks out in the Middle East or Eastern Europe or West Africa and the price of everything goes up. And if I was being brutally honest with you, that has caused us some financial stress lately."

Manolis sat back in his chair. "Thank you," he said. "I appreciate your honesty. I imagine that most construction projects go over budget."

"Mm, yes. But perhaps not like ours. There were so many unforeseen circumstances, we'd never done anything like this before, and the scope of the build changed so much along the way."

She paused for a beat. "Wait, have you had a tour?"

The three police looked blankly at each other.

"Follow me," Holly said brightly.

The dogs led the way, bounding joyously from room to spacious room. Holly described every designer and architectural feature in the minutest detail to the generally disinterested officers, although Manolis remained compelled by what he might learn about Marlowe and his second wife.

"The kitchen is sheathed in Saint Croix marble, which we chose for its bubbly seafoam appearance. The bench was imported from Jamaica and mirrors the coral reefs in the Caribbean Sea, its back left open for storage and its front carved with delicate plissé for texture. We insisted on soft grey cabinetry, deliberately subtle so as not to compete for presence."

"Presence is everything," said Sparrow.

Nestled behind the kitchen and adjoining butler's pantry was a library and reading room. Manolis scanned the shelves, thick with classic volumes and the latest hardback bestsellers.

"We were especially mindful to have atmospheric lighting in here, and you won't see any exposed bulbs or fittings," Holly said. "Day or night, light is paramount. And did you notice the design of our couloir?"

"Your what . . .?" Manolis was struggling to keep up with both Holly's descriptions and purposeful gait.

She strode towards the home's main corridor – more a tunnel, really – and presented it like the grand prize on a gameshow.

"The walls on either side are punctuated by strips of natural light that seep through these slender windows on each side and cast shadows across the floor," Holly said. "The light and shade change as the day goes by. It's like a sundial. This was my idea," she added with a note of pride.

"Where's your bedroom?" Manolis asked bluntly.

Everyone looked at him like he'd said something inappropriate to a married woman.

"If you don't mind," he added sheepishly.

The palatial master suite was the size of a large city apartment, the oversized Alaskan king mattress and bed positioned to breathe in optimal views of the Great Australian Bight. Its header, upholstered in a soft sudsy green, was illuminated by a wall light formed from a pair of giant ostrich eggs. An admiral-blue rug and sumptuous reading chairs sat alongside in perfect synchrony.

"This is my favourite room of all, I could happily die in here," Holly declared. "The ostrich eggs are individually engraved by the artist and contain unique genetic material."

"Not the artist's, I hope." Sparrow smiled.

"The eggs gain a life of their own, with perpetual provenance," Holly went on. "And the way the natural light works with the furnishings provides warmth and a sense of cocooning. You feel held, supported, emboldened. Every single window placement in the house affirms its place in nature and draws the coastline into every living space."

Holly sounded more like a real estate agent trying to sell to fastidious, globetrotting clients than she did the worried wife of a missing, potentially drowned, man. But Manolis imagined it was just her tone of voice and the vastly different circles in which she moved. She was also understandably pleased with her creation, still new and novel, which came across more as a work of art than a house in which to live and make a home.

Holly seemed to tiptoe past the other bedrooms, which Manolis guessed was where the twins inhabited their own private universes with private ensuites and walk-in wardrobes and drawn curtains. Everyone with their own space these days, and at an increasingly earlier age.

"Your house is amazing," Manolis said. "Just incredible. Can I ask about the twins' mother? Where is she?"

The question elicited a stinging, acerbic laugh from Holly, which echoed around the marble in the entryway.

"Virginia," said Lavender.

"She lives on the mainland," said Holly. "Suffice to say, we don't really get along. She's emotionally distant from the twins and hostile to Richard after an acrimonious divorce that involved Adelaide's priciest silks. I tried to be friendly, but it only brought me stress, so I disengaged. To her, I'm just the new model, which can never match up to the original."

"You're not supposed to get along with a partner's ex-partner in the same way you're not supposed to get along with your mother-in-law," said Lavender. "It's unnatural, goes against the laws of nature."

"To hell with her," said Holly. "Sorry to be so blunt, I may've had a sip too many."

"That's quite alright, you've been very helpful," the detective said. He quietly appreciated the lubricative power of alcohol on the human psyche. "And what about your husband's behaviour?"

"What about it?" Holly said.

"Did you notice any recent changes? Or any associations with new people?"

When Holly looked at Manolis quizzically, he added: "I'm trying to consider his psychological profile in the hope of better understanding his motivations."

They were now standing just inside the double doors, preparing to leave. After a long pause to gather her thoughts and composure, Holly said that Marlowe had been acting completely normal before his disappearance with no significant changes in his behaviour or interactions.

"What about friction with people already in his life, anything significant there?" Manolis asked.

He was expecting Holly to mention the *local* locals, or even just the locals, in some form or another. That was, assuming she knew the difference.

"As it turns out, the night before he disappeared, Richard did happen to mention a little trouble with a work associate," Holly said.

"Which one?" Manolis asked.

"With Grayson."

"Patrick Grayson," Lavender said.

The name meant something to Manolis. "Wait, where do I know that name . . .?"

"He was once on TV," said Holly. "Now the head chef at Richard's restaurant."

"And clearly a disgruntled employee," said Sparrow. "I know the feeling."

"I'd be keen to find out more," said Manolis.

"I don't know much, just that it involved a bad review that he somehow blamed on Richard," Holly said. "As if *he's* the one in the kitchen preparing the food."

"I can tell you more, Detective," said Lavender. "If you have time, why don't we have lunch at the restaurant this week? It would be my pleasure to have you as my guest. And I can guarantee, irrespective of any hack reviews in rags that no-one reads, the food is exquisite."

Accepting the invitation, Manolis thanked Lavender for his generosity.

"Oh, and another thing," Holly said. "A few weeks ago, we had a homemade mortar thrown onto our property."

Manolis was shocked. "A what . . .? A homemade mortar? Why would someone possibly do that?"

Holly shrugged her willowy shoulders. "I don't know. Don't worry, it didn't explode."

Manolis looked across at Noah, whose face wore a solid that's-news-to-me expression.

"We had some of our property damaged before that," Holly went on. "But then, so did all our neighbours."

Lavender weighed in: "I did, yes. But just some rotten eggs thrown our way and some paint tins stolen off the back of a vehicle."

"Any idea why?" Manolis asked.

"Probably just kids," Lavender replied. "Or a form of protest."

"Protest . . .?" Manolis sounded suspicious.

"Against our constructions," said Lavender. "Architecture critics abound."

"Where's the mortar?" Manolis asked Holly.

"Landfill," she replied.

"You really should've reported that to the police," he said.

Manolis didn't think she was telling the full story. An act of aggression like that surely represented some kind of retaliation. He'd seen it before with organised criminals who mixed with society's underbelly, with hired thugs and biker gangs and drug dealers.

"Hey, where's the koala sanctuary?" Sparrow asked, looking around.

"At the northern end of our acreage," Holly replied. "The eucalyptus plantation needs full sun to thrive."

"Of course," said Sparrow.

"Thanks for your time today," said Manolis. "We'll talk again. But in the meantime, can I ask you to prepare a few things for me?"

"Like what?" Holly asked.

"I need a list of your husband's bank accounts, business associates, and anyone who might bear a grudge. Perhaps James can help here."

"Glad to," said Lavender, shaking hands. "Anything to assist."

"I'll do what I can," said Holly, offering a sour smile. And as Manolis turned to go, she added that if he really wanted to know where her husband was located, "then a good idea might be to go and ask his girlfriend".

Chapter 6

Noah held the steering wheel with nervy fingers as they drove away at high speed, the road following the meandering arc of the surf-bound coastline.

"To be honest, I don't really know Holly all that well," he said. "She's still new and from very different stock to what we're used to around here."

Manolis thought that was an understatement of epic proportions. He'd never encountered such a palatial private home, not even in the most exclusive city suburbs investigating overdoses on the finest-grade cocaine. Those houses weren't built on clifftops overlooking the ocean, for starters, nor surrounded by tent cities. Sparrow still appeared to be in a minor state of shock.

"What's that place worth, anyway?" the young cop asked. "Five mill? Ten?"

"I wouldn't be surprised if it was north of twenty," Noah said. "Not that I really have a clue – I generally deal in thousands, at most, not millions. Either way, it's worth more than the entire real estate on Kangaroo Island combined before the newcomers arrived."

Following the climactic proclamation about her marriage, Holly's epilogue was to add that she'd only just discovered her husband's infidelity and had planned to confront him before he vanished.

"Perhaps that was *why* he vanished," Noah said. "Didn't want to face the music. Can you imagine the divorce settlement? Lawyers would be queuing up around the block to take the case."

"There has to be a prenup," said Sparrow. "The bloke would be fucking mad not to."

"Maybe Lavender was right," Noah said. "They're stockpiling ex-wives."

"Blokes like that, alpha males, I reckon it's in their DNA," said Sparrow. "They can't help it."

"Just take it easy, fellas," said Manolis. "We've only got what Holly said to go on. Let's wait until we find out more."

Noah fumbled with the shift knob, crunching the gears as he accelerated up a sharp rise in the road. The transmission groaned.

"Frankly, I don't really know any of the blow-ins at all," Noah said. "Their world is very separate from ours, and they keep to themselves. I'm surprised they don't have their own security detail."

"Or their own police force," said Sparrow.

"I imagine they're intensely private people," said Manolis. "Probably the main reason they bought land here."

"Intensely private people?" said Sparrow incredulously. "If you ask me, more like intensely private wankers."

As they circled the beach where Marlowe went for his last swim, Manolis watched the ominous waves breaking offshore. The hot wind of earlier had worn out its fury but there was still a heavy jigsaw of swell leftover from the gale. The huge brown surf rumbled and pounded into the rocks, sending cold spray shooting into the air. It was as if some malevolent force from the deep was trying to suck the entire world above into its dark abyss.

"Have you gone out and searched the water yet?" the detective asked Noah.

"Once, but it was a pretty crude attempt, the sea was rough that day," he replied.

"You don't say," said Sparrow.

"I want to give it another go," said Manolis. "Do you think a water search is possible?"

"We can try, won't be easy but certainly not impossible," Noah replied. "We did an aerial search too, in Lavender's chopper, for about half an hour. And I also put out an alert to aircraft to report if they saw anything."

"Good work."

Another circuitous bend in the road brought the vast horizon into full view. Looking out over the ocean, Noah mentioned the latest small-town rumour that suggested that even more newcomers would soon be descending upon their quiet island.

"There's apparently an exploration licence under consideration that would allow for widespread offshore drilling – oil and gas. This has, understandably, left people feeling fucking pissed. It was the same over the new seawater desalination plant that's now being built at Penneshaw."

Water was a constant issue on the island, he told them. It was largely sourced from dams and reservoirs, but residents still needed to buy it by the gallon when those got low.

"The bushfires exposed limitations in our ageing infrastructure," Noah said. "Our current desalination plant is decades old, with the new one supposed to answer all our prayers."

"Bushfires and drought," said Manolis. "Greater resilience and future water security."

"The problem is that many Islanders have concerns about noise, light pollution, environmental damage, aesthetics, and potentially even the desecration of a historic cemetery."

"All those whitefella souls, no longer resting at peace," said Sparrow. "My heart bleeds."

Massive underground pipes were now being brought over from the mainland by ferry to connect the island's communities. Public meetings were still underway, bureaucrats and engineers clashing with angry residents to secure planning and environmental approvals.

"So, you can just imagine what a ruckus an offshore drilling project might cause," Noah added.

Manolis figured that an ocean-based oil rig was at least more out of sight than a desalination plant on land. In the best light, oil rigs had a certain unintentional dystopian beauty; in the worst, they were a blight on the marine landscape. But an oil rig was also far more perilous for the environment.

"How do you feel about it all?" he asked Noah.

The island cop bit his lip. "A bit conflicted, actually. These projects can obviously have a negative impact on island life, but it also means more jobs for the local economy."

They arrived at their destination – further west, another beach, and this one even more remote and hidden. Stepping out of the car, Manolis removed his sunglasses, put hands on his hips, and squinted into the near distance. The sea was noticeably calmer here, the beach and bay somewhat protected, and he was immediately captivated by what he saw – the shapes of fins and flukes and great mammalian bodies breaching, heaving themselves out of the water in elegant arcs. He'd never seen such a display in the wild, and this was no tourist cruise.

"Hey, check it out." Manolis indicated the aquatic display to Sparrow. "It's not all bad out there in the water."

Sparrow glanced at the sea but then turned away, the marvellous sight unable to shift the unimpressed look from his darkened face.

"Where's this Skye character then?" he asked impatiently.

Skye lived with her loyal canine companion in a beach shack converted from a shipping container. She was much younger than Holly, mid-twenties, a self-exiled artist.

"She's an eccentric, a precocious talent," Noah said. "We went to high school together but she ran away from home in the final year. She's been living in near isolation ever since."

"So, she's a weirdo," said Sparrow.

"She's just different," Noah replied. "But she's still one of us – an Islander."

"Sounds like Marlowe had a local life with Holly," said Sparrow. "And a *local* local life with Skye." He chuckled at his own gag.

The situation made Sparrow recall a story from Australian Aboriginal mythology about a man with two wives.

"The women ate some forbidden fruit and tried to run away from their husband, Ngurunderi, before he tracked them down. Ngurunderi was pissed off deluxe and angrily called for the winds to raise up the sea and sweep his wives into the ocean. They drowned and their bodies were turned to stone. You remember those two tiny islands we saw crossing the Backstairs Passage?"

"The Pages?" asked Manolis.

"Yair. That's them, the women, Ngurunderi's two wives. Love triangles never work out, not even in the Dreamtime."

Noah took the lead in approaching Skye's container, stepping carefully across the sand as if to avoid leaving footprints. "Stay back, let me go first," he said. "She won't recognise you, but she knows me well enough."

Noah climbed the three steps onto the wooden deck, which creaked under his slender weight. He knocked on the fly-screen door and simultaneously called out: "Knock knock."

He stepped back a conscious metre and stared awkwardly at his shoes, head down.

"Hello, Skye . . .? Are you there? It's Noah."

Sparrow fired Manolis a look as if to say, *can you believe this?*

The wind blew across the dunes, scattering sand into Manolis's face. He rubbed his eyes, which only seemed to make things worse, pushing the fine grains in even further. He eventually blinked and flushed away the grit with some lubricating tears before returning his focus to the unfamiliar container.

Noah finally turned. "I don't think she's home," he said. "Come to think of it, if she were home, her Rottweiler guard dog would've come out barking."

"A Rottweiler?" said Sparrow. "Fuck me. We'd all have been ripped to pieces before we even reached the door."

"Nice little place," Manolis said. "Neat and tidy – modern."

Skye's abode was no ordinary shipping container – it had been upgraded to a cosy sea-sprayed home with elegant clerestory windows, skylights, vegie patch, and water tank.

"It's all renewable materials, which makes it more sustainable than any of those massive new builds, even with their triple glazing and solar panels," Noah said.

"Because they're so massive," said Manolis.

"They suck heaps more energy and leave a carbon footprint like a yeti."

"And with the same ocean views," added Manolis, slipping into the cloth hammock on the deck with an exhalation. "Just like Marlowe's but at a fraction of the price."

Sparrow tried the door; it was unlocked. "Shall we take a look around?" he asked foxily. "I mean, we've come all this way . . ."

"That's trespassing," said Manolis. "We need a search warrant."

"We're not from around here," said Sparrow, stepping inside. "We're lost, in need of directions . . ."

The container's interior was cleverly designed with light, airy colours and recycled timber throughout. A galley kitchen featured hidden drawers and hanging pots and pans. A bed was secreted into a snug loft space accessible by an in-built step ladder.

"Don't disturb anything," Manolis said. "Look but don't touch."

"Gotcha," said Sparrow. "The strip club treatment."

The interior walls were covered with Skye's artwork, along with many canvases stacked sideways. There was also a collection of surf-boards positioned on a wall-mounted rack. Manolis examined the paintings, hoping to gain an insight into the creator's mind. He was certainly no art critic, nor was he a behavioural psychologist. But he still imagined he could glean something from her choices in colour, style and imagery.

"Jesus Christ," said Sparrow. "Check this shit out . . ."

The images weren't the anticipated gentle landscapes, seascapes and anodyne water colours. Instead, they were dark and sinister. There was a distinctive series of paintings of a woman's face, always sorrowful in appearance, with grim sunken eyes, sometimes wet-cheeked as if she'd been crying, or with her mouth half open like she was in the midst of sobbing or wailing. In some paintings, it was as if she was melting into the canvas, being absorbed by it, swallowed. The colours were almost exclusively black, grey and seaweed green. There were also some troubling representations of what appeared to be maimed and dead children splashed with crimson red.

"These are stunning," said Manolis. "But yeah, I see what you mean."

Noah took a seat on a folding chair. "I heard a rumour that people from the mainland are offering to buy Skye's art all the time. Private investors and gallery curators, interior designers."

"She's clearly talented," said Manolis. "Probably self-taught."

"Hmm, not really my style," said Sparrow haughtily. "Guess I'm no fan of nightmare fuel."

"The idea of an exiled, introspective artist living on an isolated corner of a distant island, producing provocative images like this," said Manolis. "I can see the appeal to those in the mainstream. She's edgy, and so is her art."

"Thing is, Skye's not really interested in sales," said Noah. "She shuns the usual trappings of success."

"That's also clear," said Manolis.

"So, other than the obvious sexual allure, I'm not really sure what a bloke like Marlowe might see in someone like Skye," said Noah. "And vice versa."

"That said, sexual allure usually goes a fucking long way," said Sparrow. "Ask any bloke going through a midlife crisis."

Manolis shrugged. "Maybe he wanted to buy her art," he said. "If it's so highly sought after. Another shrewd investment."

"Or opposites attract," said Noah.

"Jesus Christ," Sparrow said sharply. "Are you guys blind? It's a textbook sugar daddy relationship if ever I saw one . . ."

And with that, the Indigenous constable strode back to the car with a quiet confidence, safe in the knowledge he'd cracked the case wide open.

Chapter 7

The cops strolled barefoot along the deserted beach, shoes in their hands like high-heeled girls at the end of a long night out. Manolis relished the creamy warm sand between his toes while Sparrow flirted with the uprush of swash from the incoming waves breaking offshore. He was like a small child, and Manolis enjoyed watching his colleague experience some pleasure from the ocean instead of abject terror and aversion. The day was getting away from them now, the sun low, their shadows long.

"I reckon Skye's not far away," said Noah. "We'll probably bump into her along here somewhere."

"Probably out walking her deadly mutt along the beach," said Sparrow. "Hunting for sharks. After all, it's nearly dinner time."

As they walked, a lanky individual appeared in the near distance, emerging from the surf with a macabre air. Loping along in tight black scuba gear and blocky face mask, the merman dragged a weighty net like he'd been busy harvesting briny souls. An oxygen tank added to his burden, and Manolis was suddenly acutely aware of exhaustion, which at that stage of the day was mental as much as physical.

"How'd you go today, Bruce?" Noah called out.

A so-so gesture followed, hand parallel to the sand, rocked slightly.

"That good, eh?"

The man removed his full-face diving mask, and a pair of chronically bloodshot eyes beneath a dripping wet fringe greeted the new arrivals.

"Gudday. Bruce Conway."

He was a puffy-faced abalone diver bringing in his daily haul of reclusive molluscs. The net clattered like a maraca.

"We're looking for Skye," Noah said. "You seen her today?"

"Earlier this morning. She was walking her dog when I headed out, and I've been in the water ever since."

"Looks like a good catch," said Manolis, pointing to the sodden net. "How long were you out there?"

Conway checked his chunky diving watch. "Today, just ten hours. Some days it's twelve or more. Either way, too bloody long to be hooked up to a machine on a boat that feeds me oxygen through a hose like an iron lung."

"Are you a local, or a *local* local?" Sparrow asked him pointedly.

Conway laughed, beige teeth jutting at all angles. "Just a local, I'm afraid. A second-class citizen."

Taking a seat on the sand with a relieving groan, Conway described how he grew up on the island but left for the mainland in his twenties.

"I was young, I wanted something more exciting than sea snails," he said. "I didn't find it, so I came back. Who'd of thought."

Having taken over the family business from his father, Conway now hand-harvested the dramatically camouflaged abalone and urchins off the seabed and reefy outcrops, often working six days a week. His life was dictated by the weather's fluctuations, the wind's direction and speed, to the point of an unhealthy obsession.

"The climate around here is crazy," he said. "The winds are fickle, the swells are wild, and the tides make no sense. But I've known women like this, too."

"So, why do it?" Manolis asked.

Conway blew out a long exhalation and flashed a smile. "The sex," he said. "It's bloody incredible."

He talked proudly about the sustainability of his modern abalone practice, which included helping to promote spawning by mixing together the sperm and roe. By gradually changing water temperature, this also mimicked seasonal changes and encouraged fertilisation. Abalone had historically been overfished in many countries, with environmental laws now in place to protect their numbers and stop poachers.

"I also don't use any antibiotics, none of that aquaculture crap," Conway said. "It takes a bit longer but it's an investment – mainlanders pay top dollar for a better product. Fresh from the ocean, straight to your plate, doesn't even need salt. When nature's this good, you don't mess with it." He flashed a satisfied grin.

"What's top dollar?" Sparrow asked.

"Depends on supply and demand, but on a good day, a hundred bucks a kilo. Some specialist restaurants charge fifty bucks a snail and even more for red abalone, which is more endangered. And a kilo of abalone meat alone can easily fetch a grand."

"Deadly!" said Sparrow. "You're printing it."

"Not quite, but some days are very satisfying," Conway said.

"I've never actually eaten abalone," Sparrow admitted.

Conway reached into his net and pulled out a hard and rough oval shell that he proffered like a jewel.

"Wanna try some now? On the house."

Sparrow screwed up his nose at the strange, featureless organism. It looked just like a wet alien rock, not a sought-after delicacy sold at high-end restaurants.

"Now?" Sparrow said. "You mean . . . raw?"

"Sure, straight off the shell. They're delicious, naturally buttery and salty cos of the ocean, and a great source of protein."

"Go on, mate," smiled Manolis. "Live a little, broaden your horizons. And a great source of protein."

"It's served in Japan as sushi or sashimi, the feet are cut into thin slices," said Conway.

"The feet?" Sparrow took a distinct step backwards.

"It's the feet that are most prized for eating. They use them to attach to reefs and rocks using suction."

Sparrow shook his head. "Suction, eh. I guess I'm worried they might suction to my throat and choke me. So, um, yair . . . thanks but maybe some other time."

Conway tossed the shell back into the net with a light clunk. "Fair enough, young fella. Abalone's an acquired taste, as tasty as it is creepy, especially when raw. Maybe we slip one on the barbie for you sometime."

Sparrow breathed a sigh of relief, glad to be out of the limelight.

"The red abalone live in the most dangerous waters where there's the greatest threat of shark attacks," said Conway.

"Probably why they're the most expensive," said Manolis.

"Like blood diamonds," Conway added.

He explained that shark attacks were most frequent at dawn or dusk or during the night when they tended to hunt. And they were on the rise, with unprovoked encounters more common for surfers than swimmers.

"Unprovoked attacks . . .?" Sparrow said. "Who provokes a shark?"

"Spearfishing is still the riskiest activity in that regard," said Conway. "Either way, in the vain hope that I might somehow survive this career choice, I had a shark cage built. I can now dive more securely in shark corridors. Pricey enough though, cost me twenty grand."

"Bushfire bunkers, shark cages," said Sparrow. "All puts your mind at ease, really."

With eyes fixed on the local diver, Manolis came straight out and asked about the possibility, or probability, of a shark attack on Richard Marlowe. He wanted the thoughts of a seasoned operator in these waters.

"There's definitely been attacks around here," Conway replied. "Surfers, swimmers, fishermen, boats. A few years ago, there was an abalone diver killed off South Neptune Island, a few hundred clicks west of here in the Spencer Gulf. And another diver at Coffin Bay to the north. I've had a few close shaves myself, hence the cage."

"What kind of shark?" Manolis asked.

"Great whites," Conway replied. "Shark *du jour*."

"I had a mate who was attacked surfing about a year ago," said Noah. "He was sitting on his board in the water and felt a hit on his side like he was being rammed by a semi-trailer. The bastard bit him around his back, elbow and arse, and took a big chunk out of his board. He was very, very lucky."

"If they sever your femoral artery in the water, you're a goner," Conway said. "You bleed out and die within minutes. Lucky is an understatement. And humans in wetsuits are often mistaken for a succulent seal."

"Wetsuit eh," said Manolis, remembering what Marlowe was wearing when he disappeared.

"The problem for me is that the best abalone are up against the cliffs, which means I can't always use the cage," said Conway. "But there's definitely more sharks nowadays because they follow their prey, which are moving further south to cooler ocean waters."

For abalone divers in the water for such long stretches, it wasn't just great whites that were the concern. Conway described the very real risk of decompression sickness – the bends – that came from being in the depths of the ocean for so many hours.

"Having nitrogen bubbling through your blood is excruciating," he said. "Worst pain you can possibly imagine."

"Sharks and blood bubbles – and all in the name of sea snails," said Sparrow. "Mate, you have my respect."

Conway laughed, full and throaty. "I guess that's one way to look at it, but someone's gotta do the dirty work. Like you guys. For the record, I'm genuinely sad that Marlowe's missing. He helped set me up with a wholesaler on the mainland, they take delivery of my abalone within hours. Without Marlowe, my business would be screwed."

Manolis raised a curious eyebrow. This was the first Islander to come out in public support of Marlowe. Could it be the blow-in was much-maligned? That he had actually done some good to support the locals?

"But then, I'm also annoyed Marlowe vanished cos he still owes me some money," Conway went on.

Normal service had swiftly resumed.

"What money?" Manolis asked.

"Some outstanding payments from recent sales," Conway said.

"How much?"

Conway ran a hand through his wet, oyster-grey hair. "I'd rather not say the precise sum," he replied. "But more than a few bob."

"And where were you the morning he disappeared?"

"I was actually on the mainland with the wholesaler," Conway said without hesitation. "You're free to check, I'll give you his name." He then added: "For the record."

As they stared out over the hard-blue horizon, the dot of a compact, twinjet aircraft appeared in the distance. Its blast was soon heard as it began closing in on them, passing low directly overhead. Manolis felt his hair blow back and was gripped by a strong desire to run for cover as if caught in the midst of an airstrike, machine-gun fire raining down on the beach as part of some forgotten, faraway war.

"Who the hell was that?" he asked, craning his neck.

"Not sure exactly," said Noah. "But it'll land on an unsealed road somewhere. Private planes do what they want, they don't really care for rules about take-offs and landings and regulated airspace. Speed, convenience, and tonnes of CO_2."

"People gotta go to meetings," said Sparrow. "And play rounds of golf and take holidays with their pets."

"The choppers are worse, though," said Noah. "You can't hear your-self think when one passes over."

A few moments later, a second distraction made itself known to Manolis, much more gratifying than the first. A colony of sea lions wandered onto the sand – bulls, cows and their young offspring. Manolis stood to marvel at the astonishing grey-and-cream mammals as they lumbered about on their flippers, barking and honking, some weighing hundreds of kilos. Conway explained how the pinnipeds had lived on the same stretch of brooding coastline for thousands of years. Female sea lions returned to the same breeding colony throughout their lives, and their pups did the same. Each colony and breeding site was a closed population.

"More juicy shark bait," said Conway. "Or at least, that's what the local fishermen considered sea lions until about 1945. Before that, they were nearly hunted to extinction by sealers who actually succeeded in wiping out all the elephant seals and hair seals."

Conway described how the sealers used five-metre-long lances to hunt. They waited until the elephant seals raised their left forefin before plunging the weapon deep into their heart.

"What happened when they ran out of seals to stab and dissect?" Manolis asked. His stomach turned at the thought.

"They turned their attention to whatever other wildlife they could find," Conway replied. "They traded in kangaroo pelts, possum skins, and the plumage of the albatross, which they almost hunted to extinction."

When the sealers ran out of food altogether, Conway said they began to roast wild dogs and goannas in ground ovens. They ate ant eggs and witchetty grubs. And when they ran out of fresh water to drink, they turned to quaffing seagull blood.

"Yet another regrettable chapter in the shameful history of our glorious little island," said Noah. "The era of sea rats."

Sealing proved to be lucrative, and the struggling new colony was soon competing with established hunting regions like Canada, Greenland and Scandinavia. In fashion cities like Paris and Milan, seal skins were used to make chic hats, soft gloves and stylish boots. A dozen clean skins could buy a gallon of rum for a grizzled Kangaroo Islander. Meanwhile, seal oil was a valuable commodity for use in lamps, as machine lubricant, and in soap, cosmetics and paint. The island fast became a destination for sealers, who eschewed the mainland to form their own little kingdom that they ruled like ruthless, dishevelled sovereigns.

"It explains why us Islanders continue to view ourselves as different to other South Australians, even to this day," Conway said.

Once devoid of all humans, the island sanctuary fast became a hunter's paradise. Manolis listened with a grim fascination – this was the stuff you didn't read about in the glossy tourist brochures.

"You wouldn't want to bring any of those blokes home to meet your mum." Conway laughed. "They were convicts, smugglers, thieves, philanderers and killers."

"Bad boys, eh." Sparrow smiled. "Real heartbreakers."

"They went in pursuit of profit and were happy to bend the rules in its name," said Conway. "And the Backstairs Passage offered a natural barrier to hide men from authority and protect them from capture."

These were young men full of swagger who had lived hard lives. They'd been buggered as boys, ripped off in hustles, and forced to cheat and scam their way to a better life.

"They left rainy old Britain for the freedom of sunny Kangaroo Island," said Conway. "They were refugees from their own society."

Sparrow stifled a laugh. "Imagine what it must be like being made an outcast in your own society!"

"At the time, our little island was infamously described as the most dangerous place in the British Empire," said Conway.

"High praise," said Manolis. "Congratulations."

"Because the sealers weren't advancing the cause of the civilised settlers, they had to be admonished and dissociated," said Conway. "They were Englishmen, that was certain. But they were no heroes to colony or Empire."

"Not like Flinders," said Manolis.

"A true star," said Sparrow. "Without him, where would we be."

"The island was a place of savages and barbarism, of lonely caves and impenetrable scrub and sharp knives and cutlasses," Conway said. "The men wanted to flee to isolated islands where they could pursue a life of violence outside the law. But it probably also explains the mindset today – we value our independence and prefer to avoid authority and officials."

"You seem to know a lot about this stuff," Sparrow said.

"I volunteer at the local maritime museum," Conway replied. "You should visit sometime."

He said that life on the island in those early days was exceedingly rough: heavy work and a meagre diet. The outcasts lived in crudely constructed huts made of bark, wattle and clay. Their lives were dictated by whatever they could hunt, harvest and sell. Manolis couldn't help but draw mental parallels with the island's newest arrivals, who also seemed to live according to their own rules. But how the quality of life had changed.

"The men had long, matted hair and beards steeped in oil, and necklaces of kangaroo teeth," said Conway. "They had no linen and wore clothes made of assorted animal skins, wallabies and seals and feral cats."

"Like Davy Crockett," said Manolis.

"More like cheesy versions of Robinson Crusoe with their very own Girl Fridays," said Conway.

"Girl Fridays like my aunty," said Sparrow. "It was the slave trade in miniature, hands tied behind their backs, frogmarched around in the hot sun. Abducted from their families, kept as concubines, beaten to within a fucking inch. And eventually trafficked and disposed like items of property."

"It's true that gangs of sealers had intense rivalries that regularly spilled over into deadly violence," said Conway. "The island scene was howling dogs, savage men, abused women and naked children. It was chaotic and godless."

He described how the mainland colonists rarely visited the island; the authorities in Sydney and Hobart feared the sealers, who had grown bold and powerful. In return, the sealers only ever visited the mainland in armed parties because they feared retribution by Indigenous Australians.

"There was a prevailing view that Aboriginal people couldn't be trusted," he said. "They were so violent that the government was forced to take measures to ensure the safety of the colonists."

Sparrow let rip a cynical laugh so loud that it seemed to startle the rookery of endangered seals.

"Can you blame us for being violent?" he said. "Our land and people were both stolen. Gimme a break . . ."

"The blackfellas would stab the whitefellas and then cut an incision to remove their kidney fat," said Conway.

"The ancient Greeks did the same," said Manolis. "It was a form of sacrificial offering."

"Sealing was Australia's first export industry," said Conway. "The skins were traded in overseas markets for money and goods. It's sad to imagine now but without sealing, the new colony wouldn't have survived."

He said that salt was also traded, as well as being used to cure pelts and preserve meat bound for faraway places like merry old England.

"There was once the promise of gem fields and precious metals, gold and silver, even coal," Conway said. "But none of that took off. Instead, it was sealing that pulled the crowds. The strategy was simple – the hunters would block the animals from reaching the water by getting in their way, before clubbing them on the nose, which is their most vulnerable point. This technique also caused the least damage to their pelts."

Manolis was disgusted at the thought of such unadulterated barbarity. Idyllic island life wasn't as simple as it seemed – the land was indeed, as Sparrow intimated, blood-soaked and haunted. He looked at the nearby seals with compassion.

"The slaughter was so widespread that, even today, there's some beaches where the seals refuse to go," Conway went on.

Sparrow snorted another laugh. "The seals are like me. We've inherited stress-related genes and carry generational trauma in our cells."

"Lots of hunters eventually went to Sydney or Hobart or returned home to Britain, changing their identities and keeping their dark island histories a secret," Conway said. "Not all of them took part in the abduction of Aboriginal women. Not all would rape or beat them."

Sparrow was unconvinced. "But no-one stepped in to stop the cruelty cos all the whitefellas were busy profiting from my ancestors' bush knowledge. We need reparations."

Conway agreed. "I feel for your People, mate. If it's any consolation, the sealing industry in southern Australia was the very first to consider Indigenous work to be economically valuable at all. The women's talents were hugely regarded, their essential skills in high demand, they weren't

74

just slaves, sex partners and possessions. But yeah, us whitefellas didn't understand the culture and economy of the First Australians, and through our greed, we turned the island into a fucking circus."

Sparrow nodded gently, acknowledging the recognition.

"Times are different now," Noah said gently.

"They are, but the seals are still vulnerable and preyed upon," Conway said. "Their biggest threats are probably feral cats."

"Feral cats hunt seals?" Manolis sounded highly sceptical.

"No, but they're here in plague proportions and they spread the parasite that causes *Toxoplasmosis*. On top of that, there's also the risk of seal entanglement in marine debris and fishing gear. Not to mention sharks, boats and drunk teenagers looking for entertainment."

With their round, stocky bodies and narrow flippers, the furry sea lions continued to socialise and frolic, fight and rest. They appeared seemingly oblivious to what had come before them on the island, and to what horrific events the strange fleshy humans were now recounting. Manolis sat and watched them with a quiet joy and appreciation.

Chapter 8

Manolis and Sparrow checked into their accommodation – Nails's pub.

"We're lucky to have gotten you anything at all," Noah told them. "The hotel's bursting at the seams cos of the housing crisis."

The heritage building had considerable charm, which is another way to say it was a confusing labyrinth of narrow staircases, contradictory passageways and illogical geometries that felt like they were designed by M.C. Escher. It felt more like a cold school dormitory than a cosy hotel, and was anything but practical. A barefoot, desperate Sparrow got lost trying to find the communal bathroom late at night and nearly had to pee in the pot of a dying plant, which looked like it may have appreciated the hydration. Manolis's room felt tiny – he imagined that Marlowe's acropolis would've had bigger broom cupboards. Its sticky brown carpeting sang the songs of thousands of spilled drinks, of raucous nights that got out of hand after the downstairs bar had closed. No amount of supermarket air-freshener spray could now silence their voices.

At least the place was quiet, thanks to its thick, impervious walls, their materials and construction methods a relic of a bygone age. Although it meant they swallowed phone reception as effectively as they did excess noise.

Manolis had to step out onto the street to get a signal. He smiled when he saw that Emily had finally replied to his last text.

"Hope you cleared customs okay," she wrote. "Everything I've heard about Kangaroo Island makes it sound like a paradise. Hard work for some!"

"Don't believe everything you hear," Manolis replied. "But so far, so good."

Manolis was loath to discuss the specifics of any of his police work with Emily but at times he outlined cases in more general terms. He valued her input as a sounding board but knew she was flat out with her own career and making up for his own parenting shortfalls.

With some effort and a stack of multicoloured sticky notes, Manolis unwrapped an old investigative chestnut by trying to construct a diagram of suspects on the wall of his room. It was still early days but it allowed him to visualise all the major players, the connections and relationships, in the hope it might trigger a flash of inspiration.

So far, with the exception of the massive new developments, arriving on the island felt like stepping back in time. It wasn't just the hotel's construction that was from an earlier era – so too were the local attitudes. Manolis had somehow expected it from previous cases and knew it would require both time and energy to break down those walls, perhaps almost as much as it would take to locate Marlowe. But the two went hand-in-hand – if Manolis could navigate one world, he knew he would succeed in the other. He'd seen it in reclusive migrant communities, hidden drug culture and organised crime rings. Every group was different but the dynamics were the same: there was a hierarchy and unwritten rules and resistance to outsiders. But the concept of *local* locals was especially new to Manolis. Had Marlowe tried to appeal to them, to curry favour, or would he forever be considered a *parvenu* whose money could never buy what they had . . .? Either way, the *local* locals represented an extra barrier that Manolis would need to overcome – that of history, which was inherently tethered to belonging and place. And he wasn't even sure if Noah could help him penetrate that.

*

In the morning, Manolis woke to a strange sound – silence. It was partly due to the hotel's noise-absorbing walls and partly to the hangover the locals and guests were suffering from after what Manolis had observed the night before. He'd gone to bed when things seemed to be kicking off downstairs, the beer flowing, the patrons thirsty, the stories exaggerated, the revelry in full force. Sparrow and Noah had wandered into the main bar for a curious gander, but Manolis's more advanced age and seniority had persuaded him to listen to his pillow's wise entreaties.

The lack of any hot water in the shower brought Manolis to full consciousness like a smoke alarm in the night. He dried off using a hotel towel with the thickness of cigarette paper (and also the smell). He had to knock on Sparrow's door three times – with increasing volume at each attempt – before the bleary-eyed constable appeared, complaining about the early hour and supernova sunlight. He looked like he'd been dressed by a blind man.

"Late night?" Manolis said cheerily.

"Shaddup," Sparrow grunted.

"When did you get to bed?"

"Dunno. I was busy. Gathering intel."

"Intel, eh."

"On the town. I thought you'd be pleased."

"Thanks, mate. Any luck?"

Sparrow exhaled a long breath. "I reckon we may be here a bloody while. But right now, hook some caffeine up to my veins."

"Mine too . . ."

Downstairs at the bar, a bright-faced, clear-eyed Nails was absently watching the drone of a breakfast show on the wall TV. He greeted his guests with offers of bitter instant, as black and as murky as witch's brew.

"On the house," he beamed.

"Thanks, but no," said Manolis. "Is there a café nearby?"

Nails looked offended. "Pub coffee not good enough for ya, princess?"

"We need something a bit . . . stronger."

"A *lot* stronger," said Sparrow.

"No worries. If you wander down the main drag, Elvis's café may be open. Depends on how dusty he is."

"How is it you're not dusty?" Manolis asked.

Nails smiled, showing corn-coloured incisors. "I'm a publican. And publicans drink but they don't get drunk."

The next TV news story captured all their collective attention. Nails had to hurry to turn up the volume on the remote control. It was about Marlowe's disappearance and showed some old footage of him speaking to an erstwhile politician in the world's greyest suit, shaking hands and smiling unnaturally to camera.

"With the support of the government, this infrastructure project will bring significant investment and local benefits, not only by providing job opportunities during the construction phase but also after it opens," Marlowe said. "Furthermore, it will provide essential services to tens of thousands of homes and establish an important intergenerational asset for the broader community."

In Marlowe's voice, Manolis heard the very same enunciation as captured in the simple voicemail he'd left for Holly – sophisticated, formal, refined. It made the detective wonder whether Marlowe had another verbal gear or if his singular intonation applied to all situations and circumstances. It came with a certain presence, a gravity, a flow, as if every word was carefully curated and carried more significance because of how it was said and by whom. If he were being honest, Manolis found it genuinely engaging and compelling, and could see why Marlowe had achieved so much in business. A switch to an equally successful career in politics would not have been out of the question for such a polished orator.

"Speak of the devil," sneered Nails. "There he is, our man of the moment. Excuse me while I go puke."

"Don't choke on it," said Manolis.

The police officers left the pub and headed east along the tree-lined avenue, sauntering at a slow, suitably sobering pace. The street was deserted with only a few lonely dogs roaming around, snuffling for scraps and barking at tiresome magpies. With the sun in their eyes, Manolis and Sparrow walked past the maritime museum that Conway had mentioned, which had a CLOSED sign in the window.

"What a bloody shame," sighed Sparrow.

But a mini-market was open, which they entered in case it sold freshly brewed coffee. To their collective disappointment, the cops only found tins of instant available, sitting alongside stout jars of pickled local produce swimming in brine, turnips and rhubarb and squash and strawberries. Continuing on, they soon found the café further down the street, which also appeared closed, doors locked, seating area empty. Sparrow was now determined, his course firmly set on collision with a caffeine god. He bashed on the single-paned glass with a meaty fist, making it rattle and move like a wobble board.

"We're closed," came a voice from an unseen source.

"Open up!" Sparrow called back. "Official police business."

"Mate," said Manolis.

"What? Well it is . . ."

Manolis might have chastised Sparrow for causing such a disturbance . . . if only he didn't need the inky black stimulant almost as much as his jaded constable did.

The owner of the voice soon appeared on the other side of the unwashed glass, a young barista in a skin-tight blue shearing singlet. An art gallery's worth of murky tattoos snaked their way up his sleeves and neck. His lower lip was pierced, his slender waist was tight. His eyes, framed by a pair of smart browline glasses, were nearly as red-rimmed as Sparrow's.

"Oh, it's you," the barista said. "G'day, mate. Gimme a tick, fellas. I'll open up."

He unlocked the glass door and let his grateful first customers of the day inside.

"Ta, mate," said Sparrow. "Two flat whites."

The cops took a seat at a window table. A gleaming espresso

behemoth, all boilers and pipes and tubing, was soon heard running through its warm-up cycle.

Sparrow began playing anxiously with a sachet of sugar. Manolis eyed his colleague with a new curiosity.

"What does 'oh, it's you' mean . . .?" the detective asked. "I didn't realise you had mates here."

Sparrow's pupils flicked from side to side. He looked like he was trying to string together the right sequence of words.

"S'nuthin," he said. "He was just at the pub last night. I saw him looking at me."

"Looking at you. Yeah right."

The milky coffees were soon brought over, their creamy heads trembling in the barista's unsteady hands. Sparrow took an unnecessarily large gulp, giving himself a foamy moustache. He seemed to reanimate before Manolis's eyes, the lines on his face disappearing, his shoulders relaxing. Manolis took a sip; the coffee was smooth, rich and genuinely excellent.

"You were at the pub last night," the barista said to Sparrow.

"So were you," Sparrow replied curtly.

"With Noah."

"Yair, with Noah."

"You blokes new in town?"

Manolis excused Sparrow's brevity and tone, chalking it up to the residual alcohol and lack of caffeine in his system. He made the requisite introductions.

"You're Elvis, right? Nice place, good coffee."

"I know. Single origin, fair trade."

Elvis pulled up a chair without waiting for an invitation. It came across as a café owner's right, an unwritten law, to be a guest at any table. He sat backwards, arms on its backrest, legs spread wide in a distinctly masculine pose. His chocolate-brown eyes scanned every inch of the young constable whose stare remained more focused than ever on his rejuvenating brew.

"You look like you've got a little Aboriginal in you," Elvis told him.

Sparrow's eyes seemed to double in size. "The fuck . . .?" he said. "Are you tryin' to be funny, mate?"

Elvis laughed playfully, touching Sparrow's arm. "Mate, I'm joking. I've actually got some in me, my great-great-grandmother. I'm proud of it and make no effort to hide it like some people do."

Sparrow opened his mouth to speak but Elvis interrupted. "And before you say anything, I know that having blood is different to being Aboriginal, which involves spirituality and connection to the land. I'm not saying I'm that, I don't have that, I'm not saying I'm like you at all. All I'm saying is that I don't deny my past and what your mob went through, especially here on the island."

It wasn't quite the monologue Sparrow expected and made Elvis sound like he was trying to right a past wrong on a personal level, or completing a prescribed twelve-step programme. Or, perhaps he was just especially conscious of white guilt and wanted to establish a rapport with the new arrival.

"Err . . . thanks," said Sparrow. "That's cool to hear, appreciated."

Elvis fondled his black onyx stud earring. Sparrow continued gulping his coffee like it was liquid oxygen. For a moment, it was as if Manolis was invisible.

"Saw you at the pub last night," Elvis said playfully.

"We already established that," Sparrow replied.

"No, we said you were there. Now I'm saying that I *saw* you."

"What's that s'posed to mean?"

"Well it means I was too shy to approach."

"Too drunk, you mean . . ."

Sparrow seemed to blush. It was a response Manolis had never seen before.

The Aboriginal cop blew on his coffee. "Uh huh," he said nonchalantly. *Gulp.*

"So, listen, I close up here about four o'clock. Wanna go for a drink after?"

Sparrow dove back into his coffee with a somersault and this time didn't resurface until the dregs had disappeared down his parched throat.

"Tonight . . .? Dunno, yair. Had a bit too much last night, I probably shouldn't drink again. I gotta go now, I'm meetin' Noah actually, we're doin' a recce of the island. Ta for the coffee, mate. And see ya later, Sarge."

Elvis watched Sparrow leave, carelessly shunting a table in the process and letting the door slam. His words had come out at double speed. The barista turned to Manolis, his face a mixture of astonishment and confusion.

"Shit eh. Was it something I said? I was just trying to be friendly."

Manolis savoured the warmth and flavour of his cup. "Never mind my colleague. He's not himself today. And he doesn't really want to be here anyway."

Elvis looked instantly crestfallen. "Oh? Why's that?"

Manolis explained the background.

"Shit," Elvis said. "No wonder he didn't like what I said, I came on way too strong."

"Just a bit. But he'll be fine once he reflects. You meant well."

"I'll have to make it up to him. Any advice?"

"Go slow. Give him time."

"Okay, cheers mate. Another cup?"

"Well I won't say no . . ."

Elvis disappeared behind the stainless-steel machine a second time and began working the caffeine turntables with the dexterity of an all-night DJ. He swiftly returned with a second flat white for Manolis and first doppio espresso for himself.

They opened up over coffee. Elvis said he lived in a small semi-detached house behind the café and described himself as "just a local, not one of those *local* locals".

"They're famous," said Manolis.

"Aren't they just. A-listers, VIPs. Still, I'd rather them than the newcomers. And I say that knowing that one of them's missing and that you guys are here to investigate."

"Fair enough, mate."

Elvis quickly mentioned he was at the port with Nails the morning Marlowe disappeared.

"Innocent until proven guilty, right?" He smiled.

"Usually how it works," Manolis said. "So, what have you got against the newcomers?"

Elvis sloshed his thick coffee around, aerating to improve its flavour.

"Are you kidding me? Have you seen their houses? All outrageously massive and perched up high on clifftops. They're two storms away from being declared unsafe and being slated for demolition. I just wish they'd all get washed away into the sea so their owners could feel the full effects of the global warming they're causing. But even then, the disaster relief programmes and subsidised insurance payouts would all be taxpayer-funded. But hey, the system works."

"Sure does," said Manolis.

"Stronger storms, higher seas, erosion and landslides are all the consequences of reckless overconsumption," Elvis said. "Hasn't anyone made that connection?"

Manolis assessed Elvis as immature in age but mature in conscience. Indigenous rights, climate change, sustainability, diversity. The world wasn't just about him, his motivations were more humanitarian and global, and his reasoning noble – all hallmarks of a more enlightened generation. It was an altruism and inclusiveness that Manolis hoped his own son might one day have.

"My grandparents were hippies," said Elvis. "They raised me. They came down to the island to escape the rat race in the 1960s. Never looked back. I guess I inherited their values, their weird outlook on life and the world."

"What about your parents?"

"Corporate. The less said about them, the better."

"I know what you mean . . ."

Elvis explained how the latest arrivals had destroyed the island's peaceful aesthetic with brash modern architecture. But more significantly, the size of the constructions also ruined the local environment, which had already suffered badly from the latest bushfires.

"I mean, they're welcome to come live here, everyone is. But if they're going to erect eyesores and ruin the landscape with garish mansions, at least put some effort into helping regenerate other parts of the island."

"You mean donations?"

"Or time. I mean, if money's too much to ask, if you're on skid row, ha. But just devote some time to planting trees or weeding, or help rescue injured wildlife or volunteer for the Community Fire Service. In other words, do your bit for the community like the rest of us do."

"Some people struggle with that concept. It comes from never feeling like they've been part of a community, so they can't really recognise it."

"Or they can and still choose to shun it. At the end of the day, we don't want to become a sanctuary exclusively for those who can afford it."

"Sanctuary from what? The rat race?"

Elvis laughed. As he spoke, his voice seemed to trail off in nostalgia.

"We're far beyond the rat race now. I'm talking environmental catastrophe or the collapse of society, which to me are one and the same."

The mention of the environment naturally led on to Elvis's concerns about the desalination plant and the proposed offshore drilling project. He pushed his glasses further up his angular nose.

"Of course, there's the obvious, most significant risks posed by oil spills," he said. "The contamination of marine ecosystems."

"I hear you," said Manolis. "But there's also benefits."

"Like what?"

"Resources. Energy security."

"Sea creatures don't care about resources. For them, it's only bad news. Simply setting up such a project causes toxic chemicals to be released into the water. And before even that, there's seismic blasting."

"I don't know what that is but it doesn't sound good," said Manolis.

"It's animal cruelty," said Elvis. "Large ships with massive air guns fire loud blasts into the ocean every few seconds. These sonic booms create soundwaves that penetrate deep into the seabed, and those that bounce back to the surface are used by geologists to find oil and gas reserves trapped in the ocean bedrock."

"And this is underwater mining?" Manolis asked.

"Yep," Elvis replied. "The noises are the loudest that humans can possibly make, twice as loud as a jet engine on take-off. Needless to say, that fucks up the marine life no end – it leaves whales or dolphins deaf, which ruins their navigation and communication. And it can outright kill tiny little zooplankton, which are the very basis of ocean food chains."

"You seem to know a lot about this stuff . . ."

"There's a group of us on the island, 'the greenies', if you wanna call us, who have it in our hearts. But there's heaps of people who feel the same even if they're not as hardcore."

He finished his double shot and began to clear the table. Manolis did the same, carrying his cup to the counter. Elvis began loading the dishwasher and separating the coffee grounds for composting.

"Liberal versus conservative, public versus private schools, sustainable versus non-sustainable," he said. "Our opinions may differ, I get that. But it's community that unites us. Even today, that's gotta count for something."

Little did Manolis realise it was a pronouncement whose echoes would only get louder with time.

Chapter 9

Adequately caffeinated but with a deep growl in his cavernous stomach, Manolis drove to Marlowe's restaurant for lunch. Lavender's invitation was a generous gesture and the detective was especially keen to hear more about the chef who'd had some recent trouble with Marlowe.

Naturally, Grayson's overlooked an expanse of calm, azure water. There was so much glass taking in the widescreen panorama, Manolis felt like he was ensconced in a fishbowl. The views alone would've drawn a crowd. With glossy boards underfoot, a mix of louvres and floor-to-ceiling bifolds were angled to capture every ripple, reflection and breeze from the dramatic seascape. All the fine-dining bells and whistles were in place – crisp white linen, elegant tableware, an exorbitant wine list and matching prices. There was also a "source local" ethos at play, with the daily rotating menu leaning heavily on Mediterranean influences and a focus on pristine, fresh seafood.

"What a view!" Manolis texted Emily, sending an accompanying ocean photo. "This restaurant is amazing."

"I'm at my desk eating a cheese sandwich with two-day-old bread," she replied immediately. "No need to rub it in."

"I don't mean to," wrote Manolis back. "I just wish you were here to see it."

Manolis imagined that any restaurant so close to the water that didn't specialise in seafood was anathema to the hospitality game. The menu nonetheless offered enough vegetarian options to keep him more than satisfied.

"The real magic happens here during the shift from sunset into early evening," Lavender said. "So we must have dinner sometime too."

While Manolis savoured stuffed zucchini blossoms with heirloom tomato salad, Lavender tucked into crab and swordfish, calamari and clams, honey king prawns and smoked rock oysters. Even Conway's wild abalone was on the menu, and at a price that dwarfed the other dishes like Jupiter and its moons. Other modest menu items included plump partridge and pheasant noted as being "fed with corn soaked in champagne".

"Richard and I would regularly enjoy lunch together here," Lavender said.

"Who picked up the bill?" Manolis asked.

Lavender chuckled. Some kind of in-joke was clearly at play.

"Usually whoever lost," he said. "The golf, I mean. We often played with friends and business colleagues who'd flown from the mainland for a round."

"For a round . . .?"

"Fly-in fly-out golf weekends. Breakfast beers, shucked oysters and buttery lobster tails. Richard loved to showcase the island like it was his exclusive little secret."

Or a bauble, thought Manolis. The idea of wealthy, influential men hopping aboard private aircraft to play a casual round of island golf blew his working-class mind.

Lavender sighed. He seemed to be sincerely missing his old friend and sparring partner.

"To think, we once jumped in our helicopters to head off for a round of golf," he said. "And then there I was, now using the same chopper to search for his body in the ocean."

"Marlowe's business associates," said Manolis. "How were relations there?"

"The corporate world is cut-throat. No-one gets out alive and no-one makes an omelette without cracking some eggs."

"That's a suitably vague response . . ."

"It just means that Richard was like everyone else – no saint, but no sinner either. In all my experience, that competition has never gone beyond strictly business. If anyone bleeds, it only ever stains the trading room floor."

Judging Lavender to be a shrewd and intelligent individual, Manolis considered bringing him a little further into the fold of the missing persons investigation, in the hope of securing an ally among the newcomers and getting access to deeper, more reliable information. In a setting such as Kangaroo Island, he needed to play both sides.

"Well in all my experience, in cases of missing people, what lingers more than anything is the *not knowing*," Manolis said.

"Like anything," Lavender replied. "It's awful to not have closure. The uncertainty consumes you." Helping himself to an oyster, he slurped the gooey meat down his slender throat.

"I've seen it destroy families," said Manolis. "Wondering what happened to their partner or friend or sibling or child. Sometimes for years. Sometimes forever."

"I can imagine."

"In the best-case scenario, the person will be returned to their family and friends safe and sound. In the worst-case, we at least try to give as many answers as possible."

"Is it a crime when someone goes missing?"

Manolis shook his head. "That's a common misconception. Strictly speaking, no, it's not a crime. If someone chooses to go missing and start a new life elsewhere, they have the right to do so unless they are legally required to stay, like being under court orders. And if a person gets lost or has an accident, it's a missing person case for the police to solve, but no crime, there's no defendant."

"But you must surely now have some pretty good technology to find missing people?" Lavender asked.

"We do," Manolis replied.

"Like what?"

"Well, we can't specify the exact techniques we use because some of them are also used to search for criminals."

"I understand. A splash of wine?"

"No, thanks. One thing we can try is geo-targeted text messages to all phones connected to particular mobile phone towers."

"Geo-targeted . . .?"

"They're sent to people who are within a certain distance of a missing person's last reported location in the hope they may be able to provide the police with real-time information on the ground. They're usually sent in high-risk cases – those with mental illness, people with dementia who have wandered from their homes, or young children."

"Fortunately, Richard's none of those. Or unfortunately."

A waiter in a starched uniform with slicked-back hair materialised at their table to present the next ornate course of fish and flora. Their description of the beautifully presented fare was finely rehearsed and impeccably delivered in a casual, relaxed tone. The boyish waiter kept referring to Manolis and Lavender as "friends", which Manolis found awkward but endearing. Not unexpectedly, the restaurant was relatively quiet for a weekday lunch service, the chiming of cutlery in harmony with the gently lapping waves. Manolis kept an eye out for Grayson, but there was no sign of him emerging from the kitchen.

"We can also issue press releases and post on social media," Manolis told his lunch companion.

Lavender thoughtfully sipped his wide-bellied glass of Pinot Gris. "How many people are never found?" he asked.

"I'd say only about one per cent of cases go on to be classified as long-term missing persons if they haven't been located after three months."

"One per cent? That's a good figure, it gives me hope."

"The key is to enlist the public to be our eyes and ears. Photos of missing people in places they'll see them, on a digital screen at a shopping centre, on public transport, at the cinema, or even at the start of an online video."

"It's like the modern-day milk carton."

"If you like, yes."

Lavender was referring to missing children whose pictures were once printed on the sides of American milk containers. Their faces would be seen from coast to coast every morning, forlornly staring out over people's milky corn flakes and coffee, imploring: *Have you seen me?*

"Hmm, but I think all that may be a problem here," Lavender said. "The sense of community, of connection."

"Don't be so sure," Manolis said. "I understand the Islanders organised an informal search party when Marlowe first went missing, and there's still people looking for him now as they go about their everyday lives."

With a look to the ocean, Lavender unleashed a dismissive laugh over the water. Manolis cocked his head, a questioning frown forming rows across his forehead.

"Sorry for the honesty of my reaction but we both know that's not true," Lavender said. "And frankly, if you ask me, it's the polar opposite of what's going on. If people are searching for Richard, it's simply in the hope of finding his body and confirming his demise."

He went on the offensive, pointing the finger for Marlowe's disappearance squarely at the Islanders.

"You remember the mortar tossed at the house?" Lavender said.

"I do. Is it that you suspect someone in particular?"

"No-one in particular. But it was crudely assembled, so we definitely suspect one of the locals."

"Why? What kind of mortar would a corporate type throw? Is it diamond-encrusted?"

Lavender snickered slyly and slurped his wine.

"Personally, my experience suggests an aggression like that represents some kind of reprisal," Manolis added.

"But that's the thing here, isn't it," said Lavender. "Just *our presence* on the island is treated as being an act of aggression. They want to turn this into a turf war, as if we're fighting over the control of prized territory."

As he tucked into a spooky-looking platter of black lip mussels, Lavender went on to describe the Islanders as "slippery customers, wayward and sullen, cunning and unmanageable, difficult to please and dangerous to offend".

His background in mining, exploration and other infrastructure projects meant that Lavender had a solitary focus – the almighty dollar. He described how the money recently brought into the island had improved the local economy and increased property values.

"We make these people richer, and they then have the gall to complain about us . . .?" he posited. "Hating people for saving their pennies, managing their finances and investing wisely is the new blood sport."

"Tall poppy syndrome," said Manolis.

"Taken to ridiculous lengths," said Lavender. "We've got a problem with success in Australia. You've got to keep it to yourself."

"But if the outcome is an increasingly bifurcated economy, is making vast amounts of money necessarily a good thing?" Manolis asked.

"Look, I understand there's always going to be tension when it comes to development and conservation, money and lifestyle," Lavender said. "But for God's sake, there's enough island to go around."

Gazing out over the water, Lavender reflected on Marlowe's affection for the water-bound territory.

"Richard always described it as a private paradise, and he was right, I love it here, too. It's absolutely beautiful and perfectly tranquil. Just this morning, I saw dolphins arching through the waves from my living room. It's the stuff of wildlife documentaries."

"Did Marlowe see the island as a retirement destination?" Manolis asked. "Was he coming to the end of his working life?"

"Well, one day. But not for a while, he was still very active in business. He loved the thrust and parry, and he was still at the top of his game."

Manolis ate a delicate mouthful of his butternut squash ravioli with toasted hazelnuts. The fine morsels detonated across his taste buds, then liquefied in his mouth. A benign warmth soon crawled up the back of his neck like a releasing massage.

"Increasing property prices aren't all good news," Manolis said. "It also brings higher property taxes and rising rents, which will soon squeeze people out. And I doubt they'd ever come back. It's land that builds generational wealth – especially so around here, it seems."

Lavender beamed a perfect white-picket-fence smile. "That's just economics, my friend. What's next? We'll be accused of controlling resources, stockpiling water and food and utilities, or buying up acres of land to build a new utopian settlement that operates using solely clean energy? Please. But I wouldn't be surprised, there's crackpots every-where."

The waiter materialised again, presenting Manolis with a warm, damp towel. The detective inhaled scents of lemon, myrtle and euca-lyptus as he cleansed his hands and mouth.

By the time Grayson finally made an appearance, tumbler of neat scotch in hand, Manolis had lost count of the number of artful, mouth-watering courses, including dessert, that had come his way, each paired with a bouquet of wine. It was like a famous director taking to the stage at a film festival after a triumphant premiere screening.

"Ah, gentlemen. I trust everything was to your satisfaction."

It sounded less a question and more like a statement. Lavender found his feet, as if rising to give a standing ovation. Part of that may have been due to Grayson's status as a minor celebrity. Manolis vaguely recognised his face from TV commercials and cooking shows, even if the name had largely eluded him. If it came up, he decided to explain that his demanding job and fatherhood meant he watched very little of the idiot box.

"Spectacular as always, Pat," said Lavender. "My senses are over-whelmed – sight, smell, taste, texture. And what on earth did you put in that whiting?"

"The King George fillets," Grayson said. "Pulled from the ocean yesterday. Prepared with a touch of mint and more than a touch of clarified butter."

The acclaimed chef sat, shook hands with Manolis, and proceeded to describe every course in intricate detail as if they were his own beloved children. Manolis got lost in the flowery explanations, he'd never heard so many colourful adjectives in such a short space of time, let alone to describe plates of food.

"All the produce, the vegetables and fruit and herbs, are sourced from a private garden we have right here at the restaurant," Grayson said. "We used to have something similar in the city, but down here, it's ten times the size."

"And did you like the dessert?" Lavender asked Manolis directly.

Manolis smiled at Grayson. "In fact, I did," he said. "*Baklava* and *loukoumades*. Better than my own mother could make."

Grayson's eyes brightened with appreciation, with recognition. "I always aspire to do that – the mother thing. And hearing that from a Greek, whose culture has such incredible cuisine and ingredients, I'm genuinely humbled."

He said the secret was the honey he used. "It's from our world-famous Ligurian honeybees. The strain originally came over by yacht from the Italian Alps, the province of Liguria, over a century ago, with an apiary being established in Penneshaw. And now, because of the island's isolation, these bees are direct descendants of the first colony, which makes them the last genetically pure population anywhere in the world."

"Wow," said Manolis. "I had no idea."

"Technically, Kangaroo Island is the oldest bee sanctuary in the world. The Ligurian bees feed on sugar gum eucalyptus, which gives their honey an intense, deep flavour with a hint of caramel."

Manolis found Grayson surprisingly lean and muscular for such an accomplished chef, which he put down to an unfair mental stereotype, the image of a jolly chef with round belly and tall white toque. Instead, Grayson had a sculpted coif, sharp blue eyes, a full moustache and neatly trimmed goatee, and an animated disposition. He was built for the modern media and the camera.

"For me, these days I just want the most ethically sourced, local and fresh ingredients," Grayson said. "My job is simple – get these onto the plate with a minimum of fuss. Modern food is all about the produce and producer, the chef is just a vehicle for all their hard work. Grow your own food and prepare it simply and honestly to do justice to its amazing flavour."

It was a culinary philosophy that made Manolis remember not only what Conway had said, but also his own father. As both a café owner and restaurateur, Constantinos always had a vast, lush vegetable garden on the family's quarter-acre block. It was the same for all the suburban Greeks with their feta tin pots and tomato plants tied to stakes with old pantyhose – a vestige of their life from the old country. The preparation of such homegrown fare only ever saw the addition of olive oil and lemon juice before hitting the plate. Young Manolis had turned up his nose at such "peasant" offerings, which always came across as a mortal blow to proud homemaker Maria. Little did he realise at the time what dark secret his wholesome parents were keeping from him.

"So, let me ask you then," Manolis said. "How does someone with such an uncomplicated, contemporary gastronomic view and such delicious produce possibly end up with a bad review?"

Grayson glared at Manolis, his index finger nervously tapping the table. The detective stayed cool, unflustered; he'd stared down hardened thugs and criminals before, a television chef – even the most hot-tempered and imperious specimen – held no fear.

Finally, Grayson laughed, whitened teeth, mouth agape. It was loud, purposeful, defensive, and almost tinged with a degree of hostility.

"So, you heard about that fucking review," he said. "Well, what can I say? Like literature or music or painting, cookery is like every other art form – completely subjective. Some people like vanilla ice cream, some chocolate."

"Only in this situation, the game was rigged," said Lavender.

Manolis appeared confused. "What does that mean?"

Grayson sipped his single malt and assiduously studied the sea. Pale ripples of light refracted on the surface, creating the illusion of a galaxy starscape.

"Seafood is my favourite to both cook and eat, so I always wanted to live near the ocean," Grayson said. "And down here on the island, I had a second chance to reinvent myself with a good news story. Slow cooking, quality produce, sustainably sourced. No bright studio lights, no make-up, no ads. Back to basics."

Grayson went on to describe a wage underpayment and embezzlement scandal that ultimately cost him his restaurant empire and numerous celebrity endorsements.

"But that was just the start," he said. "My wife left me, we sold our house, and my kids are now estranged from me, humiliated because of their dad's indiscretions."

As the chef spoke, reflected, Manolis finally realised Grayson's significance – his wasn't a homicide case, but it had still made headlines in both the public eye and law enforcement.

"I've only just started to be able to talk about it all, it's almost a form of therapy," he added. "And then this happens with fucking Marlowe . . ."

What little goodwill Grayson had established since that unfortunate time in his life had come crashing down when he was tarnished with a scathing review in the national media. It was negative, bitter, and further harmed his already tainted reputation. And he blamed it solely on his boss.

"The review was personal, the journalist and Marlowe have a history," Grayson said. "It had nothing to do with the food. Despite all my efforts to redeem myself and rebuild my life, I was dragged back into the gutter. And now, given what's happened to Marlowe, along with my criminal background, I'll likely be placed squarely at the top of your list of suspects."

With a look of resignation, Grayson returned his attention to the ocean, as if seeking nourishment. He exhaled and took another soothing slug of scotch. It was a crutch to lean on, one Manolis had seen in many police colleagues after traumatic incidents. Which, in a way, was what Grayson had endured.

Manolis's heart went out to him. In another universe, *he* was Grayson – an unhealthy commitment to his work, bending the rules, pushing the boundaries, always on edge, with a family disintegrating in the background. Manolis had been fortunate. Although Grayson's history was undeniable, he was still trying to atone, which Manolis respected in other offenders he'd seen convicted. But his criminal past could not be ignored.

And now, Manolis knew that the chef's frank assessment of the case was not inaccurate, and that it would take some work to dislodge the presumption of guilt from his shoulders.

Chapter 10

Noah drove Sparrow around the island, its perimeter and inland. The idea was to familiarise him with the terrain and conduct a rudimentary search for Marlowe on foot whenever they pulled over – for what it was worth. Manolis had also charged them with another search of the beach where Marlowe was last seen.

"How'd you pull up this morning?" Noah asked.

"Rough as guts," Sparrow mumbled.

"Coffee?"

"Intravenous." He didn't mention Elvis, his thoughts still too numerous and conflicting in that regard.

Sparrow was struck by the diversity of the terrain, from lush farmland to desolate scrubland, jagged coastline to white, sandy beaches, bold cliffs to the surging waves offshore. The young cop thought the boom of the waves and spumes of milky foam were both absolutely stunning and utterly horrifying. One wrong move, one trip or stumble over a rock, would surely result in his being sucked out to sea by such a powerful undertow. Who could possibly swim against that? The boiling cauldrons of frothing water an untrammelled force. Its inescapable grasp would lead to certain death in the unfathomable depths of the Southern Ocean.

Noah showed Sparrow the island's half-built desalination plant, where massive underground pipelines were being dug with even larger industrial equipment. Meanwhile, Sparrow focused on a sprawling shanty town of tents being blown about on a desolate beach.

"It's never been this bad before," Noah admitted. "And yet we're prioritising millionaires with multiple mansions over working families living in homes made of polyester. Haves and have-nots."

The bushfire damage became more obvious and grim the further west they travelled. Flinders Chase National Park was wild frontier territory, a region that still resembled the landscapes that faced the savage, long-bearded sealers. At the most southwesterly point, Sparrow marvelled at the red-domed Cape Du Couedic lighthouse, over a century old. The isolated headland looked out across the tantrums of the Southern Ocean with nothing else before Antarctica.

"Supplies used to be delivered to the lighthouse by boat once every three months," Noah said. "That was before the road was built. Can you imagine that? All the way out here but basically inaccessible, so the lighthouse keeper was essentially stuck on an island on an island. And that meant they were always vulnerable to accident and tragedy."

About a dozen conservation parks had been established on the island, along with the spectacular Remarkable Rocks tourist attraction, a collection of famously eroded granite boulders that had been shaped over eons. The contrasting colours of their black mica components, pink feldspar and blue quartz, and the orange lichen that coated many of them, gave them a distinctive character and appearance that photographers and influencers adored. They were some of the most imposing natural formations Sparrow had ever seen.

As they drove on, Sparrow asked about the island's more recent criminal history – long after the sealers and convicts and pirates had departed.

"More petty crime than anything else," Noah responded.

"Like what?" Sparrow asked.

"Burglary, criminal trespass, the odd arrest for firearms or drug offences. For a while there, family support services were sending dead-beats to the island to take advantage of cheap housing, which caused an uptick in such cases. One bloke was manufacturing booze in his farm shed, we seized hundreds of litres."

"How'd it taste?"

"I was paralytic."

"Ha. Anyway, none of that sounds especially serious . . ."

"If you want to hear about murders, sexual assaults, abductions and stonings, then no, we're unfortunately a pretty boring lot around here."

Noah spoke about the history of each region as they passed through and the people who generally lived there, who tended to be manual labourers of one form or another. He seemed to know every Islander he passed, greeting them with a wave and even stopping to chat to a few, introducing Sparrow as a colleague from the mainland helping out with the Marlowe case.

The first was a flannel-clad farmer, Wayne Boyle, with facial skin like worn leather. He lived at the dead centre of the island, not far from the sleepy township of Parndana. His family was descended from the island's very first free settlers in 1836, so he definitely qualified as a *local* local. The snowy-haired widower admitted, quite proudly, that he'd "never been to the mainland and never planned to". The island represented the unofficial birthplace of the State of South Australia, which Boyle claimed had been largely left out of historical narratives due to its shameful history.

"Ours is the only Australian state to have never received British convicts," Boyle said boastfully. "It's maybe why our accent is a bit posher, or a little more British, than other Aussies'."

Sparrow was about to say something about the British accent potentially helping the Islanders to be free of white guilt, and especially with no blackfellas around at the time, but Boyle interrupted his ruminations.

"In the same way that South Australians were segregated from other Australian colonies, Islanders were segregated from the mainland," he said. "The first settlers came in boats stocked with whaling and fishing gear. Coopers, carpenters and families lived in sailcloth tents and prefabricated wooden huts, mainly on the peninsulas at the eastern end of the island nearest the mainland."

"Wayne's family settled there before they moved inland after the war and started farming," said Noah.

"What did you grow?" Sparrow asked.

"Mainly grasses," said Boyle. "Crops of wheat and barley."

The island's heart was once rough and overgrown land with dense and impervious scrub spread evenly like a vast carpet. It had initially thwarted the settlers, who had expected something more like the gentle rolling fields of England than an impenetrable Amazonian jungle. Clearing the land was painstaking work that had to be done by hand with axes, picks and hoes. It was only after the Second World War that huge machines arrived on ships from the mainland that could swiftly clear paddocks and convert the region into suitable pastoral land. The government then laced the soil with super phosphates, anchored it with clover, and gave perpetual leases to ex-servicemen to start a new life as productive farmers.

"The families were called soldier settlers and initially lived in make-shift camps," said Boyle. "Pa's first proper residence was a brush house. It was superseded by a wooden structure, and then a solid stone residence. Which is why living in this shithole dump really gets my goat . . ."

He was referring to his current accommodation – a cramped camper trailer that had a crooked roof and flat tyre. His tone and language quickly darkened.

"It was lush and green and fertile here for decades until the bushfires roared in like a freight train from hell and turned everything black and lifeless. They flattened my house, which still had the original Tasmanian Oak floorboards. I also lost my sheds and basically all my infrastructure and machinery, half my livestock, and almost all the fucking fencing."

"Have they given you a time for the rebuild yet, Wayne?" Noah asked.

"Not yet," Boyle replied. "Maybe next century."

Fishing a crumpled cigarette from his shirt pocket, Boyle ignited it between sun-blistered lips.

"It's pretty bloody annoying seeing all those massive new builds going up near Vivonne Bay," he said. "Many of 'em sit empty, the owners aren't even renting them out, they don't want tenants to trash 'em. Not that I could afford it, but it's still bloody unfair for some people to have multiple homes when I'm forced to live in a fucking trailer."

Boyle stared out across the distant paddocks scattered with mechanical debris – tractors and ploughs and horticultural machinery of unspecified vintage – remnants of long days working alone. The old farmer had a tragic quality about him; Sparrow thought he saw a tear form in the corner of Boyle's eye. The corrugated sunflower of a windmill sat crooked in an empty field.

Boyle inhaled another lungful of strength. He kicked the trailer's flat tyre with resignation.

"Look, don't get me wrong," he said. "The community's rallied around, their generosity's been really touching, I'm grateful as hell. They brought me food and clothes when I was wiped out – even donated this old trailer. The Islander spirit, which we've had for generations, through wartime and natural disasters, shone through. It shows there's still good people out there."

Noah nodded with an air of quiet contentment. They had the island, and each other, and would defend it with every fibre in the face of oncoming danger, whatever its form. It was a bond that Sparrow found worthy of his reluctant respect, and perhaps even a little envy.

"And you also got your health, mate," Sparrow told Boyle. "You look as fit as a trout."

Boyle chuckled, embarrassed by the sudden attention. "I'm doin' okay. I put it all down to physical labour. Old-school farming, like Pa once did, always moving around. I've no bloody time to be ill, I can't afford it, and I'm grateful to everyone for their help. But this, right now, isn't sustainable."

"I reckon things'll pick up soon," Sparrow said. "The new builds are nearly finished. I saw Marlowe's the other day and it was basically done."

"Marlowe," grumbled Boyle, eyes narrow. "Don't talk to me about fucking Marlowe . . ."

"Why? What happened?" Sparrow asked.

Boyle admitted he'd had a spiteful encounter with Marlowe soon after he arrived on the island – a road rage incident that had quickly escalated, involving Boyle's boxy tractor and Marlowe's luxury sports car.

"The prick vowed to have me killed," said Boyle. "Can you believe that?"

"Jesus," said Sparrow. "Over a car?"

"Yep, over a lump of fucking metal."

"Must be some car . . ."

"Piece of foreign shit driven exclusively by corporate wankers with private jets. I was pretty shaken, I've had some run-ins over the years, I'm no soft cock, but no-one's threatened me like that over a piece of metal."

"Did you report it?" Sparrow asked.

"Informally," Noah said. "In other words, he told us over beers at the pub."

Boyle took a final drag on his smoke and flicked the glowing orange stub onto the grey earth, snuffing it out with an unforgiving work boot. No regard for fire safety – not that there was any fuel left to burn.

"I'm not like that, I can take care of myself," Boyle said. "Especially against a little prick like Marlowe. He was the same back at school, you know. Always tryin' it on."

"You went to school together?" Sparrow asked.

Boyle dipped his wide-brimmed Akubra hat and nodded. "Marlowe may be missing, he may be dead, but I'm too old to care. All I know is that a missing, dead prick is still a prick."

He echoed Elvis's sentiments that it was unfair for rich people to be able to use their wealth to buy their salvation.

"And especially when they made their money doin' shit that harmed the environment in the first place. Fucking hypocrites. They may as well use their dirty money to go buy their own private islands. Go away and leave us the hell alone."

As they drove away, rocks peppered the underside of the car's chassis like machine-gun fire. Noah spoke loudly to be heard above the din.

"The first settlers on Kangaroo Island weren't farmers, they were actually sealers," he said. "But you can't tell that to Wayne or Nails, they'll cut you up with a rusty blade."

The second Islander they encountered lived only a few minutes down the road. He was a local beekeeper, Yuri Petrov, an immigrant who once kept honeybees at his home in Russia and claimed he "fell in love" with the strain of pure-bred, disease-free Ligurian bees when he arrived on the island. Incredibly, his property had largely escaped the fallout of the natural disaster, but such was the lottery of a bushfire and sudden changes in wind direction. Some homes were spared while others were gutted.

Petrov was in his apiary when the police pulled up, tending to his rows of hives. He was wearing a soft white hat with reinforced brims and a mesh veil that protected his face and neck. Sparrow thought he looked like an astronaut surrounded by tiny orbiting spacecraft.

"The bees, they are so gentle, like babies," Petrov said. "See, I do not even need a smoker to keep them calm, and I can work without gloves."

Like a proud father, he showed them a hive frame, dripping with dark buzzing bees and golden honeycomb within its array of hexagonal cells. Sparrow tried to appear interested but all he saw were barbed stingers, venom, swelling and pain.

"This pure strain of bees is the single best thing our island has," Petrov said. "A pure strain of any species is extremely rare these days."

In recognition of this fact, a bee sanctuary status had been bestowed on the entire island, prohibiting the importation of all bee products.

"The fires destroyed so many trees and plants that the bees have since struggled to make honey," Petrov said. "We cannot bring bees in from anywhere else, it is not allowed and will contaminate the strain. We do not use antibiotics or pesticides so we need to be careful of parasites and bacteria. This past summer was very hard."

"But at least you still have your house," Sparrow said.

Removing his hat and veil, Petrov smiled, though it looked more like a sneer. His features were imposing, old world, with a hooked nose like an eagle. "This is true," he said. "God, He spared me."

The apiarist noticed Sparrow keeping his distance. "Do not be scared," Petrov said. "The bees are harmless, they will not sting you."

"How do you know what the bees are thinking?" Sparrow said. "Are you a bee? I'm fine here, thanks anyway, mate."

"Yuri sells the honey to specialty shops on the island, and also supplies cafés and restaurants," said Noah. "And what's the stuff used for healing again . . .?"

"Propolis," said Petrov. "It is a resin the bees make. It protects the hive against invaders and the elements. I use it to repair wounds on my skin, take it to ward off colds and flu, and even gargle it like mouthwash. The ancient Egyptians once used it to preserve their mummies. King Tutankhamun's burial chamber contained over three hundred gallons of honey."

"Amazing," said Sparrow. "It treats the living and the dead."

Petrov laughed. "It is true. And even after thousands of years, you could still eat the honey today."

"No expiry date," said Sparrow. "Just like convenience store food."

"When another insect enters the hive, or even something big like a mouse, the bees defend their home by stinging the intruder to death," said Petrov. "They then cover the carcass in a layer of propolis to stop the spread of disease as it decomposes."

"And I'm pretty sure my ancestors used beeswax in their rock art," said Sparrow.

Petrov stared at Sparrow with wide eyes. "Incredible," he said. "I did not know that. Thank you."

"Yuri sells queen bees, too," Noah said.

Petrov replaced the humming frame back into its slot and extracted another like he was fishing through an office filing cabinet. He studied it a moment and then proffered it for inspection.

"Here," said Petrov. "The brood nest. Look right here. Can you see the queen?"

Hesitantly, Sparrow squinted into the grist. There were so many moving parts in opposing directions that his brain hurt. To his untrained eye, the bees all looked like clones of each other. It felt like madness.

"Can you see her?" Petrov asked again.

"Umm . . . no," Sparrow replied.

"The queen is larger and longer. She has an abdomen that extends beyond her wings, which makes her look like she has short wings. And she has a shiny, black hairless back and light-coloured legs. Workers have fuzzy backs and dark legs."

Sparrow's eyes kept scanning. Was this some kind of intelligence test that he was flunking . . .?

"Is that one the queen?" He pointed desperately at a molecule amid the swarming mass.

"No, I think that is a drone, they have big eyes," said Petrov. "Look again. Worker bees are always very busy and hectic. But the queen stands still. Look for who is still among the motion."

Stillness among such constant motion . . .? Christ, thought Sparrow. Needle in a haystack, more like.

"And when the queen moves, the workers and drones make room for her to avoid hitting or bothering her," Petrov added.

After a moment more, Sparrow piped up: "I see now! There. Bugger me, no wonder I couldn't spot her, I was busy looking for her little crown."

Sparrow laughed at his own joke like it was the funniest thing ever.

"How much would one of these set you back?" he asked.

Petrov replaced the frame safely back into its slot, muting the incessant insect murmuring.

"It depends, but usually a queen is a few hundred dollars," Petrov replied.

"Fuck off!" Sparrow said impulsively. "That much for a tiny insect!"

Petrov appeared suddenly self-conscious. "Well, as I did explain, the bees are rare and pure, so the hive leader is more expensive."

"Who even spends that much on a bug?" Sparrow said.

"It is funny you say that . . ."

Petrov mentioned his latest client was none other than a local man named Richard Marlowe. Keen to establish his own Ligurian bee colony "and impress his rich friends", Marlowe reached out to Petrov, who supplied him with a fertile queen and hives.

"When his queen bee failed to reproduce, Mister Marlowe accused me of selling him a dud and threatened to sue," says Petrov. "I explained to him that some queens take time to lay eggs, especially when introduced to a new hive. They are not machines – they are animals. But he did not listen, he was not patient, and even had his lawyer write me a long, angry letter."

"That sounds like a pretty extreme reaction," said Sparrow.

"That is his world – impatience, lawyers, disagreements, arguments. I will never understand it. All that stress over a little insect, a few hundred dollars. He probably spends that much on lunch. In the end, I gave him back his money."

Petrov added that, given everything else that had recently happened on the island, he was surprised that Marlowe did not just try to import his own bees. "After all, who cares what the law says you can and cannot do or what people think of you."

"What did you do with the letter?" Sparrow asked. "Can I see it?"

"No," Petrov replied bluntly. "I threw it away in the garbage. Good riddance to bad energy."

With each new introduction, every new conversation, Sparrow was piecing together a pattern. Marlowe had not especially ingratiated himself with the Islanders, and wore a target on his back from some. Sparrow didn't yet know what to make of it. He'd need to discuss it with his more-experienced superior officer, who was no doubt sketching his own caricature of the island's strange, insular dynamics.

Chapter 11

Sparrow and Noah continued their tour of the island's fire-ravaged western end. They pulled over when they came across a park ranger tending to injured wildlife by the roadside. The ranger had the animal wrapped tightly in a fluffy bath towel, its furry face hidden from view, and was carrying it in a laundry basket. Noah introduced the young woman as Sara Fox.

"Kangaroo Island is free of all fox and rabbit pests," he added. "Which technically makes Sara the only fox on the island."

"Not for much longer," Fox said, patting her proud, pregnant belly. "There's a kit on the way in eight weeks."

Sparrow expressed his congratulations and offered to help with the basket, but Fox said it was feather-light. Its contents revealed the tragic reason why.

"It's a joey," Fox said. "A baby koala, poor little thing."

A series of yips and squeaks were soon heard from the darkened confines of the towel. The joey was pining for its mother.

"Her body's back there," said Fox, gesturing over her shoulder. Her voice carried a twinge of sorrow. "If youse can grab another basket from my car and carry her back, that'd help. She'll be limp and heavy."

"Oh," said Sparrow. "Okay."

"Be careful with her though. Her body will be needed to comfort the little one until we can get it feeding."

Sparrow picked up the doe's dead body as if she were still alive. He'd only ever seen koalas perched high in eucalypts, and usually happily asleep in a gum leaf coma. These were the crushing aftershocks from the fires seen up close, a tragedy continuing to unfold like a ceaseless tide.

The cops watched as Fox gently transplanted the joey and its dead mother into a stiff cardboard box. The baby's cries soon diminished in volume and frequency until they stopped altogether. The silence broke Sparrow's outback heart.

"The box is nice and dark, the joey should be fine until we get it veterinary treatment," said Fox. "She'll give it a once over and we'll then hopefully be able to start the road to recovery."

"How do you rate its chances?" Noah asked.

The ranger wiped the sweat from her brow and blew out a tense lungful of air. "Honestly, I don't know," she said. "I've seen so many animals that I thought would make it and yet I ended up being wrong. But also vice versa – animals that appeared to be gone and yet somehow survived. This little tyke doesn't look too bad – coat dense, eyes bright. But the loss of the mama bear throws a spanner in the works."

Fox took a seat on the tray of her ute, whose suspension buckled under her third trimester weight. Her eyes half-closed, she rubbed her swollen tummy with tenderness as if she were somehow communicating with her unborn child, sending all her hopes and prayers and questioning the world into which they would soon be born.

"Boy or girl?" Sparrow asked.

Fox looked up. "I don't know, didn't find out. Apparently, that's strange these days, most people prefer to know. I wouldn't know any different, it's my first time."

"Nice for there to be some surprises still left in the world," Sparrow said.

"That was my thinking, too."

There was no mention of the baby's father. Sparrow didn't pry.

"Every night I go home, I hope I've seen the last injured animal from the fires," Fox said. "And yet every morning, all I see is more traumatised creatures. It's like a never-ending zombie movie."

With a quaver in her voice, she talked about the diabolical conditions over the summer that led to the island apocalypse.

"It was a perfect storm, the combination of intense heat, strong ocean winds and high fuel loads."

"Had there been any back burning to clear the fuel?" Sparrow asked.

Fox showed a painful smile. "Yes and no. I tried to warn people this was on the cards, but no-one listened."

"Disaster waiting to happen," Sparrow said.

"I consider myself an environmentalist but even I know we can't just let it run wild. There was some hazard reduction burning done at the eleventh hour, but it didn't seem to make any difference.'

"That only makes things worse. You need to regularly breathe life into the land."

"You seem to know a bit about all this," said Fox.

"All blackfellas do, it's part of our growing up," Sparrow replied. "Blackfellas do something called cool burning, often at nighttime when its dewy and the winds are gentler. Very low flame height. It's basic land management. We have a cultural obligation to do it, things we're taught by our Elders and pass on to our kids to make sure the environment's healthy and the country stays safe."

"There was too much thick bracken and casuarina around over the summer," Fox said. "Invasive species take over, they choke out the native grasses."

"And the land loses its identity," Sparrow said. "Indigenous land management and cultural burning isn't just about blackfellas lighting fires willy-nilly. There's protocols, methods, right ways to do it, it's bloody technical. You gotta understand the trees and animals and breeding and bush foods and medicines and seasons, and understand that everywhere's different. And I still don't reckon whitefellas realise that."

"In the past, it would be violent and stormy, you'd get lightning strikes, and then fires would take off," said Fox. "They'd burn away a bit but you knew the wind change would come from the southwest, which would cause the temperature to drop and humidity to rise. And that was when you could finally attack the fire and put it out. But this last time, a freak wind change caused the humidity to go down, the temperature skyrocketed, and it all went to hell with so much fuel on offer."

"A really hot fire will end up encouraging plants that like hot fires to regrow," said Sparrow. "If you keep repeating that, you end up in a vicious cycle where you bounce between either really high fuel loads or really bad fires. And if you toss the blackfellas from their land, you end up with mismanagement of country."

As they spoke, a grey-brown bird with dark streaks and long legs scampered past. Its large eyes and thick knees made it look almost comical. Sparrow correctly identified it as a bush stone-curlew that builds its nests on the ground and has a distinctive mournful call. Fox was impressed.

"We blackfellas say that bird carries the spirit of death," Sparrow said. "If a blackfella sees it in their dreams, the blackfella dies."

"Birds fell out of the sky during the fires," Noah said. "It was literally raining down birds on us like roasted chickens."

"Kookaburras and owls and hawks and peregrine falcons," said Fox. "Butcherbirds, kingfishers and sea eagles. I saw roos on fire. The smoke was so thick that heaps of animals now have respiratory distress. I still have no idea how any slow-moving echidnas survived, maybe by sharing burrows."

"You can look at a bushfire as either something natural or man-made," said Sparrow. "If you ask me, it's always the latter, and it all comes from how you treat the fucking land."

"I agree, but the land's just one part of the ecosystem," Fox said. "There's also the weather, the rising sea levels and coastal erosion. These new developments are already stressing our limited energy grid, the island is seeing increased numbers of brownouts, and I don't know what's next. I've found quite a few dead roos recently – shot, not burnt. If there's illegal hunting parties, I'm yet to catch the culprits." She stroked her belly with a contemplative air.

"There's also been some logging operations underway recently, Tasmanian blue gum plantations cleared for agricultural use," Noah said. "Resulting in more injured animals."

"More koalas," said Fox. "Broken skulls, jaws, arms, hips. Or just plain dead. The harvesters ignore trees marked with tape by trained spotters to indicate they contain koalas. They're supposed to leave that tree untouched, and also the eight nearest surrounding trees. But at the end of the day, they don't care."

"How can koalas be protected by leaving a tiny cluster of just nine trees on an otherwise flattened landscape?" Sparrow asked.

Fox shrugged her round shoulders. "You tell me," she said.

"Sara's been great," Noah said. "She helped coordinate the first search and rescue party for Marlowe in the national park."

"It was a tiny area compared to the overall size of the island," Fox admitted. "But at least it was something."

She sighed and adjusted the hair tie securing her practical ponytail. Checking her watch, she got to her feet in a cumbersome motion, relieving the ute's rear suspension.

"It's been good chatting with you fellas and thanks for the help. I better get moving. This joey's got an urgent appointment with the vet . . ."

The pair's final stop was the ill-fated southern beach where Marlowe went missing. Sparrow and Noah wandered together across the dunes, their eyes fixed to the ground, their waists tethered by an invisible cord. The sand appeared wrinkled, its ridges as defined as a desert erg. By now, the cops weren't talking; they were tired of the day and of each other, with only the susurrus of the surf in their ears like white noise. It was another new face and introduction which revived their interest in proceedings.

"That's our distinguished island mayor," Noah said, gesturing with a thrust chin.

He indicated a fat bloke on the sand in a bucket hat, footy shorts and a pair of double pluggers. He had a fishing rod in one hand and beer can in the other. His sartorial splendour didn't stop there with a sleeveless T-shirt struggling to contain a sizeable gut and failing spectacularly. A hefty esky full of grog rested comfortably by his side while cantankerous seagulls squawked noisily overhead.

"Who . . .?" Sparrow asked. "Him, seriously?"

"Elected four times. Lemme introduce you . . ."

The Right Honourable Mark Murden flashed a perfect smile from beneath his toothbrush moustache, accompanied by a stiff handshake and sly wink. He offered cold cans, which were reluctantly declined due to being "on duty".

"Good to meet ya, son," he told Sparrow. "I'm part Aborigine myself, you know. One-sixteenth from Mum's side of the family."

Sparrow wondered how many more people planned to announce their Aboriginality to him, as if seeking his personal approval or eager to curry favour with a police investigator. But he was interested to hear what the island's resident politician made of the newest residents to his quiet electorate. To Sparrow's surprise, Murden said he embraced their arrival.

"It may come across as political suicide, and I wouldn't normally say it out loud to my constituents, but the new developments have only made the economy stronger," Murden said. "We could've barred the use of our tiny airstrip and jetty, vetoed construction, and mired ourselves in the past. But what good would that do, how would that help our future, our kids . . .?"

"Money talks, eh?" said Sparrow.

"Loud and fucken clear," Murden replied. "Louder than any voice, that's for sure. And Marlowe himself made some sizeable donations to the Council. He never spoke of them publicly, that wasn't his style. They were anonymous donations, and I'm only telling you now in confidence."

Murden was outspoken by nature, and he made it clear that he was anti-science and a climate change denier.

"All smoke and mirrors," he claimed. "Look hard enough and you can find scientific data to support any argument. I trust my gut. And my gut calls bullshit on it all."

Sparrow didn't know what to say in response. He doubted there was any point. Noah just bit his thumb and stared numbly into the pounding surf like he'd heard it all before, and was tired of hearing it again. To some, Murden's outlook was honest and refreshing. To others, it would be repulsive and delusional. And yet, it was clearly popular with the electorate, which was worth noting of itself. For a moment, Sparrow began to wonder if Murden's esky had some red, raw meat inside.

In the ultimate island throwback, Murden had also thrown his considerable weight behind the idea of resuming seal culling, ostensibly in defence of the local fishing industry.

"The seals are taking over the island and starting to impact our fishing hauls and small businesses," Murden said. "Contrary to popular belief, seals are not warm and cuddly and innocent creatures. They're highly invasive and aggressive mammals."

Sparrow eyed Murden's esky. Could it be he actually had some seal meat in there . . .?

"But what about your lucrative tourist industry?" Sparrow asked. "They come to see the seals, right?"

"They'd still come," Murden said confidently. "There's enough other things to see on our glorious island."

"Yair," said Sparrow. "Old lighthouses, special bees, tent cities, burnt wildlife."

Murden ignored him; he was on a roll, in politician mode.

"We recently had interest from an eco-tourism company keen to offer off-grid, sustainable tiny rentals," Murden said. "Each one will have an indoor sauna, indoor and outdoor baths, king-sized beds – and total privacy. The cabins will be solar-powered and prefabricated off-site to minimise disruption to the environment. So, you see, it's not all bloody backwards."

"Money's money, I guess," said Sparrow.

"My oath it is. But when you think about the sealing, it's the same with wallabies, which the sealers once trapped on the island. Tammar wallabies are now a protected species but their numbers have exploded.

It's the same with koalas, there's too many for the vegetation available, so people are talking about sterilisation, contraception and relocation. Personally, I think that's too much work for no tangible gain – we should be culling the bastards and selling their meat commercially to China and Asia, the markets are huge and they'll eat anything with some soy sauce and ginger."

"Wow," said Sparrow. "Just . . . wow."

"Or, at the very least, don't make it a crime to go wallabying," said Murden.

"What is and what isn't a crime isn't up to us," Sparrow said. "We don't make the laws, we just enforce them."

"And what a lot of people don't realise is that more seals also means more of something else," Murden said. "More food. And more food means more sharks. Seals are agile, so the only ones that get eaten are the ones goofing off and flopping around on the water's surface. And that's exactly what a surfer looks like to a shark."

"Nearsighted bastards," said Sparrow.

"Look, don't get me wrong," Murden said. "I bloody love this place, this island, and plan to die and be buried here. But the residents are difficult to lead, and I say that as a compliment."

Murden's focus was drawn by a sudden tug on his fishing line. His eyes lit up; had he snagged some rare, endangered fish species? He fought it for a moment, reeling it in and letting it out, wrestling with the line, before feeling it go slack again. Cursing his luck, he returned to his beer can and their debate.

"Frankly, the biggest threat to our tourism industry – more than any reduced wildlife or supposed 'global warming' – is the rise in juvenile crime," he said. "Ask the hard-working constable here, he'll tell you."

Noah nodded reluctantly.

"We discussed that," Sparrow said.

"I'm planning on petitioning the State government for more resources to tackle the problem," the mayor said. "Our island is always an afterthought when it comes to the allocation of funds from the government, all they do is take their full entitlement in taxes but give nothing back – our roads are the worst in the State. They also interfere and regulate our land use, I've had a bloody gutful."

"More police," said Noah. "Now *that* is something we can agree on."

"More cops, yes," said Murden. "But not just that – also more social workers, teachers, counsellors, mental health professionals, drug and alcohol centres, family support services, coaches and sporting teams. Basically, whatever ensures our kids get back on the straight and narrow. Punitive measures aren't a deterrent – the earlier a youth enters the justice system, the more likely they are to have behavioural problems and reoffend."

Sparrow had to reluctantly agree. He was once a troubled teen and since joining the police, he had seen first-hand what a difference such support services made. The mayor wasn't on the same philosophical wavelength as Sparrow but he still seemed to genuinely care about his populace.

"Look around the island, do you see any grand old mansions or homesteads or historic public buildings?" Murden said. "No. Without any mineral wealth to dig up, all we've had is agriculture and aquaculture."

"In other words, bugger all," said Noah.

"But things are changing, there's massive new homes being built and the desalination plant is coming along nicely," said Murden. "These construction projects have dragged us into the new century and created jobs to give our young people a purpose and a future."

"Well, yair," said Sparrow. "And the plant is designed for water security and will provide greater resources during bushfires, right?"

"Yep, and gives agriculture and tourism a boost," said Murden. "But the desalination plant is just one piece of the puzzle. There's also logging operations underway on the island and an offshore drilling project in the works that will further bolster the economy."

"So, you support those projects as well?" Sparrow asked.

Murden didn't stutter. "My bloody oath, I do," he said. "Unequivocally, wholeheartedly. They'll create high-paying jobs for skilled workers, generate significant income, and re-establish our island identity. If we're serious about the future of our kids and our island, it would be negligent not to. Resources like oil and gas simply have to be in the frame, the world still needs non-renewables and will do so for a bloody long time."

Sparrow wanted to ask what kind of world would be left for the children to enjoy if fossil fuels kept being mined and burned at an unremitting pace. But again, he didn't know if there was any point arguing against a popular politician whose mandate was clear. Murden struck Sparrow as a man of action who was used to achieving results. Come election time, there needed to be tangible results he could point to. It was more influential than any talk could ever be.

Murden inspected his line, now hanging limp, disinterested. He sipped his beer and stared into the distance.

"There's a school of sharks out there feasting off a stranded whale carcass," he said.

"Really?" Noah said. "I hadn't heard."

"Floating about a kilometre from shore, having a great ol' time, filling their guts like drunks at an open bar. There's a warning out for swimmers and surfers to stay away."

"And for sickos to flock," said Sparrow.

"The whales are migrating to Antarctica," said Murden. "More whales are actually a sign of conservation success, but it also means that more will die from natural causes during their journeys. The rest is just the cycle of life."

The men continued talking, shooting the shit, the waves breaking around their ankles and dumping clumps of dirty seaweed on the sand. And then, Sparrow saw something.

"Wait, what's that . . .?" he said.

Appearing like a flare amid the profound blue, a bright yellow surfboard was floating recklessly towards them on the incoming tide.

Chapter 12

It was Sparrow who inspected the washed-up surfboard first, noting that its primary structure was intact with the requisite number of fins (three) and shape (torpedo). It was a concerning discovery considering Marlowe's yellow surfboard had also gone missing the day he disappeared.

"I don't think there'd be many boards on the island with such a distinctive colour," Noah said. "I certainly haven't seen any."

"It could very well be custom-made," said Sparrow. "Like everything else he owned, it'd cost a bomb."

Sparrow consulted Holly's beach photo that Manolis had shared. "Yair, looks like it could be the same board," he said.

"Will you fingerprint it?" Murden asked.

Sparrow shook his head. "I doubt we'd get anything. The ocean's high salt content and all that time in the water will have fucked the chance of any decent prints."

"Marlowe could've been out on the water and just lost his board," said Noah.

"Or it could have floated across from the mainland," said Murden. "Across the firebreak."

"The what?" asked Sparrow.

"The Backstairs Passage," Noah replied. "Another name the locals sometimes use. Kind of ironic though in light of recent events."

118

"I reckon both those possibilities are pretty unlikely," said Sparrow. "I reckon this could be the first indication of a body in the water."

"Or someone discarded it to dispose of the evidence," added Noah.

Sparrow held up the board; its leash remained attached.

"Hmm," he said. "That's a bit strange. The Velcro cuff is still fastened."

"Either way, we haven't yet conducted an ocean search," Noah said.

Sparrow was loath to go anywhere near the water, but agreed that that should probably be their next move.

"I'll ring the boss," he said. "He needs to know about this."

Checking his phone, Sparrow saw it had no reception.

"It's the beach," said Noah. "Drops in and out depending on where you are and the weather conditions at the time."

With the light fading, they conducted a rudimentary search of the beach with Murden's assistance, but failed to find anything more on the sand or shore. The police departed with the valuable yellow board wedged inside Noah's vehicle, its tri-fin configuration resting on the floor, the passenger seat down as far as possible, and the seat belt strapped tight. Sparrow was scrunched in the back, gathering his mental notes to properly brief Manolis and trying to surf the waves of nausea that came from the rutted government road.

They headed out early next morning – Manolis and Sparrow by land, warm coffees in hand, Noah by sea, thermos of black tea, with both parties agreeing to rendezvous at the same stretch of southern beach.

"Hopefully Noah's not too long in coming," Manolis said. "We can search the area in the meantime."

"More beachcombing? Awesome."

"Nice job again, mate."

"Right place, right time. But thanks – someone had to be there. There's clearly more to Marlowe than meets the eye."

"By the time we're called in, there always is."

The day was overcast, the sky and sea the same indistinct shade of heavy, mournful grey. At the beach, Sparrow showed Manolis where they had searched, where the surfboard had washed in, and where the island's mayor had offered them beer and expert scientific insight.

"I still can't quite believe it," Manolis said. "When you first told me, I thought you were yanking my chain."

"Sadly, no," said Sparrow. "Christ, my imagination's not that fucking good."

"I guess we're a broad church . . ."

"Even if it includes clubbing seals to death."

Hearing Sparrow describe Fox and her doubts about impending motherhood amid the chaos of bushfires, climate uncertainty and island transformation transported Manolis back to when Emily was pregnant and the feeling of nervous anticipation they had naively felt. They'd prepared meticulously for the labour and birth, learning about breathing techniques and the like, going to evening antenatal classes and shopping for Swedish baby carriers and highchairs that developed both eating and social skills. Even still, they were completely unprepared for the reality of looking after a newborn, the sleepless nights and difficulties with feeding, and Emily's isolation and postnatal depression. Caring for a baby had stopped career-driven Emily in her tracks. Instead of constantly trying to push forward in her legal trajectory, she became more aware of wanting to build a foundation filled with values and love for their son, and that came from the bottom up. Manolis regretted not doing the same, not stopping himself, not being more aware of the real and tangible change in his life. He wondered whether Fox's partner – if she had one – was of the same mind and making the same mistakes.

Noah soon arrived in his underfunded police boat. It was a tinnie – a small aluminium dingy with a single outboard motor. And it altogether didn't appear up to the challenge of the large ocean swells on offer.

"Um, boss," said Sparrow hesitantly. "If it's okay, I might sit this one out."

Based on the seaworthiness of the vessel on offer, Manolis secretly wanted to do the same. If only they could take out Marlowe's luxury superyacht instead. Captain Volavola smiled invitingly and fired a naval salute, the palm of his hand facing down towards his shoulder, before he gestured for them to join him aboard the good ship.

"Yeah, okay," Manolis reluctantly told Sparrow. "You can sit this one out."

"I'll search the beach again, there's decent light now," said Sparrow, trying to be helpful.

"And then go see if you can find Skye," said Manolis.

"Righto."

With some doubt and hesitancy, Manolis took a cautious seat in the front of the tinnie. The bottom of the boat felt incredibly flimsy beneath his feet – just a thin layer of aluminium between him and the almighty ocean – while his centre of gravity suddenly felt uncomfortably high.

"Just hold on tight," was all Noah said as he powered the outboard into the open water.

"No life jacket?" Manolis asked, looking about.

There was a long pause before Noah responded. "We'll be right."

Manolis and Noah headed out, with a relieved Sparrow waving them goodbye and good luck. They were searching for anything floating in the water that looked distinctive – identification, a wallet, clothing, or even a body. The coastline presented itself like a broken wall of bold rock while the ocean was rocking and rolling with a heavy metal beat, making Manolis feel queasily aware of his own mortality. With such distractions and unease, he found it increasingly difficult to concentrate on the police work at hand. Noah described the day as "calm", which made Manolis wonder what kind of swell he would consider as "rough". The outboard motor sputtered at times, prompting Noah to admit reassuringly that "it can sometimes be unreliable".

After searching all morning, they failed to identify anything that didn't look like it already belonged in the ocean. The tinnie had been buffeted mercilessly by the waves and had nearly capsized on multiple occasions. With every passing minute, Sparrow seemed to be proven shrewder in his judgement call. Manolis felt light-headed, suffused with sun and a sense of failure. Finally, gratefully, they came across another boat – one that was better built to handle the conditions.

"It's the Nankervises," said Noah. "Father and son, lobster fishermen."

Erik and Erik Junior helped the newly established water police aboard their more stable fishing boat. For the first time in hours, Manolis felt his heart return to his chest.

"We've been on the lookout all week and haven't found a thing in the water," said Nankervis. "And nothing on the rocks and beaches."

"The ocean, the swells, the weather," stammered a pale-faced Manolis. "How the hell do you do it every day?"

The bearded, beanie-clad seafarer offered Manolis a bottle of tepid water and a ginger lozenge to soak up his nausea, both of which the detective accepted gratefully.

"Can you imagine what it must've been like for the earliest sailors?" Nankervis said.

The island was notorious for shipwrecks and drownings, its coastline synonymous with destruction and death. Its insular shelf was rough and serrated like a hacksaw blade.

"In the island's history, there's been some eighty ships go down," Nankervis said. "When you think about it, that's about one every three years."

He described the 1899 shipwreck of the Scottish barque *Loch Sloy* in Maupertuis Bay on the southwest coastline as the island's deadliest, with some thirty souls being harvested by the jagged reef in the darkness of pre-dawn.

"The clipper overran her distance when trying to pick up the lighthouse at Cape Borda and was wrecked on rocks a few hundred metres offshore. She was too close inshore and the light was hidden by the sheer cliffs. Not far from here, actually."

"That's comforting to know," said Manolis.

"There were only four survivors, none of whom remembered how they actually got ashore," Nankervis said. "It's pretty ridiculous when you think about it – once upon a time, the most dangerous part of the six-month sea voyage from England was the very last day before you found land again. And that's assuming you survived the cholera and scurvy and starvation and rats."

"Take-offs and landings are always the riskiest parts of flying," Manolis said. "Same thing here, I guess."

The region surrounding Kangaroo Island came across as Australia's own version of the Bermuda Triangle. Perhaps, thought Manolis, that somehow explained what had happened to Marlowe – he'd been sucked through a vortex into a parallel universe, never to be seen again.

"The shipwrecks are now as much a tourist attraction as anything else," said Noah. "Scuba divers, tropical fish, coral reefs."

Nankervis screwed up his face. "I dunno what's so appealing about a place of death," he said.

Manolis spared a thought for Sparrow and his allergy to the island for similar reasons.

"The shipwrecks are memorials," Nankervis added.

"It's part of history," Manolis said. "Everything's so much safer nowadays, cars, ships, planes."

"And lighthouses have more sophisticated instruments, including brighter lamps," said Noah.

"Yeah sure," said Nankervis. "But the rocks are still the same, still razor sharp and deadly. They haven't smoothed them out or filed them down over the years. And there's still boatloads of fishermen trying to make a living from the sea. Mistakes happen all the time – it then just comes down to blind luck. If it's not your day, you're dead."

Nankervis's summation seemed to make the swell pick up a notch, the fishing boat rocking like a bell-buoy in a storm. Erik Junior stared benignly at his feet, his pimply face barely visible beneath a long fringe of smooth teenage hair. Manolis sucked harder on his lozenge.

"My dad was a shipbuilder," Nankervis went on. "But it's too much for me, I'd rather just be catching things than building them. Lobsters are easy once you've got all the gear and their meat always fetches a good price. But things are changing."

"How's that?" Manolis asked.

"The ocean's warming up, which makes sea creatures head for cooler waters further south," Nankervis said. "It makes our catches smaller, and in turn inflates prices."

Nankervis went on to describe Marlowe as "a valued customer" who bought fresh lobsters straight off his boat.

"He was buying for his restaurant but also for his dinner table at home. He paid top dollar every time and sometimes even came out on the boat to help haul in the latest traps."

"Jesus," said Manolis. "He came out here . . .? Why would he possibly do that?"

"People fish for a hobby," Nankervis replied.

"Yeah, but how many head out to deep, rough water like this . . .?"

"He said it gave him a rush. The power of the waves, the thrill of the pursuit, the joy of the catch, to know he'd brought it in with his own two hands."

Manolis remained sceptical, surprised, but imagined that even the richest, most distinguished men occasionally liked to get their hands dirty, and also maintain some semblance of connection with "the common man".

"Marlowe said he felt more alive on the boat, and I saw it with my own eyes," said Nankervis. "The sea has a way of making everyone seem equal. Out here, he was just like us, his wallet was no use. Plus, I liked the bloke's company. Even with my own son on the boat, it still gets pretty lonely out here."

Back on terra firma, Manolis was tired and wet and despondent but ultimately relieved to have regained control of his jelly legs and surging stomach acid. Having failed to locate Sparrow or reach him on the phone, he decided to drive to the Marlowe stronghold to discuss the discovery of the yellow surfboard. But it was two unfamiliar faces who met him at the heavy double doors.

"Holly's not home," said one.

"No-one is," said the other.

The strangers introduced themselves as Luigi Rossi and Juliette Lemieux – they were Marlowe's architect and interior designer, and also husband and wife. Based on the mainland, they were regularly flown over by direct helicopter to project-manage and consult.

"You have keys to the house? You have access?" Manolis asked.

"Well, yes of course," said Rossi, adjusting his bold, blue-framed eyeglasses. "We still have work to do." He sounded displeased and anxiously rubbed his billiard ball head.

As they walked Manolis back through the house, they described its many exclusive features, of which they were understandably proud, in meticulous detail.

"The building's striking design meshes effortlessly with its challenging topography," said Rossi. "Being asked to design in such an exposed position makes this construction like no other, an unrivalled private home. It's a fitting homage to its naturally magnificent surroundings, it enhances the landscape, and it will never, ever be replaced."

"Like the Acropolis," said Manolis.

Lemieux wore her silver-grey locks in a short bob, tousled and carefree. Breezing through the interiors in her tailored pantsuit and dramatically pointed pumps, she looked like she'd just stepped from the pages of a glossy magazine.

"Each space merges soapy marble and stone with smooth concrete to convey a feeling of calm," she said. "Meanwhile, bleached and washed timbers, linen, and crisp surfaces provide pause."

"I like pause," said Manolis. "Pause is vastly underrated."

"Elsewhere, a sense of surprise can be found, from the rounded bulkheads and elegant balustrades to the timber battens that line the ceilings inside and out," Lemieux said. "It's innovative yet intimate."

Manolis loved their descriptions, delivered with bombastic panache. They weren't just flaunting an inanimate structure – they were selling emotions, which were far more powerful and persuasive.

"Precise sun and weather control is achieved through full-height sliding timber screens," said Rossi.

"And custom-made furniture from across the world was the icing on the cake," Lemieux went on. "All the blinds, curtains, carpets and joinery have been painstakingly handmade, making this the complete luxury package. Beautifully considered and flawlessly executed."

They arrived in the living room, which boasted a suspended wood fireplace as its centrepiece, floating like a flying saucer. The room's vast windows offered panoramic sea views and allowed the light to stream in like something otherworldly.

"You've certainly done an amazing job," said Manolis. "Unique design and exceptional craftsmanship. From speaking to Holly, I know she absolutely loves it."

Lemieux snorted an impolite laugh. Rossi rubbed his designer stubble in frustration.

"Holly is a bitch," said Lemieux sharply. "Pardon my French, but she's made our lives a living hell."

Manolis furrowed his brow. "Wait, how so?" he asked.

"Excessive workloads, unreasonable demands, impossible deadlines," said Rossi. "I could fucking go on."

"The scope of the project changed so much along the way," said Lemieux.

"We tried to rein her in but she insisted and demanded the work be tendered at far less than it would actually cost," added Rossi. "Her husband was pressuring her."

"Pressuring her? Holly told me the house was a joint project . . ."

Rossi and Lemieux laughed in unison, as if sharing a private joke.

"Is that right?" said Lemieux. "Hardly. Marlowe's too busy with work. He gave his trophy wife carte blanche to design the project however she wanted. He said it would keep her occupied, give her a focus. But she got swept up in it, and she was out of her depth, which meant the scale and cost blew out."

So Holly was lying, thought Manolis.

Looking around, the detective could not deny that he genuinely admired the space. "But the house is a true work of art," he said. "No matter how inexperienced Holly might have been."

"Sure, but at what cost?" said Lemieux.

"Our souls," moaned Rossi.

"Holly took micromanagement to a new level," said Lemieux. "It became nanomanagement."

"So, why do it?" Manolis asked. He suspected they had their professional portfolios in mind, architectural awards and the like.

"Well, it's not every day you have the opportunity to work on a grand clifftop home overlooking the ocean," said Rossi pragmatically. "For our résumés, we'd be mad to say no. And financially, it's been the job of a lifetime."

"But one thing's for certain," said Lemieux, voice firm. "We'll never do another job for these people ever again, no matter what ridiculous money they might offer."

Chapter 13

That evening, Nails's pub was heaving with thirsty patrons, the six o'clock swill in full effect despite the fact the pub still had many hours before it actually closed. The cash registers were ringing, drinks were sloshing, and the toilets were overflowing. Nails was out from behind the bar, holding court at his table of choice with a select group of binge drinkers and alcoholic friends, feeding their collective habit and at the same time adding an extra storey to his house – he'd show those new arrivals how it was done.

Sitting at a nearby corner table, Manolis and Sparrow tried to close their ears to Nails's tall tales of football and fishing conquests, but it was proving impossible to brief each other properly on the day's developments. Eventually, they took their drinks and went outside, sitting in the shade of a coolabah tree around which Nails's surprisingly salubrious beer garden rotated.

"Marlowe's architect and interior designer seemed pretty ticked off," Manolis said.

"But quietly, they're prob'ly laughin' all the way to the bank," said Sparrow.

"I reckon. And I had no idea there were so many different shades of white . . ."

"Are you kiddin' me? All blackfellas know that . . ."

The police were combining their daily briefing alongside a pre-dinner drink, with Noah having invited them around for a home-cooked meal with his young family. Given the limited menu at the pub's bistro, the vegetarian in Manolis was especially grateful. The island was taking shape to them now, the dynamic between the residents, and the personal, racial and class tensions that existed; some were new, while old grudges died hard. A couple of locals who were also cleansing their thirsts said g'day as they sauntered past – Boyle and Conway among them. Unsurprisingly, there were no "blow-ins" to be seen.

"Okay, so, tell me more about Skye," Manolis said to his colleague.

Manolis was especially keen to hear about Sparrow's encounter with Marlowe's supposed love interest, which had taken place earlier in the day.

Sparrow concentrated on his beer, a local drop with which he was clearly unfamiliar. His facial expressions and slow sips suggested he wasn't a fan.

"Not much to say really," he said. "She didn't want a bar of me. No surprise there. She was evasive, cagey and pretty uncooperative."

"Right," said Manolis. "So, of course, you used your finely honed police interview skills of persuasion and negotiation in order to crack an uncooperative witness . . .?"

Sparrow slurped his beer. "Bleh," he said. "Not buying this one again."

"Mate . . ."

Sparrow held the glass up to the light to examine the consistency and colour of his beverage.

"Constable," said Manolis. "C'mon now, focus."

"I am focusing. Hmm, maybe the lines need cleaning . . ."

"Is that all there is to report?"

"Well yair, Skye said she didn't need to speak to me and didn't wanna talk about Marlowe, and frankly, didn't wanna have anything to do with him anymore either."

Manolis tasted his whisky on the rocks. It was bland, too.

"Okay. And what was her tone?"

"As bitter as this fucking beer."

The senior detective thought they sounded like the sentiments of a woman scorned.

"Marlowe was clearly in over his head with whatever romantic involvement he'd engineered with such a young woman," Manolis said.

"But I did like her art," said Sparrow. "Her guard dog, not so much. The mutt kept growling at me, I thought he was gonna rip me to shreds at any moment."

"Who's this, is this Skye . . .?"

The voice from behind belonged to Nails, who had crept up on them once more. Manolis wondered how much of their conversation he'd overheard, and whether sneaking up like that was a deliberate ploy the innocent-faced publican regularly used in his domain.

"Umm . . . yes," said Manolis. "The constable met with her today."

"What'dya reckon, eh? Bit fucked up in the head?"

"I've seen worse," said Sparrow diplomatically.

"Well I sure as hell haven't, at least, not around here . . ."

Nails proceeded to pull no punches in calling Skye "mentally disturbed", "a freakshow", and "a recluse for a reason".

"That girl's just not right, she's completely unhinged," he said. "I mean, see what she named her dog . . ."

Manolis looked at Sparrow blankly. The young cop sighed.

"Satan," Sparrow finally said. "The dog's name is Satan."

Manolis asked about mental health and counselling services on the island, which only made Nails laugh until his eyes disappeared. He took a long draught on his beer.

"That there's your mental health support," he said. "Delicious."

The more the publican spoke, the more Manolis questioned what Marlowe could have possibly seen in a girl like Skye. Perhaps it was her untamable nature that drew him in . . .? Powerful men like Marlowe might relish such a challenge in the same way they were happy to brave the frenzied ocean and catch their wild dinner with their own two hands. It was the thrill of the chase, above all. Regardless, Manolis was left feeling disappointed to hear such a disapproving, negative assessment of Skye.

"All communities have their issues," he said. "No matter who you are or where you are, people can still get help."

Sparrow chimed in. "I actually found Skye to be pretty normal," he said. "She has a cool outlook on the world and hasn't bought into the whole material wealth thing. Not necessarily my cuppa tea, but I dunno if that makes her mentally unstable either. But enough about that, there's more important matters to discuss – like, can I get a refund on this beer?"

The sound of a vehicle blaring its horn from the road interrupted proceedings. The policeman in Manolis prickled at the disturbance before he realised it was simply announcing the local footy team's triumphant arrival at their prized watering hole, rowdy and thirsty and ready to celebrate a big afternoon win against their archrivals. A horde of sweaty young men, some still in their grubby footy kit and boots, piled out of a rust-ridden minivan and proceeded to serenade the beer garden with a rousing rendition of their club song at the highest volume. Nails was swiftly in the thick of things, roughly grabbing blokes by their guernseys in a show of camaraderie and strength, and belting out a second verse that only former club legends knew. The youngsters loved it and hailed Nails as their hero, which brought the desired effect from their club sponsor of "free drinks!" being declared.

The team's irrepressible captain led the charge. Full of swagger and confidence, Elvis strode over to Manolis's table.

"Hey mate," he said to Sparrow. "Buy you a drink?"

Sparrow held forth his half-drunk schooner. "Already got one," he said.

"Then buy you the next one. And maybe you join me and the boys for the night? I can introduce you around . . ."

Sparrow eyed the assemblage of fit and muscular footballers with some interest.

"Love to but I can't," he replied. "I got a prior engagement."

Elvis looked at Manolis. "He really does," the detective sergeant confirmed. "It's not just an excuse, Noah and Tessa are hosting us for an early dinner."

Elvis crossed his oiled, sleeveless arms across his barrel chest, making his biceps appear bigger than they were. He looked vascular, jacked. Like a peacock fanning its tail feathers.

"Early dinner?" he said. "Righto then. So, come back later tonight?"

"Unlikely, mate," Sparrow replied.

"Then what about a raincheck?"

Sparrow looked Elvis up and down, the footballer's shiny, bulging arms catching the light.

"Yair okay," Sparrow breathed. "C'mon Sarge, we better go."

With a wry smile, Elvis left to rejoin his abandoned crew, while Sparrow decided to abandon his disagreeable beer. As the officers left the pub, they heard the boisterous footballers egging on Nails to drink his first shoey of the evening, and saw Murden arriving to partake in the celebration in his official mayoral capacity.

"I hope you boys like curry," Noah said. "And these are traditional Fijian-Indian dishes."

Noah's weatherboard home was simple yet inviting. The selection of delicacies he'd prepared included chicken curry on the bone, a seafood curry made with prawns and ling, and for Manolis, two vegetarian curries, one with pumpkin and potato, and one with pea and spinach. All were served with fluffy white rice and oven-baked naan and roti.

"My absolute favourite is the goat curry," said Tessa. "It's the one that Noah and the kids love too, but we thought it too rich to serve today."

"Goat curry," said Manolis. "Sounds like what Greeks would make as a fusion food."

"Or feta cheese paneer," said Noah.

Sparrow proposed a toast, which somewhat surprised Manolis until he realised his colleague was enjoying not just the warmth of the hospitality but also the stunning taste of Noah's homebrew.

"It's still just a hobby," the local cop admitted. "But one day, you never know. Microbreweries and craft beer are taking off, including here on the island."

"Homemade curries and homebrewed beer," said Manolis. "Constable, I am impressed."

Tessa smiled. "There's a reason I married him."

Blonde-haired, blue-eyed Tessa had grown up on Kangaroo Island. She now reflected glowingly on the uniqueness of her youth.

"The island's a beautiful place to either be a kid or raise kids," she said. "In such a small community, my experience is that people are more accepting and forgiving because you've got no choice other than to get along. You just have to find common ground, something that ties you together. And I've been fortunate to find that here. I wouldn't live anywhere else and I plan to die here, too."

Tessa's two young sons looked up from slurping their cold mango lassis, their eyes wide with distress.

"Gee, darling," Noah said. "Talk about getting morbid."

Tessa hugged her children tight for reassurance. "Oh, you know what I mean. We absolutely love it here, don't we boys?"

They nodded dutifully, in unison. With mixed heritage, they had exotic hybrid features that defied convention.

But Tessa lamented the likelihood of their striking sons one day leaving the island, as so many others did.

"Most young people are dying to explore what the world has to offer by the time they've reached their twenties," she said, helping herself to a coconutty prawn. "They leave for the big smoke, for the glamour of Adelaide."

Noah snorted a laugh. "Sure. Glamour."

"Relative glamour," Tessa added. "Or they go even further afield, to other cities and other countries. But it's funny how many I've seen return due to the pull of family or the land or the ocean. I've seen it in heaps of my girlfriends."

Manolis had seen it in Emily, too. The desire to ground herself, to be kinder to her body and soul, to slow down and teach young Christos the values in simpler pleasures, in home, to prepare him for the future.

"My wife's the same," Manolis said. "Our son is her everything."

At Tessa's request, Manolis proudly showed her a photo on his phone of Christos looking cute and precious.

"Motherhood is like a sisterhood, and especially here on the island," said Tessa. "We're all fighting the same fight, living the same daily struggle. The women here are strong and inspirational. It takes a lot of guts for a woman to live on a rural island, which is still seen as man's territory."

"So, where'd you crazy kids meet?" Sparrow asked the happy couple.

They looked at each other adoringly. "At football, if you can believe it," Tessa replied.

"Well, not quite," said Noah. "It was at the pub, where most island relationships seem to start."

"Yeah, but it was after a big win, which I watched," Tessa said. "I was so nervous approaching him, he'd played so well that day, everyone wanted his attention . . ."

Noah blew on his fingernails and pretended to buff them on his shirt in a gesture of modest showboating. "Can you blame her?" he said coolly. "She was star-struck. It was love at first sight."

"That's not what my mum and dad thought," said Tessa. "Dad, especially."

She spoke frankly about her parents' disapproval of their mixed marriage.

"It's not their fault, it's a generational thing," Tessa said. "And times are changing. Younger people are now starting to wear their convict heritage with pride, embracing who they are, and it's the same for Indigenous ancestry. They even get tattoos now. It's edgy and interesting, not boring and shameful."

Sparrow acknowledged the more nuanced outlook. "Old habits still die hard," he added. "If we deny that racism is still alive and well, then we don't know ourselves."

"Well, Dad changed his tune a bit," said Tessa. "Especially when he tasted Noah's beer."

Manolis reflected on his own family history and the recently identified Indigenous presence that stemmed from his aunt accidentally falling pregnant. Was this the moment to share it, to finally tell Sparrow what had happened in the past . . .?

Tessa noticed her sons had finished eating and were starting to get distracted and playing with their food at the separate kids' table.

"Bath time, boys," Tessa told them firmly. "Let's go. Now."

Under some protest, she ushered them off to the bathroom, from which rushing water and squealing and chastising was soon heard.

"Witching hour," said Noah.

"You've got a great little family," said Manolis.

"I'm very lucky. Tess is the glue, she does so much. I do what I can but usually just end up feeling guilty most of the time."

"I know that feeling," Manolis said. "How does she feel about you being police?"

Noah poured himself some more beer from the unlabelled brown longneck. "Hates it."

"Seems to be a universal feeling among wives and partners," Manolis said. "Young Sparrow, take heed."

"Ha," said Sparrow. "Noted."

With Tess and the boys having departed to commence the evening bedtime routine, the conversation turned to suspects, motives and the investigation.

"I want to talk to Skye myself," said Manolis. "I still think those closest to Marlowe remain the most likely suspects."

"There's a fair bit goin' on," said Sparrow. "With mistresses and unpaid debts and road rage and bad reviews and righteous greenies and pissed-off designers and dud bees."

"You've been paying attention," said Manolis. "Good to see. But there's also valued customers and old mates and anonymous donations and a loving family."

"What's the case history of missing persons like on the island?" Sparrow asked.

Noah leaned back in his chair. He clasped hands behind his head and considered his food-spattered ceiling.

"To be honest, it's sketchy," he said. "Not cos our record's poor, more cos there's hardly been any."

He went on to describe a few runaway teenagers or mislaid drunks who were found within a couple of days. Marlowe had already been missing for much longer.

"There's only so many places you can hide on the island before someone finds you," he said.

"Many more places off it," added Sparrow.

Manolis tapped the table with a nervous finger. "We need those phone records," he said.

"I'll chase the service provider," said Noah.

"And bank records," said Sparrow.

"Yep," said Manolis. "Though the phone ones are usually more informative – they reveal the minutia. Going through those micro conversations reveals the full story."

Just as a young child let out a strident scream in the bathroom, Noah's phone pealed to life. He answered on the second ring.

"Hello . . . yes . . . yep . . . right. Perhaps no surprise. On our way."

Beep.

Manolis and Sparrow stared at their host inquisitively, who stood and started stacking the dirty dishes.

"Quick, gimme a hand to at least clear the table," Noah said. "That was Nails at the pub, we gotta go."

"What's up?" Manolis asked. "Is it a lead?"

"Fraid not," Noah replied. "Just the usual policing garbage. The footy team's celebrations have gotten out of hand, there's been assaults and vandalism, and the long arm of the law is needed to restore order."

Chapter 14

The drinking and revelry at the pub had been building to powder keg levels all evening. The combination of grog, masculinity and aggression had conspired to bring out the worst in young brains and shredded bodies. But what had really lit the fuse was the arrival of the opposition football team on Nails's doorstep.

"There was some controversy in today's game apparently," said Noah. He gunned the speeding paddy wagon en route to ground zero, its hazy headlights slicing through the darkness like dull knives.

"A disallowed goal?" asked Manolis. "A referee's mistake?"

"That would've been preferable," replied Noah. "Instead, we had our captain coathanger a rival midfielder, knock him out cold, start a melee, avoid being reported, and then ungraciously celebrate with taunting and showboating."

"Captain . . .?" said Sparrow. "You mean, Elvis?"

"There's a reason they made him captain," Noah replied. "Spiritual leader."

"And clearly a good sport," said Manolis.

"I know," Noah said. "But I remember what it was like playing, the adrenaline and emotions take over in a close win."

Descending on Nails's pub was an act of provocation from a defeated foe and came with a hardness and commitment that paralleled any sporting contest. If they couldn't win the sanctioned game, they at least wanted to conquer the unsanctioned fight. Manolis mused on the territorial aspect of it all, of one group invading the space of another, much in the same way the rich new arrivals had upset the long-term Islanders. It was an act of vengeance and, for a vanquished opposition, a means for regaining a fragment of self-respect. It was parochial, it was insignificant, but at the same time, it was everything.

"Any idea of the damage?" Manolis asked. "To either man or property?"

Noah swerved to avoid an unidentifiable lump of fresh roadkill clogging up his lane.

"Nails didn't say," he replied. "But judging by past experience, we should expect the worst."

Pulling up at the pub with an anguished rasp of brakes, the cops found a scene of mayhem and destruction. There were broken windows, splintered furniture, mortally wounded schooners, and so much needlessly spilt beer at the altar of male pride. The local team were looking decidedly worse for wear, with blood-splattered faces, torn guernseys, shattered knuckles, and even more crooked noses than usual. But, sizing up the roughly similar state of the enemy forces, it was still hard to tell who exactly had won the off-field war.

"Fuck me," said Sparrow. "Looks like the scene from a barroom brawl. Which, I guess, is precisely what it is."

A shirtless and bloodied Elvis was at the very centre of the action, his fists still hungry for more. Having been targeted, he had brought his crunching physicality to bear and obliterated opposition players for the second time in one day.

"Just get him the fuck out of here!" said Nails, indicating his club captain. "The drunk prick is the reason all this happened."

Extricating Elvis from the gory tableau was the equivalent of cutting the red wire on a ticking bomb. The combined efforts of Noah and Sparrow were both needed to restrain him and crudely bundle him into the back of the wagon like a lump of battered meat. Sparrow felt Elvis's arms – they were as firm as iron girders, and his muscles as taut as drum skins.

"Fucken lemme go, you arseholes! Don't fucken touch me!"

His protestations were not received sympathetically by the boys in blue.

"But I did nuthin' wrong! Those cunts came at me! Why are you locking me up?"

"I know, mate," Sparrow said calmly. "It's grossly unfair."

"Let's just sleep it off for tonight," said Noah.

"Whose fucken side are you blokes on anyway?" asked Elvis.

"We're on no-one's side," said Sparrow. "Only the law's."

He smiled as he slammed the door shut. On the other side, Elvis continued his stream of four-letter words.

Back in the front bar, the casualties were dispersing like the wounded from a battlefield. Manolis approached Nails who had a swollen eye and was missing a front tooth that he claimed was an implant following an old football injury. He was holding a cold can of medically approved beer to his temple.

"Any charges you wanna lay?" Manolis asked. "There's lots of property damage and also assault. Best you finger them now before everyone wanders off."

Nails's reply came with the hint of a new toothy whistle: "What's the point . . .? Anyway, I know all their families."

Standing on a rickety but unbroken chair, Manolis ordered everyone to go home. "It's been a long, tiring day, fellas," he told them. "Well played, hit the showers."

A few players from the opposing team fired him dirty looks and middle fingers as they stumbled off into the night nursing their wounds and injured pride. They would all hurt doubly the next day.

An unruffled Conway wandered over, his face and beer both amazingly intact. He decided to offer his own low-key take on proceedings. Boyle had wisely left the pub before the trouble kicked off.

"Besides the two teams going at it, Elvis decided to take the opportunity to tell Murden off for letting the blow-ins ruin our island," Conway said. "He's done so before, of course, but not to this extent."

"The Council could've rejected the development proposals but Murden pushed them through," added Nails. "The prick didn't even announce the applications publicly so people could object."

"A year ago, we had one approved private helipad on the island," said Conway. "Now, we have fifteen. In a year's time, we'll have fifty."

"Suddenly, everyone needs one," said Nails. "Vineyards, tourist operators, boutique accommodation, private fucken beach owners. The ferry ride across the firebreak is too much for them."

"The Council's got unlimited power, they're not accountable to anyone," said Conway.

"I think helipads are pretty easy to build," said Manolis. "No hangar or structure, just a concrete slab or even a flat bit of grass."

"And once you get approval, you've got it forever," said Nails. "It's not like a dog licence that needs to be renewed every year."

"Better one airport than a hundred fucking helipads," grumbled Conway.

"But that's not good business, mate," said Nails. "Rumour has it that Murden's been lining his pockets this whole time. And when you see how shiny his new car is, I fucken believe them."

"There's even more developments on the way," said Conway.

"Like what?" asked Manolis.

"Like resorts and apartments and a world-class golf course. The course will cost tens of millions and will include fairways that run along the clifftops."

"And it'll mean more private choppers and planes, and more noise," said Nails. "Fucken hell. The whole island's going to shit."

"Where's Murden now?" asked Manolis.

Nails gestured over his shoulder. "Out back."

"Out back where?"

"On a sick bed in the janitor's closet. He's got double vision. Copped a few injuries."

"What kind of injuries?"

"Cheek lacerated from a glassing, and his nose could be broken. Elvis nailed him in the eye pretty sweet."

"Jesus . . ."

At the police station with its freshly repaired roof, Elvis was helped along by the accommodating police duo. By now, the pugilist was floppy and close to unconsciousness, and thus ultimately calmer. He slumped like a ragdoll against the scratched and scuffed wall of the foul-smelling drunk tank.

"Murden's a fucken dinosaur," he slurred. "Head in the fucken sand. Deserves everything he gets. Fuck him."

With a tea towel soaked in warm water, Sparrow wiped Elvis's handsome face clean of streaked blood, dried sweat and assorted encrusted grime. Elvis kept his head slung low the entire time, his long curls hanging like drapes over his rugged features and pinched-tight eyes. Sparrow handed him a glass of water and two painkillers.

"Take these and drink this," Sparrow told him. "*All* of it."

Elvis opened his tacky eyelids reluctantly and tossed the pills down his gullet. He chugged the water down like it was a beer, throwing his head back in a violent, careless motion. He retched once, twice, before wilting back into position. His glazed eyes appeared like mail slots, struggling to focus on Sparrow.

"You're gorgeous," he mumbled.

"You're drunk," Sparrow replied.

"And horny."

"And drunk."

"But you *are* gorgeous."

"I know I am. But is that your best line? I bet you say that to all the guys . . ."

"C'mon man. Don't make me beg."

"You're not even my type. Sleep it off, sweetheart. Goodnight now."

He handed Elvis a plastic bucket and clanked the door closed. Flicking off the lights, he plunged the room into a profound darkness in which no drunkard could possibly escape oblivion.

Noah was concluding a phone call when Sparrow emerged.

"That was Manolis. He said Murden's injuries are bad, really bad, he's lost a lot of blood. And he thinks he's at risk of losing an eye, there's swelling and bruising and the socket looks fractured. Manolis has called for him to be airlifted to the mainland by medical chopper for emergency hospital treatment in Adelaide."

Sparrow's jaw hung slack, he seemed to momentarily forget how to blink.

"Holy shit," he said.

"There's also now talk of potential charges for assault and even grievous bodily harm." He shrugged. "Which is fair enough, really."

The next morning, Manolis and Sparrow staggered downstairs to the pub, tripping on the thickly carpeted stairs in the process. They were battling the formidable forces of being overtired and underslept.

The devastation that had been wrought appeared even worse in the new daylight. Nails was picking his way through the ruins like a man searching for survivors after an air raid. With eyes aflame, he looked like his head hadn't touched the pillow at all. Manolis and Sparrow grabbed some brooms and garbage bags and bent their backs to try and help restore order.

"Cheers, lads," said Nails. "Really appreciate it."

The trio worked silently, without a word being passed, like hungover university students cleaning up after a monumental housewarming party, praying that the landlord would give their bond back.

They soon adjourned to the front bar. The job was still far from done, but at least they'd made some visible progress.

"Thanks again, fellas," said Nails. "Hopefully the insurance company doesn't screw me over from here. Coffee?"

The police officers looked at each other seriously.

"Elvis will still be comatose," said Sparrow. "And even if he's not, he wouldn't be at work. Hell, I know I wouldn't, in all honesty."

Manolis nodded. He turned to Nails, a look of resignation on his stubbly face.

"Sure," he sighed. "Two instants, thanks mate."

"Comin' right up," the publican replied cheerily. "And a hair of the dog for me . . ."

Manolis's phone rang. It was Noah at the station. They spoke for about a minute while Sparrow considered Nails's choice of beverage and whether it was preferable to prospect of instant coffee.

"Good news and bad," Manolis told Sparrow. "The bad news is that the café is indeed closed, Elvis is still dead drunk. He's pretty green – had to use the bucket a few times overnight. But the good news is that the search warrant for Marlowe's house was just approved by the magistrate. We'll head back over there after we down this witch's brew."

"Let's just go," said Sparrow. "Surely Holly can whip us up something tastier than instant . . .? Their coffee machine looked like it was worth more than my monthly rent. Just say something urgent came up."

Manolis stopped; his colleague had made a very insightful point. But then, his eyes softened, his shoulders slumped.

"We should stay," Manolis replied, tone measured. "Sometimes, you gotta take one for the team."

They had to wait a long time before Marlowe's double doors finally swung open. They were greeted by another unexpected face.

"Dad's not here," said Allegra, before adding: "Lolz."

She turned and walked away in her delicate bare feet, staring into the chasm of her phone and leaving Manolis and Sparrow on the doorstep.

They watched her sashay up the staircase in her designer robe, hair swaying from side to side, and disappear into the never-ending vastness of the house.

Sparrow swept his hand forward, presenting the interior to Manolis. "After you, good sir."

Manolis took a hesitant step inside, followed by his colleague who proceeded to embark on a cheery, echoey whistle inside the polished entrance hall. Manolis went to fire him a scowl of disapproval before he heard the clamour of a much louder argument emanating from another room. Following the source of the disturbance, the police officers came across a swimsuit-clad Holly in the kitchen with Lemieux, a vigorous, animated discussion over curtain fabrics rending the air between them. Maple and Banjo Marlowe lay with their fluffy heads on the ground, seemingly bored of the conversation.

"Uh, hello, sorry to interrupt," Manolis said tentatively. "Allegra let us in."

Sparrow stood beside him, eyeing the shiny coffee machine with intense longing.

"I was just leaving," said Lemieux. She sounded breathless, relieved for the opportunity to depart, her high heels click-clacking across the cold, smooth floor. The front door slammed with a force that seemed to blow back Manolis's hair.

"Well, now that that unpleasantness is behind us . . ."

Holly sounded flustered. Giving a forced, embarrassed smile, she adjusted her triangle bikini top so it was sitting straight.

"Hello, gentlemen," she continued. "Good to see you again. I was just about to hop in the spa after morning yoga. To what do I owe the pleasure?"

Manolis thought the whole situation came across as somewhat macabre: the disrespectful teenager, the bickering over furnishings, the upmarket wellness routine. Was this really a home where a beloved family member had recently gone missing . . .?

The senior detective let a light frown downturn his features. "Good morning, again. Sorry for dropping by unannounced and interrupting, but I'm afraid there's something you need to see outside."

Holly's sun-kissed complexion took on a sudden ghostly appearance. The dogs looked up, their ears rotating like satellite dishes.

"Oh," she said. "That doesn't sound very promising."

"Right this way . . ."

In the teardrop driveway, Sparrow unstrapped the yellow surfboard, carefully extracted it from the car, and stood with it by his side. Holly blinked twice, deliberately and sluggishly, taking in all the visual information. Then she held a trembling hand to her mouth as the emotion and worry overcame her. Manolis was almost relieved to see it.

"That's his," she said. "That's Richard's board. I'd know it anywhere. Where did you find it? God . . ."

The Samoyeds barked loudly; they had recognised it, too.

Sparrow explained. "He may have just lost it," he said, trying to reassure her. "It got washed out with the tide and then brought back in again."

"Then where the *hell* is he . . .?"

"We're doing everything we can to find him," said Manolis. "And that includes needing to do this. I'm sorry."

He showed her the search warrant, which did nothing to improve her emotional state.

"This is important for locating your husband," Manolis went on. "You don't need to leave, you can stay, but most people prefer not to be around while we conduct our work."

"How long will it take?" Holly asked.

"As long as it takes, I can't be definitive," Manolis replied. "The search just needs to be ongoing and continuous. Given the size of the house, it could be longer than usual but we promise we'll be as quick and as tactful as possible."

The family, along with their phones and devices, decided to head for the rooftop balcony while the search got underway. Wearing a surly expression under his baseball cap, Roland kept his head low, avoiding eye contact with the police. He was dressed in a replica American basketball singlet that showed his skinny arms, a pair of maroon trackie daks, and flat-heeled slides that he barely lifted as he walked.

Allegra eyeballed Sparrow and pointed a finger in his face. "Don't you dare touch my bras and panties, pervert," she warned him.

"Wouldn't dream of it," he said, rolling his eyes.

Noah arrived to help with the search. The enormity of the house made the task onerous, even with the rubber-gloved officers working diligently in separate sections. Sparrow kept getting lost in its various wings and levels and wondered if a floor plan was available. Every room was immaculate, with the stratospheric price tag of its furnishings and accoutrements lost on the unassuming police officers. Manolis found drawers and cupboards stuffed with luxury items, rings and bracelets and jewellery. Sparrow had never seen so many clothes in his life, and all from instantly recognisable European and American designer labels. Holly seemed to have a thing for handbags and shoes; Allegra, beauty and make-up; Roland, sneakers and sports jerseys. As befitted an alpha male in the financial world, Marlowe's weakness appeared to be business suits and exquisitely crafted geometric wristwatches, feats of fabric and engineering, homages to tailoring and horology. On the bedside table was a reading pile that provided a window into Marlowe's mindset: ghostwritten biographies of busy entrepreneurs and vacuous celebrities, treatises on investment strategies and politics and the environment.

After an hour of exhaustive searching, the police finally came across each other in the grand billiards room. The table was the size of a swimming pool, intricately carved, with eight mahogany legs as thick as tree trunks.

"Anything?" Manolis asked Sparrow.

"Yair, heaps," he replied. "Tens of thousands of dollars' worth."

"I meant of significance."

"Then nah."

"Me neither," said Noah.

Manolis thought that a search of the entire property would likely need a separate visit and more hands on deck.

"Keep looking. Top to bottom."

Manolis checked in on the family. Toilet breaks were allowed on request and with an escort.

"Not long now," Manolis said, and raced back inside.

And he was right. A few minutes later, Sparrow hit pay dirt.

"Sarge! In here . . ."

Manolis and Noah rushed to Marlowe's study.

"Look," Sparrow said.

Hidden away in the desk's bottom drawer, beneath a pile of business papers, was every modern businessman's must-have combo – a silver handgun and a bag of white powder.

Chapter 15

With what seemed to be a key piece of evidence in hand, Manolis's spirits were immediately buoyed. Taking a seat in Marlowe's leather ergonomic chair, he felt its impossible comfort and leaned back with satisfaction.

"Great work, mate," he told Sparrow.

The young cop smiled smugly to himself, enjoying the moment.

"Is, um, the firearm loaded?" Manolis asked.

Sparrow stopped smiling. "Shit. I didn't check."

Manolis checked. Sure enough, the handgun carried a full complement of cartridges.

"Crikey," said Noah.

"Ready to rock 'n' roll," said Sparrow.

Positioned at one end of the house, the study's elevated position overlooking the ocean meant that Marlowe quite literally had a prestigious corner office at home.

"It's a bit intimidating to imagine that Marlowe had a fully loaded firearm in the house," said Manolis.

"Depends on his business," Sparrow said.

"Could he have used it to hunt?" Manolis asked.

"Hunt what?" Sparrow said. "Seals, roos, creditors . . .?"

"It doesn't strike me as that kind of weapon," Noah said.

"Plus, even if he did hunt, why keep it loaded like this?" asked Manolis.

He held up the sealed plastic bag of powder. "And what about this? Do you reckon this is powdered sugar?"

"Baking soda," said Sparrow. "Marlowe liked to make blueberry muffins. With frosting."

Opening the bag slightly, Manolis inhaled deeply. "Surprise, surprise," he said. "The devil's dandruff."

He sealed the handgun and powder in two separate evidence bags.

"Send these off to be analysed," he told Sparrow. "And also, check if Marlowe has a licence for the firearm. But for now, let's go have a friendly chat with the others."

The police returned to the rooftop balcony, where they found Marlowe's family grateful to see them. The relief was short-lived once Manolis presented the seized items for their consideration.

"Why in the world does your husband have a loaded firearm in his study?" Manolis asked Holly. "And do you have any idea what this powder might be?"

The Samoyeds snarled at the items, their highly sensitive canine noses on red alert.

Unsurprisingly, a stunned Holly denied all knowledge. Allegra looked bored to death. Roland offhandedly asked, "Did you just plant those?"

"Easy, mate," said Noah. "You don't know what you're sayin'."

"Yes, I do," he said confidently. "Spill."

"Son, accusing the police of perverting the course of justice through false, planted evidence is a serious allegation," Manolis intervened. "It's not to be made lightly."

With a sneer of contempt, Roland looked down at his phone, his eyes chastened, seeking validation in the screen's warm glow, the predictable online world.

"Excuse us a moment," Manolis said to the family.

He gathered his troops in close and spoke in a low voice. "I don't believe her," he told them. "How could she not know that—"

The trill of Noah's phone interrupted Manolis's reasoning. It was Murden calling from his convalescent hospital bed on the mainland.

They spoke for about a minute, with Noah mostly just listening before hanging up.

"What's up?" Manolis asked him.

"Good news," said Noah. "Our illustrious mayor needed two bags of blood but he's gonna be fine. X-rays show a busted nose and also an orbital fracture but he's avoided surgery. He just can't sneeze for a while or his face will shatter into a thousand pieces."

"I guess that's a positive outcome," Manolis said. "And what about Elvis, is Murden going to press charges?"

"More good news, no charges," Noah replied. "Murden said that 'boys will be boys' and he admitted that he also got up to similar mischief when he was younger."

"I don't know how breaking two facial bones is possibly considered mere mischief but that's great news for Elvis," said Manolis.

"And good news for us," added Sparrow. "Less paperwork."

Noah explained how Murden felt like he was living up to the island's violent past, almost as if he was somehow honouring those troubled times by not involving modern jurisprudence.

"Strange reasoning," said Manolis. "This isn't the nineteenth century."

"It's also how he leads, governs, plans," said Noah. "He's an old-school operator."

"We noticed," said Sparrow. "Seal clubbing comes next."

A second call ushered Noah away. Another minute.

"Sorry about this," Manolis said to Holly and the twins. They took little notice, having started an argument over the discovery of the seized items. Accusations flew like salvos in a skirmish. By now, Maple and Banjo had lost interest and left in search of crunchy dog biscuits.

Noah hung up. "That was the phone company," he said. "The call data is available."

"To the station," said Manolis. "We can pick this up later. Leave them here to squabble."

*

A bruised and surly Elvis was finally released from the drunk tank. He'd used the bucket a couple more times and now stank like Satan's armpit. Manolis cheerily told him that Murden wouldn't be pressing charges, and to go and buy a lottery ticket for all his luck. Noah fetched a mop and some bleach.

"And behave," Manolis told Elvis. "Stick to kicking goals on the field."

Elvis barely acknowledged him nor his own good fortune. He was so hungover and disinterested, he wasn't even in the mood to flirt with Sparrow, who seemed slightly disheartened.

"If anyone needs me, I'm gonna spend the day recovering at the beach," Elvis announced as he staggered out the door. "In other words, collapsed on the sand with the biggest electrolyte drink I can find."

Armed with a selection of petrol station snacks, the police settled in to analyse Marlowe's CDRs, which documented his telecommunication transactions, voice or text, but did not include the content of those transactions, for privacy purposes. The data recorded phone numbers, start times, call durations, and sometimes even location information. With so many minute details to pour over and somehow integrate into a narrative, Sparrow looked distinctly underwhelmed.

"Mate, you should be excited," Manolis told him. "This is a goldmine. In among all this data is a nugget, something that reveals Marlowe's relationships and behavioural patterns and helps us identify the most likely suspects. Humans can lie but the data doesn't."

It sounded compelling, the prospect of joining the dots to reveal a guilty caricature. But Sparrow clearly didn't relish the idea of sitting in a chair all day to manually cross-check two interminable lists of numbers.

"I was never good at maths," he said. "These days, there's gotta be some computer program or artificial intelligence that can do this shit."

"In the underfunded world of law enforcement . . .?" said Manolis. "Mate, you're hilarious."

Fortunately, with three pairs of eyes working in tandem, and fuelled by processed sugar and refined salt, it didn't take long for a pattern to be revealed. For all his complaints and supposed inabilities, it was Sparrow who identified it. In the lead-up to Marlowe's disappearance, there was a distinctive series of late-night calls to a number that was soon identified as Skye's.

"There's the girlfriend," said Manolis. "But that's a strange pattern alright."

"Is it?" Noah asked. "Surely late-night calls are part and parcel of such an affair."

"Keep going," Manolis told them. "But that's enough for me. I'm heading out."

Grabbing Noah's car keys, he drove at speed through the scorched landscape noir to the island's western end. And this time, he found Skye on the wooden deck outside her converted shipping container working on new art. Her Rottweiler from the underworld sat loyally by her side, snarling at the incursion. Skye rubbed the animal's gargoylish head in reassurance, seeking to soothe the savage beast. She was dressed in a black neoprene wetsuit, and her hair was still wet and salty after a surf in the ocean.

"Hello there," Manolis said, keeping his tone friendly. "My name's Detective Sergeant George Manolis and I'm—"

"I know who you are," she said without looking away from her sketchpad.

"Nice to meet you, too."

"And I know why you're here."

Skye had a confidence that Manolis expected, but an appearance that took him by surprise. She had a carefree blunt bob of beachy blonde hair that perfectly framed a heart-shaped face. Her bare, waiflike arms bore tattoos inspired by nature – mountains, turtles, mushrooms. A stainless-steel nose stud caught the light in a way that kept drawing Manolis's attention against his will. He was determined to stay conciliatory and warm but at the same time he realised that Skye's boldness and intellect were a force to be reckoned with.

"Okay then," he said. "Well, that makes things easier. Can you then tell me about—"

"Am I under arrest?"

"Sorry . . .? Arrest?"

"Yes."

"Well, no . . ."

"So, I have the right to silence? I don't have to answer any of your questions?"

Her tone was light, airy and enlightened. Manolis shook his head in disbelief.

"Well, yes, you're correct," he said.

Skye kept scratching away with her charcoal stick. "And you can't officially drag me to the station for interview unless I'm under arrest?"

"That's also true. But people often make statements."

"Voluntarily, though."

Manolis smiled painfully and shifted his weight between his feet.

"Miss, I'm just trying to do my job here. And we can do this the easy way or the hard way. Personally, I know which I prefer, and which I recommend to you, too."

Skye stopped her sketch and finally looked Manolis in the eye.

"Like I told your nosey partner, I don't really want to answer any questions about Richard Marlowe, and nor do I want to have anything more to do with him," she said firmly. "And the same goes for you or anyone else. So, if you don't have any official paperwork or a charge to lay, I'm sorry you wasted your time coming all the way out here."

She returned her focus to her art. As if to underscore her dismissal, Satan unleashed a low, menacing growl from deep within his throat that Manolis felt in his bones. The dog's teeth appeared like sharpened blades interlocking in a saw-like fashion, his thick, sticky drool hinting at a potential rabies infection.

Manolis started on a slow pace of the deck. It was a deliberate tactic to establish a foothold on hostile territory and demonstrate his composure and cool even if it risked making him a moving, more appealing target for Satan.

"Okay then," Manolis said. "I'll head off. But before I go, I need to tell you one thing."

"What's that?" she asked, head down.

"Just that you're now the prime suspect in Marlowe's disappearance. So, any refusal to answer questions today isn't a good look for you should things blow up tomorrow."

Skye smiled to herself. Manolis was playing *that* game, which he acknowledged was a weapon in his law enforcement armoury that was always at his disposal. And despite her better judgement, Skye couldn't help but engage.

"Is that right . . ."

"It is, yes," said Manolis.

"Prime suspect, eh. And why is that exactly?"

"Well, two reasons. First, we have reason to believe that you and Marlowe were in a relationship, but subsequently had a falling-out. And second, the call data we've analysed shows a distinctive series of transactions with you just before he disappeared."

Skye stopped sketching and let out a laugh that was loud and cynical. It startled Satan who sniffed the air intensely. Manolis couldn't quite see what she was working on but it appeared to be the start of another disturbing face.

"Wow," she said. "Just wow. To both those reasons."

"Then you deny you were an item . . .? Frankly, I was a bit surprised myself. From what I've seen and heard, you and Marlowe are poles apart."

Skye put down her sketchpad and charcoal and swung around to face Manolis. She sat forward, propping her elbows on her legs and clasping her fingers together as if in prayer.

"We are, that's for sure," she said.

"Then what? Did he support your artwork and creativity?"

"He's an art lover, yes. He's got a big collection. As for me, I could appreciate his power and influence, but not for the reasons you might think. I've got everything I need, I don't want for any more shit in my life."

"Then what do you want?"

"To make change. To sway his principles and beliefs towards something more humanitarian and altruistic."

"That's very noble of you but it sounds like a tall order when it comes to a man like Marlowe."

"I can be very persuasive." She gave a disarming smile, arching her eyebrows.

"The locals around here don't seem very welcoming to him," said Manolis.

"I can't blame them. But at the same time, they don't really welcome me, either. Any point of difference is frowned upon."

"I noticed."

"And I'm not like them."

"I noticed that, too. Do you live here by yourself?"

"You know I do. Just me, my puppy and Mother Nature. I'm used to it by now, being around my own company. And through his connection with me, I like to think that Marlowe established a renewed appreciation for island life and the natural world all around."

Skye stared softly at her small feet, her toenails painted ink black. Manolis hoped she might elaborate on her personal circumstances, her lone wolf status, what it was like to be a woman on this remote, unforgiving island. But she defiantly said no more.

Manolis wondered whether any connection between Marlowe and Skye came from their similar status as island outsiders, as two black sheep, albeit different breeds. Their backgrounds and worlds could not have been more contrasting but a common foe meant they found common ground in the most unexpected of places – at the even more remote end of a remote island. They shared stories, moaned about the locals, learned each other's histories, and perhaps even went surfing and walked their pack of dogs together. It would not be entirely surprising if all that were to somehow evolve into flirtation and a romantic involvement.

"Look," Skye said. She ran her hands through her hair, sucking in a sharp breath. "Make me your prime suspect or public enemy number one or whatever you call it. I'm used to it and fine with it. I've nothing to hide and know you're simply a cog in a machine doing your little job."

On hearing that, Manolis felt a cramp of annoyance in the middle of his forehead. His "little" job was his everything – both his passion and his pain. He quickly pushed his irritation aside and refocused on the matter at hand.

"I love my job," he said assuredly. "As police, we are committed to maintaining safety and security of the community. And I'm sorry but this is just where things stand right now."

Manolis's phone rang, he stepped away to answer. It was Noah.

"We just received an anonymous tip-off," he said. "Someone rang to say we should go check out Petrov's property."

Manolis scanned his thoughts. "Which one is Petrov?"

"He's a local beekeeper. And apparently, the dumb bastard has been going around the island boasting about something he stole from Marlowe's house."

"Okay, cheers. I'm leaving now."

Manolis fished out his car keys. "Thanks for your time," he told Skye. "We'll talk again."

Skye nodded silently. Satan barked deafeningly.

"Oh, and Detective," she said. "One more thing . . ."

"What's that?"

"The next time you set foot on my property without me here and without a lawful search warrant, I'll have your community-minded arse charged with trespassing."

Chapter 16

Manolis met Noah at Petrov's property in the dead heart of the island, parking by the roadside. Leaning against the bonnet of his car, the local cop briefed him on the beekeeper's recent history with Marlowe, including the spat over the dud queen.

"What's Petrov's background?" Manolis asked. "Has he always been a beekeeper?"

"Nope," replied Noah. "Before he came to Australia and Kangaroo Island, he was in the Soviet Army."

The idea of a military man did not appeal to Manolis. His experiences suggested they were a breed apart from ordinary civilians – even hardened criminals – thanks to years of ferocious self-discipline, rigorous training and habit forming, both physical and mental. It was a mindset driven by accountability and consequences and directed at overcoming obstacles and preparing for the unknown, which might sometimes include nosey police investigations.

Settling on a strategy, the officers drove onto the property, rattling across the corrugations of an old cattle grid. They spotted a space-suited Petrov again attending to his hives within sight of his house. He proudly showed them off to the new face in Manolis, who took a genuine interest, all too aware of the crucial role bees played in maintaining stable ecosystems.

"Of course, there are many animals that pollinate plants," said Petrov.

"Bats, beetles, birds, butterflies, wasps. But bees are the most important of all, and humans have been working with them for thousands of years."

"Healthy bee populations are needed for sustainability, there's better food security and biodiversity," said Manolis. "We've always known this, but we seem to have lost our way recently."

"And I love working within such an ancient practice," said Petrov. "As a Greek, you would appreciate this, too."

The Ancient Greeks, he explained, saw bees as closely linked with the birth and death of the soul. They were a symbol of immortality because wild hives were often located in cracks in rock walls or in caves.

"The Greeks imagined those to be entrances to the Underworld," Petrov said. "Their philosophers believed that humans could be re-incarnated as bees, or that bees carried the tiny souls of those who had not yet been born."

It was a nostalgic, romantic idea that had Manolis yearning for a simpler time when he was more likely to believe such stories. He could see how myths of this kind offered the comforting notion of a grander plan for the universe, one that was immutable and beyond human control. But they also inadvertently urged respect for these humble winged pollinators of flowering plants.

"In more modern times, I heard a story about an Athenian beekeeper who slipped cards bearing religious icons into his hives to bless his bees and their yearly honey production," Petrov said. "Every spring, the same mysterious phenomenon occurred: the bees made their honey-comb around the pious images, meticulously avoiding covering them. It is almost as if they did so out of reverence."

As if part of a rehearsed routine, Petrov showcased the contents of his own hive, with Manolis failing at "spot the queen" almost as spec-tacularly as Sparrow had.

"Wait, are you Orthodox?" Petrov asked Manolis directly.

Manolis's eyes darted to Noah, who returned a look of confusion. His religion wasn't a question Manolis was usually asked in the modern world. He'd been brought up Greek Orthodox by his devout mum, made to attend Sunday services and fast on holy days. And while he didn't actively practise as an adult, he'd never renounced his faith, either.

"Err, well, I was raised Orthodox," said Manolis. "So, yes, I guess I am."

Petrov smiled warmly. "Then we are like brothers," he said, putting his arm around Manolis's shoulder in a show of camaraderie. Manolis felt his Red Army muscles envelop his smaller frame. He wondered whether Petrov would've automatically done the same if he learned Manolis was ex-military, and likely depended on his country of allegiance. Were the Greeks and Russians friends or foes . . .?

"But I am being rude," Petrov said suddenly. "Please come inside for a drink. Or I can make you a traditional Greek coffee if you like?"

"Fantastic." Manolis smiled.

The country kitchen was tightly packed with more individual items – pots, pans, spice containers, tinned goods – than Manolis had ever seen in such a small space. An unnamed marmalade cat stalked the culinary maze like an orange ninja, somehow bending and guiding its lithe body around every obstacle and leaving them in their haphazardly arranged place. Petrov prepared the brew in his well-used *briki* like an old-school operator – using cold water, not stirring the ground coffee and sugar granules too much, giving attention to forming the creamy *kaimaki* foam on top. It was near perfect, even by Manolis's lofty standards. Noah didn't think it was too bad, either. After he rinsed the *briki*, Petrov flipped it over to show Manolis the words MADE IN CZECHOSLOVAKIA on its base.

"Please try this also," he said, presenting a thick glass plate with thin slices of homemade honey cake. Taking a forkful, Manolis found it luscious and not overly sweet with a light texture and just the right moisture level.

"An old Russian recipe using Italian honey made in Australia," Petrov said. "We call the cake Medovik, which means honey. The secret is a tiny amount of bitterness from only very slightly burning the honey during preparation before pouring it in. And the quality of the honey, of course.

Much of the world's honey is now fraudulent, it is adulterated, bulked out with cheaper sugar syrup. That is another reason why our island honey tastes so good."

As they sipped and tasted, chewed and swallowed, Manolis scanned the interior of the house with interest. In addition to crammed and dusty bookshelves, assorted knick-knacks and framed photos, there were numerous items of Russian military paraphernalia on display.

"There is a lot of mindfulness and focus required for beekeeping," Petrov said. "When you work the hives, you cannot be thinking about anything else. So, it is very good to manage stress."

"I can imagine," said Manolis. "How did you first get into it?"

"Beekeeping has been used for therapy, especially for treating post-traumatic stress disorder in military veterans," Petrov replied.

"Did something happen to you during service?" Manolis asked.

"Not to me, but to many of my comrades," Petrov replied. "They started beekeeping and said good things so I thought to give it a try here."

Manolis wasn't entirely convinced. After another mouthful of cake, Noah finally said:

"Yuri, I'm afraid this isn't a social visit. We're here about Marlowe."

Petrov smiled knowingly. "I thought so. How can I help? Has there been a new development?"

Manolis sat forward and straightened his shirt in a business-like manner. "My colleagues have informed me that you and Marlowe recently had a financial transaction that turned sour."

"Yes, we did. But it was resolved."

"Can I ask what happened?"

"I sold Mister Marlowe a queen bee for his hives. When she failed to immediately reproduce, he accused me of selling him a dud, of trying to rip him off. He threatened to sue me, so I refunded his money, a few hundred dollars. Mister Marlowe did not understand that some queens just take time. I understand his hives are now thriving."

Manolis jotted down notes, but everything he was hearing was consistent with Sparrow's briefings.

"It was messy for a while, but as I said, it was resolved," Petrov repeated. "And that was all that happened between us. I did not know Mister Marlowe very well otherwise."

"That's not the word on the street," Noah said suddenly.

Petrov stared at him blankly. "Sorry . . .?" he said. "What street? I am confused."

"He means that you've been going around bragging about an expensive item you stole from Marlowe's house," said Manolis.

Petrov looked down. He casually reached for his cup and slurped with force. He then nodded silently, as if digesting the accusation alongside the coffee. Manolis didn't know if he was about to deny all knowledge. When Petrov finally spoke, his words were slow and his voice was steady.

"You must understand, I do not normally do this. But I felt wronged and saw a wrong occurring."

Manolis waited for more from the beekeeper but all that was forthcoming was another long sip of coffee.

"Okay," Manolis finally said. "Go on."

Petrov eased back in his wooden chair, making it squeak under the increased pressure.

"So, what happened is that I went to Mister Marlowe's home to discuss the purchase of the bees and hives. This was around the time his lawyer sent me an angry letter. I soon realised I was getting nowhere with a man who came across as wholly unreasonable. I was in the army and I am trained to improvise and adapt when faced with adversity. When I saw a free moment, I decided to claim a souvenir. I saw it as a form of reparations. It is not like he would miss it." He paused. "Has he missed it? Did his wife complain to you? Or was it someone else?"

Petrov began to mumble in Russian. Manolis thought he was quietly speculating as to who may have gone behind his back and told the police.

"Unless, of course, they told someone who then told us," said Manolis. "Word gets around on a small island."

"Either way, someone has talked," said Petrov. "There is a rat, an informant."

Manolis wondered why Petrov would admit his theft publicly at all – after all, it wasn't the wisest tactic for any criminal. Was it a deliberate strategy with a view to undermining Marlowe's prestige and endearing Petrov to the locals? Unless, of course, Petrov somehow *wanted* to be caught. Manolis had seen it in some cases he'd worked, it was a complex emotional mindset deeply rooted in criminological psychology. It was usually linked to a desire for acceptance among criminal peers, or a bid to gain street cred. Sometimes it was to instil fear in people, or even to taunt the authorities. It often came across as simply "dumb behaviour", but in Manolis's experience, most convicted criminals were guilty of precisely that.

"What did you steal?" Noah asked. "What was this souvenir you claimed?"

Without a word, Petrov stood, shunting his chair back across the grimy linoleum floor. He vanished into another part of the house like a spectre melting into the shadows. Manolis momentarily wondered if he needed to give chase in case Petrov was attempting the world's least subtle escape attempt. But he soon heard rustling and the sound of footfalls on the wooden hallway floorboards. Petrov stepped forward and placed the stolen item onto the kitchen table like a coveted trophy.

"That looks vaguely familiar," said Manolis.

"It should to you, yes," replied Petrov. "It is from our Eastern Orthodox Church."

The memento was a long-stemmed chalice cup, about a foot tall. Gold, intricately decorated, engraved and bejewelled, it caught the afternoon light to glow like a fiery torch.

"I was unhappy when I saw that Mister Marlowe had this item in his house," Petrov said. "I consider it sacrilege."

"What's it worth?" asked Noah. "Thousands? Tens of thousands?"

"The value is not my concern," Petrov said. "It is what the cup represents. To Mister Marlowe, it was likely just a souvenir of his international travels on a first-class ticket, a bauble, something to showcase and brag about. But to me, it has a deeper meaning, connected to culture and faith. Someone named Richard Marlowe has no right to have something like this in his private home. It is like some kind of cultural takeover."

Manolis nodded gently. "Be that as it may, we need to see this objectively, without emotion or any feelings of unfairness or propriety. Technically, this item belongs to another person and it needs to be returned to its rightful owner."

"But it was not his to begin with . . ."

"Be that as it may . . ."

Petrov exhaled. "I see. Will there be further ramifications? Will I be charged?"

"I'm not sure," said Noah.

"Usually, yes," said Manolis. "But you have been forthcoming with information today so let me discuss the issue with the owner, they will have a say given the value of the item and its theft."

Petrov threw back the remainder of his coffee, holding the cup to his lips for some time – it made him appear like he was drinking the thick grimy sludge at the bottom. He then threw his head back a second time, only now in disbelieving laughter, as if possessed by a spirit, or even a demon, before regaining his composure. Manolis thought it made him look borderline maniacal.

"I understand," Petrov said. "But you have to ask yourself . . . By reporting me to you for something so trivial, is someone trying to protect themselves in relation to another, more serious matter?"

It was a question that stopped Manolis in his tracks. The Russian had made a good point. And it had not gone unnoticed that the tip-off had been anonymous. But it all made Manolis feel decidedly uneasy – the visit to Petrov hinted at even more fractures and divisions on the island, which was the last thing the police needed after the events at the pub. The presence of the new arrivals was at the root of all manner of ructions in the small community.

"Personally, I think Mister Marlowe went swimming and drowned," Petrov added. "The waters surrounding us regularly claim victims, unfortunate as that may be. This is why I do not go anywhere near them and live as far away as possible, in the dead centre of the island. I know I had nothing to do with his disappearance. My theft of the chalice cup is another matter entirely. I think you are wasting your time looking for a culprit, but at the same time, the phone call you received is not insignificant."

Sparrow had been following the jagged coastline for nearly an hour, a loop that had taken him dizzyingly clockwise. His neck muscles had begun to hurt with strain from constantly looking left towards the water. He'd already pulled over several times, got out, looked around, cursed, and kept driving. He was following a hot lead, searching for something that only he knew.

His next stop was at the northeast tip of the Dudley Peninsula, not far from the ferry terminal, a place near Penneshaw Beach called Frenchman's Rock. He finally spotted his target across the road and up on a small hill overlooking the placid expanse of Hog Bay.

"What do you fucken want?"

Elvis was all stretched out on a long wooden bench facing the ocean. He looked like he'd made it his recuperative bed for the day, a bundled jumper for a pillow, soaking up the sun like a lizard. He was wearing a pair of futuristic, oversized mask sunglasses that offered maximum shade for his eyes.

"Nice glasses," Sparrow said.

"They help me see through the bullshit," Elvis replied. "I repeat – what do you want?"

"I wanna check up on you," Sparrow replied.

Elvis unshackled a dismissive laugh. "Like you were checking up on me last night, eh?"

"Come on, mate. Nails called us. You were outta control. All you blokes were."

He handed Elvis a large bottle of water and took a seat without invitation. Elvis sat up with a groan dredged from the weary, hungover depths of his soul. He cracked the bottle's plastic lid and sucked down half the contents like it was nothing.

"You come here often?" Sparrow asked.

Elvis exhaled. "Good line. And I do actually."

"It wasn't a line. I even checked for you at that really white beach with the maze of caves."

"Stokes Bay?"

"It was a pain in the arse to access."

"It always rates highly as one of Australia's top beaches."

"So, why come here instead?"

"The significance of the place. See where I'm sitting?"

Sparrow admired the wooden bench. With smoothed, curved features, it was intentionally artistic and unexpectedly comfortable.

"They call this the Contemplation Seat," Elvis went on. "It was made by a local woodcarver from a fallen gum tree and deliberately positioned to look out over the ocean crossing – a gun-barrel view of the Backstairs Passage."

"Why's that?" Sparrow asked. "To contemplate seasickness?"

"The seat is meant to be a memorial to all the Aboriginal women brought to the island by the sealers before settlement. The idea is for people to sit and contemplate the stretch of water that turned those women into prisoners, the one-way journey from the mainland."

Sparrow read the sign alongside that acknowledged how the women "made shelters, hunted, gathered and cooked food, found water, made clothes and rugs, tracked missing people, and acted as partners for the men". He was so moved by the unusual yet poignant monument that he had to wipe an unexpected tear from his eye. Elvis noticed and respectfully removed his snow goggles.

"Mate, you okay?"

"Yair. Just . . ." He paused to regain his composure. "Just my aunty was one of those stolen women. Well, not my actual aunty, but one of my ancestors."

"Shit. I had no idea."

"It's one of the reasons why I didn't really wanna come here. For my mob, it feels like this place is cursed."

Elvis slid across and gently put his hand on top of Sparrow's.

"Mate, that's really crap to hear, I'm truly sorry. But the seat is meant to kick-start reconciliation and healing between the local Aboriginal people and broader island community. There's been a big effort to recognise the contribution of women like your aunty and what they meant to island life. There's now also creeks, gullies and paddocks with names that recognise Indigenous women."

Sparrow processed the shift in thinking, the evolution of mindset. He remained cynical, but couldn't help but be genuinely touched by the memorial, which was both significant and organic.

"It's a beautiful gesture," he said.

"It's fitting," said Elvis. "Like I said, I come here often, not just when I'm hideously hungover and I want to die. I just sit and think."

"Think about what?"

"Everything. About being alive, being here, being free, being myself. The sacrifices of the past, the gift of the now, and the promise of the future. And just being grateful for it all."

They sat without speaking for a while, listening to the wind's gentle susurration and lapping of the waves. The atmosphere and solemnity of the moment was soon washing over Sparrow who became reflective, introspective, feeling both mortal and vulnerable. Elvis put his athletic arm around the young cop and took his weight.

"Why are you such an arrogant arsehole?" Sparrow asked. He sounded frustrated.

"I don't mean to be," Elvis replied. "People have told me it's because I'm a deeply insecure arsehole and I'm always trying to keep people from seeing that."

Away from the crowds and distractions and dripping testosterone, the pair finally began to open up. It was a chance to get to know each

166

other personally, more intimately – their histories and personalities, likes and dislikes, beliefs, values and fears. Sparrow saw something in the extroverted, flirtatious, complex Elvis, but still wasn't quite sure how to proceed.

Chapter 17

The atmosphere was appropriately muted at the devastated pub that evening as punters and police gathered to eat and drink and chinwag and, where appropriate, brief each other on the case. Manolis shared a few text messages with Emily before he entered the building with its impenetrable walls.

"You've been quiet," she had written. "That worries me."

"I'm okay," he replied. "Just been focused on the case, I'm having trouble gaining traction, there's still too many loose ends."

"Hang in there. You've cracked so many cases, this one may just take a bit more time."

"I know, I'd rather it took less."

"Christos misses you."

Hmm, why didn't she write "I miss you", Manolis wondered.

"I miss you both," he wrote back. "Love you."

Manolis waited but there were no more replies. With an air of disappointment, he pushed open the pub door and shambled inside.

He found Noah sitting with a pair of pre-ordered drinks. Manolis thanked the constable and pensively sipped his whisky and cola; the sugary mixer at least energised the blandness of the booze and blunted what little alcoholic taste it otherwise had. Meanwhile, Noah hoovered up his foamy schooner like a camel refuelling at an oasis.

Manolis looked around the harshly lit room, his eyes sore and scratchy. "Where's Sparrow?" he asked.

"Late," Noah replied.

"I can see that. Where *is* he though?"

"Said he was going out to follow up on a lead."

"A lead . . .? He didn't mention anything to me."

"Must be deep undercover work if not even his boss knows about it."

"He's cagey at the best of times. Still young and unsettled – he had a troubled time as a young fella," said Manolis.

"What happened?" Noah asked.

"Dysfunctional community, social issues, didn't get much support or many opportunities."

"That's pretty shit but also pretty common for Indigenous communities. And Sparrow seems somewhat fired up about that."

"Can you blame him? I can't. First Australians have been a footnote in this country for years."

"Making an Acknowledgement of Country is one thing but it's just a token gesture when there's still deaths in custody, high unemployment and poverty, and low life expectancy."

"Sparrow is good when he focuses on his work. I'm glad he's taking it more seriously these days."

"Hence the undercover assignment," said Noah. "Following his nose." He quaffed his ale with eyes closed to enhance its taste.

Nails seemed to be keeping a low profile behind the bar – pouring the odd beer, absently checking his phone, staring into space, sweating into his already stained shirt. His eye had blown up nicely overnight into the size and shade of a blue-green emu egg while his toothless whistle was now even more pronounced and melodious. The contrite publican acknowledged the cops with a polite nod and warm "gudday" but largely kept his distance for a change. Manolis wondered whether his subdued nature was due to a rapidly blossoming gum infection.

"Hopefully the bloke's insurance comes through without much hassle," Noah said.

"Sobriety insurance," said Manolis.

"Like a hospital gown, you can never have enough coverage."

"Speaking of which, we need to look into whether Marlowe had a will and life insurance policy."

"A man like that, with assets like he has, I imagine he's insured out the wazoo."

"Me too, but the devil's in the details, the small print. Same with a will. You'll be surprised how some are drafted – the legal language and technicalities, or the people who suddenly come out the woodwork claiming to be beneficiaries."

"In Marlowe's case, with so much on the line, I'm predicting there'll be blood on the Persian carpet."

Manolis slugged another grim mouthful of his drink, wincing at the sickly sweet stale taste. He reconsidered the menu, which still had just as few vegetarian options as when he'd looked a few minutes earlier.

"If Marlowe's disappearance was down to foul play, I still think it would be someone known to him," Manolis said. "Someone close to home."

Noah shook his head. "I reckon we can't completely rule out a random event," he said. "Shit happens."

"Or it doesn't. I think that—"

Their deliberations were cut short by the pub doors flying open and almost off their hinges. A seething Patrick Grayson was stood in the doorway, hands on hips. He addressed the bar in no uncertain terms.

"My restaurant's been desecrated, vandalised. That's my livelihood being messed with, and that's not on. Disgusting graffiti on the walls and a rotting pig's head dumped on my doorstep."

He made it clear who he felt was responsible and demanded to speak to the publican.

Noah put down his half-drunk beer and leaned over to Manolis. "Speaking of shit happening," he whispered. "Should we . . .?"

"Wait," said Manolis, reluctant to get involved. "Let's just see how this plays out."

Noah explained how Grayson was a profoundly private person these days, away from the public eye, so his arrival at the pub was decidedly uncharacteristic and also signified the gravity of the misconduct.

"Plus, it's downright provocative," he added. "It's planets colliding."

Hearing the commotion from a back room, Nails marched right up to Grayson to block his path. They stood a foot apart like two bull elephant seals preparing to square up on the sand. Grayson was the taller of the two, but he still seemed to shrink an inch. What few patrons were in the pub set aside their pints and plates to take in the impromptu live entertainment from their ringside seats. Round one, *ding ding.*

"What the fuck are you talkin' about?" Nails said. "I've been here all fucken day, I did no such thing."

"Bullshit," said Grayson. "You're lying."

"Look around you. My pub was trashed, too."

Grayson examined the scene but wasn't buying it. "Looks like you just run a crappy, second-rate establishment. Either that or you orchestrated it yourself for the insurance claim."

Nails's reaction was neither immediate nor expected. After taking a moment to comprehend the absurdity of the accusation, he smiled, baring broken yellow canine teeth. He then laughed out loud, roaring, showing Grayson the outline of his tonsils and the bile rising in his throat. But both responses felt acutely unsettling and were quickly replaced by a cold, unflinching stare. This had clearly been simmering between the two hospitality barons for some time, with Nails now relishing its inexorable boil-over.

"Yeah yeah," Nails sneered. "Sure thing, mate, sure thing. If only I were as smart as you. Maybe next time, to really maximise my profit margin, I'll somehow accidentally forget to pay my staff, too."

Grayson pursed his lips and nodded lightly, as if acknowledging the verbal blow. He was trying to suppress his hurt; Nails had touched a raw nerve. The publican was up for it, he was happy to punch below the belt, and wanted to see if his airbrushed, corporate adversary would fold or fight. Even with Nails's lingering injuries, Manolis could tell he was desperately hoping for the latter.

Grayson held up a hand in apology. "Fair call," he said. "I hope people can one day forgive me for my past indiscretions but I know there's still a way to go."

"A long fucken way to go," said Nails.

"I just wanted to make an honest crack of it here, a fresh start."

"Nothing's ever completely left in the past, mate."

Grayson narrowed his eyes. "You wanted an all-out war from the day I arrived. You hate my restaurant, my food, my clientele, and everything I seem to represent."

Nails shrugged his round, featureless shoulders. "It's true, I can't deny any of it. You're a cancer on our little island. But that doesn't mean I would take it so far as to vandalise your joint. That's lower than a snake's gut. At the end of the day, I'm just like you – a small business owner tryin' to make ends meet. But there's one big difference between us – my business practices are honest."

Grayson scowled. "Screw you," he said. "Arsehole."

"Fuck you, too," said Nails.

Manolis watched as the thickset publican unfurled and loosened his stubby fingers. They were gnarled from years of being broken on the football pitch, improperly healed then broken again. He then curled them into a concrete fist that he cocked back in readiness.

"Okay," Manolis said, nudging Noah into action. "Now."

The senior detective had seen enough. Noah was forced to forsake his beer and back up his colleague as they intervened to avoid the needless destruction of more mismatched furniture and delicate eye sockets. They pushed in between the two combatants, watching them breathe carbon dioxide into each other's faces.

"Okay now, fellas, let's not do anything rash or jump to any conclusions," said Manolis in his calmest, most diplomatic voice. "Before anything else happens, we need to see some proof. Accusations are just words – they carry no legal weight. Let's go to the restaurant and have a look at the damage, take some photos of the graffiti and pig's head, take samples, all that should provide some clues. I can take down some details for the report on the way."

Manolis hoped that showing the chef he was taking the incident seriously would mollify Grayson. But he remained dubious, reluctant.

"You're just wasting my time," he said. "I already know the culprit. He's standing right in front of me. I can still smell the pork on his clothes."

"I'm offended," said Nails. "That's just my natural musk."

With a view to diffusing some tension, Noah decided to point out the ongoing problems with disillusioned, marauding youths on the island. Vandalism and wide-ranging anarchy were high on their agenda of chaos.

"It's probably just some bored kids," Noah said.

"Or bored footballers," said Nails. "They're still kids, only slightly bigger and stupider."

"It's nothing personal," Noah told Grayson. "This week it's your restaurant, next week it'll be the school or police station or my house."

"The law doesn't help things," said Nails. "Young 'uns are becoming more brazen every year, they know their behaviour isn't an offence under a certain age and they're instead offered intensive therapy. Therapy! That's your hard-earned taxpayer dollars at work right there."

While the tense negotiations over an uncertain peace treaty continued, a sheepish Sparrow slipped through the pub door unnoticed. He stood awkwardly by the wall, watching proceedings with arms behind his back, uncertain of whether to make himself known to colleagues or remain on standby as surprise backup if mediation efforts failed. As he was still considering his options, the door behind him opened to reveal Nankervis, a stressed and panicked look on his face. He pulled Sparrow to one side for a quiet word before they disappeared back outside together.

Meanwhile, at the court of arbitration, a frustrated Grayson upheld his accusation, while Nails continued to deny any involvement.

"Look," said Grayson, "do I need to take matters into my own hands?"

"Whoa, easy now," said Manolis. "That's never the answer."

"Circumventing the law again," said Nails. "What a surprise from you lot. We got laws here on the island. Didn't you invading barbarians get the memo?"

Sparrow suddenly appeared by Manolis's side, pulling him into a corner of the pub while Noah continued the hair-trigger discussions between the two aggressors.

"Jesus," said Manolis, tone low. "You scared the shit out of me."

"Sarge," Sparrow said. "I gotta show you something."

"Mate, where've you been? Not bloody now. Can it wait?"

"Yair bloody now. And privately. And no, it can't wait."

But it was too late – Erik Junior had already marched into the bar carrying a tattered old tartan blanket in a tight bundle, with his distressed father a step behind.

"Junior found this on the beach tonight," Nankervis said.

The lobster heir handed the irregularly sized package to Noah. The local cop stared at the blanket gravely as the police and patrons gathered around. A strange hush gripped the small crowd, the hostility between Grayson and Nails suddenly forgotten.

"What?" asked Manolis, trying to look. "Found what, what is it?"

Nervously unwrapping the ragged bundle, Noah revealed its hidden contents.

"Is that . . .?" said Manolis.

"Holy fucken shit," said Sparrow. "No way . . ."

Noah's arms seemed to tremble under the weight as the realisation dawned – he was holding a severed human foot.

Chapter 18

The entire pub seemed to push aside their half-drunk schooners and half-eaten sirloins and gasp a collective intake of air. Forming a tight group, the Islanders gathered around to cop an eyeful – after all, it wasn't every day that a dismembered human appendage was put on such public display. With grave eyes, Manolis looked up at the tiger shark mounted above the bar, hovering like a storm cloud.

By now, the foot had been removed and lay flat on its tartan blanket, toes pointed out, where it was met more with morbid fascination than outright revulsion, tapping into the same part of the brain that allowed humans to enjoy blood sports in ancient coliseums or modern basements. And of course, it prompted immediate speculation as to the identity of its unfortunate owner.

"It's gotta be Marlowe's," said Nails bluntly. "I mean, whose else could it be? Shark attack. How else do you lose a fucking foot?"

"Ripped clean off by seven rows of serrated teeth that can always regrow," said Nankervis. "Blood doesn't congeal in water."

"The poor bastard probably bled out," Nails added.

Manolis knew the publican was merely verbalising what everyone was thinking, including him, especially given Marlowe's misplaced surfboard had also been washed up on the shore. The multimillionaire had vanished during a dawn swim to ease away his corporate stress, and now a detached right foot had been found. Had it been bitten off like a delectable appetiser and floated away, or regurgitated in distaste by a predator with a more discerning palate? It was unfortunate, it was tragic, but sharks still killed a handful of unsuspecting Australian swimmers every year, with dawn notorious as a favoured hunting time.

"There's more sharks in the ocean now than ever before," said Noah.

"I thought they were endangered?" Manolis said.

"Not around here," said Nails. "Plague proportions."

"Thanks to conservation efforts, shark populations have actually increased," Nankervis said. "Predators are a sign of a healthy ecosystem. If they can thrive, it shows the broader marine environment is in good nick."

"But no wonder there's also more attacks," said Nails. "It's simple maths."

"It's not just their numbers," said Nankervis. "Sharks are now bigger than ever. They're getting monstrous in size and becoming more aggressive and predatory."

"Monster sharks," said Sparrow. "There's two words you never want to hear put together."

"How is it they're growing bigger?" Manolis asked.

"Radioactivity," said Sparrow.

"Growth hormones," said Nails. "In our food, and then they eat us."

"It's actually because of the protected no-fishing zones," Erik Junior blurted out. "We need to obey them."

"Junior's right," said his father. "The sharks take advantage of abundant food sources and gorge on more prey, which makes them both longer and wider. I've seen great whites six metres by three. They're also now coming closer to shore."

"And starting to roam in packs," Erik Junior added.

"Packs?" Manolis said. "Aren't sharks meant to be lone predators?"

"That's bullshit," said Nankervis. "An old sea myth. Rather than competing with each other or hunting alone, sharks know that they can get more food if they work together. It means they can take down big prey like whales, which become an all-you-can buffet. Another reason why they're now so bloody big."

Manolis reflected on these colossal sharks, more muscular and hostile than ever, joining forces to roam the cold southern waters. It sounded like they were an unstoppable force. What could possibly match such leviathans . . .? Perhaps a military-grade submarine with a reinforced hull. Certainly not a middle-aged businessman with a slick black wetsuit and canary yellow surfboard.

"I also heard about sharks high on cocaine going batshit crazy in the water," said Erik Junior.

"Cocaine?" Manolis asked. "Are you serious? How . . .?"

"Bales of coke get dumped in the ocean by drug smugglers who are scared of getting busted by the navy," Erik Junior said. "Sharks eat anything, so they chomp on them and it sets their brains on fire, like catnip to cats."

"Monster sharks in packs high on blow," said Sparrow. "Fucking beautiful."

He leaned in to examine the foot more closely. Its shape, features, skin colour.

"Well, one thing's for sure – it's definitely from a whitefella," he said. "So, it's at least got that going for it."

Manolis had never seen a severed foot before, and chances were no-one else in the pub had either. It looked almost unreal, like a prop from a theatrical performance, all pale and grimy and slightly misshapen. Despite its decomposing state, Manolis got a distinctly male vibe due to the foot's length and breadth. It had no distinguishing characteristics – tattoos or piercings or painted toenails – and retained its requisite number of digits. And somewhere, somehow, someone was missing it.

"How long's it been detached from its owner?" Noah asked.

"Hard to say, I'm no doctor," Manolis replied. "That's why we need to get this to the lab quickly for proper analysis."

"I wonder if it has any fractures," said Noah.

"The lab boys can image that and also analyse its shape," Manolis replied. "It looks like a bloke's foot to me. I reckon a woman's would probably have a different shape, the arch and ball."

"Fetishist," said Sparrow.

"I'm no forensic pathologist but what I very much am is a criminal investigator," Manolis said, ignoring Sparrow. "So, I'll need to see where the foot was found."

Speaking on behalf of his son, Nankervis described the location, which was a different beach from the one where Marlowe had vanished and his surfboard had washed up.

"Whereabouts on the beach?" Manolis asked. "On the sand or rocks or in the water?"

"The sand," Nankervis said.

"Where on the sand?"

"Down near the water."

"Rather than it being further up the beach?"

"Yep. We reckon it likely washed up on shore."

Manolis rubbed his rough jaw, stubble emerging. "Don't be so sure," he said. "It could've always been buried somewhere near the water and dug up."

"Dug up after being buried?" said Sparrow. "Say, by a dog? Maybe even a hungry Rottweiler?"

Manolis shot him an icy glare. Sparrow acknowledged the slip, but it wasn't like Skye hadn't already been discussed as a prime suspect by the townsfolk.

"Why didn't you call us before handling such precious evidence?" Noah asked Nankervis.

"We tried to ring but we couldn't get reception," he replied. "You know what it's like on the beaches. But we were fully aware of what we were doing and careful to only handle it with fishing gloves. If it makes any difference to something that looks like it's been floating around in the ocean for a while."

Surprisingly, the beach in question was nowhere near where Marlowe went swimming; instead, it was on the opposite side of the island, on the northern coastline.

"Well, that's pretty bloody interesting," said Sparrow.

"It might mean something, or it might not," said Nankervis. "The foot could've been floating for days in the water and been carried hundreds of miles by ocean currents and tidal flows. It's not surprising for objects to get caught up in huge eddies and travel around in circles, we see it on the boat all the time."

With no proper evidence container to hand, Nails produced a sturdy black garbage bag and offered his secure pub fridge for foot storage before transport to the mainland for analysis could be arranged. Failing to see a viable alternative, Manolis reluctantly agreed, then proceeded to measure the foot using a self-retracting metal tape measure also provided by Nails. The confirmed length made him even more sure it belonged to a man.

It had been an eventful evening of unplanned entertainment – a faceoff that threatened to explode, followed by a B-grade horror movie. With the live performances all but over, the punters began to disperse. Sensing the shift in mood, Manolis tapped his whisky glass loudly with a teaspoon to gain their attention. He was acutely aware of the power of gossip and how quickly word could spread within a community, and especially in the era of social media.

"No-one is allowed to talk about what you've seen here today," he told the pub. "I'm sorry but this is an ongoing police investigation and we can't risk jeopardising its progress. Anyone who talks about this may be charged with obstructing or hindering an investigation. I repeat, *no-one* is to talk about this until the police make a public statement. As the old saying goes, loose lips sink ships."

Seeing their blank or unimpressed expressions, and hearing the tone of their grumbles and discontent, Manolis wondered if he was asking the impossible. If someone talked, Manolis would be powerless to prove their identity – there were just too many possibilities.

Grayson, the forgotten man, suddenly piped up to remind people that a disembodied foot wasn't the only potential crime committed that day.

"What about my restaurant? The ugly graffiti's still there and the disgusting pig's head is really starting to stink."

"What about cooking a meal with it before it goes off?" Nails suggested helpfully. "Oven-roasted pig head is a delicacy, crisp up the skin and ears nicely, meaty snout and cheeks, mmm. Or even just make some stock or brawn." He gave a greasy smile.

"I'll make *you* into stock or brawn," Grayson muttered.

"Alright," Manolis said sharply. "Enough, you two. You're behaving like children."

He turned to the bar. "Folks, can I please ask for volunteers? Some Good Samaritans who wouldn't mind being generous with their time to help with the mess at the restaurant. I'm sure Nails and Constable Volavola can provide some cleaning supplies."

Noah looked confused; Nails stunned. But both finally nodded.

Unsurprisingly, Manolis's appeal fell on deaf ears. He was preaching to the wrong choir.

He turned to Sparrow and spoke quietly. "No love from the locals."

"No shit," Sparrow replied.

"Over to you then, mate."

"What . . .? You're kiddin' me, right? I bring in a key piece of evidence and this is the thanks I get?"

"You hardly found the foot yourself," Manolis said. "And anyway, I need Noah's local knowledge at the beach. Sorry, mate. Police work isn't always glamorous."

'More like it never is," Sparrow grumbled.

With mop and bucket and detergent in hand, Sparrow begrudgingly headed off with Grayson. Nails bid them adieu, wishing them all the very best in their search to find the culprit with a royal wave and an upturned middle finger.

Together with the Nankervises, Manolis and Noah headed to the northern shoreline where Erik Junior had found the human foot. The deserted beach was windswept and darkening, the light fading fast. Spreading out, working in pairs, they searched the area with supermarket torches but their anaemic beams illuminated nothing of interest – only rocks, seaweed, shells and sand.

"There's really not much around here at all," said Noah. "There's no houses or businesses or even any interesting landscape. It's just dry coastal scrub."

"The waves can be pretty rough," said Nankervis. "The winds around this part of the island are always wild and unpredictable, we've nearly come a cropper a few times."

"Capsized?" Manolis asked.

"Or run aground. The rocks offshore are like a metal rasp. It's ship-wreck central."

"What about sharks?"

Nankervis shrugged. "No more or less than anywhere else. In other words, plenty of the buggers."

Manolis asked Erik Junior to describe the moment of discovery in the hope of latching on to something tangible. He hoped that returning to the right location might trigger the kid's memory to reveal something new, something Manolis had seen with many other witnesses. But instead, Junior suddenly seemed to clam up and spoke with a decided unsteadiness in his cracking adolescent voice.

"I saw what looked like a shell or a rock. But as I came closer, I saw it was a human foot severed just above the ankle."

"Which way was it lying?" Manolis asked.

"Lying . . .? Huh?"

"I mean, which way was it positioned. Was it standing up or was it lying on its side or—"

"It was lying on its side. The first thing I saw were the sole and toes. I didn't actually believe what I was seeing until I came up close. It's not what you usually find on a beach."

Manolis wondered if the poor lad was traumatised, which he'd also seen with other police witnesses, particularly younger people.

Using a roll of yellow gaffer tape, they cordoned off the area, declaring it a crime scene. The exact spot where the foot was found was now underwater thanks to the incoming tide. Noah volunteered to stay the night and ensure the beach stayed secure.

"Mate, are you sure?" Manolis asked.

"I got my swag and some water in the back of my car," Noah said. "And I quite like camping on the sand. Reminds me of my youth, we did it all the time." He then added: "I'll just quickly call my wife and see if she'll be okay with the kids overnight. Just need to find some reception . . ."

Manolis said "of course", recognising a marital consciousness that he had once lacked as a hard-working cop and absent husband. He wondered how Emily was faring with Christos all week – if he was behaving, if he was unwell, if she was stressed at work, if she was coping at home. He'd hear about it all later but already felt his guilt rising.

The detective turned to Nankervis. "I'd like to conduct a search of the water out there," he said.

"Not now, I hope," the fisherman replied. "It's too dark. Tomorrow, in the new light."

Manolis looked around, surveying the scene, hearing the wind wail and the waves thump, and reluctantly agreed. They called it a night.

Chapter 19

The next morning, with most of the pub still sleeping off the night's revelry and grog, Manolis and Sparrow headed for the beach with a care package of food for Noah. Most of it was sourced from the early morning petrol station, its proprietor still only half awake, but Sparrow claimed their meat pies were "criminally underrated".

"Glad it wasn't me out there on the beach," he added. "Evil spirits are busier at night, there's always more opportunities for mischief in the dark."

"Hopefully Noah was fine," said Manolis. "It wasn't too cold. So, there you go, being on pork patrol wasn't such a bad thing."

Sparrow said it was a couple of hours of intense cleaning at Grayson's restaurant with mops, buckets, soap and scrubbing. "Luckily, the graffiti was still pretty fresh. For the more stubborn stains, we used baking soda and bleach and even more fucking elbow grease."

"How was Grayson by the end?"

"He wasn't entirely happy, but at least he'd calmed down a bit."

"Consider that a win. And as reward . . ."

The detective said he was charging Sparrow with the vitally important task of delivering the foot for forensic analysis, along with the white powder found at Marlowe's house.

"Enjoy your time off the island," Manolis said.

Sparrow couldn't hide his smile.

"It's possible that from an analysis of the foot, especially its bones, we can determine if there was active blood flow at the time it was articulated," the detective added.

"What's that mean?" Sparrow asked.

Manolis was working the steering wheel hard, slaloming around clumps of new roadkill that had appeared overnight.

"It means there are sophisticated lab analyses that can be done to determine whether a person was alive or dead when an element, like a hand or foot, was lost," he said. "I don't fully understand them myself, but it's proper forensic science – indisputable."

"Yair, sure," said Sparrow. "Until expert evidence is found to contradict the other expert evidence."

"So cynical, young Sparrow. So cynical."

"What about more body parts washing up?"

"If it was truly a shark attack, then it's perhaps a surprise that more of Richard Marlowe hasn't yet surfaced."

"Unless the rest of him was consumed by the shark."

"Or sharks, plural."

"Or megasharks."

"So, yeah, maybe more pieces will come," Manolis said. "Nankervis was saying something about ocean currents and tidal flows. I didn't entirely follow him, but I reckon an expert like an oceanographer would know better than me."

"More experts. Awesome."

"And even then, the waters around here sound like they're pretty unstable so who knows. You'd probably also need to consider what other scavengers or predators were in the area at the time, and how long the body was submerged in the water. The ocean's a big bloody place."

They found Noah huddled in his sleeping bag, staring out at the ocean, bleary-eyed. His mood brightened when he saw his colleagues, and even more when he saw the breakfast bounty they'd brought.

"It's servo coffee," said Sparrow. "And a bit cold by now."

"It's still coffee," Noah replied, taking a big sip.

"Anything to report overnight?" Manolis asked.

Noah shook his head. "No more body parts and not a soul to be seen. But it was nice to watch the sun rise over the water again."

"And at least it didn't rain," Manolis said. "Although the forecast said there's some storms rolling in later today."

With the aid of daylight, they conducted another search of the beach and also the shoreline, turning over what felt like every grain of sand. Once again, it proved fruitless.

"As I was driving back to the pub last night, something occurred to me," Manolis said. "It's that we probably need to consider the remote but real possibility that the owner of the severed foot may still be alive."

"Aye aye, Captain Ahab," smiled Sparrow.

Manolis glared at him. "I'm being serious, son. We need to check in with local hospitals and clinics on the island, and also on the mainland, to see if any patients with matching injuries have presented. And we need to find out if anyone else has gone missing, especially ocean swimmers."

"Sounds like a lot of work," Sparrow moaned.

"I can make some enquiries," said Noah.

"Thank you, Constable," said Manolis. "Whoever's foot was found could be being tortured somewhere on the island."

"In an isolated shed or underground basement," said Sparrow. "Their body parts scattered around the island one by one. Next they'll mail a finger to the police station – a middle finger."

"Or they've already been murdered, and their foot was kept on ice for a while," Noah said.

"The foot and ankle are pretty complicated, the bones in that part of the body," said Manolis.

"Maybe Marlowe wanted to disappear and he paid someone to cut off his foot to put us off the scent," added Sparrow. "To fraudulently collect insurance."

"Or evade some kind of major debt," said Noah.

"Or criminal prosecution," said Sparrow.

"Or it's actually the foot of some island drifter who has been paid off," said Noah. "I know a few . . ."

"A conspiracy!" said Sparrow. "Now you're talkin' . . ."

As if freshly powered by an unexpected fuel source, wild new theories began taking flight. They were more interesting than any mere unfortunate accident, the narratives more compelling. All Manolis had proposed was another perspective, as unlikely as it seemed, but the notion of a plain-old, garden-variety shark attack had, it seemed, sunk to the watery depths.

"Well, all that's certainly possible but it sounds unlikely," he said. "I'm just saying to keep an open mind. In my whole career, I've never come across a fake suicide. Anyone who did that would be feeling trapped in a desperate situation they've assessed incorrectly."

"Though I reckon drownings would actually be a popular way to do it because they provide plausible reason for the absence of a body," said Noah.

Manolis recalled a story about a famous Canadian case where multiple disembodied feet had washed up on the British Columbia coast over a number of years, including a number of matched pairs.

"A root and branch investigation by the coroner ruled out foul play. They concluded that the feet came from people who were killed either in accidents or died by suicide, and they'd become detached during decomposition because the ankle bones are relatively weak. Many of the feet were still in running shoes, which have air bubbles in their soles that make them more buoyant. But the human body is pretty buoyant, too, so it could be as simple as that."

Even with so many theories circling, Marlowe's disappearance still loomed large over all of them, and Manolis knew what he had to do next.

"Oh. Oh God. First the surfboard, now this. It's only getting worse."

Sitting at the breakfast bar in her shiny marble kitchen, hands clasped around an enormous mug of warming herbal tea, Holly turned pale. Manolis knew her mental state was a priority. He took the time to speak with her sensitively and answer all her questions as reassuringly as possible. Somehow, her hair and face remained immaculate throughout. She inhaled deeply, both the liquid and its aroma, a blend designed by wellness experts specifically for stress relief and inner calm. Manolis wondered if there was a concoction formulated for dread and mourning; it wouldn't surprise him. Nearby, Banjo and Maple sat on a lounge, their heads thrust forward, triangular ears listening to every word.

"We're doing all we can, the investigation remains ongoing and is my sole focus right now," Manolis said. "There's plenty of alternative explanations we're considering, too. So be worried, naturally. But please don't let this consume you."

"How could I not . . ."

Holly's olive-green eyes turned glassy, her pupils dilated. Manolis handed her an aloe vera facial tissue from the box on the countertop. She dabbed at her eyes assiduously.

"Just remember to breathe," he told her. "Deep breaths, in and out."

"Yes, I know how to fucking meditate," she snapped. "I teach yoga, remember."

With some irritation, Holly produced her phone and showed Manolis a short video of Marlowe and his twins beneath a towering Christmas tree with a thousand blinking lights. He was wearing a polo shirt and cargo shorts and laughing with contentment as he watched them enjoying their new toys, his eyes bright, his tone relaxed. Manolis liked what he saw – the normally serious and focused Marlowe sounding happy and carefree loose during a traditional holiday.

"This was a few years ago," said Holly, wiping away an emotional tear. "I've watched it a lot in recent days. Look at how happy he is. God, I need a drink."

"Have one later," said Manolis. "Right now, I need your help."

"You need *my* help . . .?"

"Yes . . . Sorry, I know that sounds strange right now. But in order to keep things moving, we need your assistance with two things, and they are things that only you can provide."

"Like what?" Holly asked warily.

Manolis outlined his first requirement, which had two components. Holly looked at him gravely and nodded, before standing up and walking stiffly down the house's main corridor. The Samoyeds followed her, skipping lightly on their paws. While Manolis waited, he stood before the wall of windows, taking in the expanse of perilous ocean below. The skies were clouding over now, growing greyer and darker like a ceiling of slate.

After a few minutes, the dogs scampered back with Holly who was now carrying a pair of well-worn weekend boat shoes. They were leather, had exposed stitching, and were the colour of desert sand. Manolis could picture Marlowe pairing them with a pair of cotton shorts or unstructured blazer, his ruffled hair blowing coolly in the wind.

"Will these do?" Holly asked.

"Perfect, thank you."

He carefully measured them and wrote down their size in centimetres. Holly watched him soberly, eyes wide and serious as if Manolis was conducting an autopsy.

"Does your husband have any distinguishing marks on his feet or ankles?" Manolis asked.

Holly shook her head, her expression and gaze remaining fixed.

The next item Holly handed over was Marlowe's oyster-shaped hairbrush. It had a two-tiered bristle structure that massaged the scalp with every stroke and an ergonomic grip that sat easily in the palm. But most importantly, it held stray samples of Marlowe's hair for DNA analysis. Manolis washed his hands with an exfoliating soap in the cast-iron farmhouse-style sink and let them air dry. Applying sticky rubber gloves, he carefully extracted the thick grey strands using a pair of fine-tipped tweezers and stored them in a resealable plastic bag.

"Excellent, thank you very much," he told Holly. "Now the second requirement is a bit more complicated . . ."

Holly listened closely and again nodded her comprehension. She thought for a moment and rubbed her temples before taking off back down the length of the hallway. Banjo and Maple resumed their comfortable positions on the lounge, lying on their shaggy sides and closing their gentle eyes. They were soon breathing deeply, their stomachs rising and falling. Manolis watched their effortless tranquillity with some envy.

A pair of footsteps were soon heard growing louder along the corridor.

Holly reappeared first and stood awkwardly a few seconds, waiting by the refrigerator's touchscreen control panel. Manolis was already prepared with his buccal swab-sample-collection kit.

"Hello, son," he said. "This won't hurt a bit."

Young Roland looked up from beneath the protective brim of his American baseball cap. He had a dazed look in his eyes. "I'm not in trouble, am I?" he asked, voice weak.

"This isn't about you, mate. It's about your dad."

"You wanna collect my DNA? Is that allowed? That's, like, my personal property, isn't it?"

"You got something to hide, son? Afraid you might show up in our database?"

Roland's eyes grew wild, darting between his evil stepmother and the nosey interloper.

"Aren't there laws against this? Have you got a court order to collect my DNA? I think I need our lawyer here first. Holly, what's his name and number?"

Manolis's powder-blue fingers held out the swab stick and screw cap tube. "This won't hurt a bit," he said.

"Don't you dare touch me," Roland said. "That's assault." He turned to Holly. "Can't you get bloody Allegra to do this? She's family, too."

"She's on the toilet," said Holly. "She's not feeling well."

"Time of the month," said Roland. "Perfect timing."

"Roland, please . . ." Holly's tone turned frustrated. "The detective is just trying to locate your father, not pin you for being a ratbag. Please just give him a swab and pray to God that the DNA doesn't match."

Manolis proffered the collection kit again. "Do it yourself, son," he said. "I won't lay a finger."

Reluctantly, Roland took the stick and tube. "How do I do it? It's not up my arse, is it?"

"Well, you can if you really want to," said Manolis. "But your mouth is fine."

Following Manolis's instructions, Roland first washed his hands. He then peeled back the plastic from the opposite end of the swab tip. Holding the stick in the middle, he rubbed the side of his inner cheek for about half a minute and then placed the tip into the tube. He then sealed the tube tightly and handed it to Manolis.

"Thank you," said Manolis. "You've both been very helpful. And now, I have just one final thing . . ."

Reaching into his backpack, Manolis produced the chalice cup that Petrov had stolen from Marlowe, placing it carefully on the marble benchtop with a hefty clack.

"I believe this is yours."

Holly looked stunned; Roland, confused.

"Well then," she said, picking it up, admiring it, checking it was intact. "It is indeed ours. It went missing from the foyer. Thank you very much. How did you get it? Who stole it?"

"I'm afraid I can't say," Manolis replied. "It was a condition of having it returned voluntarily."

Holly studied his face, her eyes narrow. "That's okay," she said slowly. "I think I know . . ."

"Right then," Sparrow told Noah. "I'm off."

Back at the beach, Sparrow hopped in the car and revved the engine with a heavy foot. True to the island's history of interesting geographical names that reflected local events, the police had unofficially named the location as "Severed Foot Beach". Sparrow's plan was to first return to

Nails's pub and secure the valuable human cargo in an esky full of ice. He'd then head to the station to collect the white powder, and finally catch the salvation ferry to the mainland.

"I don't really want to lose my lunch on another crossing of the Backstairs Passage," he added. "But I'm glad to leave the island, even if just for a short while."

"Suck on some peppermint or ginger," Noah said helpfully.

"Island of the dead," Sparrow muttered. "Do you know, I haven't seen a single unadulterated blackfella since we got here. Plenty of mongrels but no pure-bloods. Now then, please excuse me while I go collect a disembodied foot."

He accelerated away at speed.

Manolis returned to Severed Foot Beach to meet back up with Noah, whom he found chatting with the Nankervises, pointing to the skies and the watery horizon. Having threatened all day, the first droplets of rain were now beginning to fall and the wind was starting to howl.

"The forecast's not looking good," Nankervis said. "If we're gonna head out on the boat to search, it's now or never."

"Much appreciated," said Manolis.

Nankervis eyed the overcast skies and darkening clouds doubtfully, then returned his gaze to Manolis. "Okay, mate. Your call."

"I think I better head home," said Noah. "Have a shower, freshen up, see if Tessa still recognises who I am."

Manolis checked his phone – still no text replies from Emily. His fears for his marriage were already heightened but when it came to being reminded about it, the pain became torturous.

On board the lobster boat, Erik Junior strapped Manolis into a vibrant orange life vest with a yellow whistle. The more experienced father and son were travelling commando; that is, without any personal floatation devices. The detective positioned himself on the stern while the Nankervises went about their duties and steered the boat out to sea. Compared to Noah's flimsy aluminium tinnie, the fishing boat felt like a grand ocean liner. But Manolis was reflective, staring out into the vast expanse of cheerless ocean, thinking about the task ahead, the needle in the haystack, and going over everything that had brought him to such an uncertain moment. The missing businessman, the island, the locals, the *local* locals, a chalice cup, a yellow surfboard and a severed foot. It made his head hurt just trying to process it all.

A sinister rumbling powdered the grey-black sky. And then, the immense ocean transformed itself into something rough, turbulent, the waves jagged and irregular, pushed by millions of invisible competing forces. It made the boat lurch from side to side, reacquainting Manolis with the first familiar but unwelcome pangs of nausea.

Chapter 20

With the fishing boat continuing to jumble through the waves, Manolis forced a series of deep, steadying breaths into his lungs and tried to focus on the undulating horizon. He was sitting down now, his legs having lost all strength and coordination, his muscles and bones feeling like they'd liquefied into a useless mass. But the extra oxygen wasn't helping, and his symptoms didn't improve when he closed his eyes, the conflicting messages being sent by his senses to his central nervous system flowing like an open channel. He was wet and weak and cold and hot all at the same time. Any sight of land had disappeared some time ago. At least Manolis's life vest meant he wouldn't die by drowning; just from dehydration and severe abdominal cramps.

The Nankervises continued their nautical tasks like it was another day at the office. Erik Senior was the helm, arms flexed, gaze steely, steering as best he could, trying to give the impression of having some semblance of control, while Junior was working the deck with youth and vigour. No doubt they'd experienced such conditions a thousand times before and potentially a hundred times worse. Their guts were now fortified with iron; only their boat shearing in twain would see them bat an eyelid.

In between waves of swell and motion sickness, Manolis was still somehow able to spare a thought for Sparrow, who would've been enduring the same torture across the Backstairs Passage strait – and hating it even more. It was a reflection that helped Manolis feel, if not less vulnerable, then at least less alone. This was supposed to be a search for clues but at that moment, in those weather conditions, the only thing Manolis was searching was his soul.

"Wait," the detective muttered to himself.

He found his feet and attempted his best imitation of poultry – body moving, head still – in the hope it might lessen his seasickness. Nankervis suddenly appeared on the deck, stopping when he saw the sight of Manolis in action.

"What are you doing?" he asked above the roar of the waves and wind.

"Trying to harness my inner chicken," Manolis said. "It stabilises your vision, and is apparently good for motion sickness."

"Inner chicken, eh," Nankervis said. "Never heard that one before. But I've only been a fisherman for decades.'

Seeing the captain on deck made Manolis wonder who had command of the boat, even if control was merely an illusion in such rough seas. Nankervis's eyes looked wide and haunted; something was very wrong.

"Sorry to cut the search short, but we better head back," he said. "I just heard on the radio that a severe weather warning has been issued. There's a strong cold front bearing down on us, with predictions of five-metre swells and winds of up to 30 knots."

It was all wrapped up in naval and meteorological language, not all of which Manolis understood, but that didn't sound very positive. He promptly stopped his chicken dance and straightened up.

"As a result of this weather warning, all commercial ferry services have been cancelled," Nankervis added. "Boats are advised to return to shore."

"Oh-kay . . ." Manolis said. He sounded anaesthetised.

"And there's also been a warning against any coastal activities like surfing, fishing or swimming," Nankervis said.

Manolis seriously doubted whether Sparrow would be keen on swimming to the mainland with a severed foot strapped to his back.

This was a logical headache that Manolis hadn't anticipated, one that reinforced the drawbacks of their current geographic location. But in the face of a raging Mother Nature, he was powerless to argue. And almost relieved at the outcome.

"We'll come out another day," said Nankervis. "I'll turn her around and head for the nearest safe shore. Just hold on tight, this could get dicey."

The boat bludgeoned its way south, smashing through the waves like a rugby player clattering through loose tackles. Manolis steeled himself physically and mentally, gripped tight his body and mind, and reminded himself that every passing second was one second closer to safety. The sweat of nausea had been replaced by the sweat of apprehension. He was being jostled in every possible direction and angle, and while he tried to anticipate the boat's next movement to minimise the impact, predicting the most treacherous waves was like trying to identify where landmines were buried with no metal detector. Nankervis appeared to have no such worries as he gunned the engine to the hilt in a dead straight line, preferring to skip over the waves rather than avoid them, or simply barrel and crash straight through them. Manolis was in no position to question such tactics and simply prayed to every Greek god that the experienced seafarer knew what the fuck he was doing.

At last, the sweet sight of land came into view. Manolis was preparing to exhale when a sucker punch came from the starboard side. It was a wall of water – potentially even a skyscraper – or so it seemed to Manolis who felt the boat rock and almost stall in the piss-angry sea. An almighty dump of water hit the deck, knocking Manolis down and again drenching him all over. As he blinked the water out of his eyes and regained focus, he looked around and realised that he was the only person on deck.

"Junior . . .? Junior!"

Erik Junior had fallen overboard and was now being battered by the ferocious swell. All Manolis saw was a head and a hand flailing from side to side, clawing at the waves and then disappearing into the blue-grey drink. Manolis wasn't sure what to do, his head on a swivel, he'd never been called into such an urgent rescue situation. He was a competent enough swimmer, and his instinctive reaction was to try to reach the boy. But jumping into such a seething vortex didn't seem an especially wise move and would probably just result in one extra coffin being required.

Manolis figured there was also a risk of hypothermia given the temperature of the southern waters and the thin clothes Erik Junior was wearing. The colder the water, the faster someone would become exhausted or even unconscious, dramatically slashing survival times. Visibility was poor and only seemed to be worsening. Fast and decisive action was required.

"Man overboard!"

Manolis's exclamation came out almost involuntarily, like "Fire!" or "Call triple zero!" in another kind of emergency.

"Man overboard!" again.

"Shit!" said Nankervis, slowing the engine. "Where?"

"Um, I think port side!"

Nankervis circled back hard towards his son, then swiftly appeared on deck beside Manolis, staring out over the water.

"I can't see him," the fisherman said. "Junior! Junior!"

For a second, Manolis had lost him, too.

"There!" he said, pointing. "He's there. See him?"

Erik Junior signalled again, gesticulating wildly. If he was calling, no-one could hear him above the yowling wind and pounding water.

"I see him," Nankervis said. "Stupid bloody idiot had to wear a dark shirt . . ."

"Stupid bloody idiot had to not wear a life vest," said Manolis.

"That's cos we only have one," Nankervis added. "Quick, take it off, you'll need to toss it to him. Whatever you do, don't lose sight of him, or he's fucked."

Manolis unclipped the vest while Nankervis returned to the controls. He needed to manoeuvre the vessel into position alongside Erik Junior, preferably into the wind, and avoid coming too close and risking a propeller strike.

"Guide me!" called Nankervis.

As a fellow parent, Manolis knew what was at stake and the pressure that both fathers were under. For the detective, it meant channelling what skills he had at hitting a target. But this was no familiar firearm he was holding, so his muscle memory was non-existent.

"Hang on, Junior!" cried Manolis as the teenager momentarily disappeared under the water again. "Hang in there, son . . ."

Erik Junior was now really struggling, the ocean and storm proving too much for even an experienced swimmer and fisherman. Manolis himself felt overwhelmed by the enormity of the waves, the sudden power of Mother Nature, and was almost swept overboard on more than one occasion, which would've proven utterly catastrophic. And every time the boy's head disappeared under the surface, time stood still for the detective until he reappeared.

Nudging the boat into position was proving a challenge in such lashing winds and rolling swells, even for such a proficient sailor as Nankervis. At times, he had to put the motor in neutral to avoid the propeller turning his son into human pâté. Erik Junior was still bobbing up and down in the waves, swallowing gutfuls of toxic brine. Manolis knew he had only one chance with the life vest – he needed to either hit Erik Junior dead on or land it in his very near vicinity, within arms' reach. Did he need to account for the wind and aim to the left or right . . .? Probably. If he missed and the vest floated away, there would be no recovering it, or Junior by extension. And even if his aim was true but his timing was off and Junior went under the moment he threw the vest, the lifeline would float away to oblivion by the time he resurfaced.

"Okay?!" yelled Nankervis over the blare of the motor and surge of the waves. "Ready . . .?"

"Ready," Manolis growled through his teeth. "One . . . two . . ."

He loosened his shoulders, pulled back his arms, and letterboxed his eyes. Erik Junior was only about five metres away, but it felt like a universe. Both he and the boat kept moving, shifting and then reshifting. The variables multiplied tenfold, and so had the difficulty.

"Three!"

Manolis hurled the life vest as hard and as straight as he could. With his breath held, he watched it sail through the air, at the mercy of the wind and rain, before it splashed into the water immediately in front of Erik Junior. He snatched at it and secured it close to his body. Manolis released the tight ball of tension caught in his lungs with a gasp.

"He's got it!"

"Thank Christ," grumbled Nankervis, killing the motor.

Manolis waved exuberantly, with relief, as he watched Erik Junior slip one arm into the flotation vest, then the other, before pulling it up over his shoulders and clicking it secure. Nankervis appeared and threw him a thick braided rope, and together they pulled him to the side of the vessel and then up onto the deck over the stern. Erik Junior was gasping and coughing, shivering and sobbing all at the same time. Nankervis was also shedding tears, hugging his beloved son tightly to his chest and calling him "a bloody idiot".

"You okay, mate?" Manolis asked.

Erik Junior nodded warily, his face a shade of white and green. "Th-th-thanks," he stammered.

"Strip," Nankervis told him summarily, handing over a silver space blanket. "Can't have you freezing in wet clothes."

Junior was soon down to only his cartoon-themed jocks, wrapped up in the thermal blanket. Manolis stayed beside him, lying flat on the deck for stability and balance while Nankervis fired the engine and hammered it all the way back to shore. Safe again, standing on dry land, it was clear the boat's hull was damaged from the physical ordeal, battered like a boxer, and that everyone was soaked and spent.

"Let me drive you to the local doctor for a check," Manolis told the pair.

"We're fine," said Nankervis. "He's fine. Aren't ya, son? We'll just head home and rest up there with some painkillers: paracetamol for Junior, pale ale for me."

"Are you sure?" Manolis insisted. "It's no trouble at all. I mean, the lad nearly died—"

"I said *we are fine . . .*"

Manolis sensed they needed space, to come together as a family. He had a mind to comment on the lack of adequate maritime safety equipment, flotation devices, distress flares and radio beacons, but he knew that this was not the time. He was genuinely concerned for Junior though – the poor kid had swallowed a lot of dirty, salty water.

The detective returned to the pub through blasting wind and driving rain, dodging newly fallen tree branches and even power lines lying slack on the road. Dark shadows had quickly accumulated in heavy belts and streaks, in broad masses and abrupt breaks, making the normally idyllic island appear almost unrecognisable and brooding.

"Jesus. What happened to you, Sarge?"

Sparrow looked stunned as Manolis entered the front bar. His superior didn't answer.

"You hear the news?" Sparrow continued. "All the ferries are cancelled. So, we're stuck here on this mass grave until the end of time."

"I did," Manolis finally said. "And I've done some thinking. I reckon the only way for you to get the evidence to the mainland for analysis is by taking to the air."

Sparrow stared at him with some bewilderment. "Wait . . . you're serious. You seriously want me to go up into the sky in this bloody weather? Can't we just wait the storm out like normal, sane people?"

"Afraid not, mate. The forecast says it'll be here a while. I don't see any other option. Either a light plane or helicopter. In this weather, it'll be just as choppy as being on the water, only you won't capsize and drown."

"But we might just fall out of the fucking sky and crash," Sparrow said.

He shook his head in disapproval, in negation. It was, after all, his valour on the line, along with his skinny young arse.

"Well, it's either that or you swim for it," Manolis added.

He went on to make the point that the island's recent transformation into a bolthole for the rich might finally prove to be of some benefit.

"Lavender's got a chopper," Manolis said. "He's Marlowe's old mate, he told me he'd do whatever he can to help find him. And he's already used it once before to conduct a search."

"But unless someone blabbed, Lavender doesn't know about the foot," said Sparrow. "Do we tell him about our mission to the mainland?"

Manolis paused. "Hmm, you're right," he said. "We'll need to be a bit vague when we ask, but emphasise the importance of getting to the mainland today so that he helps us."

With the storm unrelenting, Lavender said he would be more than happy to help the police in their investigation. The trio were standing under his gable-roofed pergola overlooking the leaden ocean below, the cold southerly prickling their faces.

"I'm a highly experienced helicopter pilot," Lavender said confidently. "I earned my licence a decade ago, a birthday present for my fiftieth. There's a landing pad in my backyard."

"Is it seriously safe up there?" Sparrow asked. He wanted Lavender to say no.

"Extremely safe," Lavender replied cheerily. "Modern choppers are worth hundreds of thousands of dollars, and some of them millions. For that price, they come equipped with the latest technology. They can fly smoothly even in bad weather. And mine has advanced avionics, outstanding manoeuvrability and emergency floatation devices. It also has an energy-absorbing fuselage, crash-resistant fuel cells, and the best safety record of any helicopter in the industry."

"Crash . . .?" said Sparrow. "Did you say crash?"

"I said crash-*resistant*," smiled Lavender. "The only time I'd be even remotely concerned is if it was frosty or foggy. And even then, it would be tricky but not impossible – the windshield is heated and the blades can be de-iced. I've flown in far worse conditions than this, I can assure you. We'll be right, the flight's not long anyway."

Sparrow eyed the skies ominously. "I'm almost as nervous a flyer as I am a sailor," he said.

"We'll be right," Lavender repeated. "Trust me."

"You'll be fine," Manolis told his colleague. "And thanks, mate."

Lavender's helicopter had room for two pilots, eight corporate passengers or four VIPs, and a lot of crocodile leather golf bags. An on-board refrigerator kept drinks chilled. The cabin was large, glassy, sound-proofed and vibration-free. Sparrow strapped himself into his shoulder harness with inertia reel, securing it tight. He made a mental note of the portable fire extinguisher and first-aid kit in the cabin, even if they were basically redundant in the event of a major air emergency. Lavender slipped on his sleek headset, conducted his pre-flight instrumentation checks and examined the weather radar. With the push of a few buttons, the twin turbine engines started, the rotor blades blurred, and they lifted effortlessly into the whirling air. Lavender flicked on the windshield wipers and gave an awkward thumbs-up gesture; Sparrow crossed himself, despite being non-religious. Manolis waved them off with his own silent prayer for their safety.

They headed out over the water at a velocity that had Sparrow sinking into his leather backrest seat. He stared down into the depths of the ocean but quickly changed tack when he felt dizzy and instead decided to focus on the jittering horizon. Meanwhile, Lavender eyed Sparrow's all-important cargo with some longing.

"So, what's in there?" he asked. The chopper shuddered, lurching from side-to-side in the buffeting winds.

Sparrow wanted to be ambiguous and say little about the case but felt acutely vulnerable so high up in the air. Even after a few tension-releasing breaths, his voice still came out shaky:

"And I can definitely trust you, right . . .?"

Chapter 21

The light on the Saturday morning was watery and only reflected the view through Manolis's bedroom window. He stared out the rain-spattered glass at the storm, which continued to bucket down in biblical proportions. He thought about Sparrow, what fresh level of hell he'd put the poor constable through, but reminded himself that if Sparrow wanted to make it as a serious police officer, a comfort zone was out of the question. Manolis had tried calling his errant colleague a few times since he saw him disappear over the squally horizon in Lavender's chopper but with no luck – he was probably out of range or charge. The detective assumed he would've heard about a major air disaster by now.

Manolis lay on his marshmallow soft mattress, worn of all support, and turned on his side. The pub's electricity was now out, likely due to damaged power lines overnight. As a result, it felt like a day of consolidation, of reflection and analysis, after the hectic events since the foot was found. It was the police's best lead but they still needed evidence-based confirmation of its origins from the forensic lab on the mainland. That could take some time, depending on the exact pathological condition of the appendage, alongside any backlog in workload. Staring at his diagram of suspects on the wall, Manolis tried to make new mental connections. In his experience, the best investigative breakthroughs came in quieter moments of contemplation when links could be drawn between suspects and motives. And the soft pitter-patter of rain on the window and pub roof only lent itself to a moment of reflection.

Things weren't quite adding up. Holly's reactions, Skye's attitude, Grayson's restaurant, Petrov's bitterness, the locals' resentment, alcohol-fuelled violence and severed body parts. As much as the island felt like a tight-knit and supportive community, it was also equally dysfunctional. Manolis couldn't quite believe that that was solely down to the presence of one man and his way of life, which by most measures was considered exceedingly successful. He suspected there were deep-seated issues under the surface, things he couldn't yet see. It left him feeling unsettled – the realisation that there was a curtain he hadn't peered behind. And, in the case of the *local* locals, that he may never get to pull aside. Perhaps, thought Manolis, he should consult with one of those self-proclaimed psychic mediums on social media – after all, they seemed to have all the answers.

Manolis had a short and bracing shower in the communal bathroom and prepared to go downstairs. But as he was heading out, he saw Sparrow's door creak open and a familiar face emerge from inside. It was Elvis, wearing only a pair of boxer shorts and a mischievous smile.

"Oh . . . hi there," Manolis said innocently.

"Gudday."

"I didn't realise you were staying here."

"I guess you could say that," Elvis replied, eyes bright.

"Heck of a storm, eh. Did your place get damaged, is that why you're here?"

A second smile from the dishy barista. "Umm . . ."

Sparrow's door swung open again and this time it was the man himself, and wearing only a crisp white bath towel tied around his slender waist.

"Mate," Sparrow said. "I was just gonna—"

He looked up and saw Manolis, whose face now wore a wry smile of its own.

"Oh. Hiya, Sarge."

"Constable. Good morning. I didn't realise you were back."

"Last night, yair." He sounded sheepish, eyes downcast.

"You survived."

"I did. Lavender's a good pilot."

"I've been trying to call you."

"Sorry. My phone's out of charge."

"That explains it. What about at the lab, any news?"

"All delivered. They'll let us know when it's ready."

An awkward silence filled the tight passageway. Elvis looked like he wanted to make a run for it. In the end, he backed away one step at a time, brushing a light hand across Sparrow's torso, teasing his finely trimmed abdominal hair, and into the darkened room. And yet, it was Manolis who felt like he was interrupting and should excuse himself.

"Excellent work, Constable," he said. "Thanks again. Keep me posted."

"I definitely will."

Sparrow receded into the room, closing the door with a gentle click. Playful snickering was soon heard on the other side. Manolis stepped away.

As he descended the pub's uneven stairs, the detective smiled to himself. He was genuinely pleased for Sparrow and the new romance that had somehow blossomed when Manolis wasn't looking. He knew Sparrow had experienced intense difficulty in forming relationships in the past, and was all too aware of his antipathy towards the island that stemmed from its lamentable history. At least now, there was something positive he could enjoy. There was a slight worry that Sparrow's involvement with a potential suspect might compromise his investigative skills and impartiality, but Manolis pushed those concerns aside for the time being, happy that Sparrow was having some carefree fun at last. It was something everyone deserved in life, and which even left Manolis feeling a little envious.

Downstairs, he found Nails sipping a medicinal morning bourbon instead of his usual morning beer.

"Cos the bloody power's out," he grumbled. His injured eye was still bulging with pressure and appeared like a second head.

"Hopefully it gets restored soon," said Manolis.

"I'm not holdin' out much hope. The rain's good though, should fill up the dams and take the stress out of the trees."

Manolis collected what newspapers and magazines were left discarded in the pub and took them upstairs. The reading material helped kill an hour as the storm seemed to lose some of its potency, the wind and rain diluting to a breeze and showers. But a certain restlessness soon arrived in its place, which prompted Manolis to head out for a slow drive to survey the state of the island for himself.

Emily had texted, which brought a gratified smile to Manolis's lips.

"The news is showing some pretty wild weather down there," she wrote. "I hope you're safe."

"As houses," Manolis replied. "The case has taken a turn as well so let's see where things now lead." He then added: "You're a wonderful mum and doing a great job. Hug Christos for me."

Manolis had seen Emily doubting her parenting skills, always questioning herself, wishing she could do more in the face of unreasonable pressure and impossible expectations. It was the modern mother's curse, the lack of self-care combined with crippling insecurity, something Manolis understood but could never quite fathom given how devoted he saw Emily was to raising their son. The only complaints and doubts were ever hers, which Manolis could never seem to dislodge. He'd now come to dread major occasions – Christmases, birthday parties – which always involved more of everything, including stress. Christos seemed perfectly joyful and happy without all the trimmings. At school and home, he was always gently encouraged to be himself, to ask for help, to use his words. And yet, his parents invariably failed to do the same.

Cleaning his windscreen of fallen leaves and twigs, Manolis saw a sorry-looking Murden crossing the puddled street. The mayor's face and head were all bandaged and stitched like he was a civil war soldier returning from the front. But his mood seemed to brighten the moment he saw the city detective.

"I'm back," he beamed. "Not necessarily better than ever but I'll survive."

"Good to see you," said Manolis. "How'd it all go?"

"I must say, I tip my hat to our medicos, the attention and care I received. The craniofacial and eye surgeons were world class. Not to mention the transfusion nurses and the three pints of blood they gave me – absolutely delicious."

It was a remark that made Murden sound less like a mayor and more like a vampire. The image stayed with Manolis a moment.

"Thanks for not pressing charges, it makes our lives a little easier," the detective said. "But if you change your mind and do want to hold Elvis to account, that's also fine."

"Boys will be boys," said Murden, repeating his earlier sentiment that reached Manolis indirectly. "Anyway, I'm glad to be discharged and back on my feet – and back on the island to help my people with the clean-up."

Manolis wasn't so sure. "Man of the people," said the mayor. And yet Manolis only heard it as "it'll probably still come down to the community to restore order after yet another natural disaster". He wondered where they would find both the will and the energy in the wake of the recent bushfires. Would the blow-ins pitch in on a practical, or even financial, level? It seemed unlikely.

"I'll do whatever I can to help," Manolis told the mayor. "Another pair of hands, a donation, whatever you need."

"Thanks a lot, mate." He shook Manolis's hand, attempting to crush it. "Once we know the extent of the damage, the road ahead will become clearer."

"Actually, I'm just heading out for a little drive now," Manolis said. "I'll see what I can see."

"Ha. Appreciated, ta muchly."

As Manolis accelerated away, Murden's parting words were taken by the wind:

"At least the bloody hippies can't pin the storm on global warming like they could the fires!"

Touring around the island, Manolis was pleased to see the damage wasn't too catastrophic. A few roofs and parked cars had been broken by fallen trees and flying branches, and even more power lines were down. The roads, which were still largely empty of cars, were strewn with debris, natural or otherwise; some were altogether impassable due to collapsed, thick-trunked eucalypts and required long detours. Crews with chainsaws and trucks would be needed to deal with the immediate hazards on public land and to clear roads, driveways and pathways for access. Labourers and electricians would be busy for weeks. It seemed the island had been largely spared but Manolis still wondered how its scores of homeless residents sheltering in thin synthetic tents had fared in such an aggressive storm. Especially with all the newfound lakes of water that lay stagnant, soon to become home to hordes of fledging mosquitoes with a thirst for blood.

Two figures standing on a lonely dirt road, cars parked parallel, appeared as Manolis rounded a sweeping bend, tyres sinking into the softened clay. He recognised their distinctive outlines from a distance: a rounded and pregnant Fox alongside a hunched and elderly Boyle. Manolis pulled over and eased a tanned arm out the window.

"Glad to see you're both safe and well," he said. "How'd you fare during the storm?"

Boyle muttered to himself and shook his head. "Bloody awful in that flimsy trailer," he grumbled. "I thought I'd get blown into the sky like the wicked fucking witch. I would've given anything to be in a secure house with fixed foundations."

He described how he'd once gone to Murden for housing assistance. "I asked our esteemed mayor to write a letter to all the non-resident ratepayers asking if they could see fit to *at least* rent out their holiday homes. Or, if he wanted to go even further, to slug absent owners with financial penalties and increase land taxes on non-first homes."

"Any luck?" asked Manolis, already sure of the answer.

Boyle crumpled his face in frustration. "I may as well have been talking to a brick wall. Property has become an addiction, a costly habit, for those who can afford it. This is now like the Middle Ages with feudal landowners, lords and knights, and then peasants like me."

Meanwhile, Fox was angry that the government had cut the funding for rangers. "Either that or Murden mismanaged the money," she added.

"That'd be my bet," said Boyle.

"There's talk of taking our glossy black cockatoo to the mainland, tempting them to cross the Backstairs Passage," Fox said. "They've been extinct there for decades."

"Glossies are endangered even here," said Boyle.

"But I don't see it happening unless more resources are spent managing the environment," Fox added. "Instead, it's all left on the shoulders of the low-ranking ranger in her third trimester."

Fox was annoyed that she couldn't help clean up as much this time by virtue of her physical condition.

"I feel like a pregnant whale now," she said. "My ankles and feet are killing me and it's getting harder to sleep. The baby's kicking like a full forward."

With his advanced years, Boyle was also limited in how much he could help. Manolis was struck by how measured and nuanced his response to the storm was. He had seen more seasons and natural disasters than perhaps any other Islander, armed with the hard-won wisdom of generations and a stoic resilience in the face of adversity.

"It all feels a bit different this time around," Boyle said. "Like we've reached a tipping point. These new developments have changed the face of the island forever, which is something I never thought I'd say. There's no going back now."

Driving further, Manolis encountered Rossi and Lemieux on the southern coastline road outside Marlowe's property. He flashed his lights as they approached and flagged them down. Lemieux lowered the tinted car window with a smooth hum. With a gargantuan grille, polished rims, and exaggerated proportions, the black SUV was the kind of vehicle that belonged in a Presidential motorcade.

"All good?" Manolis smiled. "How'd you cope with the storm? The island's a bit of a mess so it'd be good to have some help to clean up the—"

"Marlowe's house is fine, thank Christ," said Lemieux, teeth white. "We just visited to do a top-to-bottom inspection."

"Not a scratch," added Rossi. "We're so relieved. All that hard work could've been ruined but it's fantastic to see the house and grounds are untouched and fully operational, which is a testament to its design and construction."

"The house is rock solid, made for all conditions," Lemieux added. "Built with the best, strongest materials. It came at a hefty price but it's built to last."

Manolis was tempted to ask whether the house could withstand a thousand-degree bushfire inferno like the one that recently engulfed the island. But then, he imagined it probably had some kind of futuristic insulation or advanced technology that made it genuinely bomb-proof – an invisible force field imported from northern Europe or the American military.

"That's good news for Marlowe's family," Manolis said. "But seriously, there's trees and power lines down around the island, scraps and rubbish everywhere, we could do with some help to—"

But Rossi and Lemieux just sped away, leaving Manolis alone with his good intentions and a lingering sense of hopelessness.

The detective continued along the coastal roads, looking out over piles of garbage washed up on the island's shores by the pounding waves and surging ocean swells.

"Like space junk," Manolis muttered to himself. "The past returning to the present."

There were old fishing nets and tonnes of discarded plastic, bits of broken wood and petrol cans, endless hazards for the fragile aquatic ecosystems nestling among the rocks. Manolis was left feeling down-hearted and depressed. Parking the car, he stepped onto a deserted beach to try and clean up what he could. Alongside all the human waste, there were also piles of dead sea creatures, fish and crabs and tangled octopuses. Manolis soon realised the enormity of the task and gave up in disappointment, slumping onto the sand. He'd need gloves and garbage bags, and also to clone himself about a thousand times over to even make a dent.

Manolis reflected on his own actions over the years. Had he been kidding himself in thinking he was doing his small bit for the environment? He diligently recycled his milk bottles, glass jars and even plastics, and yet still continued to contribute to the consumption of fossil fuels by driving his car, using gas heating and regularly upgrading his phone. He felt even more despondent now.

Returning to his vehicle, Manolis started the engine, igniting more non-renewable resources and further turbocharging emissions. With an air of resignation, he shifted into gear and commenced the slow drive back inland. Where the hell he was heading now, he wasn't entirely sure. Things appeared to be out of his control on so many fronts. Manolis thought of home, of his family, and his ongoing responsibilities on the mainland. At least there, he could potentially make a difference and help his wife in winning the domestic war. The island didn't feel real – it was a fantasy world.

As Manolis materialised into a pocket of mobile reception, his phone started beeping with a frantic backlog of voicemails and missed calls. Pulling over and applying the handbrake, Manolis broodingly listened to the recordings:

"Hello, Detective . . ." It was Noah. "You better ring me urgently, as soon as you get this message. Thanks."

"Detective, are you there? Please ring me."

"Detective, it's me again, call as soon as you get this."

Noah answered on the first ring. He was hard to hear over the sound of waves crashing and fizzing in the background.

"You better get here right away."

"Why, what's up?"

A pause, followed by a sigh.

"We found a body."

Chapter 22

Together with Sparrow and Noah, Manolis convened at a remote beach on the island's north, many miles away from where Marlowe went missing, on the opposite southern shoreline. It was still grey and drizzling as they looked out over the colourless ocean. The name of the watery expanse was not lost on Manolis – it was called Investigator Strait.

Noah looked stony-faced. "There's an ambulance on the way," he said.

"What about the coroner?" Manolis asked. "Did you notify them?"

"Yep."

Sparrow wore a serious frown and stayed surprisingly quiet, in stark contrast to his usually chipper demeanour. He kept any sardonic comments inside his head, but Manolis knew he would surely have some, along with his many new reasons to be cheerful. He wondered if Sparrow's sombre mood somehow reflected the place that the island occupied in his heart through its tragic history.

There was an unexpected absence of wind, the sudden stillness of death and loss of human life having seemingly descended. It appeared the body had washed up in the throes of the storm, along with half the rubbish discarded into the Great Australian Bight, it seemed. Who knew how long it had been floating out there at the mercy of harsh meteorological elements and ocean currents. It was bound to find land sooner or later if it wasn't consumed by a sea creature or smashed into fragments. Perhaps it had floated across from the mainland. Either way, it had ended up in the water somehow and never made it out again. Or so it seemed.

The body had been found by Conway, who was the only witness to interview. He now stood by awkwardly, waiting to be questioned and appearing stressed by his grisly discovery.

Manolis took the lead, delegating tasks left and right. "Secure the scene," he told his colleagues. "Police tape, photographs, notes, sketches, overhead and elevation. Keep the scene in the same condition as it was first found, disturb as little as possible, keep your hands occupied with something or otherwise in your pockets. We only get one shot at this, so we need to make the most of it. We can't have any evidence destroyed or inadvertently left behind."

Sparrow looked up from his compass, finding his voice. "What evidence?" he asked. "It's just a body washed in by the tide."

"That's how it appears, yes," said Manolis. "But what if someone dumped it here?"

Sparrow didn't respond, his eyes downturned, and kept scribbling away in a spiral notebook.

Manolis typically began a crime scene investigation with a walk-through of the area where all the apparent actions associated with the crime took place. This was normally a fairly time-consuming process but in the case of a dead body on an isolated shoreline, it was more straight-forward. Manolis paid careful attention to the sand and placed a marker wherever there was something of interest, but there was little of note. Removing his shoes and socks and rolling up his trousers to his knees, he strode out into the cold shallows. With the swash constant, wiping the evidentiary slate clean every other minute, Manolis could only hope for something else to wash up on the shore. But it didn't.

"Photograph wide first," Manolis told Noah. "Then medium range, then close."

"I brought a ruler as well," Noah replied.

Manolis approached Conway, who was standing back on the beach. "So then, Mister Conway. Tell me how you found the body."

Conway appeared nervous. "You don't think I had anything to do with it, do you?"

"I never said that. I just want to know the circumstances behind your discovery."

It all sounded incredibly formal, and in stark contrast to earlier, casual conversations about island life. But then, this was a major development in the case that obviously entailed a more official exchange.

"Well, I'd finished diving for the day, filled my allowed quota of abalone as prescribed by law," said Conway. "Check my net if you want, I never harvest more than what is allowed."

"That won't be necessary," Manolis said.

"And since I didn't end up as shark bait after eight hours down there, I was in a pretty good mood. I came in from the water and saw the body lying on the sand. Simple as that, really."

"Uh huh. And when you went out in the morning, the body wasn't on the beach?"

Conway looked at him with a slight frown. "If it was, I would've reported it, don't ya reckon?"

"Mister Conway, please," said Manolis. "Cut the sarcasm. A man is dead and this is standard police questioning."

Conway looked down at his bare feet and fidgeted with his fingers. Grumbling to himself, he went and sat on the sand to watch the police work.

Manolis again addressed his colleagues. "Wear gloves and collect the most fragile evidence first. Use separate plastic bags to prevent cross-contamination. We'll need to air dry everything when we get to the station or else microorganisms will grow."

Manolis looked out for suspicious signs and red flags, including anything to suggest the body may have been positioned there intentionally. But other than a set of footprints, which Conway claimed were his, the sand appeared undisturbed in every direction. No tyre marks from vehicles or bikes. Manolis closely examined the amount of sand on the body, trying to estimate how long it had been on the beach, supposedly no more than Conway's claimed eight hours. There were no signs of wounds or trauma or bite marks but it appeared to have been in the water for some time. Clad in a torn black wetsuit, the body was bloated, discoloured and slightly decomposed. There were no bullets or casings nearby, nor any toolmarks on the body.

"You gonna take prints?" Sparrow asked.

Manolis sighed. "We could try, but probably no point. The wetsuit will need to be analysed more carefully for hair, fibres or broken fingernails in case there's something tiny we can't see."

Much like a bullet had individualising striations on it, so did fingernails. A broken nail found at a crime scene could readily be matched to an individual. It was the science of human ballistics.

"So, we need to consider both the identification of the perpetrator and the identification of the body," Manolis said.

"What's the bloody point . . .?" Conway sang out from his dune. "It's pretty clear it's Marlowe."

Manolis looked across at Noah, who was nodding in solemn agreement. Significantly, the body's right foot was missing.

Manolis consulted the photo of Marlowe on the beach; the wetsuit appeared the same. "Albeit black and generic," he muttered to himself.

"And it looks like a shark attack to me," Conway continued. "Four species account for the vast majority of fatal attacks on humans: the bull shark, tiger shark, oceanic whitetip shark and great white. These waters are infested with whites. They're the reason I had the cage built."

Manolis resisted the urge to speculate, and yet, the evidence was undeniable. Slowly, one piece at a time, the missing man had washed back onto the island: surfboard first, then appendage, and then the rest. But it could still have been a homicide, something Manolis was more attuned to investigating than a wild animal attack.

"What is it with these sharks?" said Sparrow. "Growing bigger, hunting in packs. The homicidal maniacs of the sea."

"I heard they've started testing surfboards with LED lighting underneath to deter shark attacks," Noah said. "The lights disrupt the ability of sharks to see silhouettes against the sunlight above, so they no longer see it as prey."

Conway countered by saying that sharks had a bad rep based on only a couple of species. "They're actually really important for the environment, and there are hundreds of species out there that are now considered at risk. Sharks play a crucial role in the health of our oceans and reefs. Changing the balance of the marine life at the top of the food chain would have major repercussions at the bottom."

Hearing a more balanced take pleased Manolis. The most extreme standpoint was that humans didn't belong in the sea at all, which was the shark's natural home.

"They're just going about their business," Conway added. "They don't come onto our territory, do they? Saunter into our living rooms and get comfortable on the sofa? So, if we go into theirs, we should just leave them alone. That's what I always try to do."

"And yet, you have a shark cage," said Sparrow.

"Well, yeah," laughed Conway. "I don't really wanna end up as a hors d'oeuvre."

"Humans gotta hate something," said Sparrow. "It used to be spirits and demons and witches, now it's sharks and snakes and bloody kangaroos."

Manolis examined the body's wrists, which appeared bare.

"Strange," he said. "Holly said Marlowe wore a black sports watch when he went to the beach, but there's no sign of it on the body."

Manolis wondered how Marlowe's watch was fastened to his wrist. A rubber strap with a pin and holes? Velcro? A sturdy metal clasp?

"It could've just washed away like his surfboard did," Noah said. "Such a small object would be hard to find, assuming it ever washed up at all."

"We may need a metal detector," said Sparrow.

"And if Marlowe went into the water on the other side of the island, could his body really have travelled so far?" Noah asked.

The surfboard was found near Marlowe's home but his foot and then his body had washed up a considerable distance away. Manolis wasn't so sure that was likely or even possible, but he recalled what Nankervis, an experienced fisherman, had said about ocean currents and tidal flows.

"I can confirm that's certainly possible," said Conway, another seasoned sea dog.

The ambulance arrived, and a pair of young, muscular paramedics loaded the body for transportation to the local island hospital in Kingscote. Sparrow was again given the role of honoured escort.

Noah's phone rang, surprising them all by having reception. He spoke low into his handset for about a minute then turned back to Manolis.

"It's the state coroner's office," he said. "They said a forensic pathologist will travel over from the mainland tomorrow to conduct the autopsy to determine the precise cause of death. He's one of their best doctors, apparently."

Even with confirmation from Noah and Conway that it was Marlowe's body, Manolis still needed formal identification from a family member. This would mean a visit to his new widow.

"Until I speak with Holly, there can be no public statement," he told Conway.

"Cross my heart, hope to die," Conway replied.

He stood and walked over to the dead body. Looming over it, he spoke:

"I guess there's now no chance I'll see the money you owed me, you fucking bastard."

And with that, Conway departed the scene.

A chopper suddenly whupped the air, black and gleaming, shooting across the sky directly above the crime scene. It was more fresh island traffic, new money, but Manolis felt self-conscious, like a celebrity busted by paparazzi.

"Good thing the body's already gone," he told Noah. "But let's finish up and get the hell outta here."

Manolis and Noah went to see Holly, wearing their most sombre and grave expressions. She was in the spacious living room with her freshly groomed dogs, their thick double coats shining and glossy. A fruity-looking drink in a tall, tinkling glass was cupped in her left hand. She was sitting with Lavender and watching the capricious weather outside.

"Sorry, but we need to speak with Holly in private," Manolis told him.

"Yes, I understand," Lavender said, standing promptly. It was clear that he sensed there had been a major development in the case.

The detective sergeant inhaled a deep breath and again took the lead, briefing Holly on the beach discovery. As she wiped away tears, he asked if she felt she could identify the body.

"In so many ways, I've been dreading this moment," she sobbed. "I knew it would come. Dare I say it – it's almost a relief."

That sounded strange to Manolis. Surely a relief would be to have your beloved spouse returned safe and sound.

To minimise the shock, Manolis explained what he was about to present to Holly, what she was about to see. There were strict protocols around such procedures given the potential emotional and psychological impact on the relatives.

"I'm going to bring up a series of digital images on my phone," he said. "These were taken about an hour ago at one of the local beaches. I want you to view them at your own pace, only swipe when you feel comfortable."

He presented his phone to her face down on the coffee table, sliding it across the single slab of sugar maple. Holly glared at it like it was a loaded gun with the safety off.

"At your own pace," Manolis repeated, tone measured.

Holly needed several fortifying slugs of her drink before she could pick up the phone, and even more lungfuls of air before she could finally look at the photos. She recoiled at the sight and then broke down, hands to her face.

Manolis gave her a moment, conscious that everyone handled grief differently, whether it was with shock and numbness, sadness and denial, anger and guilt, helplessness and yearning.

"There's grief counselling available if you need it," said Manolis gently, even though he wasn't sure it was.

"I want to see him," Holly said, reining in her tears. "In real life, not a two-dimensional digital image. Take me to where he is, the morgue or hospital or wherever I have to go. I just need to see him . . . *now*."

Having seen similarly distressed family members before, Manolis didn't think that was a wise idea. It was too soon. She needed at least a day to process such life-shattering news.

"Before I can tell the twins, I need to see him," she added. "Until I do that, with my own eyes, I'm not going to tell them. And I think they need to know. After all, he was their father."

She paused, before adding:

"And I want to be the one to tell them, as hard as that will be."

It was an ultimatum that tipped the scales in her favour. The children were a factor, and if anything, the most significant parties of all who should be forefront of mind. Holly was Marlowe's partner, but he was their blood. Manolis watched her hug the Samoyeds for reassurance and comfort.

"Okay," Manolis said. "If you're sure. You *are* sure?"

"Very," Holly replied. "Absolutely."

"Then let's go."

The police drove Holly to the hospital along the island's tree-strewn roads. Manolis watched the widow in the rear-view mirror, her vacant gaze fixed on the blurred landscape out the window, face pale, expression blank and unflinching. Manolis recognised it as the face of someone utterly overwhelmed with emotion and sorrow. If he could somehow reach inside her head and harness the electricity firing between her synapses, he imagined it could possibly restore the island's lost power. Memories of moments together and conversations shared. But also, the shock of the now, and preparing for an uncertain future that was about to begin with a traumatic but necessary encounter.

Under the indifferent eye of a bored intern with a bad haircut, Holly and the police were shown into the gelid hospital viewing room. A harsh fluorescent light buzzed above their heads. With the flick of a wrist to unzip the body bag, the intern showed Holly her late husband's body. He was stretched out on a stainless-steel gurney, grains of sand still embedded in the ridges of his face, toes of his remaining foot splayed. Holly now caved in a second time, collapsing in on herself, and finally into the somewhat awkward arms of Sparrow standing alongside her. She had no more strength to give and he was wholly unprepared.

Manolis's phone rang, echoing loudly and obnoxiously in the clean, antiseptic room. He checked the number.

"Excuse me," he told the others. "I have to take this."

It was the forensic lab on the mainland – the results were ready.

The severed foot matched the DNA sample taken from Roland Marlowe, and the white powder was chemically confirmed as cocaine. It was all a bit of an anti-climax now.

Manolis said a simple "thanks" and numbly hung up.

Chapter 23

The next day, the police were at the station completing administrative tasks – paperwork, evidence filing, phone calls, and more bloody paperwork. The discovery of the dead body, most likely the result of a wild animal attack, seemed to suck the oxygen from the investigation and kill all forward momentum. In his many years as a homicide detective, Manolis had never had such an outcome; there had always been at least one perpetrator. And there was here too, but as Sparrow had said, what were they supposed to do, arrest a shark for being a shark and doing shark things . . .? The senior constable was right, it was a ludicrous notion, made doubly unfathomable by Manolis's love of animals, which left him feeling somewhat conflicted. The shark could be hunted down of course, in the same way a vicious dog mauling a young child could be destroyed. It would be photographed and showcased across the media, both mainstream and social, and likely would attract global coverage given Australia's reputation for shark divers and croc hunters and snake enthusiasts. But that wasn't police work, which was more focused on the human causes of dead bodies, and always brought with it a forest of paperwork to which Manolis was naturally allergic. Deep down, his mindset had now become more aligned with Sparrow's. All he wanted was to leave the insular little backwater as soon as possible to return to his family and forget he'd ever wasted his time on Kangaroo Island.

Meanwhile, Sparrow appeared to have gone the other way, done a full half-turn and was now keen to stay on the rock. He told his colleagues as much at their morning briefing.

"You changed your tune," Manolis told him.

"What can I say?" Sparrow smiled craftily. "The island and all its hidden charms have finally grown on me . . ."

But Manolis knew the real reason. He felt nostalgic about the idea of a summer romance, which was what appeared to be on the cards. His only concern, which he was yet to voice, was that it could get in the way of professional responsibilities. But given the direction in which the case was now inexorably heading, it hardly seemed worth raising anymore. Let the kid enjoy his fling.

"Poor Holly," Noah said. "She was pretty distraught."

"It's heartbreaking and tragic," said Manolis. "And you can only imagine how his kids felt. But the absolute worst feeling is needing to tell parents when a young child has died."

"I'm lucky to have never been in that situation," said Noah.

"You changed your tune," Sparrow said to his superior.

"Sorry, what . . .?" asked Manolis.

"About Holly. Thought she was the prime suspect."

Manolis chuckled. "Mate. That was just experience talking. It's hardly gonna apply every time."

"Maybe she fed him to the shark," said Sparrow. "That'd be something, eh. She and the shark are in cahoots."

Manolis discussed the forensics results, which were met without much interest, let alone fanfare. He again thanked Sparrow for all his toil and endeavour at the mercy of the angry meteorological gods.

"What about a funeral?" Noah asked.

"A funeral can't be scheduled and the body can't be released to the family until foul play is completely ruled out," said Manolis.

"Holly mentioned the idea of a memorial service," said Noah. "At least in the short term."

"That'd be hugely popular around here, I'm sure," said Sparrow. "Well attended, moving, emotional."

"The pathologist is due later today from the mainland by ferry," said Noah.

"Hopefully they don't take long in coming to a conclusion," said Manolis.

Murden arrived, slightly less injured and more healed than the day before, his face still heavily bruised. He'd come to pay his respects and thank the police for their hard work.

"Helluva tragedy," the mayor said, mournfully removing his fishing cap. "Bloody sharks."

"Sharks," muttered Manolis.

"I only knew Richard Marlowe a relatively short time but he was a highly charismatic individual, a wildly successful businessman, and a dedicated father," said Murden. "I was proud to have known him."

Murden sounded like he was rehearsing a eulogy, or perhaps about to grant a state funeral. Wouldn't that prove popular, Manolis thought. But he was more annoyed by the fact that Conway had clearly spilled his guts across town. Half the island probably knew of Marlowe's demise by now, if not all.

"Look, deep down, I know Marlowe wasn't hugely popular, but neither am I," Murden said. "And like me, his contribution to the community is huge. Once people realise that, they'll see things differently. His loss to the island is truly immense."

Murden began to reflect on the island's history of shark attacks, saying they were "always takin' our best and brightest" and that he'd "hunt the bloody bastards into extinction" if he could.

"The cause of death is still unknown," said Manolis.

Murden laughed, his lungs crackling. His Adam's apple bobbed in his thin throat like a chicken pecking corn.

"Be that as it may, I'm considering installing shark barriers on certain beaches and even shark nets," he said.

"The problem is those nets catch all kinds of other marine life," said Noah. "Sea turtles, dugongs, rays, dolphins, seals. Even whales and harmless hammerhead sharks. These are all threatened species and they're usually dead by the time they're found."

"You can't make an omelette without breaking a few eggs," said Murden.

Manolis was mildly horrified by what he was hearing – both the claims and the commentary.

"One of the saddest things I ever saw was a baby dolphin who had drowned in a net like that," said Noah. "It had scratches all over it from its mother trying to set it free."

Murden stepped forward and, without regard for role or rank, jabbed his index finger provocatively into Noah's chest.

"Better a few fucking fish die than more people," he said unequivocally.

"Dolphins are mammals, like humans," said Noah. "And there are alternatives."

He went on to describe drone surveillance systems and "smart" drumlines that instantaneously alerted operators of shark incursions via satellite-linked GPS communications.

"You're proposing to use technology that's a hundred years old," Noah said.

Murden laughed again. "Well then, mate," he said. "Best you find the money to pay for all that modern tech eh! All I've got money for is nets. And our sugar daddy in Richard Marlowe is gone now, so that tap's run dry."

His respects now fully paid, and with more important people to talk down to and places to be, Murden left the police to their wearisome paperwork.

Later, they were visited by a black-suited, red-eyed Lavender, who was also visibly saddened by the passing of his old mate and sparring partner. Seeking comfort, Holly had told him what happened, confirming his suspicions all along.

"I was emotionally prepared," Lavender said. "Holly thought she was but really, she wasn't."

"How's she doing?" Manolis asked.

"She swam to the bottom of a Magnum, I'm afraid. Give her time. She'll eventually ascend."

"Of course."

Manolis thought that champagne was a strange choice for a grieving widow, but each to their own.

"It's still hard to believe I'll never see Richard again," Lavender said. "We drove one another to better ourselves and do good things. Life has a bit less meaning now."

"What are you working on these days?"

Lavender described his latest project, a high-cost exploration venture for offshore drilling.

"I had heard about this," said Manolis. "I didn't realise you were involved."

"It's one of many pies for my fingers. It's still early days, a long-term project, but it'll also bring sustained regional security for oil and gas resources. Australia used to be a self-sufficient country but now we rely heavily on imported oil, which is bad for business."

Manolis was surprised to see the station's heavy door swing open and Allegra poke her uncertain face through.

"Allegra's with me," said Lavender. "I told her to wait outside a few minutes while we spoke."

Marlowe's only daughter appeared almost unrecognisable from the edgy, confident teenager Manolis had seen every other time they'd met. She was dressed conservatively, almost demurely, in a flowing polka dot dress with a high neckline and low hemline, her hair pulled back with an elegant silk headband. It was a look so cool it appeared retro. Manolis wondered if that was what she was aiming for, perhaps even ironically. Or maybe it was her best attempt at a mourning outfit.

"Allegra, we are so very sorry for the loss of your father," said Manolis earnestly. "Our condolences. As police, we did all we could to try and find him alive."

She acknowledged the sentiments with a polite nod but then appeared awkward, her eyes shy, her body language hesitant.

"Go on then, love," Lavender said. "Tell them what you told me."

Allegra's gaze bounced around the room, between each of the law enforcement officers and her late father's confidant. Manolis assessed that trust boundaries were being tested in real-time.

"Err . . . umm . . ."

She looked back at Lavender, who again prompted her with a slight smile of encouragement.

"Do you remember that bag of white powder you found at our house?"

She blurted out her question at low volume and high pace. Manolis almost had to ask her to repeat it in order to understand. Sparrow scrunched up his face.

"Yes, we do," said Manolis. "What about it?"

"It was mine," Allegra said meekly. "I didn't want Dad's memory to be made all dirty like that. It's just some coke, a friend gave it to me. We do it sometimes for fun but know we need to stop. And I will, I promise, I know it's wrong. I've learned my lesson. Am I going to be in trouble?"

"Allegra came to me earlier today and volunteered that information all on her own," said Lavender. "She told me that she loved her father and didn't want him to be remembered as a drug user. I encouraged her to come clean to you in the hope she wouldn't be in any hot water as a result."

The police exchanged glances. Allegra kept her head down, her eyes on the scuffed vinyl floor.

"What do you say, gentlemen?" Lavender went on. "We hope Allegra's honesty counts for something. Everybody makes mistakes – the important thing is that she's acknowledged it like an adult and she's willing to change her behaviour. Personally, I am very proud of her and I know her father would be, too."

Allegra's eyes were moist with tears. She clasped at a silver locket hanging around her neck.

"Dad gave me this for my sweet sixteen," she said.

Manolis again eyed his colleagues before clearing his throat. "We're going to need to discuss this a moment," he told Lavender and Allegra. "Excuse us."

They adjourned to the kitchenette and closed the door, their voices low.

"Throw the book at her," said Sparrow. "Full force of the law."

"I couldn't disagree more," said Noah. "She appears genuine and remorseful."

"Genuine and remorseful my black arse," said Sparrow. "It's all a carefully rehearsed act from a privileged little private school turd. Today, it's a small bag of coke; tomorrow, it'll be a suitcase of hash or a kilo of homemade meth or boosting luxury cars."

"The poor young girl just lost her father," said Noah. "Surely that's gotta count for something."

"Poor young narcissist, you mean."

"She shouldn't be tarred with a record for life cos of one mistake."

"If it's good enough for black kids," Sparrow said. "Different rules for nepo babies, it seems."

"Enough," said Manolis. "Give me a minute."

He knew it would be up to him to make the call, the deciding vote.

Manolis strode to the sink and poured himself a glass of water that he drank with slow, deep sips. He took a moment to reflect on affluent families and the problems wealth brought with it. His experiences suggested the parents were generally absent, both physically and emotionally, which left the children with anxiety, depression or substance abuse, and a deep-rooted fear of weakness and failure. Families like the Marlowes functioned more like a business than a community, which made real bonding difficult.

Manolis rinsed his glass, returning it to the drying rack. "Okay," he said. "Let's go back."

They approached Lavender and Allegra, who were now sitting on a pair of wonky plastic chairs. Lavender stood to attention and gestured to Allegra to do the same.

"Having consulted my colleagues, we acknowledge Allegra's bravery in stepping forward, her honesty in admitting she's wrong, and her willingness to learn from her mistakes," said Manolis. "But there's no such thing as 'just some coke' – it's all harmful, illegal narcotics. From what I've seen, in the long run, nothing good ever comes from illicit drug use. Your dad would want you to achieve great things in your life, you're in a privileged position with opportunities that other kids can only dream about."

He paused. Allegra's eyes were wide, her mouth hung slightly open. She was a vessel taking it all in, awaiting the executioner's blow. Sparrow and Noah glared at each other, wondering on whose side of the fence Manolis would land.

"So," continued Manolis, "if you are truly sincere in your promise that you'll quit messing with this stuff, I think we can let you off with a warning."

Allegra squealed, jumping in the air and clapping her hands with delight. She embraced the police one by one, which left Manolis feeling slightly embarrassed and Sparrow visibly annoyed. Allegra acted as if she'd won a prize on a game show. And while that grated a little, Manolis acknowledged she was young and energised. Sparrow, on the other hand, wore a deep, black scowl that spoke volumes for his disappointment in how the white man had abused his position of authority.

"You must really love your dad," Manolis told Allegra. "Again, I'm sorry for your loss."

The day's last visitor was the forensic pathologist from the mainland, an elderly chap named Jock Chesterman. He wore check shirt and tan trousers and carried a battered suitcase in one hand and an even more antiquated Gladstone bag in the other. He handed them both to Sparrow to carry, repeatedly calling him "boy" in the process.

"Be especially careful of my portmanteau, boy," Chesterman said. "That was my father's and all my medical tools are in there."

"Yes, master," Sparrow said, tongue firmly in cheek.

Chesterman announced that he planned to stay overnight so they all agreed to start fresh in the morning. Manolis thought he smelled a whiff of booze on Chesterman's breath.

"He looks, uh ... highly experienced," Sparrow whispered to Manolis.

He was referring to the good doctor's resemblance to a living corpse, all bones and drawn skin and dark, suffering eyes.

"Probably what makes him such a good pathologist," Manolis said. "Decades of work and attention to detail."

He estimated Chesterman's age to be somewhere in the late eighties, and perhaps even the nineties, but he had a fire about him, a sparkle in his eyes.

"I've worked many shark attacks over the years, boy," Chesterman proudly told Sparrow. "If anyone's going to know a shark attack, it's me. So, where's the pub? I'm dying of thirst . . ."

The cops took Chesterman to Nails's hotel, where it was Sparrow's turn to buy the first round.

"I'll have a dark ale, boy," Chesterman told him. "The darker the better."

"Yair right, ya ol' coot," muttered Sparrow under his breath as he headed for the bar.

As they took their seats, Manolis couldn't help but notice a small celebration underway at a nearby table. Beers were being clinked and backs slapped, rounded bellies pulsing with laughter. The group included Elvis, Boyle and Conway. It turned out the table were "toasting the shark", in other words, actively celebrating the demise of Richard Marlowe.

Manolis locked eyes with Conway, whose immediate expression was one of guilt.

"Mate," Manolis said to him. "I thought I could trust you with the news about Marlowe."

Conway slapped Manolis's back hard. "Maaate," he drawled. "Lighten up, eh. This is a good day, a really, really good day."

"You crossed your heart."

"That I did and for that, I'm sorry. But I'd had a few drinks, my tongue was loose . . ."

He presented his wrists to Manolis, held together in mock surrender.

"Slap some irons on me, if you have to. Haul my arse to jail!"

His drinking buddies roared with laughter, which only made Manolis feel inadequate and powerless. From a legal perspective, there wasn't much he could tangibly do in such circumstances, and it would probably be more effort than it was worth. Better to address the table with a few choice words:

"Frankly, I think a celebration like this is in pretty poor taste. A man is dead and you're toasting that?"

More laughter, this time with Sparrow joining in, his arm tossed affectionately across Elvis's shoulders. Manolis shook his head with disappointment.

"You let that little rich bitch off the hook," Sparrow told his superior. "If this is the end of days, I may as well kick back and enjoy the ride."

As the evening unfolded, the drinking and revelry continued. Chesterman downed two bottles of red wine on his own while he regaled his colleagues with stories of dead and mutilated bodies and unexpected discoveries within internal human cavities. Manolis imagined you needed a sense of humour to work as a forensic pathologist, though it seemed to help if you were also a high-functioning alcoholic.

Checking the time, feeling the heaviness and fatigue in his body, Manolis prepared to retire to his room. But just then, the pub doors swung open and an unfamiliar face entered, an older, immaculately dressed woman who exuded both refinement and financial wealth. She was accompanied by a man in a formidable three-piece suit who had one of the most spectacular comb-overs in recorded history.

"I'd like a room for the night," she said to Nails.

The publican looked her up and down like he was sizing up a piece of prime rib. "I reckon you're in the wrong place, ma'am," he said.

"No, we insist," the suited man said swiftly. "Here is fine."

"Certainly then," Nails said, forcing a haughty smile. "Under what name shall I book?"

"Virginia," she replied. "Virginia Marlowe."

Chapter 24

Marlowe's ex-wife had arrived on the island with her solicitor and personal adviser, Ian Tudge, King's Counsel. They ordered gin and tonics. Manolis made a beeline for their table and introduced himself.

"My condolences on Richard's passing," he said.

"Ha," she snapped. "You can only mourn your ex so much, but thank you all the same."

Virginia said her primary reason for coming across from the mainland was her children.

"I've come to support the twins through this traumatic time."

"Oh really?" Manolis said. "I thought you and the kids weren't all that close?"

"Excuse me . . .?" Virginia replied. Her tone was sour. "I utterly adore my children. Who the hell said that? Must've been Holly, that cow. I wonder if her nose has fallen off again . . ."

Manolis felt like he'd stumbled into the middle of an old feud. Family relationships were complicated, and after a death, when respect was questioned and inheritances were on the cards, people revealed their true colours.

"Look, I actually am deeply saddened to hear of Richard's untimely demise," Virginia said, tone softening. "He was still so young, we're the exact same age. We had our differences, and we loved each other once, which can't be forgotten. We grew apart over the years but I always admired his determination and confidence, which served him very well in life."

Tudge nodded furiously in agreement, supporting his client's viewpoint in the same way an adviser might when a politician was speaking. Manolis wasn't sure what to make of Virginia. Was she feigning her sentiments? Had her daughter – her flesh and blood – done the very same earlier in the day when she showed contrition for her drug use? Were two generations of Marlowes pulling the wool over Manolis's eyes? The detective was both curious and suspicious about Virginia's motivations given the contents of Marlowe's will and the presence of her prestigious silk.

"And of course, we've come to discuss the will with the executor," Virginia said.

"Of course," said Manolis. "And who is that?"

"A man named James Lavender. Have you met him? Like Richard, I've known James for years. He's a trusted friend and perfect for the role given the financial complexity of Richard's estate."

The next day, Chesterman conducted his detailed external and internal examination of Marlowe's body in the bowels of the hospital. He was ably assisted by Manolis and Noah, who labelled a body diagram, took photos and wrote notes as Chesterman dictated. Sparrow, meanwhile, had excused himself.

"What's wrong, boy?" Chesterman asked him accusingly. "Got a weak stomach?"

"No, I'm good," he replied cheerily. He leaned in closer to Manolis and said: "Maybe I'll take some leave and stay on the island a bit longer." He then sauntered away with a skip in his step.

"Where the hell's he going?" Chesterman asked. "There's work to be done." He opened his Gladstone bag and extracted his gleaming tools of the trade: saws, shears, scissors and forceps.

"I think he may've found true love," Manolis replied.

"True love, eh. No such thing. Still, good luck to him, must be one lucky girl . . ."

Under the buzzing fluorescent lighting, Chesterman began by noting the body's details: weight, height, length, eye colour, hair colour, ethnicity, sex, and approximate age. He then carefully removed Marlowe's torn wetsuit with a pair of heavy-duty dressmaker's shears and handed it to Noah.

"You can probably give that to his widow as a keepsake," he said.

"Pretty morbid keepsake," Noah replied.

"You'll be surprised what some family members want to keep," said Chesterman. "When a loved one dies, people want to maintain some kind of connection. It's understandable, of course, but borne of a sad, pathetic desperation. Death is an inevitable part of life. It's just life ending, the natural denouement."

It was the kind of frank, unsentimental assessment that could only come from a forensic pathologist who had spent decades with corpses as co-workers.

"Hmm," he added, inspecting the body. "He's a cleanskin, not a single distinguishing scar or tattoo."

Prior to cutting, Chesterman asked Noah and Manolis to lift Marlowe's torso up off the metal table. The dead body was heavy, with no longer any resistance to gravity, and required some strain and effort. Chesterman then slid a distinctive rubber block underneath to extend the arch of Marlowe's body and provide greater access to the chest and abdomen.

"There." He smiled, admiring his unblemished canvas. "Beautiful. Let the dance begin."

Chesterman began the chest and abdomen autopsy by making a large Y-shaped incision, the two arms of the Y running from each shoulder joint to meet at the sternum, with the stem running down to Marlowe's lower abdomen. The cuts produced little blood – without a beating heart, the only impetus came from gravity. This pattern of incisions allowed Chesterman to examine the organs in situ, which meant removing the rib cage. Using a medical saw that resembled a small pruning shear, he cut the sides of the chest cavity, leaving the ribs attached to the breastbone but removing the entire frontal ribcage as one impressive chest plate.

"How's it look?" Manolis asked.

"Heart and lungs are badly decomposed," Chesterman said. "But nothing to write home about."

The skilled pathologist said there was no need to examine the face, arms, hands or legs internally, although he took several X-rays to scan for bone abnormalities or foreign objects, including a few of the severed leg. He used a handheld ultraviolet black light torch to scan for specific residues like gunpowder.

"The time the body was supposedly in the ocean makes a lot of this analysis completely redundant," Chesterman reflected, before adding: "But still essential, there's boxes need ticking."

The abdominal examination was next. Chesterman freed the intestines by cutting along the attachment tissue with a sword-like scalpel. Manolis held his nose. Even after so much time, there was a distinct smell. But the liver, stomach and spleen were all normal.

"Brain autopsy?" Chesterman asked himself. He then shrugged. "Come this far, I guess."

Manolis watched as Chesterman carefully made a triangular incision across the crown of Marlowe's head, from the bony bump behind one ear to the bump behind the other. He then opened the cranium using another cold saw that cut bone but left soft tissue unharmed. The brain's blobby architecture came into view, which Chesterman examined with a circumspect finger, making an unsettling squishy sound.

"Normal again," he said. "Ho hum."

Whistling as he worked, Chesterman harvested tissue samples from each major organ, which he briefly examined under a small microscope he'd also packed in his weighty Gladstone. He tried to collect bodily fluids – blood, urine, bile from the gallbladder, vitreous gel from the eyes – but found it nigh on impossible. Noah labelled each sample to be sent for analysis to check for any infection, changes in body tissues and organs, and chemicals such as medications, drugs or poisons.

"It's a multi-pronged approach," said Chesterman. "Microbiology, histology, toxicology and pharmacology. But frankly, probably all completely unnecessary. To me, this preliminary assessment makes it look like your bog-standard, run-of-the-mill, fatal shark attack. Sorry if that disappoints you, chaps. You can always try and apprehend the shark, I guess. Charge it with murder, or at least manslaughter."

He placed the organs in individual plastic bags to prevent leakage and returned them to the body along with the breastbone and ribs. Lining the body with wads of soft cotton wool, he sewed it shut with a long baseball stitch and needle, and washed it clean for the funeral director in case the family desired an open-casket funeral.

Chesterman thanked the police for their assistance and time. He cleaned his implements under a running tap with liquid detergent, scrubbed his hands with the same yellow detergent, and packed his hefty Gladstone bag.

"I'll write up my report and be in touch once the lab results are in, it should only be a few days," he said. "The full results may take about six weeks or so. Give my best to the love-struck boy."

While Noah drove the respected pathologist to the pier to catch the next ferry back to the mainland, Manolis dialled his supervisor to brief him on the new developments. "The case is likely wrapping up," he said.

Porter thanked him for the update and applauded his detective sergeant's police work. "And pass on my compliments to Sparrow, too," he said. "He's come a long way and much of that is thanks to you."

"He's a good kid," Manolis replied. "I'll just tie up some loose threads here and look to head back to base soon."

Manolis drove to Grayson's to follow up on the vandalism, and was pleased to see it had been cleaned of paint and pork and largely restored to its former glory. He found the chef sitting alone with a glass of sparkling wine, overlooking the terrifyingly beautiful ocean.

"Just drinking it in," he said. "Both the Prosecco and the view. Perhaps for the last time."

"Oh really?" Manolis asked. "What's up?"

"I can't pretend that Marlowe's passing isn't significant, because it is. He was the reason I came here – now, the restaurant's future is uncertain. And I already went through one financial collapse with my previous business, I don't think I can handle another."

"So, what next then?"

"Dunno yet. Haven't decided yet. Was hoping the wine might help me decide. Maybe head back to the mainland, buy some land, take things slow. Live self-sufficiently, champion local produce and organic food and seasonal harvests. Try to patch things up with my family, and keep my head down. There's not much left for me here."

"That still sounds like a pretty good life."

Grayson smiled to himself. "It does, eh," he said. "But I can't help but feel a bit resentful over how it all worked out. I blew my chance, my fifteen minutes. In another universe, I would've run a dozen bustling city restaurants across the globe, had TV shows, a regular cooking segment on morning TV, won awards, written cook books, done charity work, and had my face plastered across jars of signature brand pasta sauces."

"Those bottled sauces are garbage," Manolis said. "But you can still do charity work. Maybe open something like a soup kitchen?"

"That thought had occurred to me, too."

"It may help the bitterness fade. Which I'm sure it will with time. Good luck."

Grayson held up his glass in agreement. "Saluti," he said, guzzling his wine. "To Marlowe."

As Manolis departed, he heard the remorseful chef pour himself another fizzing glass of memory eraser. That night, he would drink himself to oblivion, but the next morning would be reborn, ready to turn the page on a new chapter. And Manolis was completely at peace with that.

Back behind the wheel, with light rain again falling on the car's chipped and grubby windscreen, the detective returned to the northern stretch of beach where Marlowe's dead body was found. He wanted to examine the scene a second time, with fresh eyes, in case he'd missed any crucial details. In Manolis's experience, the first time on a crime scene always carried an emotional element, a shock, even after so many years and cases, which somewhat clouded judgement and analysis. A second look through a clear, sober lens always revealed something new and unexpected.

But the novelty on this occasion was even more unforeseen. From a distance, Manolis was surprised to see that people had laid remembrance flowers on the sand. Like any blow-in, Marlowe was barely tolerated, let alone well liked. But perhaps his death had allowed the Islanders to privately reflect on the sanctity of human life, despite the public celebrations. Manolis went over to examine the individual items and bouquets, their inscriptions and messages, but then saw someone emerging from the water with a surfboard and striding for the scene. It took him a moment to recognise the individual, clad in a wetsuit with wet strands of hair . . .

Skye, crouching at the site, crossed herself and seemed to say a few quiet words. Manolis watched her a while from the cover of some thick scrub, considering whether to approach her. But it might be seen as intrusion, and he preferred to be respectful and let her grieve in her own way during a private moment. The end of the line had a way of healing old wounds and making people contemplate both the sheer fragility of life and the devastating finality of death.

Manolis headed to the pub for another nightmarish vegetarian meal of miscellaneous ingredients and questionable origins, of grey-brown mushrooms and wilted spinach and a bloody massacre of ketchup on white rice. He thought about discussing the menu with Nails in the hope it might improve for the next sucker keen to cleanse their arteries. Grayson's certainly had the upper hand in that culinary space, but then, it had the advantage in all of them – meats, desserts, sides and drinks, not to mention service and décor and overall hygiene. But Nails's pub offered an indefinable rustic charm, it was a throwback and more affordable, even though the meals were more likely to show up on your yearly physical. It was altogether one of many aspects of island life that Manolis looked forward to leaving behind on his return to the mainland.

Noah was sucking on a beer when Manolis arrived. "Just a swifty tonight," he said. "Domestic duties await."

"Who says you can't parent better with alcohol?" said Manolis. "Any sign of Sparrow?"

"Do you need him? I reckon he's shacked up over at Elvis's."

"So long as he's staying on the straight and narrow . . ."

Manolis eyed the main room, which featured the usual assortment of barflies nursing their pints and schooners like they were mother's milk. But then, a face caught his eye, looking him up and down. Virginia was soon closing in, looking slightly dishevelled in appearance and clumsy in stride but with a determination in her eyes.

"Has the autopsy been completed yet? Are the results ready? What's going on with my husband's body?"

"*Ex*-husband," said Noah.

"Missus Marlowe, good to see you again," said Manolis. "In all my years, I don't think I've ever been accosted about an autopsy before. Even the dead deserve a moment's peace, don't you think?"

"Don't be silly," she snapped. "Without the autopsy results, the death certificate can't be issued, and that means the will can't be administered."

It was clear she'd had a few cold shandies that had lowered her inhibitions and loosened her tongue as to her priorities and focus. Tudge appeared, Johnny-on-the-spot, to calm her down.

"My sincerest apologies, gentlemen," he said. "We don't mean to exert any undue influence. Happy to let the official process take its natural course."

"Why such urgency anyway?" Manolis asked.

"There may be an issue with the will," Virginia blurted. "We'll be contesting it."

Tudge glared at her for saying too much and quickly escorted her away, in the face of clear reluctance and vocal protest.

Manolis and Noah exchanged looks of confusion. Issue with the will . . .? What the hell was happening?

"Didn't you hear . . .?"

It was Nails with a pair of menus listing the evening's lacklustre offerings. He'd overheard something and was keen to enlighten the police as they considered their orders.

"You mustn't have heard," he went on. "The will named Marlowe's children, which included Skye. Apparently, she's his daughter from a secret affair. Now watch them cannibalise each other as they fight over their inheritance. Eat the rich, I say."

Chapter 25

The next morning, Manolis sought enlightenment at Skye's converted shipping container. At first, he received the welcome he expected – unapproachable, uncooperative, hostile, and with Satan growling at the perceived threat like a hellhound guarding an Underworld gate. Manolis stood back an extra metre from the wooden deck and spoke even louder to be heard over the thundering waves. Skye sat with a big mug of fresh tea clasped between her fingers, blowing on its tendrils of steam.

"First of all, my condolences on the passing of your father," he said.

"So you heard," she replied.

"I saw you on the beach where he was found, you looked like you were paying your respects. It makes even more sense now."

"The secret's out."

"Second, I need to apologise for last time we spoke."

"Uh huh . . ."

"You were our prime suspect then, but I need you to understand, that was only because of the evidence we had at hand."

"Can't a girl talk with her dad on the phone? Can't we hang out? Does everyone have to think we're fucking?"

She grizzled her frustrations at her parochial island world, its obsessions over the lives of others and its insular protectiveness of a miniscule patch of insignificant turf.

"I know," Manolis sighed, relaxing his shoulders. "I'm sorry, it's a pretty awful situation for you. I wish I could say more than that."

Skye rubbed Satan's demonic head firmly in what appeared to be a kind of massage, which seemed to reduce his ferocity level from outright homicidal to merely aggressive. She invited Manolis to sit, which he did, on the step, albeit slightly warily. She took a deep sip of herbal tea and let out a full body sigh that seemed to carry both physical and emotional tension.

"Dad and I were connecting, you know. We were making up for lost time."

In Manolis, an outsider, Skye suddenly realised she had a sympathetic ear. Someone safe she could open up to, who didn't take sides, and who was about to depart the island anyway. He was the equivalent of a one-night stand.

"I grew up as an only child, raised by Mum, who was my universe. She said that my dad had abandoned us. 'Just you and me against the world, baby,' she always told me. But things changed when she met another man who effectively became my substitute father. I guess Mum was lonely, she needed companionship, I can't blame her. There was just one problem – Mum wasn't enough for him . . ."

Mum's new beau was soon paying Skye too much attention, and in an intimate, unwanted way that no teenage girl truly desires. Skye had tried to oppose him but felt distinctly powerless against an older, smarter, more physical man. When the abuse was revealed, her mum then took matters into her own hands.

"She went at him with a shotgun, aimed it squarely at his balls," Skye said. "Mum didn't fuck about, she didn't mince words, that was her strength. And that was the end of it, the coward ran for the hills. But it probably also explains why I am the way I am."

Manolis felt a familiar pain in his forehead, a hot flash of tension that came when he learned of a cruel injustice in the world that went unpunished. He made the tentative suggestion of counselling and support services.

"Too late for that," Skye said. "I'm over it."

Manolis wasn't sure she was. "Where is this arsehole? Was he charged for what he did to you?"

"He was, but the charges were dropped," she replied.

"Then let me reopen the case, let me hold him to account for what he did to you," Manolis said. "It's not too late for that."

"What evidence is there? It's Yuri's word against mine. And frankly, I don't want to relive the nightmare." She sipped her restorative tea.

"Who . . .? Wait, you mean Yuri Petrov, the beekeeper?"

Skye nodded, eyes to the ground, staring into another dimension and time. Satan growled with the savagery of an escaped tiger.

"I felt this huge level of shame and blamed myself and soon became anorexic," she said. "Typical teenage pain, in other words."

"Petrov . . . Jesus."

It wasn't long after the incident with the shotgun that Skye ran away from home and sought out her biological father, who her mum said was on the mainland.

"That was a headache and a half, tracking him down. One dead end after another. And then, to find out he was loaded. I stood no chance of penetrating his world. A poor, estranged daughter from a summer fling didn't go down well with a new family and a new life. I came across as an opportunist when all I wanted was to get to know my fucking dad."

Marlowe shunned his daughter, having moved on with a new partner and a pair of perfect twins. Having gone to the effort of establishing a base on the mainland, Skye attempted a fresh start in the big smoke, away from the trauma of her island past. It became a decade of questionable share house rentals and creepy flatmates that left Skye preyed upon, chronically penniless, and clinically depressed. But it was even worse news that finally returned her to island life.

"Mum was diagnosed with pancreatic cancer," Skye said. "Stage four, highly aggressive, with a five-year survival rate of one per cent. In other words, she was a goner."

"And there was no-one else to look after her?" Manolis asked.

"Just me. Mum's death rocked me, it impacted my thinking and choices. One of the last things she said to me was to live my life, not work my life."

But there was a surprise face at the funeral – Richard Marlowe, paying his respects. He later initiated contact with Skye to say he was considering his own return to the island.

"Our relationship blossomed," Skye said. "Dad had changed and finally became a father to me. Perhaps he'd finally learned how to with his two other kids."

Despite their different worlds, Marlowe and Skye found a common emotional frequency. Together, they seemed to bring out the best in each other, which came from the appreciation of a slower pace of life.

"I helped improve Dad's surfing, while he supported my art," Skye said. "He loved being a free spirit and wanted to embrace my kind of lifestyle, away from the cut-throat corporate world in which he reigned."

"The rich man wants to live like the poor man," said Manolis. "Simply and without the worries."

"Yeah, but he still wants the rich man's bank account," Skye replied. "Anyway, Dad was keen to experience something more humanitarian and altruistic. He had a renewed appreciation for the natural world. He was growing older and starting to have second thoughts about his work priorities and projects, including a new drilling project that was supposed to happen offshore. The animals in the ocean are struggling to adapt to rising ocean temperatures and other threats like fishing. Can you imagine the environmental damage a project like that would cause?"

"I've heard rumours about that project," Manolis replied.

Skye groaned. "I've grown so bloody tired of island rumours. Rumours are what made people think we were in a relationship. And I can see why people believed them, but the reality was nothing like that."

"So, can I ask, why were you so reluctant to talk about Marlowe?"

"I thought people would say I had something to do with his disappearance given I was supposedly his lover," she replied. "I wanted to distance myself – the less talk, the better."

Manolis reflected a moment. "But being evasive only implicates a guilty conscience," he said.

"I know, but I also knew I was innocent," Skye said. "Thing is, Dad's disappearance left me feeling abandoned again. It brought up all this past hurt in the same way I felt traumatised when people said I was his mistress. And I didn't need any more negative energy in my life."

The sudden roar of a speeding car hitting the brakes and pulling up in a rush interrupted their intimate conversation. The driver's side door of the luxury SUV flung open and Virginia stepped out, deadly high heels and deadlier pantsuit, marching straight up to Skye with no regard for her property or the salivating beast that stood to attention, nostrils flaring. There was no sign of Tudge anywhere on hand to placate his client, which made Manolis suspect that Virginia had disappeared without his knowledge, gone rogue. When Satan bared his serrated yellow teeth and thick ropes of saliva in her direction, Virginia shushed him like an unruly child. She then launched her verbal attack on Skye, calling into question her paternity claims and insisting she take a DNA test.

"Your mother was a gold digger and a common whore," she spat.

Satan grew aggressive and defensive of his owner, and his studded collar needed to be tightly restrained by Skye.

"My dog could rip you to shreds," she said.

"If your inbred mutt so much as breathes on me, I'll have him destroyed," Virginia replied coolly.

With the case winding down, homicide detective Manolis didn't especially want to be caught in the middle of an inheritance dispute. It wasn't his forte. But he made a mental note to discuss with Noah the potential for ongoing conflict over Marlowe's will.

"I'm more his blood than you could ever be," Skye said. "You're just a woman he was sleeping with. Once."

"Excuse me . . .?" said Virginia, tone incredulous. "I am the mother of his only children, I raised them from babies."

"Correction, they're not his only children – I am his child, too."

"Their blood is my blood."

"That's true. But *you* are nothing."

"How *dare* you . . ."

Manolis stood, arms outstretched, a peacemaker imploring for ceasefire.

"People, please. There's nothing we can resolve here today, but we can make things worse for ourselves by doing something physical or violent that makes me have to get involved. So, let's just retreat to our respective corners until the bell rings for round two."

Manolis wasn't quite sure what "round two" would involve – lawyers, judges, courts, geneticists – but he didn't really want to be there, either way.

"See you soon," Virginia said to Skye with a threatening smile.

Skye let Satan's booming bark be her retort. Virginia spun the wheels on her SUV to underscore her displeasure and disappeared back into the nearby bushland.

Manolis looked at Skye. "Sorry that happened," he said.

She continued to stare into the scrub. "Not your fault," she said simply. "And fuck that bitch. I should slash the tyres on her luxury gas-guzzler."

"Don't do that," said Manolis. "But I was meaning to ask you about something else."

"What's that?"

"About your dad being taken by a shark. You surfed with him. How was he in the water?"

Skye returned to her tea, now cold. "He was a competent surfer and an even stronger swimmer. But in the face of a hungry great white, who stands a chance . . .?"

"What about you, ever have any close calls?"

"Not personally, no. And all I can put that down to is dumb luck."

Manolis retrieved his wallet and handed Skye a card with his phone number.

"If there's anything you need, or that occurs to you, don't hesitate to call."

Skye thanked him and Manolis saw her smile for the very first time – her teeth were crooked but held a certain charm.

Manolis's next stop on his farewell tour wasn't originally on the schedule but the detective made sure to carve out time. He found Petrov nurturing his hives, absorbed in a miniature world where he was a god presiding over even the queen's royal reign.

"I'm heading off soon," Manolis told him. "Leaving the island."

"Oh, right then," Petrov replied, tone uncertain. "Good then. Nice to have met you." It wasn't an invitation for further conversation. It was a "don't let the door hit your mainland arse on the way out".

"Nice to have met you, too," said Manolis. "I just came by to discuss the cup you stole."

"Oh. Right."

Manolis paused, watching for changes in Petrov's body language or expressions. But he stayed like a statue, only his chest rising with each intake of breath.

"The good news is that no charges will be pressed," Manolis said.

"Oh. Excellent then, thank you," Petrov said, and returned his focus to his cherished bees.

"But that's on the proviso that we discover nothing else you've done," Manolis said.

"Yes, of course," Petrov replied, eyes firmly on his winged charges. "Well, I have nothing to fear there."

Manolis shifted his weight between feet to something more comfortable and placed a hand on his hip. He wanted to show he was in no rush and wouldn't be hurried along.

"That's good to hear," Manolis said. "And you would've also heard the news about Marlowe, no doubt . . ."

"I did. Very unfortunate for him."

Manolis waited for elaboration but there was nothing forthcoming, no "sad" or "tragic" or anything freighted with emotion. He couldn't quite tell if Petrov was being sarcastic given their history.

"To say the least," Manolis said. "A man lost his life."

"People live, people die," said Petrov, examining some precious honeycomb. "That is life."

It was the kind of cold, clinical response Manolis might have expected from a military man, or the lack of any true remorse may have simply reflected the behaviour of a genuine psychopath. Then again, the patrons had been celebrating in the pub. In truth, it was an island-wide blowout, and it was obvious why.

"Fair enough then, mate," Manolis said. "I spoke with his daughter earlier, she was a little more upset about it all. Perhaps you know her? Her name is Skye . . ."

At that moment, Petrov finally looked up. His expression also changed from disinterested and distracted to serious and intense.

"I do," Petrov said calmly. "The charges were dropped there, too."

"Then I guess you have nine lives," Manolis replied.

"Unlike the chalice cup, I was proven innocent of all wrongdoing."

"That's not the same as charges being dropped."

"And I think the sexual assault of minors is utterly abhorrent."

Manolis approached Petrov, standing in his personal space. The dull drone of bees seemed to lower in intensity, as if setting the stage for what was to come.

"I swear, if I discover any evidence that you had interfered with that girl . . ."

"Which you certainly will not."

Manolis didn't like Petrov's confident tone, but he knew that cases of sexual assault were rarely reopened. It usually required fresh DNA evidence or proof of bribes or cover-ups for silence. But if Petrov had stolen personal property and committed rape, it begged the question – what else might he have done in his life?

"The only thing worse than a murderer is a child sex offender," Manolis said with conviction. He trudged back to his car, dodging bees that encircled him like fighter jets defending their airspace. Petrov watched him go without another word.

Manolis had to pull over a few minutes later on an empty dirt road when his phone rang – he recognised Chesterman's number.

"The autopsy results are ready," the pathologist said. "Sooner than I imagined."

He said that there were no drugs or poisons found in Marlowe's system.

"Although the body was floating around in the sea for some time with all those minerals and salt, so those results don't mean all that much," he added.

"Fair enough," said Manolis, shoulders slumping.

"There were also no indications of any disastrous medical episode like a cardiac arrest or brain aneurysm."

Manolis knuckled his hot eyes in defeat, letting the facts sink in.

"Thanks very much for all your hard work," he told Chesterman. "I really appreciate the—"

He was wrapping up the conversation and about to hang up when Chesterman talked over him.

"But there was also something I didn't expect," he said.

Manolis snapped his eyes open. "And what's that?"

Chesterman cleared his throat with a phlegmy cough that kept Manolis on tenterhooks and only heightened his nervousness.

"To be thorough, I went back and examined the severed foot that was found, and conducted some further lab tests," Chesterman said. "As it turns out, there was no active blood flow at the time the foot was articulated."

Manolis stared into space, trying to process the physician's findings. Just then, a mob of muscular kangaroos bounded across the road, six or seven, paws and tails skipping across the dusty surface. They captured Manolis's attention, distracted him.

"Detective . . .?"

"Err, sorry," Manolis said. "I was just thinking. No active blood flow? What does that mean?"

"From an anatomical perspective, it means the deceased was already

249

dead when the foot was lost, and most likely when it was then taken by a shark," Chesterman said.

"Uh huh, I see. So, what does that mean exactly?" Manolis again asked.

"Tangibly, not very much," Chesterman replied. "Many shark attack victims die from drowning. But in this case, it means that I noted the official cause of death as drowning, not shark attack."

Manolis didn't know what else to say. One way or another, no matter how you sliced it, Marlowe's death sounded entirely accidental, and beyond the realms of homicide.

"Thanks again for all your time and effort," the detective said and hung up the phone with an impotent finger.

Chapter 26

Manolis had to sit with his full weight on his suitcase to get it to zip closed. He chastised himself for always overpacking, which stemmed from a worse-case scenario mindset, always planning for contingencies. It also came from procrastinating over his preparations due to feeling stressed and overwhelmed in other areas of life. In his defence, he hadn't known what to expect from his latest assignment, and in the end, this island of impenetrable mystery and lingering trauma and treacherous waters and acute community change hadn't disappointed.

With the discovery of Marlowe's body and Chesterman's autopsy report, it was officially time to return to the mainland. It had only been a short mission but Manolis had nonetheless missed his family, with a big part of him relieved to get back. But the other half remained unsatisfied.

"Drowned," Manolis muttered to himself. "Jesus . . ."

Reflecting, he repeated something that Holly once told him: "The water brought him peace." It was an offhand remark that underscored the importance of life's simple pleasures, but had also proved to be prophetic.

With a light sigh, Manolis took down the diagram of suspects he had constructed on the wall of his room. It was undercooked, still rudimentary, and now utterly useless. And yet, he still felt a niggling doubt, like a stone in his shoe, over all he'd seen and heard. There were so many unanswered questions, especially when he focused on the small details. Marlowe's wristwatch was never found, while the Velcro cuff on his surfboard remained fastened. If Marlowe had drowned, wouldn't his watch have remained on his wrist, and wouldn't the cuff have come undone . . .? Of course, it was possible the watch had simply floated away and was still in the ocean somewhere, or down at its cold bottom, in the same way it was possible his foot had been bitten off by a shark and the cuff had simply slipped off his leg. All possible, even probable occurrences. But it was just speculation and unless new evidence came to light, Manolis knew the case would be closed. The relatives were already fighting over the inheritance, picking away at an especially meaty carcass as families – and vultures – tended to do. But that was all work for lawyers and not police to sort out, unless things took an especially vicious and unexpected turn. Manolis had already briefed Noah on such potential and he hoped it wouldn't come to such an undignified conclusion. But given what was at stake, he wasn't so sure.

Heading downstairs for the last time, Manolis saw Nails in the front bar and thanked him for his hospitality. He returned his room key with its clunky, numbered plastic tag – no sleek, unlabelled electronic swipe card here. Manolis didn't mention that he wouldn't be returning any time soon to order from the pub menu, but admitted to himself the hotel had a quintessential colonial appeal and history that most of the country now sought to erase. No wonder Sparrow had been so quick to seek out Elvis's digs instead.

"I guess Marlowe wasn't all that bad," the publican said.

Manolis was surprised at his tone. What a change from the ghoulish celebration that Manolis had witnessed only a few nights earlier. He put it down to human nature, to the vanquishment of a foe, to the loss of meaning and drive, and to a reflection on the futility of it all – territoriality, hate, life, death.

"When all's said and done, he was just another bloke, like any of us," said Manolis. "He had good luck and bad, wins and losses, triumphs and mistakes and regrets. A life fully lived."

"And one helluva legacy. For our island, I mean."

252

Nails looked at Manolis seriously, eye still slightly swollen, and sipped his mug of black instant sludge with a ruminant air.

"What's that?" Manolis asked.

"I dunno exactly. But I reckon the horse has bolted. Still, it's a relief to know there's not a murderer out there knocking off residents."

"Murderer shark, maybe," said Manolis.

"That's the same thing," said Nails. "And it's simply business as usual around here."

They shook hands for what Manolis saw as the last time. As he departed, the detective doffed an invisible hat to the tiger shark above the bar.

Manolis stopped at the servo to fill his empty tank with unleaded and his empty gut with processed snacks. To fuel his brain, he'd grab a real coffee at his next stop. The price of petrol was outrageous, the oil companies gouging left right and centre. It was more than his police salary could reasonably afford; perhaps he would look to upgrade to an electric vehicle, which Emily had mentioned more than once. As Manolis waited for the bowser to activate and his bank account to empty, he saw Nankervis and Erik Junior appear from inside, each with a cola in their hands. Junior couldn't wait, cracking his icy-cold can and chugging thirstily. Manolis stopped them, and Junior told him he was faring well after falling into the ocean and nearly drowning.

"That's a relief," Manolis said.

"Without your help, the boy could've suffered brain damage, and may have even lost his life," Nankervis told him.

"It's a shame I couldn't help Marlowe in the same way," Manolis replied. "Out of interest, the day he drowned, do you remember what the water conditions were like?"

The father and son looked at each other with Nankervis recalling the weather was perfect that day – sunny and still and warm.

"More than anything, it's the wind that causes waves," he explained. "And there wasn't a breath that day."

"Our catch was bloody huge as a result," Junior added.

Manolis shook their hands, wishing them the best of health and luck in the water.

He dropped by Elvis's café for a last delicious brew, which the grinning barista proffered "on the house". Elvis sung a little tune as he wiped down the plastic tables, clearly in a good place with life and the universe. Sparrow was also there, all hopped up on high-quality caffeine, hanging on like a groupie, and all touchy-feely with his new beau.

"I'll be taking some immediate leave, boss," Sparrow informed Manolis. "Hope that's okay."

"I guessed as much," Manolis replied. "Approved."

The detective had been disappointed by Sparrow's initial loss of interest in the case – he saw it as unprofessional and was worried about his less experienced colleague letting his investigative abilities become compromised as key suspects emerged. But given how things had worked out, Manolis felt comfortable enough to lower his guard.

"At least something good has finally come out of our island adventure, eh Sarge?" The young cop beamed. He put his arm around Elvis's supple waist, pulled him closer and kissed him hard on the lips, teasing at his labret.

Manolis could only nod and return the smile. It was nice to see Sparrow so happy and content – the kid deserved it. The detective picked up his coffee and headed for the ferry terminal.

Leaning through Manolis's car window, Noah saw him off at the other end. "Thanks again for all your help," he said.

"Stay in touch," said Manolis. "Give my best to Tessa and the boys."

The morning ferry had just arrived, crammed with passengers and vehicles and cargo. Bundles of long pipes like drinking straws were unloaded on the backs of trucks.

"For the new desalination plant," Noah muttered.

Manolis drove his vehicle into position to be loaded on board alongside trucks, trailers, boats and other cars. He marvelled at the process – like reassembling a geometric puzzle into a tight space. Collecting his boarding pass, he took a modular seat inside the terminal and rested his feet on the smoke-grey carpet. With his first sip of warm coffee, he seemed to properly exhale for the first time in ages. It was a mental process of expunging the solved case, the old world, and preparing himself for the new. It was a world scheduled to start the moment he set foot on the mainland – he'd organised to meet Emily for a few days in the Fleurieu Peninsula region, nature walks, boutique wineries and glittering beaches. Their son was staying with his aunt – Emily's sister – and her family. It was an impulsive decision to book a luxury eco-cabin, but Manolis knew he wouldn't regret it, he knew they needed some time together, especially after the time apart. And spontaneity always has a way of creating memories.

Checking his phone, Manolis saw he had reception and decided to make one final call. Holly answered on the third ring.

"How are you and the kids doing?" Manolis asked.

He heard her sigh as one of the Samoyeds yapped in the background.

"As well as can be expected," she said. "Though the kids are still in shock, they've barely left their rooms, even less so than usual. It's the most traumatic event since their parents got divorced. But at least their mum has come by."

"All okay there? I know Virginia can be somewhat . . . emotional."

"To say the least. But we've put our differences to one side given the circumstances."

"For the kids."

"Yes. And I reached out to Skye, too. She's family, after all."

"That's encouraging to hear," Manolis said. Perhaps, he thought, there was still some hope for this cold, fragmented clan.

"Richard left me the house," Holly said. "Of course, I'll now have to sell it, there's no way I can pay the mortgage otherwise. But what would I need such a big house for anyway when it's just me and the dogs . . .? And Richard was right when he said it was pushing us further apart instead of bringing us closer together."

She explained how the rest of the estate was left to his three children in equal shares. "But Roland and Allegra haven't yet reached the age of maturity so their shares will be held on trust by their legal guardian," Holly said.

"Who's that?"

"Who do you think? Virginia, of course."

Manolis sipped his double shot espresso, drinking in the stimulant alongside the information.

"Either way, all our lives have changed," Holly went on. "There's so much to sort out now, Richard achieved so much in his life, which makes untangling it more complicated."

"I can imagine. Actually, while I have you, there's a couple of tiny things that have been troubling me . . ."

"About Richard?"

"Yes. Do you mind if I ask? They might come across as strange requests . . ."

"After this ordeal, I don't find anything to be truly strange anymore."

"Thank you. Well, the first was his surfing technique. Do you perhaps remember how he stood when he rode his board, did he have a regular stance or was it a bit goofy?"

Holly went silent, before Manolis finally heard her say "ahh" and realised she was finishing a drink. Of what, he didn't know.

"Sorry, I don't quite understand the difference," she said.

"Did he lead with his left or right foot on the board?" he explained. "A goofy-foot surfer stands with their right foot forward and their left foot back, which is the opposite of a regular stance. Can you picture him on the board, how he stood?"

Manolis was trying to get a sense of how Marlowe attached his leg rope and cuff, which was still fastened when his board washed up. After taking a moment to consider, Holly replied:

"I'm picturing him standing with his left foot forward."

Manolis sighed his disappointment – it meant Marlowe had a regular stance, with his right foot tethered to the surfboard, which was consistent with the same foot being severed. He was hoping it might've been goofy.

256

"Thanks," he replied. "And the other thing was his wristwatch, which was never found. I know it's a really small detail but do you know what kind of band it had, how it was fastened to his wrist?"

Holly wasn't sure. "I'd only be guessing," she said. "Sorry."

"It's alright, I didn't expect you to know."

"But at least we can have a funeral now."

"That's important, don't underestimate its impact . . ."

Manolis remembered his own father's funeral, how important such send-offs were in the Greek Orthodox community to bring a restless soul the peace it needed. Manolis had thought it was all for show, all bullshit, until he realised the benefit to the grieving family left behind. Whether it was laying a body to rest in the ground or cremation and the scattering of ashes or organising organ and tissue donation, it brought with it a sense of closure, and in some instances even tangible benefit to the lives of others.

"It's an ending," Holly said. "Can't have a beginning without an ending. And to be honest with you, there were moments when I wondered what life might be like if Richard was *never* found, if he always remained missing. And that, somehow, felt much worse than even a bad outcome."

Manolis wished her well and said she could call him anytime. She thanked him and hung up.

He finished his last warm mouthful of coffee and boarded the ferry, settling in for the unpleasant journey back to the mainland across the choppy Backstairs Passage strait. At least the wind was calm, which increased Manolis's chances of keeping down his stomach contents. He sat outside to keep sight of the horizon and chewed on a ginger and lemon lolly infused with propolis. Filling his lungs with salt, Manolis hoped the combination might altogether lessen the unpleasantness of the sea voyage ahead.

As the ferry rode the waves, Manolis couldn't help but notice a bleach-haired, barefooted surfer dude sitting opposite him. He was wearing a colourful Baja hoodie and baggy boardshorts and staring intently at his wristwatch, making it beep incessantly. Seeing what appeared to be a curious middle-age tourist watching him, the surfer opened up a conversation.

"This new watch is sick," the dude said. "All these features and data, you've got to get one."

For a moment, Manolis wondered if this was a paid promotion, like attractive young girls in a nightclub drinking the latest alcoholic mixer.

"I can imagine," the detective replied. "Mine has one feature – it tells the time. And even then, only barely."

The surfer laughed, a nasally, staccato type giggle that made him sound stoned. The intensity and duration of his reaction suggested that he may very well have been under the influence, because it was more than Manolis's joke deserved.

"That's cool, man," the surfer said. "Mine's got all these health sensors, heart rate, blood oxygen levels, ECG, it even tracks sleep stages. But it's the water features that are the shit."

"What shit . . . ?"

The surfer's eyes lit up under his long fringe of messy blonde bangs. "Yeah, man. Like the low and high tide times for any surf break on the freaking planet. It's got wave counters, wave height, wind speed and direction. There's sunrise and sunset times, moon phases, barometer, weather forecast, and all sorts of other stuff, too."

"Everything but pizza delivery."

The stoner dude again giggled stupidly. Manolis wondered if he really did have the munchies.

"It's probably got a button for that, too," the surfer said. "But what's really cool is that it tracks how far I've surfed and swum using GPS. I can see how far and how fast I surfed on every wave, how many waves I caught, and the total wave time and distance. With my old watch, I couldn't take it into water and had to download the activity data to my phone. Freaking ancient technology, man. This new one syncs with my phone and sends it all in real-time."

Manolis's eyes suddenly sparkled.

"Mate, hey, can I just take a quick look?" he asked.

"Knock yourself out, dude . . ."

The surfer passed the watch across while Manolis activated his phone. Scanning his collection of digital images, his eyes settled on the photo of a smiling Marlowe on the beach with his yellow surfboard. Focusing on his wrist and zooming in to magnify the image, Manolis squinted hard to compare the watches.

They appeared to be identical.

Back on the island, business was proving slow at Elvis's café. An already jittery Sparrow prepared himself yet another delicious coffee.

"What a bludger of a day," Elvis exhaled in frustration, bored.

He perused the local paper, flipping casually through its meagre pages. He only stopped to read a story about the continued progress of the island's offshore drilling project.

"Hmm," he said.

"What's up, babe?" Sparrow asked.

"This sounds morbid but with Marlowe dead, I thought the drilling project would've been killed off, too," Elvis replied. "I guess I was wrong."

"Hey, I've got some receipts here," Sparrow said. "Where's the stapler?"

"Check through that drawer there, the top one . . ."

Sparrow rooted around in the drawer for a while but was unable to find what he was looking for. Instead, his hand clasped a wristwatch that he held up for Elvis to see. Shiny and black, it caught the light, reflecting it back at him.

"Nice watch," Sparrow said. "Looks pretty schmick and sporty. This yours?"

"Aw yeah," Elvis said. "Glad you reminded me. Someone left that behind in the shop recently. It looks new, like it might be worth something, so I hung on to it in case the owner returned."

Chapter 27

From the top deck of the ferry, Manolis recognised Emily's silver-grey SUV on the mainland, catching the afternoon light like a mirror shard. She was leaning on the bonnet scrolling on her phone but waved and smiled when she saw him, clearly looking forward to their upcoming time together.

But Manolis now had other ideas. He was first to alight from the ferry the moment it docked, racing out ahead of the tourist parties with their cameras and backpacks and wide-brimmed hats. Rushing straight up to the ticket counter, he paid for a return fare back to the island on the very next crossing.

"And do you have a vehicle?" the attendant asked.

"Yes," Manolis replied. "It's already onboard."

"Wait, what . . .? How? Excuse me . . ."

But he didn't wait to explain, jogging onto the mainland to rendezvous with Emily and present her with the unexpected change of plans. He was slightly breathless by the time he reached her but needed as much time as possible to explain what had happened in the hope it might soften the blow. He didn't expect it would, but still needed to try.

Emily lifted her retro square sunglasses onto her head as Manolis emerged, greeting him with a smiling pair of piercing blue eyes. She was wearing an olive-green tank top that exposed her tanned shoulders and arms, a pair of much-loved blue jeans, and open-toed sandals. Her shoulder-length hair was wind-blown and messy, which gave her an altogether relaxed appearance fitting for a short break from busy professional life and parenting. Manolis embraced his wife tightly and pecked her on her sweaty cheek.

"I missed you so much," he said in her ear.

"Me too," she replied. "This was a great idea."

"I know. There has, unfortunately, been a slight change of plans . . ."

"What's up? Is it the accommodation? I bet they stuffed the booking, it always happens . . ."

Taking his wife by the shoulders, Manolis explained the situation. As his words fell out, Emily's expression changed from expectant and optimistic to shocked and confused, and eventually resigned and disappointed. Manolis told her that he was following a lingering feeling, a hunch that there was more to Marlowe's death than an unfortunate drowning.

"And this despite the pathologist's official report?" Emily asked.

"I know, I know," said Manolis. "But the activity tracker on Marlowe's watch might hold the answer if it uses the same technology as the one on the ferry."

Manolis explained that it wouldn't even be a case of finding the missing watch – given the new technology, the data would've already been sent to Marlowe's phone. As long as he'd used the tracker the morning he disappeared and it reliably connected to the GPS on the island.

"I just need to check the phone, and I know where it is," Manolis said. "It's all those juicy ones and zeros of data that hold the answer."

Emily was listening with her arms crossed in annoyance, looking at Manolis for a very long time.

"You haven't changed one bloody bit," she snapped. "How stupid do I feel . . ."

She went to storm off. Manolis had to grab her by the arm to stop her progress, which she did not appreciate.

"George. Please let me go."

"Em, please, gimme a chance," Manolis said.

"I am," she said. "I want you to go. Just go and do whatever the hell you have to do."

"Aw hey. Not like that."

Looking deep into her eyes, Manolis summoned all his charm to explain that he truly understood the mistakes he'd made in the past when it came to his work commitments and his neglect of family life.

"I can assure you, I fully appreciate what you and Christos have been through," Manolis said. "Even being there on the island this short time has helped drive that home. I know you've given me another chance and I'm committed to making this work."

She looked at him hard, assessing, gauging her trust.

"Please believe me when I say I am absolutely not the same man," Manolis went on. "I promise you. I'll make it up to you. But right now, I have to get back to the island and see if my hunch is true. A man died, and a killer may be free. I wouldn't do it otherwise."

Emily looked over his shoulder at the docked ferry bobbing about in the water.

"Then let me join you," she said.

Manolis hadn't anticipated that. And while the island certainly was a holiday destination in its own right, the nature of his investigation and the storm damage meant it probably wasn't the most appealing time to experience it.

He held Emily's hand, gave it a squeeze. "Normally, I'd say yes," he began. "The island is certainly unique, I'll give you that. But honestly, after what's gone down, I think it's safer you go."

"Go? Go where?"

"To where we booked, the cabin. Enjoy some me-time there. Read, relax, eat, sleep. All going well, I reckon I'll be able to join you soon. But either way, I promise I'll make it up to you."

Emily snatched her hand away, striding with determination for her vehicle. Manolis ran after her and gave her a hug as she reached for the door.

"I'm so, so sorry," he said. "I have changed, you will see."

She kept her arms stiffly by her sides, then drove away without another word or backwards glance. Manolis watched her leave, waved and blew a kiss, before bolting back to the ferry.

On the island again after another crossing, and now doubly nauseous, Manolis dialled Noah.

"There's been developments," he said. "I'm back on the island."

"That was a quick turnaround," the Islander cop replied.

"Unexpected, yes. I need you to chase something down . . ."

"Oh, right. Well then, I'm all ears."

He asked Noah to search online for the model of Marlowe's phone and then meet him at Holly's house.

"What's this all about exactly?" Noah asked.

"I'll explain in person." *Click.*

Manolis then rang Sparrow, who was technically on leave and, unsurprisingly, not answering his phone. The detective drove on, heading west and south, without leaving a message.

Back face-to-face again, Manolis explained his thinking in the living room. He spoke like the clappers, at the speed of thought. Holly and Noah stared at each other like Manolis was slightly unhinged and borderline obsessive. As if sympathetically, the Samoyeds tilted their fleecy heads in confusion.

"I just won't rest until I've turned over every stone," Manolis said. "This is a long shot, but it might shed some light on what happened to Marlowe and how he might've drowned."

"Or you could be barking up the wrong tree," said Holly. "Reopening fresh wounds."

She admitted to still being upset and a little reluctant to proceed while she remained in the process of healing, but at the same time she understood that Manolis was only trying to help find the truth.

"I'm sorry to drag things out," Manolis said. "I don't want this to be any more traumatic than it needs to be but I wouldn't have gone to all this effort if I didn't think it was worthwhile."

Holly's gaze bounced between the two officers, doubtful and uncertain. But then she slumped her shoulders and sighed, half-closing her eyes. When she opened them, she stood to her full height.

"Okay. Wait here."

Banjo and Maple followed Holly down the corridor to the bedrooms. There was no sight nor sound of the twins. Manolis and Noah exchanged uncertain glances. To pass the time, the local cop drummed a slow military beat on his knees with his palms. Manolis thought Noah looked tired and wondered how Tessa and the kids were faring. The detective tried to block out thoughts of his own family and what he'd need to do there to redeem himself. It wasn't catastrophic or irrecoverable – he hoped.

It was two more drum solos before Holly reappeared, slim black mirror in her palm. She held it out to Manolis, who received it gratefully.

"I honestly didn't even realise his watch was an activity tracker," the widow said. "I mean, he never told me his daily workout or anything like that, the metrics. I imagine most people would brag if they set a personal best or whatever. I know I would."

Her response made Manolis wonder if Marlowe even used the tracking function – he could've simply bought the most modern sports wristwatch that his hefty wallet could afford, consistent with the rest of his life. The best of everything, but not necessarily across everything.

Manolis tried to activate the phone but its screen stayed dark.

"I've not charged it," Holly said. "Almost out of respect."

Manolis recognised such behaviour – like grieving parents who left their dead children's bedrooms in the same state, frozen in time. It was both touching and heart-wrenching.

"And I know Richard used to keep it locked," Holly added.

"That's the task now, to unlock it," said Manolis, wiping it clean of dust and oily residue with his shirtsleeve. "Once we do that, we'll be able to see if there's any activity data."

He described how the phone would now be sent to the computer forensics crime lab on the mainland.

"They have the tools, the specialist software, that can crack even the most secure encrypted modern phone," said Manolis. "The problem is time. It could take a while."

"How long you reckon?" Noah asked.

"A day, a week, a month, a year," said Manolis. "Or, worst case scenario, not at all. It all depends on the phone and the level of security. They're getting more advanced these days, artificial intelligence, et cetera. And the police technology is always one step behind."

Manolis explained that the computer software tools worked to first remove the limit that phones imposed on passcode attempts. Stage two was to then sequentially enter passcodes until the phone unlocked.

"Because of all the possible combinations, a six-digit passcode apparently takes on average twelve hours to guess," Manolis said.

"What if it is more than six digits?" Noah asked.

"A ten-digit code can take as much as twelve years. If that's the case, suffice to say, we're screwed."

They both looked back at Holly for insight. "Sorry, I've no idea how long Richard's code was," she said. "Or what the hell it might be."

"A birthday?" Manolis asked. "One of the kids' birthdays? Or yours? Or the dogs?"

"You could try them, I guess . . ."

She told Manolis the relevant digits, which he wrote down – at the very least, he wanted to charge the phone and enter them before handing it over to computer forensics. It was the simplest, quickest solution that Manolis would be remiss not to try even though he imagined a man like Marlowe would use something less obvious to secure such a treasure chest of personal information.

At the back of his mind, Manolis was worried about taking up valuable police resources trying to crack a phone with state-of-the-art security features, given the autopsy report and the chances that Marlowe hadn't even used the activity tracker. But what Emily would've described as his "stubborn determination" meant he still wanted to roll the dice.

Manolis pocketed the shiny device and stood. "Thank you," he told Holly. "We'll be in touch if we learn anything new."

"God. That's not, is it? It can't be . . ."

Driving east back across the island to the ferry terminal, Manolis narrowed his eyes and eased his foot off the accelerator. He was approaching a figure shambling along the dirt roadside, and the distinctive lurching gait suggested it was someone familiar.

Manolis pulled up smiling in a cloud of dust. He rolled down the passenger window.

"Well, bugger me," he said. "It is."

Sparrow was carrying a forlorn jerry can in his right hand. He turned lethargically, fatigue chiselled across his sweaty face.

"Need a lift?" Manolis asked.

"Sarge . . .? Jesus, what the hell are you doin' here?"

"Long story. Hop in."

As they drove, Sparrow explained that he'd run out of petrol.

"I figured," Manolis said. "But where?"

"I was on my way back from a nearby beach. Just went for a dip."

"Swimming at the beach, eh?" Manolis grinned. "Well, look at you. All of a sudden, a water baby."

"Blame Elvis. He took me there yesterday, bloody awesome little spot, calm waves and clear water. And it was hardly a swim, more of a splash about and float. And shark-free."

"You seem pretty smitten there, mate."

Sparrow smiled to himself. "We're just enjoyin' each other's company. That's all, nuthin' serious."

"Don't be like that. I'm happy for you."

"Thanks, Sarge."

"I tried to ring you earlier."

"No reception on the beach, hence needing to walk my sorry black arse home. What brings you back anyway, did ya miss me?"

"Like the deserts miss the rain . . ."

Manolis went on to detail the wristwatch theory he'd formulated, the smart technology and activity tracker.

"Legal cases are getting more sophisticated these days, more focused on tech," he said. "Mobile phone calls, text messages, GPS data and vehicle monitors are all used as evidence."

"Personal activity trackers are next level," said Sparrow.

"So it seems. I definitely know of cases where defendants were either convicted or acquitted thanks to their own activity tracking data. But I've not heard it used for murder victims in working out what happened to them."

He passed his phone to Sparrow to show him a photo of the surfer's watch alongside the old image of Marlowe wearing his. The young cop studied it a while, his electrically charged mind ticking over, and then stared out the window.

"Hey, mate," Manolis said. "What's up, you okay?"

Sparrow blinked. "Aw yair," he said. "I'm alright. I just thought I saw a king brown slither into the scrub out there . . ."

Dropping Sparrow off at the café, Manolis wished his colleague well. "And if you see or hear anything," he added.

"Yair yair," Sparrow said. "I know."

The detective continued on his way to the ferry terminal with Marlowe's phone all set for delivery.

Elvis's metallic green ute was in the driveway but he was nowhere to be seen. Sparrow ducked into the café and tried to busy himself with cleaning and restocking but soon succumbed to curiosity. Searching through the top drawer, he found the watch, and his heart sank when he realised it was the same distinctive model of wristwatch.

Elvis said that someone had left it in the café. But what if he was lying . . .? There was always a chance it wasn't Marlowe's watch but the ramifications were significant if it was. Either way, Sparrow knew he needed to do something – to either inform Manolis or properly discuss the watch with Elvis. But which option, who . . .?

"Shit shit shit," Sparrow said, rubbing his hot cheeks.

This was a test of character and professionalism that the young cop hadn't faced before. There was one time in Cobb when he'd needed to assist in the arrest of a young cousin after an aggravated assault with a steel claw hammer, but it was no-one he particularly liked, so no thing. Elvis was different. The café was empty and showing no signs of life.

In the end, and despite his better judgement, Sparrow's heart won out over his head. He decided to ring Elvis.

No answer.

Sparrow looked around, a rudimentary search – the back of the café, the semi-detached house further in behind – but was unable to find him. The universe was clearly hinting at something. Activating his phone, Sparrow decided to call Manolis and provide a situation update.

"Christ, mate," Manolis said, still at the ferry terminal. "Why didn't you tell me this earlier?"

He was annoyed and Sparrow knew it.

"I . . . I wasn't sure," he replied. "About the watch – or what to do."

"And where's the watch now?"

"In my pocket."

"Well, I'm bloody glad you told me. You were honest, you did the right thing. I'll be there soon. Stay alert."

Sparrow exhaled and shuffled numbly to wait at a table outside the café. Wherever he was, Elvis surely wasn't far away, and he would need to be kept occupied, and potentially even confronted.

Just then, Sparrow heard a car door slam and an engine rev. He spun his head round to see Elvis's ute appearing from the driveway in a mad, uncontrolled rush. Sparrow went to stop him, running fast, bashing on the passenger window. But Elvis just ignored him, slipped the ute into another gear, and accelerated away at speed.

Chapter 28

When he arrived at the café, Manolis found Sparrow slumped like a drunk in the gutter. He looked dejected and defeated, head slung low. He was resigned to his fate, ready to face the music from his senior officer, who assumed his own look of disappointment and loss when he learned what had happened.

"Elvis has done a runner," Sparrow said. "He must've overheard me talking to you on the phone. I'm so, so sorry Sarge."

"*Gamoto* . . ."

Manolis cursed out loud in Greek. Sparrow didn't understand the detail but recognised the context and apologised again.

"I should've told you sooner, in the car, privately," he said. "We wouldn't be here in the shit now."

"You're damn right you should have . . ."

Manolis wore his irritation like a cheap suit. His hunch had been proven correct, and simply confirmed his suspicions that there was more going on.

Sparrow stood and arched his back, which made a sharp cracking sound. He rubbed his jaw anxiously and looked in both directions up and down the empty road.

"Which way did he go?" Manolis asked.

The senior constable pointed east and, trying to be helpful, began to speculate on why Elvis may have fled.

"He could've been shit-scared. Or pissed off cos I broke his trust."

"Or because he had a guilty conscience," Manolis said, speaking from experience. "C'mon, son. Don't be so naive. I know you don't wanna believe it but that's the first and only place my brain goes."

Sparrow looked brooding and sullen, his eyes dark. "You just don't know him like I do," he said.

"Well, that's a given. But if he's got something to hide, I know *his type* intimately. Are you suggesting he didn't have a grudge against Marlowe?"

"Oh no, that was fucken legit alright. In fact, it may've run even deeper than we realised."

Sparrow proposed they search Elvis's house. "He gave me a key, you know," he added.

"Tempting," said Manolis. "But it wouldn't be admissible as evidence, we'd need a search warrant. Don't get ahead of yourself, mate. We need to obtain evidence legally or it can't be used in court. You know that. By the book or not at all, enough fucking mistakes."

Sparrow cast his eyes down. "I was just tryin' to help, Sarge."

Manolis could tell the young constable regretted his lapse of judgement but still wasn't thinking clearly.

"Does the café have any CCTV so we can see who left the watch behind?" Manolis asked.

Sparrow shook his head. "That's assuming the yarn Elvis told me is true," he said.

He seemed to be trying to defend his new lover, but to Manolis, it just sounded like he was digging the hole deeper. And the senior detective didn't like it. During the entire time on Kangaroo Island, Manolis had been mulling over whether to tell Sparrow about his father and Jimmy Dingo. But at that moment, he thought to take the grim revelation to his grave just like Con had.

"Mate," he said. "Whatever you had with Elvis, he may genuinely be annoyed that you breached his trust. But the fact you didn't tell me earlier means that *I* now have trust issues *with you*. You let your heart control your head, your judgement's clouded, you're all over the fucking place. It's unprofessional as hell."

"Unprofessional? Me?" Sparrow said. He took a combative step nearer his superior officer, standing in Manolis's comfort zone. "You're the one that let that narcissist rich bitch get off scot-free despite admitting to having a bag of blow. A black kid would've never gotten away with that, they would've been locked up for nicking so much as a durry."

"That's got nothing to do with this investigation," Manolis said, eyes narrow.

"Bullshit," Sparrow replied.

"I know you went rogue on your last assignment and did some shit there that was also unethical. And I looked the other way before, earlier in this investigation. But I can't anymore. Step back, please."

Manolis had let his frustrations bubble over, his face hard-lined and austere. Sparrow had never seen him like that – restrained fury – and seemed to shrink an inch. In facing the music, it seemed to be louder than he had predicted. He took a deliberate step backwards.

"Sarge . . .?" Sparrow stared at him with shaken, pleading eyes.

Manolis exhaled. "Look, if you truly wanna help, just go wait in your hotel room," he told him.

It was clear – Sparrow had now become a liability, which suddenly seemed to anger him, too. He kicked the ground in disgust to underscore his annoyance, sent loose pebbles flying.

"All I was doing was trying to be with someone. And now you want to make me feel like shit for that."

The partners were at loggerheads, a rupture that had been brewing for some time. Sparrow backed away a few more metres before turning and picking up speed, striding off with purpose to distance himself from his tormentor. Meanwhile, Manolis remained steadfast, watching him go. He felt a pang of guilt for the confrontational approach he'd taken, but at that moment, he saw no alternative. A foul-smelling dust hung in the air, which was uncharacteristically still.

Checking his phone and seeing it had precious bars of reception, Manolis dialled his only other island option.

"All of a sudden, we've got a manhunt on our hands," he told Noah.

"The island's only so big," Noah replied when Manolis had explained the situation. "And yet, there's still so many ways to escape it."

He pointed out the obvious water routes, with the mainland being accessible using either a boat or ferry.

"There's also the air," Noah went on. "Planes and choppers."

"Less likely," Manolis said. "You go to the ferry terminal. And don't just watch out for drivers, I need you to search their cars for stowaways as well."

"Where's Sparrow?" Noah asked.

"Not feeling well," Manolis lied. "He's resting in his room."

Manolis knew he needed manpower to aid in the search for Elvis and was slightly worried about his own welfare, and also the safety of others, if the football captain was unhinged or panicked and acted on impulse. Manolis had already witnessed Elvis's physicality and capacity for violence first-hand and he didn't need a repeat screening.

"I've got an idea," Manolis added.

His next call was to Murden, whom he asked, in his mayoral capacity, for civic assistance and local reinforcements.

"I knew it," Murden said. "I bloody knew it. The bloke was always a thug."

Manolis wondered whatever happened to "boys will be boys", but Murden was now on the offensive and appeared to be taking things personally. Either way, he was willing to help Manolis's cause.

"Leave it with me," Murden said. "I'll make some calls, get some shit happening."

Manolis headed out eastwards to scour the island's towns and roads and beaches, which was the most he could manage in his car. It replicated Elvis's mode of escape but there was no guarantee he hadn't already ditched his vehicle for some other form of carriage – by sea, by air, or overland by foot. It could have been hidden in scrub, a mate's garage, or under a synthetic car cover. Manolis might have already driven past it and not even realised. His firearm was ready in case of a confrontation, but Manolis was loath to use his weapon, which was only issued as a last resort if another human life was in danger. A car pursuit was more likely, in which case Manolis would look to shoot out Elvis's tyres, though this still came with a risk of accident and physical injury. But then, he'd also seen instances of otherwise placid people becoming almost unrecognisably aggressive and violent when cornered. Desperation and chemical changes in the brain led to poor decision-making – not unlike the effect being in love had on besotted police constables.

As he drove, Manolis spotted a barefooted Skye and a seagull-chasing Satan walking along the stretch of beach nearest their shipping container – the friendly Rottweiler had remnants of white plumage on his face. The detective pulled over, told her what had happened and asked for her assistance in locating the fugitive.

"I'll try to keep an eye out," she said. "Elvis is no shrinking violet."

She described how she'd seen him at recent numerous island protests and public meetings over development and logging proposals.

"He was very vocal and argumentative, to the point of being intimidating," Skye said. "He's young and fit and feels indestructible."

"I can imagine," said Manolis.

Skye said Elvis had sometimes demonstrated in front of the new island developments, waving handwritten placards and blasting loud music from his ute.

"The thing is, I supported absolutely everything he said," Skye added. "Just, perhaps, not quite how he said it."

They went their separate ways. Manolis drove inland, flagging down other vehicles to spread the word and check their occupants. Some appeared red-eyed and sluggish, as if driving over the blood alcohol limit or under the influence of narcotics. But at that moment, Manolis had no capacity to police the traffic laws – he let them drive on with silent prayers for safe travel. He was now fighting, and losing, a battle that was proving to be too much for one man. Manolis even contemplated recalling Sparrow to active duty from his hotel room, but had serious doubts over the wisdom of such a decision. In the end, he ploughed on, and could only curse Sparrow to the skies.

He decided to ring Holly with an update – her husband's death might not have been a pure accident, and a new suspect had suddenly emerged. Even though he knew it would subject her to an emotional rollercoaster, it was motivated by concerns for her own safety should Elvis end up doing something even more foolish.

"Oh God," Holly said. "Do I need to be worried? What about the kids? Do we need to hide somewhere or to protect ourselves somehow?" Her voice was unsteady.

"No, and just stay calm," Manolis said. "As the saying goes, be alert, not alarmed. I've no intel to suggest that you or the twins might be targeted. Perhaps I'm being overly cautious but I thought it best to keep you informed. There's a criminal suspect on the run. So, I'm telling you what I'd tell anyone in such circumstances – lock your doors and keep an eye out for anything suspicious. If there's any developments at my end, I'll call."

He hung up. They'll be okay, he told himself. Their house was secured like Fort fucking Knox. They probably even had a few other fire-arms stashed away in some secret location that Manolis and the others hadn't found during their search. And given all its other state-of-the-art features, the house most likely had a fortified panic room tucked away somewhere, reinforced with sheets of steel, Kevlar or fibreglass, secure and bulletproof.

"If things start to get dicey, they can always go hole up in their private bushfire bunker," Manolis said to himself. "Wonder how many hours oxygen they've got stored down there . . ."

Driving on, now heading into the denseness of the national park, Manolis reconsidered his colleague, who was mostly likely sitting in the bar at Nails's with a cold one in hand, hopefully reflecting on what had happened. Sparrow often bragged about possessing skills as an Aboriginal tracker that he learned from his mob. They would certainly come in handy if Elvis was on foot. In the same way the first Indigenous women on the island once helped the sealers source food and build shelter, trackers were also used to explore the landscape. In particular, Aboriginal outback troopers under the command of colonialist police were deployed to locate missing persons and escaped prisoners, capture bushrangers, and disperse other groups of Indigenous peoples. Sparrow claimed he had finely tuned powers of surveillance and scrutiny, that he could deduce the subtlest traces of human behaviour from whatever was out of place. Long blades of agitated grass, scattered branches, even a few grains of sand. That was all it took, a minor disruption to the natural order – anything that made contact with the earth left its mark. It was a philosophy that only underscored the sacredness of the land to its Indigenous people. The infamous nineteenth-century outlaw Ned Kelly was apparently more afraid of Aboriginal trackers than anyone else – he knew he could outfox a fellow white man, but an Indigenous tracker was in another league and able to call on powers unavailable to whitefellas. Admittedly, Sparrow's boasting about his tracking skills only came out after a few Friday knock-off beers, and Manolis had yet to see his tracking skills in action first-hand. It could've all been bullshit on Sparrow's part. And there was still a risk that Sparrow was compromised. For all Manolis knew, the young cop had already been on the blower to Elvis, helping him remain one step ahead of the authorities.

Surfing a rise in the dusty road, Manolis heard his pocket start ringing. He pulled over and safely answered his phone.

"Sir, additional troops have now been dispatched to the field, sir." Murden spoke in an intentionally roguish military tone.

The reinforcements included Ranger Fox, who was using her intricate island knowledge to comb its remote and desolate corners, while Conway and the Nankervises were out patrolling the waters. The city detective was more used to sniffer dogs on the ground, search teams marching in straight lines, high-powered spotlights and whupping choppers in the sky. But it was good to know he had *some* backup, at least.

"Awaiting further orders, sir," Murden added.

"That's great," Manolis said. "Thank you for your assistance."

"And Lavender's also gone up in his helicopter," Murden said. "So, we have the land, air and sea all covered."

Manolis was genuinely surprised. He had never anticipated such a community response. He thanked the mayor for his time, efforts and influence.

"I'm just heading out now in the car myself," Murden said. "Don't worry, we'll nick the little bastard soon enough, you mark my words . . ."

But the day was getting away from them now, the sun sitting heavy and low. Manolis continued on, angling towards its descent in the western sky. The night made everything harder, bringing with it poor visibility and the emergence of assorted predators in the water, on the land, and in the pubs. Feeling guilty for having had a pregnant park ranger dragged into proceedings, Manolis went looking for Fox and soon found her on a strip of beach on the island's western tip. She was hunched over, crouching on the sand, which made Manolis panic and rush to her side, expecting something to be wrong. Was she having contractions, had the stress of her work and the manhunt brought them on, was the baby coming early . . .?

As Manolis came closer, the true reason for her position became apparent. It was a baby alright, but of a different kind. The ranger was tending to a long-nosed fur seal, its tiny face and head distorted and bloody, its soft, pink-yellow brain exposed to the salty elements.

"Dead," Fox sighed. "Separated from its parents and clubbed to a bloody death."

"Jesus Christ," Manolis said.

"Another one needlessly murdered for a laugh."

Manolis felt sick to his stomach.

"By whom? What lowlife did this?" he asked, crouching down.

"Probably a bored teenager or young male, drunk or high or both," Fox replied. "To think that in this day and age, people still get a kick out of such senseless cruelty."

Manolis couldn't quite believe it – the barbarism, the throwback to

277

the island's contemptible past that it had worked so hard to distance itself from.

"They probably thought they were being edgy and cool, not callous and cowardly," Fox went on. "Showing off to their mates, living up to island history. Still, we should be thankful."

"Thankful? What the hell for?" Manolis asked.

"At least this one is properly dead. Skull crushed, forehead caved-in, arteries severed. Looks like they used a galvanised steel pipe or some such. I'll spare you the grisly details but I've often come across some baby seals that are still alive, writhing in pain. I've had to finish them off myself, which is fucking heartbreaking."

Manolis tried not to picture what that was like but his imagination was too powerful. He looked around but the beach was deserted. "Where's its parents?"

Fox shook her head, making her blonde hair swish. "They probably tried to help and then swam away to save themselves. C'mon, gimme a hand eh. We need to remove the carcass from the sand before the evening scavengers arrive."

With the gentleness of a parent nursing their own human child, Manolis took the slippery seal into his strong arms. Its wilted, lifeless body and empty eyes crushed his soul. He'd never held a seal before and to do it under such circumstances was almost surreal. Carrying it like fine china across the uneven sand, Manolis placed it in the back of Fox's car, into the same cardboard box that usually transported koala casualties. The dead seal only weighed a few kilos and fit snugly, its spine curled into the shape of a crescent moon. Manolis brushed away the grains of sand that had stuck to his now salt-stained shirt.

"Between this and all the animals killed in the fires, I can't see an end in sight," Fox said. She exhaled a long stream of tight air. "I need a break. I'll be grateful for maternity leave."

Through his own experience, Manolis knew a newborn child didn't represent very much of a break – if anything, Fox's responsibilities would only intensify to astronomical, around-the-clock proportions. But from the perspective of her own mental wellbeing, seeing a baby grow into the world would be infinitely more uplifting and fortifying than trying to empty a bottomless pit of wounded and perished native animals.

Fox secured the back of her ute and started the engine. "Sorry I couldn't help more to find Elvis," she said.

"I really appreciate that you even tried at a time like this," Manolis said.

Fox rubbed the perfect sphere of her belly. It nearly pressed up against the steering wheel.

"If you happen to find out who the hell did this today, call me," said Manolis. "I'll deal with it personally." He gave her a card with his number.

"You'll press charges?" Fox asked.

"This is wilful mistreatment of animals under the Animal Welfare Act. It comes with the potential for heavy fines, but there's also a chance of jail time."

Fox snorted a laugh. "Might send a message to those knuckleheads out there. This isn't the first seal I found in this state and it won't be the last."

"In case I don't see you again, good luck with the birth," Manolis told her.

"Thanks," she said. "I think I might be needing it." She departed in an easterly direction.

With the daylight all but gone, Manolis drove around for another fruitless final hour. There was no sign of Elvis, and the detective was left cursing the fact he'd likely escaped the island and was even now disappearing into the interminable depths of the sprawling mainland, with its infinite number of hiding places – cities, towns, outback. The investigative advantage that came from a confined island community was gone, and now he'd have to contend with the vast island continent that floated alongside it. Emily was also somewhere on that land mass, likely still cursing her bull-headed husband's name. With a sigh of resignation and regret, Manolis flicked on his yellow headlights and put a pin in the day.

A minute later, his phone rang. It was Noah. Manolis pulled over sharply, the car enshrouded in a cloud of coarse bull dust.

"It's Elvis," the local cop said.

"What about him?" Manolis growled. "Where is he?"

"In custody. I found him hidden under a blanket in the boot of Nails's car. He was trying to help him escape to the mainland on the day's last ferry."

Chapter 29

"Excellent work again, Constable," Manolis said. "And they're in separate rooms?"

"As requested," Noah replied.

In the kitchenette, Manolis fetched a coffee-stained mug from the drying rack. He filled it with tepid, police station water in preparation for the interview process ahead. He'd already directed Sparrow to bring in two cola cans and two packs of jelly snakes to supply caffeine and sugar – he needed his suspects to be alert and receptive. Sparrow himself had been decidedly obliging following his recall to active duty, doing whatever he was asked and even showing Manolis that he'd deleted Elvis's number from his phone without prompting. But he sensed that Noah's police work had earned him clear teacher's pet status with their superior officer. As a result, Sparrow knew he would need to redeem himself in other, as yet undefined, ways.

Elvis and Nails had been detained but not yet formally arrested. Elvis's vehicle was found abandoned in a remote corner of the island, concealed by a dense thicket of black-green scrub. Knowing Sparrow couldn't be involved in any interrogation, Manolis instead charged him with another task.

"You let me down recently," he told the young cop. "Time to make amends. Can I trust you with this . . .?"

It was another courier job. Manolis handed over Marlowe's phone and watch in sealed plastic bags and asked Sparrow to escort them to the mainland for lab analysis.

"This could crack the case wide open," he warned.

Sparrow looked at the sleek digital devices with clear, sober eyes.

"You can count on me, Sarge," he said with confidence. "And ta for the second chance."

Manolis watched Sparrow go, a spark in his eyes and with a renewed sense of purpose. Such a mission was as tedious as it was routine, but at that moment, it was just what Sparrow needed. With the passage of time, the detective had reflected on how he saw police duty given his own chequered personal history, and had softened his view towards his less experienced colleague. Manolis conceded that he often took his sense of duty too far, which was harmful to his own mental health and led to unrealistic expectations of others. Sparrow had fucked up, that was without question. But he was only human – like Manolis, like anyone.

As they prepared to enter the first interview room, Noah stopped Manolis with a light tug on his sleeve.

"This'll be a bit strange for me," he said. "I've known these two blokes for a bloody long time but never in this capacity."

"They've been in strife before," Manolis said.

"Well yeah, they have. But never something like this, something so complicit and serious. Maybe another officer should be involved . . ."

"I want you in there," Manolis reassured him. "Just stay professional. You're in another role now, so just picture yourself wearing that hat. And personally, I'd prefer if we kept things non-confrontational. In my experience, establishing trust and a good rapport with suspects always yields better results no matter who's in the hot seat – a hardened thug, smooth corporate type, or even a familiar face. I've had them all, trust me."

However, as he was the outsider, Manolis also said he was willing to adopt the role of "bad cop" if things stalled during interview.

"They won't expect it from me," he said. "And I can turn it on if I have to."

Manolis told Noah of his theory that both Elvis and Nails were potentially involved in Marlowe's demise.

·"After all, it's more likely for two people to be able to overpower one. And by virtue of asking Nails for assistance, Elvis may have made our job easier by leading us to his accomplice."

Noah nodded his understanding. It was time. With the metallic click of the door handle, they entered the room.

First up, the prime suspect. Elvis sat with his chair facing backwards, his legs spread on either side, body hunched forward, glasses and eyes down. It was a typically petulant pose straight from the back row of a high-school classroom that immediately raised Manolis's hackles.

"Turn the chair around," he told him. "Sit straight, sit up."

"No," Elvis muttered. "Fuck you, suit."

"Fine," said Manolis, taking his own seat. He offered the stimulants, helping himself to a green-coloured snake.

"Mm, lime," he said. "My favourite."

"Yuck," Elvis said, snatching at a dark-red snake. "Everyone knows raspberry's the best. Who even likes lime . . ."

At least he was talking, thought Manolis. A good sign. He'd seen plenty of suspects not say a word for hours or only communicate through their legal representative. The room was perfectly drab and featureless.

"Me," Manolis replied. "I like lime." He bit the snake with some delight, anchoring its reptilian head between his incisors and stretching the body out in an exaggerated ripping motion that looked painful for the jelly.

He began the interview proper by innocently asking Elvis why he was hiding in the boot of Nails's vehicle aboard a ferry bound for the mainland.

"Strange way to make the journey, if you ask me," Manolis said. "Surely a seat on the top deck overlooking the water is far more pleasurable."

"I get seasick," said Elvis. "It's a strategy to avoid that, I've done it before. Lying down flat, the darkness. Works a treat."

Manolis and Noah couldn't help but snicker. Elvis was trying to take shelter in humour, and to a certain extent it was working.

"What's wrong with leaning back in a seat with an eye mask on?" Noah asked.

"We actually thought you might've been trying to save a few bucks on the fare," Manolis said.

"True that," Elvis admitted. "It's been a really bad year for business."

"You just need to harness your inner chicken," Manolis said.

"My . . . what?" Elvis asked, his tone confused.

Manolis decided to play it straight. "Never mind," he said. "Look, this is what we know – that you were seen fleeing your house in a mad hurry, and your car was later found concealed in a secluded location. Why did you leave it there and board the ferry? And please don't tell me you couldn't find a car park . . ."

Elvis cracked open his cola can, sipped the sweet syrup reflectively, careful with his words.

"Who saw me flee in a mad hurry? Gimme a name. And the entire island is secluded. My car ran out of petrol and I didn't want it stolen. Cars get nicked all the time round here. And anyway, I was heading to the mainland to visit a friend . . ."

Elvis continued to be elusive with his answers; Manolis continued to press him.

"Some evidence has recently come to our attention, a personal item that we believe was owned by the deceased Richard Marlowe, who recently disappeared," Manolis said. "Can you explain why it was in your possession?"

Without warning, Elvis's evasiveness transformed into hostility.

"Look, cut the crap, I know what this is about," he said. "This is about that fucking watch. Like I told that treacherous little traitor Sparrow, someone just innocently forgot it on a table in my café. And I don't know how I can prove that to you."

"Well, actually, you can," said Manolis. "What efforts did you make to find the owner?"

"Did you put up a sign in your shop window, or post something on social media?" Noah asked.

"Did you think to hand the item in to the police and report it that way?" said Manolis. "That's how you can prove that someone left it in your café."

Elvis stared at his cola can, a hangdog expression across his face.

Manolis stood and commenced a slow pace of the room – another trusted tactic that sometimes helped to disarm his suspect.

"The fact you did a runner looks pretty bad for you," he told Elvis. "And your personal grudge against Marlowe gives you a motive."

"Alright, alright," the young barista said. His voice held a note of sudden panic, an unexpected urgency and defensiveness. "I knew he was one of the people involved in this new offshore drilling project. Bloody Murden as well, dirty little lapdog that he is. And it's true that I had spoken out against it, along with many other island developments in the past, including the new mansions that were recently built. But all that is a million miles away from going out and bumping someone off. One is freedom of speech, which is perfectly legal. The other is the worst crime imaginable."

Elvis spoke with a clarity that sounded convincing, if a touch rehearsed. But Manolis stuck to his script.

"That's all very true but what doesn't help your cause is your history of violence," he said. "I saw it first-hand. I mean, *you hospitalised the mayor*. Who even does that? He could've charged your skinny hipster arse with assault causing grievous bodily harm. That's a serious crime."

"I've no regrets," Elvis said, voice surly. "Someone had to stand up to him. He's a greedy prick hell-bent on destruction."

Taken together, Elvis's profile, combined with a clear motive and evidence that connected him to a man who disappeared before turning up dead on a beach, made a compelling case for any prosecuting lawyer.

"Congratulations, Mister Carter," Manolis told him. "You are now defendant material."

"I'm honoured," Elvis sneered.

Manolis reached for the door handle, which also indicated he'd reached the end of both his questioning and patience. He gestured to Noah, who exited first.

"And because you've already shown you're a flight risk, I'm placing you under arrest," Manolis said.

"The fuck . . .?" Elvis said, eyes wild. "What charge?"

"What *charges*, you mean. Here's four for starters: avoiding police, hindering an investigation, being a stowaway, and suspicion of involvement in a major crime."

"You've got to be joking. You goddamn miserable piece of—"

Manolis missed Elvis's trail of expletives but heard the fist-pounding and foot-kicking against the locked door.

"He'll be fine once he calms down," Noah said. "Could take a while though with all that sugar we gave him."

"Yep," Manolis replied. "Now time for episode two. Hopefully it's as good as the pilot."

Nails straightened up both his posture and disposition the moment the police entered the room. Manolis immediately sensed this would be an easier process and after Elvis, he prayed he was right.

"Hello, Mister . . . umm . . ."

Manolis looked at Noah with a puzzled expression. The detective genuinely didn't know Nails's surname. He'd only ever heard his sporting nickname bandied the whole time he'd been on the island.

"Longbottom," said Noah with a wry smile. "Lucien Longbottom."

"Lucy, if you prefer," said Nails. "I know I don't."

"Mister Longbottom is fine," said Manolis. "Okay then, so if you answer all our questions honestly, then hopefully we can help each other."

"Shoot," said Nails.

"Mister Longbottom, we'd appreciate an explanation. Can you tell us why you were caught helping a wanted man on the run from authorities cross to the mainland by concealing him in the boot of your car?"

Nails swiftly denied any wrongdoing. "Elvis came to me for help because we're mates," he said. "He didn't tell me details, I didn't know

286

he was involved in any criminal activity. But I helped him because he's helped me in tough situations before, and I trusted him."

"You're a loyal friend, and that's very commendable," Manolis said. "But surely it wouldn't have been unreasonable to assume that Elvis was involved in some kind of trouble with the law if he was seeking to escape the island undetected, no?"

Nails tapped the table with an apprehensive index finger. "I dunno," he replied. "I didn't ask."

"You didn't ask him . . . ?"

"Well, no. When does someone ever ask a mate if they broke the law? And would he even have told me if he had? Probably not. I sure as hell wouldn't."

"So, don't ask, don't tell, eh?" Manolis said.

"Or perhaps you already knew what was going on and you just don't want to tell us now," Noah said.

"Steady on there, Noah mate," Nails said. "Jesus, whose side are you on here anyway?"

"You sound like you've had some experience in this kind of thing, Mister Longbottom," Manolis said. "How many people have you helped sneak across to the mainland before? Or vice versa – how many have you brought to the island under cover? Or have you yourself travelled in the back of someone else's car?"

"None of the above," said Nails. "I'm just a loyal friend, like you said."

Manolis leaned in close until he could taste Nails's foul-smelling breath.

"You're full of shit," he told him. "Elvis already told us what went down."

Nails drew tight his already thin, mail-slot eyes. "Horseshit," he scoffed. "I'm not falling for that."

"Lying to a police officer during an investigation is a crime," Manolis said.

"I'm *not* lying," Nails spat.

"Maybe we ask you to submit to a polygraph test?"

"And if I say no?"

"Then you look guilty."

"Horseshit," Nails repeated.

"I've heard enough," Manolis told Noah. "Book him, Constable."

"What's the charge?" Nails asked.

"Assisting an offender to escape apprehension."

Nails bashed the table with a thick fist. "This is fucking bureaucracy madness," he said. "It's police harassment. All I was doing was trying to help out a mate and now I'm being labelled as a common criminal."

The publican paused in thought. "What's this all about anyway, what the hell did Elvis do to warrant this much attention? Is this about bloody Marlowe again? I thought they said he drowned, case closed."

Manolis sat back in his chair and crossed his arms. "Okay then. Tell me – what do you know about a black sports wristwatch?"

Nails's frown bounced between the two cops. "Wristwatch? What about a wristwatch? I know I have one, right here. It's more silver, though."

He rolled up his sleeve to demonstrate. Manolis looked at Noah, who shrugged.

"So, you've no idea about the sports watch?" Manolis asked again.

Nails shook his head firmly. "I keep bloody telling you, I was just helping a mate. Are your ears painted on?"

Manolis stared hard at Nails, trying to read his expression and body language, looking for any sign of deception. Nails was twitching with nervous energy, like he was about to self-combust.

"Arrest him," Manolis said at last. "I've had enough. Lock 'em both up."

Nails flashed a painful, disbelieving smile, which was more like a weird rictus grin.

"Who the hell do you think you are?" he hissed. "After all the hospitality that I showed you at the pub, all the assistance and advice. You can't arrest a bloke for doing nuthin'. Who's your commanding officer? I want his name."

Manolis stood, straightened his shirt with a flattened hand and finished his mug of water. "I'll be sure to put you in touch," he said as he left the room. Another series of angry four-letter words followed him out the door.

Returning to the kitchenette, Manolis rinsed his mug clean and placed it upturned back into the drying rack. Checking his phone, he saw no new messages. It was still radio silence from Emily who hadn't yet replied to a single one of his apologetic texts or penitent voicemails.

Chapter 30

The police officers reconvened at Noah's weatherboard abode for a bite and debrief. Tessa was making dinner this time – the Australian weekday staple of jaffles.

"Personally, I think toasted sandwiches are an underrated delicacy," Manolis said.

"Versatile and comforting," said Tessa. "And mine have three different types of cheese, all of them from the island."

Manolis's preference was always to include salty Greek feta in the toasties he made at home. Tessa's had gooey avocado, acidic sauerkraut, and some kind of sharp homemade pickle relish that balanced the creaminess of the oozing cheese and oily fruit. Manolis devoured his sandwich and went back for a second helping. He watched the kids do the same, asking their mum for more toasties with baked beans and thick-cut cheddar.

Noah sipped his foamy schooner of homebrew and blew on his sandwich, tendrils of steam rising from its melting insides. After an unsatisfying initial outcome, he was convinced they finally had a solid lead in the Marlowe investigation. Manolis agreed.

"But it's not enough," the detective said. "We still need more evidence, either to implicate Elvis and Nails or absolve them."

"There's still the autopsy results," Noah said. "They say Marlowe drowned. It's there in black and white."

"I know," said Manolis. "But there must be a logical explanation."

"He could've simply been held under water in the surf," said Tessa. "Or weighed down in some way."

The police both looked at her with some surprise.

"Sorry," she said. "Just trying to help."

"No, you're right," said Manolis. "And we did think of that possibility."

He recalled Erik Junior's harrowing overboard experience and how drowning was a form of death by suffocation.

"Water in the lungs interferes with breathing, they become heavy, and the person convulses before falling unconscious," Manolis said. "When oxygen stops being delivered to the major organs, the brain begins to hallucinate before shutting down completely."

Seeing the children listening, and the confused and slightly alarmed looks on their faces, Manolis apologised – it wasn't appropriate family dinnertime conversation. Tessa kissed her sons adoringly, who continued to chew their soft yellow cheese.

"Why don't you guys go outside and eat?" she told them. "The evening's warm, just take your jaffles."

The children headed for the yard and were soon heard chattering and giggling.

"But the theories are interesting," Manolis admitted. "Drowning someone in the ocean is almost a perfect way to commit a murder because it's practically untraceable."

"Marlowe's body bore no signs of struggle, no bruises or marks," Noah said. "That goes against the use of force."

"Then there's still more to it," Manolis said, tormented tone. "But we should probably talk in detail another time. Until then . . ."

He charged Noah with the task of chasing down the suspects' alibis – both Elvis and Nails claimed to have been at the port the morning Marlowe disappeared, collecting an early delivery from the mainland – two small businessmen helping each other out.

"It's very convenient that they were together," said Manolis. "But it may actually be true. So, we need independent proof, some signed paperwork or a confirmed sighting by a third party."

"Okay," said Noah. "What about Sparrow?"

"No word yet," said Manolis. "I'm assuming no news is good news, the process just needs to run its course."

While Noah went in pursuit of more information, Manolis turned his attention to identifying a motive. Here, the island's rapid development, including the ongoing seawater desalination plant and proposed offshore drilling project, came into sharper focus. The detective had always known that change was a major sticking point for the locals, and especially the *local* locals. But perhaps he had never truly appreciated the extent of its impact.

"What do you think about the direction the island is heading in?" Manolis asked Tessa.

She shrugged. "Personally, I'm glad to see some change," she said. "There's a lot to love about our little island, but we can't remain wedded to the past. We just need to make sure what happens is balanced and considered or else we'll end up ruining things for the next generation."

Manolis's first stop was at the office of the island's esteemed elected representative. Dressed in a sweat-stained polo shirt and matching chino shorts, the Right Honourable Mark Murden continued to talk up the island's "incredible progress" and how it was "actually dinosaurs like Elvis and Nails" who were holding it back with their antiquated values.

"And I say that wearing my mayoral hat firmly," he added.

On this day, Murden's headwear was a ventilated trucker cap with a pink cartoon prawn on the front.

"These exploration and drilling programs will indirectly provide jobs and supply-chain opportunities for Islanders and their businesses," he continued, chest out. "Transport and logistics, fuel and resources, food services and construction. But there's also going to be a new island support base with a wharf and helipads."

"And all that will create jobs," said Manolis.

"Precisely. The guaranteed investment in the search for oil and gas across the Great Australian Bight following the grant of permits is worth over a billion dollars."

"Jesus. I didn't expect that much."

"And that's a conservative estimate. If planned exploration drilling leads to new energy projects, it'll mean commercial and employment opportunities, resource security, infrastructure, exports, and a broader tax base. And because it's way out at sea, we're lucky not to have to deal with any of that traditional owners bullshit."

Manolis frowned, his expression doubtful. "Well, I guess that's one way to look at it. Environmentally though, people are worried."

"I'm well aware of the concerns of our resident eco-warriors," Murden replied. "But there's both national and state legislation in place to ensure the safe and effective environmental management of these sensitive marine reserves. Companies have to submit detailed bids for each exploration area, with no offshore activity allowed without stringent regulatory assessment and ongoing compliance and inspections. Frankly, our island's ecofascists have exaggerated the risks. Mining permits aren't given to cowboys, and don't let any fucken greenie or leftie tell you otherwise."

"So, what happens now that Marlowe's not around?" asked Manolis.

Murden scratched his chin nervously. "I think it's absolutely crucial the project still goes ahead and I have every confidence it will, even without Marlowe's experience and influence."

Manolis's next stop was to see Lavender, whom he knew was involved in trying to secure the exploration licence to commence offshore drilling. They spoke in Lavender's home office, its walls replete with framed photographs, modern artwork, vintage books and higher education certificates. One entire wall was a single windowpane that ushered in another astonishingly blue ocean view.

"It is certainly my intention to commemorate Richard's memory and secure his legacy by completing this vital exploration project," he said, gazing out over the water. "It's something he believed in wholeheartedly, its impact will be enormous, and it's the least I can do for an old mate."

"That's very admirable of you," said Manolis.

"And I can't thank you enough for not giving up in seeking to find the person responsible for his death, you've really gone above and beyond."

Manolis looked slightly embarrassed. "Not really," he said. "We're just doing our jobs. It's you I have to thank for helping with the search."

"You know," Lavender said, "I am familiar with these individuals . . ."

"Who?"

"The two chaps you currently have detained."

"The island's a very small place, it seems. Off the record, how would you describe them?"

Lavender flashed a knowing smile, displaying those flawless teeth. Then he swallowed, considering his words.

"I don't mean to speak ill, but since you ask, I've had numerous unsavoury altercations with these undesirables, the details of which I'll keep to myself," he said. "Richard did, too. They made our arrival on the island as unpleasant as they could. But we tried to rise above it and focus on more important things like business interests and lifestyle, rather than wasting our time on petty matters."

He spoke like someone focused on results, on bottom lines, in the realms of both commerce and justice.

"The offshore Bight represents one of the world's last under-explored petroleum basins," Lavender continued. "The first seismic survey was conducted in 1966, with about a dozen offshore wells having been drilled since. The only deepwater well was abandoned in 2004 because of harsh weather conditions. Rigs cost hundreds of millions of dollars to build but once operational, they contribute hundreds of *billions* to GDP. Ours is being assembled right now in Korea and it's currently ahead of schedule."

"And all this is happening without the approved exploration permits in place?"

Lavender swallowed again, this time seemingly more out of uncertainty than confidence.

"It's just a matter of time before we get the formal green light," he said. "No reason to delay progress."

Manolis seemed to be getting mixed messages depending on the source. He decided to seek out Skye again, who had confided that her father had experienced some doubts about his many projects. He found her poring over a canvas, another disturbing artwork in progress, while Satan gnawed on a bone the size of a railway sleeper.

"Well, I don't mean to big-note myself, to take any credit," she said. "But I like to think my influence opened Dad's eyes to the environmental damage that such an initiative would cause."

She mentioned how the proposed drilling area to the island's west was surrounded by fragile marine zones. These included regions for southern right whale calving, blue whale foraging, sea lion breeding, and a refuge for dolphins and penguins.

"The Great Australian Bight is one of the most unspoiled marine environments in the world," Skye said. "It's home to more unique species than the Great Barrier Reef."

Manolis recalled the island's genetically pure population of Ligurian bees, also the last in the world.

"I had no idea," he said. "I mean, I knew there was incredible aquatic diversity . . ."

"If there was an oil spill, it'd be an ecological nightmare."

Skye described a catastrophic oil rig disaster off the coast of Western Australia in 2009. The Montara rig caught fire and then exploded, spewing several thousand barrels' worth of oil into the Timor Sea every day for three months. The resulting slick killed seaweed crops, destroyed fishing grounds, and polluted waters as far north as Indonesia, leaving them filled with dead fish and other sea creatures.

"The exploration company pleaded guilty to charges under environmental laws and was fined hundreds of thousands of dollars," Skye said. "It then sold the rig in 2018."

Manolis eyed the ocean. It appeared clean and clear and calm. Marine wildlife and vegetation were thriving in their natural habitat, in conditions that were conducive to life, growth and regeneration. He couldn't quite imagine the scene awash with toxic hydrocarbons or the kind of devastation that would wreak.

"And the Montara spill occurred at a depth of only a hundred metres," Skye continued. "Can you imagine what a deepwater oil exploration well to a depth of several thousand metres might be like?"

"At least there's now environmental protections in place," Manolis said.

Skye laughed harshly, causing Satan to look up from his toothy chomping.

"All bullshit," she said. "Dad agreed, he said that companies can buy their way around all those requirements with smoke and mirrors and more expensive lawyers. Another big accident is inevitable. It's not a question of if – it's when, where, and how fucking bad."

Was Marlowe committed to these major projects or not? Manolis didn't know who to believe. The conflicting accounts he was hearing painted very different pictures, depending on the source and the interests at play.

He sought out one final reference in the hope it might prove definitive. Holly looked drained – both physically and spiritually – at the prospect of continued questioning, none of which would bring back her husband. Manolis apologised for the interruption, which she entertained on her doorstep and in her tight activewear straight from yoga.

"Unfortunately, my husband didn't speak to me very much about his business interests," she said. "He kept them private."

"Did you ever ask him?" Manolis said.

"Once or twice, yes. But he was so elusive I just gave up in the end. The last thing he wanted to talk about when he got home was work, and he only ever spoke in very broad terms. Who knows, maybe he didn't trust me. So long as the bills got paid, that was all that mattered."

Manolis found that a little surprising, but then, he imagined a man with the stature and wealth of Marlowe had a complex professional life with financial tentacles stretching in infinite directions, domestic and international. And some of it would've surely been sensitive material tied up in commercial confidentiality.

And yet, he seemed to somehow speak with his once-estranged daughter about his business interests. Did that simply reflect the adage that blood is thicker than water? Or that Marlowe felt more comfortable with someone less familiar, like a taxicab confessional free of judgement and history? And in what detail did he discuss . . .?

"Oh wait, now that you mention it, something just occurred to me," Holly added.

Manolis raised his head with interest. "What's that?" he asked.

"The day Richard went missing, he failed to turn up for a meeting at a ministerial office. I know this because they called and I answered his phone."

"You answered his phone . . .?"

"I didn't often do that, but it was an unidentified number. He was missing and I thought he may've been calling his own phone. Do you think it means anything?"

The detective rubbed his rough grey stubble in thought. "I don't know, it's possible. Or it may just reflect a missed appointment, like a routine dental check or car service. We've got his call records on file, so we'll be able to track down the source."

Just then, Manolis's own phone rang. "What timing," he told Holly. "Excuse me . . ."

Manolis stepped away, turned to face the curved teardrop driveway. It was Sparrow. "Hi, Sarge," he said brightly.

"G'day, mate. What news?"

"So, the boys in the lab have successfully unlocked Marlowe's watch and phone," he said. "We'll be able to access the activity tracking data."

Chapter 31

It was a scene now familiar to Manolis – standing on a paradisal white beach, staring out over cerulean water, trying to somehow piece together a gruesome criminal puzzle. The picturesque island locations changed, but the frustrating task remained the same.

At least this time, he had new weaponry at his disposal.

The near-deserted beach was the one where Marlowe had disappeared after wading out for his dawn swim. Other than the three police, there was a retired couple strolling with a shaggy wet hound, and a pair of surfers wading out into the waters. In his hands, Sparrow held the two electronic devices with the potential to reveal what had happened in the time before Marlowe's bloated corpse had washed up in the storm.

"Fire it up," Manolis told him. "The watch first."

Sparrow handed Noah the phone and began working the watch with both sets of fingers, pressing its tiny buttons and high-resolution touchscreen with the dexterity of a croupier. After about a minute, Manolis leaned in.

"Mate, you sure you know what you're doing there?" he asked.

"Yair, just gimme a sec," Sparrow replied.

Manolis looked at Noah. "He can't stuff it up, can he? Accidentally delete the data?"

Noah shrugged. "I guess he might," he replied. The soapy surf hammered like cannon fire.

"Bloody piece of shit . . ."

Sparrow was getting visibly frustrated, his fingers fidgeting, his face contorting, outwitted by what was admittedly a state-of-the-art smartwatch designed by the world's intelligentsia.

"Maybe we should consult the user manual," Manolis suggested helpfully. "Is there one?"

"No, wait, I got it," Sparrow said. "Okay, so what's been pissing me off is that there's tracking data in here, but not from the bloody day that Marlowe disappeared."

"Shit," said Manolis. "Really? Look again."

"I've been trying but there's nothing. Look at the dates."

"Still, at least we know he was using the tracking function," said Noah.

"But not for the single most important day," said Manolis.

He cursed in Greek. He was counting on modern technology joining all the dots and finally leading them to the culprit.

"What's the error rate on these activity trackers anyway?" Sparrow asked.

"Wait a sec," said Manolis. "Are the archives in there? What do they show?"

With a few more clicks, Sparrow scrolled through the saved activity data from earlier dates.

"It's all here," he said. "It shows true dedication to exercise and vitality of which I'm hugely envious."

The watch had recorded daily activity patterns both on the beach and in the ocean.

"Looks like exercises, jogging and sprints on the sand, and then swimming and surfing in the water," Sparrow said as he scrolled.

"So, either Marlowe didn't turn on the tracking function that final day or it didn't connect to the GPS," said Manolis.

"Either way, we're screwed," Sparrow said. "Fucking computers."

"Wait," said Noah. "Not necessarily. Try the phone."

"What's the point?" Sparrow replied. "Doesn't this newfangled technology mean it syncs automatically with the phone? Isn't that the selling point? The data will be the same."

Gripped by an atom of hope, Manolis impulsively snatched the phone from Noah's palm and turned it on. He entered the hacked passcode and saw the black screen come to life with a digital image of Roland and Allegra as young children in matching festive outfits in front of a Christmas tree. The screen then populated with a palette of colourful apps like fireworks exploding. Manolis swiped until he found the icon for the activity tracker and let his finger momentarily hover above, as if bracing himself for the outcome. With a sharp intake of breath, he narrowed his eyes and pressed down with a combined sense of trepidation and anticipation.

It took a moment for the connection to be made but then, the screen was filled with colourful graphics and in-depth data. Manolis was gripped and kept swiping with urgency, searching. And then, there it was – the information from the very morning Marlowe went missing, showing his precise movements. Manolis couldn't quite believe it.

"Eureka," he breathed.

"What the hell . . .?" said Sparrow, crowding alongside for a gander.

"Take a look," Manolis said. "This is the day he vanished, right? The same morning, see the time. It's the very last entry logged in the phone."

Noah crammed in around the screen's blue light. "Wow," he said. "You're bloody right."

The data resembled all the other days that had been captured, which suggested a defined exercise routine to which Marlowe adhered with military discipline. Manolis wondered if an expensive personal trainer had been involved in its initial design.

"Of course, we're assuming this is genuinely Marlowe's activity on the day he went missing and not his watch strapped to someone else's wrist," Sparrow said.

"Good point," said Manolis. "At least it's the same pattern of exercise. That's got to mean something."

"But no guarantee," said Sparrow.

"Yep. It's a leap we have to take. I'm willing to go with it."

They proceeded to walk towards the site of the first exercise sequence, which showed a series of lines on the sand parallel to the shore.

"Some stretching and light jogging along the beach, it seems, to warm up the ageing muscles," said Manolis.

The police looked to the water, with Manolis pointing in multiple directions. It appeared that Marlowe had headed out into the ocean; further rows of lines ran parallel to the shore.

"Swimming," said Manolis. "Side to side, left and right, largely avoiding the force of the waves."

Heading back to the beach, to the very first spot where the tracking began, Marlowe paused momentarily before returning to the water for a third sequence of squiggles. These were now perpendicular to the shore and, laid over the previous series of lines, formed an elegant crosshatch pattern on the digital screen.

"Looks like he collected his surfboard and caught some rewarding waves out and back," said Sparrow. "A warm-down and reward for all that earlier physical effort."

Still staring down at the phone, Manolis strode towards the water. He seemed to move involuntarily, as if drawn by the dead man's trail. He didn't even notice the wet dog that raced up for a friendly sniff before being quickly ushered away by its elderly owners. Manolis stopped just short of where the swash was lapping onto the shore. Without warning, he swung back to face his colleagues with a look of revelation and enlightenment.

"You know what this all means?" he said.

Sparrow and Noah exchanged glances, unsure of whether to respond. In the end, Manolis delivered the verdict.

"To me, it means the data on Marlowe's wristwatch was *purposely* deleted, only they didn't realise that it had already been sent to his phone on the beach. And that suggests premeditation, manipulation and foul play. They just made a mistake in trying to cover it up."

As the realisation sunk in, the police's collective level of adrenaline went up. What Manolis was proposing suggested very firmly that they were dealing with a homicide, not just a tragic accident.

"A murder," said Noah. "Far out. So, was it a targeted killing or something random? Do we need to make a public statement, reassure the community in case there's a killer now on the loose?"

Manolis kept peering at the phone, turning it at different angles to avoid the glare of sunlight. "Hold your horses," he said. "The data doesn't just stop there. Hello then, what's going on here . . .?"

All the other entries showed only the regular morning workout on the beach and opposing water. But on this last fateful day, Marlowe's regular lines and squiggles were followed by a long arc leaving the beach and then heading back into the water a second time from a different location.

"Now why the hell would he do that? Where does this go?" Manolis asked.

The police trooped along in single file, with Manolis leading the way, following the curved line mapped out on the phone. As he walked, Manolis swore he could feel his pulse in his fingertips as he held the precious device.

"He could've simply forgotten to turn off the activity tracker after his workout?" Sparrow asked.

"Maybe," Manolis replied. "But he remembered every other day, he was diligent in keeping track of his efforts."

They continued trudging along the beach, their feet sinking and slipping in the soft sand.

"Marlowe was moving incredibly slowly here," said Manolis.

"Likely buggered from his morning exercise," said Sparrow.

The arc led them along an overgrown coastal path to a secluded location with an old wooden jetty jutting out into the waves. Manolis took a tentative step onto its weathered boards, feeling it buckle and sway with the movement of the tide. The data suggested that Marlowe re-entered the water from the jetty.

"Only this time, it's pretty much a straight line, and further out into the ocean than where he would usually surf," said Manolis.

"A boat," said Sparrow.

They both looked at Noah for enlightenment. "Smaller boats can certainly access this location," he said. "But the rocks and jetty make it near impossible for larger vessels."

"Or maybe a jet ski," Sparrow added.

"To me, this pattern suggests the most likely place that Marlowe drowned was out to sea in much deeper, more treacherous water," said Manolis.

Noah scrutinised the data more closely. "So, if you think Marlowe drowned out there, in the ocean, with a shark severing his foot and his body washing up a week later, why does the activity tracker show him returning to land?"

The three police continued walking, this time heading inland, across driftwood and sand dunes and fallen branches, through the robust seaside greenery, mostly spinifex with blades like echidna quills. After climbing a steep incline, they emerged on the nearby coastal road that accessed Millionaires' Row. The last recorded activity followed the road west before vanishing altogether.

"This must be where the invisible connection to the phone back on the beach dropped out, so the tracking finally stopped," said Manolis.

He eyed the empty road in both directions with curiosity and apprehension.

"Search the area," Manolis told his colleagues. "I'm now declaring this a crime scene."

The cops fanned out, eyes focused to the ground, scouring like bloodhounds on a fresh trail. Manolis wasn't sure what the hell they were looking for – something distinctive, potentially; something incriminating, ideally. But there was only the natural world all around, dirt and grasses and rocks and twigs, not even a single discarded wrapper, let alone a personal item. The road was also free of obvious tyre marks or any distinguishing features like accident shrapnel. The overall outcome was disappointing but after all the time that had passed, it was by no means surprising.

"No CCTV out here, I'm guessing," Sparrow said. "So, what now, Sarge?"

Manolis ran his dry hands through his rough hair, making a scratching sound. Rather than focus on the twinges of defeat, he instead preferred to celebrate the fact that it had still been a ridiculously fruitful day.

"Well, two things," he said. "First, let's take a moment to piece together our new theory about Marlowe's demise. Now, I could be wrong, but if I were a betting man, it looks to me like Marlowe was somehow taken out in a boat before he had his wristwatch removed and his surfboard dumped in the water. He was then pushed overboard into the ocean and his surfboard dumped in the water, with the culprit then returning to land and driving away, blissfully unaware that everything was being quietly recorded by the wristwatch they had kept as a souvenir. Later, when they realised it was tracking their every move, the data was deleted from the watch, but it had already been sent to the phone, which was sitting safely on the beach alongside Marlowe's sandals and towel for his widow to collect. Frankly, if I were a bad guy, this isn't something I would've foreseen either – it's next level stuff. But as the good guys, it appears that technology has come to our rescue, but only off the back of fine investigative work. So, well done fellas. Excellent police work today."

Manolis let the new scenario hang in the air. Sparrow and Noah nodded their heads lightly as they digested their superior's words and pictured the scenes he was describing.

"Yair, I can buy that," Sparrow said. "But what's the second thing?"

"Our next stop," Manolis replied. "Out there."

With an outstretched arm, shaking slightly, he gestured offshore. The vast and perilous Southern Ocean rumbled all around them.

Chapter 32

With hands on hips, Manolis eyed the watery expanse below, his nostrils suffused with a fresh investigative scent.

"When can we go out?" he asked his colleagues. "Now? Can we go right now . . .?"

"Out where?" Sparrow asked, scratching the back of his neck.

"There," pointed Manolis. "To the spot where the phone indicates Marlowe probably drowned."

"What the hell for?" Sparrow said. "You're not gonna see anything, there's no clues or evidence."

Manolis held a determined look in his eyes. "I don't care, I still want to go. I'll swim out if I have to. I need to see it."

He wasn't serious about actually wading out into the ocean to such a critical depth where death would surely await, but Manolis wanted to underscore his resolve. He knew he wouldn't find anything of use in the water at this late stage, but he still wanted to get a sense of the area, the lines of sight, the motion of the waves, the light, et cetera. It was all relevant intel to piecing together the investigative puzzle. And he finally had a chance to inspect the actual scene of the crime, which had proven so elusive in the Marlowe investigation.

"Mate, and I say this out of love and respect," Sparrow said. "If you head out there, we'll just end up with one more dead body on our hands."

Noah found his voice: "Sarge, if you really wanna go out, I can fetch my tinnie," he said.

"Yes," the detective said instantly, snapping his fingers. "Positivity, thank you."

Sparrow shook his head in disagreement. Manolis didn't relish the prospect of taking to the groggy water in an aluminium tub, but at that moment, his drive outweighed his common sense. Meanwhile, Sparrow seemed to lose all colour.

"I dunno what you're gonna see out there, boss," he said. "There's nuthin'."

"Don't be so sure," Manolis replied.

"Either way, I think it's best if I just stay here on the shore and keep looking," Sparrow added.

"I know, I know," Manolis said. "You and water."

"Not just that," Sparrow said. "Me and living. And I only wish the same for you . . ."

With a faux salute, Sparrow wished Manolis and Noah bon voyage as they set out from the rickety jetty in an even more unsteady tinnie into the unpredictable swells of the Southern Ocean. Part of Sparrow knew he should accompany them in his role as dedicated police investigator and colleague. But on this day, the young cop's desire for self-preservation was too strong. And while Manolis would've appreciated another pair of eyes on the water, he acknowledged it wasn't worth the bother if it meant another stomach being emptied into the sea.

Seeing he had a single bar of reception as they prepared to set sail, Manolis seized the opportunity to make amends with his wife. He rang a day spa he'd used before and ordered Emily a beauty and massage voucher for immediate electronic delivery. She'd not yet replied to any of his messages and Manolis knew he was well and truly in the doghouse and needed to get creative. It was an obvious gesture, an admission of guilt, but at that moment, something bold was called for. The progress they'd made in the investigation was encouraging and justified his decision – at least, to him. But he knew he needed to continue the forward momentum in the vain hope he could vindicate that choice to his justifiably aggrieved wife.

Sparrow kicked around in the sand a while, pretending to search but all the while distracted by his inner voice. He slumped to the ground, craving a wistful cigarette to quieten his racing thoughts and burning emotions. His recent interactions with Manolis and Elvis had messed with both his head and heart, respectively. Sparrow felt both inadequate and inconsolable and had barely given himself any time to process. It had been a challenge to open himself up to romantic involvement in the first place given his lifelong experiences in his blinkered hometown of Cobb. The outback was still evolving in terms of diversity. Sparrow had had his fair share of black eyes and public humiliations, jeers and insults. He'd taken it all in his youthful, resilient stride, but now he was older and more seasoned, and perhaps more cautious as a result. Regrettably, he felt that any future attempts at accessing his padlocked heart might be akin to cracking a safe.

On a professional level, Sparrow also had doubts, and had begun to altogether question if he was even cut out for the police caper. Following an imperfect investigation in Cobb, Manolis had plucked him from badlands obscurity and brought him to the big, bad city, where he'd promptly bitten off more than he could chew. An innocent teenager had been killed, an almighty weight his conscience still carried, while Sparrow's unorthodox investigative methods had earned the ire of his superiors. It was an unenviable track record any way you looked at it. Perhaps he'd overestimated his abilities or ambitions – after all, his training as a cadet had been two-fifths of fuck all in a dead-end town. Manolis had been understanding and forgiving, but Sparrow still knew he was letting the side down, including at that very moment on the sand. And that was what burned him the most, that unlike everything else he neglected or fucked up in his life, this wasn't just about him anymore.

"Hey, howsit going?"

A voice from behind broke his sorrowful reverie. Sparrow turned to see the two Nankervises, father and son.

"Oh, hey," Sparrow replied. "Not bad. I'm just chillin'."

"We're just heading out to check our lobster pots," Nankervis said. "The boss is out there on the water, too."

"On the water . . .? Wow, I thought he had enough last time."

"I heard about that. Glad you're both okay."

Nankervis clipped Erik Junior playfully across the back of his solid teenage head.

"The clumsy little bastard has had a bad run recently. Been sucked under twice. Your detective mate helped save him the first time. And the second time, a trap line got wrapped around his ankle and he was pulled overboard."

"What's that?" asked Sparrow. "Sounds awful."

"That's cos it is . . ."

Nankervis described how they placed lobster traps on the sea floor in groups of around twenty. They were connected via a trap line to a buoy so they could retrieve their catch at the end of the day. But there was a risk of getting entangled in loose line on the deck, getting pulled overboard by the traps under tension at sea, and then drowning when you couldn't free yourself from the line or were unable to reboard the vessel.

"We needed to cut the fucking line to save Junior from drowning," Nankervis said. "Waste of a perfectly good line."

"Better than wasting a perfectly good Junior," said Sparrow.

Nankervis said most entanglements happened when setting or moving gear, when the most length of line was lying loose on the deck. Erik Junior had been laying new traps and, like many young men, hadn't been paying enough care and attention. Since whales had the potential to get entangled, Nankervis said there was now research into developing traps that somehow avoided ropes.

"Is it possible to catch fish or lobsters without rope?" Nankervis asked rhetorically. "That's like saying drive to work, but don't use any wheels. Rope is one of the first technologies fishermen ever used, it's fundamental."

Sparrow thought a better analogy might be driving to work without leaded petrol, which eventually gave way to unleaded fuels, hybrid vehicles, and then fully electric and even automated cars. But he kept his thoughts to himself.

Erik Junior showed Sparrow his leg. A deep red and purple mark encircled the swollen ankle.

"Junior was lucky his foot wasn't ripped clean off," Nankervis continued. "End up like bloody Marlowe . . ."

Out on the water, the papery tinnie rolled across the waves, rising and falling with the movement of the tide. Manolis felt his stomach surging in every opposing direction and tried to stay focused on the tracking data in his palm, ensuring he guided Noah to their target position.

"Here," Manolis said. "Stop right about . . . here."

Noah killed the engine and let the boat float to a natural stop. Bobbing up and down in the surf, the officers inspected the location immediately around the tinnie, which left Manolis feeling somewhat deflated.

"It's just water," Noah said. "What did you expect to find? A blood stain?"

It was just a feeling Manolis had; another hunch, based on previous experience and something approaching a sixth sense. He had a sense that he could always glean something from the air where a crime victim died, a shift in the molecules, in the aura of a space, what that person had been through. But that area just wasn't often out at sea where factors were so changeable.

Manolis held a hand up to his eyes to shield the glare from the water. He looked in every direction, surveying the scene, checking for any vantage points on the island.

"I can't see any houses from here," said Manolis. "That's a shame."

The only likelihood of any witnesses was another passing boat or an observer on the mainland, a beach walker or overland hiker with a pair of binoculars or a long camera lens handy.

"What a bloody perfect location for murder," Noah said. He sounded almost proud, or at least, mightily impressed. "Who's going to see you out here? And there's no risk of leaving any trace."

"At least, not in the water," said Manolis.

"The water covers all and sees nothing."

The ocean was cold and very, very deep; Manolis tried not to think about it. With the wind picking up, the whitecaps took shape all around them, while the choppy water made the tinnie rock. Manolis grabbed onto whatever he could in a desperate attempt to feel grounded.

"Marlowe could have been either deliberately pushed in or he accidentally fell in because of an altercation," Noah said speculatively.

"That's consistent with him having no other physical injuries, as the autopsy revealed," Manolis said.

"He could've jumped in the water to escape his captors – he was a strong swimmer," Noah said.

"Then his body probably would've needed to have been weighed down," Manolis said. "And your wife's already onto that possibility."

"There were no emergency calls on the morning in question, I checked," Noah said. "There was no accident or incident reported."

"Here's an idea," said Manolis. "And this may sound crazy, but is it possible to source a list of island boats that can successfully moor at that old wooden jetty?"

He paused to let his query sink in. Noah's pupils danced with curiosity and contemplation.

"Surely there would be registration details on file," the detective continued. "Then, we'd just need to cross-reference the size of each vessel to come up with a list of suspects."

Noah blew out a long lungful of air, which became a light nod of skepticism and doubt.

"Mate, there'd be hundreds, maybe even thousands of boats," he replied. "Even tiny tinnies like this one. It'd take forever. You'd almost have a better chance trying to identify the registered cars in the area."

It was a response that elicited Manolis's own frustrated sigh, like a balloon deflating. So close yet so far away.

"Not to mention all the unregistered boats – and cars, for that matter – that we have on the island," Noah added. "We gave up trying to keep track."

"I see," Manolis said numbly.

Leaning over the side of the tinnie, he stared into the sea's abyssal depths. The unevenness of the water's surface cast streaks of light and shade that caused the albedo to fluctuate and left him feeling light-headed. Considering his murky reflection, he pondered the impossible likelihood of dredging the ocean floor. But even if they could, what would they be looking for . . .?

Just then, there was a sudden splash a few metres away, then silence. Manolis swung around to study the surface of the water, which he saw was slightly rippling.

"What was that?" he asked.

"What was what?" Noah replied.

"In the water."

Noah stared. "I don't see anything. A fish?"

Manolis stared into the ocean again, eyes desperately scanning. "I swore I heard something over here or—"

Out of the corner of his eye, Manolis saw something break the surface of the water. It then vanished momentarily before reappearing with a vengeance like a knife through a bedsheet. It was a sharp triangular fin.

"Is that . . . is that what I think it is?" Manolis asked nervously.

Back on land, Sparrow saw the Nankervises returning triumphant from the water. They carried their heavy traps, lobsters bulging inside, claws and antennae and armour-plated bodies squeezed in tight. He watched them closely, his mind working. They smiled and waved to him.

"A bloody good haul today!" Nankervis said. "And as an added bonus, Junior didn't even drown."

Erik Junior gave the thumbs-up gesture. Father and son carried on up the beach.

Sparrow continued to think, his brain slowly making connections linking all he'd seen and heard.

And then, he snapped his long dark fingers in realisation.

"Holy fuck," he said to himself. "That's it. That's the answer."

Chapter 33

Manolis's world seemed to suddenly narrow, concentrate; everything else, all sounds and sensations, melted away. It was now just him in the boat and the fin gliding through the water like it was air. Manolis shook with uncertainty and terror as his mind went to the darkest places.

"It's probably not a dolphin," Noah said. His words were heavy and intended to be helpful, but to Manolis, they were anything but.

"How can you tell?" the detective asked.

"Dolphins move their flukes vertically up and down to arch their bodies through the water. But this one is turning near the surface and at speed. Anyway, just stay calm and relaxed. No matter what it is, we should be safe in the boat."

Manolis looked around him. The aluminium shell suddenly looked even more thin and penetrable.

"How'd you figure that?" he asked just as the fin again vanished beneath the surface. Manolis would've expected its absence to have been reassuring, potentially even encouraging, but in reality, it was even more disconcerting than its presence.

"It's like when you get stranded in the desert," Noah said. "People always end up in strife when they panic, make bad decisions and leave their vehicle. Same thing here."

A moment later, something charged the side of the tinnie with a solid thump, bringing immediate clarity to their dire situation. It felt like they'd been rammed by the steel hull of another boat or submarine or torpedo.

"Okay, that's definitely no dolphin," Noah said, voice panicked.

With another breach of the ocean's surface, the animal finally revealed itself. It was a shark, just as Manolis had feared. Its reinforced skin was rough and scaly, a streamlined, predatory matrix designed to decrease drag and turbulence and allow it to swim (and stalk) faster and more quietly, ambushing its prey from below. The creature was several metres in length; unsettlingly, almost as long as the tinnie itself. Its tail resembled a serrated hunting knife. Manolis felt his very life force drain away at the sight, at the realisation. He could handle vicious outback roos, and perhaps even wild mountain bears. But this was the world's deadliest predator, with a jaw like a steel trap, and they were encroaching in its watery domain. Manolis kept losing sight of the massive fish as it disappeared beneath the waves, circling, diving and scheming. And even when it did appear above the surface, it blended perfectly into the dark water so it was near impossible to see.

"That's another reason why sharks are such good hunters," Noah said. "They're camouflaged from every bloody direction."

The shark did a big lap around them, about a ten-metre circuit, moving in a series of formidable zigzags. Manolis struggled to fathom how fast it was moving – it didn't make sense to his brain to see something so big move so rapidly. Like a blunt missile equipped with heat-seeking capabilities.

"It's probably a great white", Noah said. "But it's probably also just curious, that's all. So again, don't panic, we should be safe in the boat. We just need it to realise what we are – humans, not seals."

Faced with the prospect of this mighty marine predator, Manolis wasn't so sure that patience was the answer. He recalled Nankervis's comments about sharks growing larger and more aggressive thanks to protected no-fishing zones.

"Perhaps it's some other kind of shark?" Manolis asked hopefully.

"I doubt it," Noah replied. "You can tell a great white straight away by how round they are. They've got a big barrel body and a huge fucking head designed to bash and crash."

The encounter was terrifying but at the same time, Manolis knew he was witnessing a unique spectacle of nature. He found himself fearing for his life and questioning his choices, and yet remained totally enthralled, the conflicting emotions reflecting a body in overdrive, with adrenaline levels that had reached stratospheric heights. He felt his pulse throbbing in his temples and throat and wondered whether he might pass out. In some ways, it was a preferable outcome – like being put under general anaesthetic to avoid the stress of either the subsequent surgery ahead of an operation. Only in this case, he saw little prospect of waking up on the other side.

Jesus, thought Manolis. What would it feel like to be eaten alive? Would it be slow or swift? Would it hurt or would he lose consciousness before any pain registered? Would his body parts ever be recovered from inside the shark's intestines or would he be slowly digested, dissolved in stomach acid strong enough to liquefy metal? He tried not to think about it and instead pressed himself against the hull of the boat.

"Do you have any shark repellent?" he asked desperately.

"No," replied Noah. "Look, if it comes down to it, we can shoot it."

Manolis shook his animal-loving head. "I'd rather not, and anyway, I don't have my weapon. Start the motor, let's just go."

But Noah was reluctant. "A moving propeller is only likely to be mistaken for prey," he said. "And that's when things can turn bad, when a shark's not sure what its facing and decides to explore with its mouth. Babies do the same thing."

Manolis wasn't sure that was the most appropriate analogy, but he knew that adolescent sharks were probably even more curious than adult specimens, and equally deadly. This shark, on the other hand, appeared fully grown – or at least Manolis didn't want to imagine it could get any bigger.

"Mate," Manolis told Noah, "sorry to say but I'm willing to take my chances."

Without waiting for a reply, the detective yanked hard on the motor's pull start rope. There was an anguished whirr but the rusty mechanics failed to fire. Manolis tried again and again, tensing his arm and pulling more desperately each time. Noah watched quietly, arms folded, respecting his superior's rank. But all Manolis's efforts succeeded in doing was fulfilling Noah's prophecy. The shark struck the boat a second time, only now with more force and at the rear end, propelling the tinnie forward. Manolis took the brunt of the impact, his feet and knees shaking as he tried to maintain his upright position. But with the boat rocking beneath him, Manolis lost his balance and was sent flying backwards into the ocean, the freezing cold water enveloping him as he flailed and fought to get his head above the surface and suck in a life-giving breath.

"Fuck!" Manolis spat, kicking wildly.

The fall overboard had been uncontrolled and clumsy, with Manolis smacking his ribs hard on the water's surface. He clutched at them as he kicked with his legs, conscious of attracting even more attention from below and desperate to return to the safety of the tinnie, which suddenly appeared like a fortress relative to his current situation.

"Here," Noah said. "Grab on to me."

He leaned over the side, offering a pair of brawny lifeguard arms. It was an arduous process returning Manolis to the tinnie, with the risk that it could capsize with too much force and leverage. But the detective sergeant eventually scrambled to safety, wet, shaken and out of breath.

"I'll call Sparrow," Noah said impulsively. He was also panting, chest heaving.

Unsurprisingly, at that distance out to sea, there was no reception. And much like its owner, Manolis's phone was soaking wet and inoperative. He scanned the water for any sign of the shark, or even its fin – but both had vanished. It was as hopeful a sight as it was unsettling.

"Shit," Manolis gasped. "Are we okay?"

"No," replied Noah. "We're still stranded and the bastard could be back at any minute. I told you not to try to start the motor." He sounded distressed and annoyed in equal measure.

Trying his phone a second time, Noah was amazed to have a signal, and even more astounded when Sparrow answered. The reception was poor and the line cut out after a few seconds of garbled conversation, with Noah unsure of whether Sparrow had fully understood their plight. In the meantime, Manolis had seen that the fin had resurfaced and was now circling them with intent, the shark's black glassy eyes trained squarely on the boat.

"Call again," Manolis told Noah.

It went straight to voicemail this time, where Noah left an urgent message.

"So, what now?" Manolis asked.

"We wait," Noah replied. "And pray the bastard loses interest."

Fearfully, and with their wet clothes precipitating a chill, they sat silently in the stranded tinnie, feeling the surging swell beneath them and watching the orbiting great white like a sniper taking aim. Thoughts of Richard Marlowe and investigative police work had suddenly become very distant.

"Apparently, sharks are like dogs," Noah said reflectively.

Manolis kept watching the water, eyes like satellite dishes. "Uh huh," he said. "Wait, what does that mean?"

"It means they have different personalities – there's good ones and bad ones."

"Here's hoping this one's not an arsehole . . ."

A few more tense minutes passed with the fin disappearing from view before reappearing in another nearby location. It didn't look like the shark was losing interest, while the mounting unease was making Manolis lose his mind. As a cop, he wasn't used to feeling so helpless.

"Sharks apparently have a highly refined electromagnetic sense they use for navigation across long distances," Noah said. "They also use it to detect weak fields that living things produce. Unfortunately, that just so happens to be the same electric field replicated by an aluminium boat."

"Great," sighed Manolis. "So, it thinks we're a delicious school of fish."

Noah nodded. "Probably more like a fat juicy seal or a small whale," he said. "Plenty of those around here. Humans have too many bones to digest, sharks much prefer large, fatty animals. Makes sense really – even I don't like eating a bony fish, getting a jagged piece stuck in my throat."

Manolis wondered how the hell Noah was able to stay so cucumber cool and conversational. Had he been in such a situation before . . .?

"If worse comes to worst and we do end up in the drink, just remember to spread your arms and legs out wide," Noah said.

"Spread them wide? Isn't that like inviting the shark to take a bite?"

"It's actually a way to alert them that we're *not* a seal or whale . . ."

Noah's advice barely had time to settle before a third approach by the shark hammered in, this time resulting in a bent propeller blade. Manolis let out a pressure-releasing shriek at a volume and pitch he never thought possible.

"Good thing the motor was already stuffed," said Noah.

He tried Sparrow again; no answer.

They watched the shark's broad body glide effortlessly through the water, a perfect blend of graceful beauty and overwhelming horror. Manolis was especially nervous when the shark passed directly beneath their boat. It was soon nudging at the hull, rocking the tinnie back and forth.

"Holy shit," Noah said. "I didn't expect that. The bastard's trying to tip us out!"

Manolis tried to stay seated, to stay calm, to keep breathing through his nose. His actions were an essential factor in the shark losing interest but he was finding it near impossible to remain still in the face of such an unyielding and crafty threat. He felt like he was suffocating, like the shark had a hold of his throat and was slowly squeezing the life out of it.

Looking around the tinnie, Manolis started considering what they could use as a weapon or toss out of the boat to scare the shark away. He was loath to do the creature harm, but at that moment saw no other choice.

"I can punch it in the nose," Noah said, cracking his knuckles.

"Go for the eyes," Manolis said. "Surely, they're the most vulnerable spot, the most sensitive body part."

"Or the gills," added Noah.

As the shark circled back at a wicked pace, flicking its powerful tail, Manolis braced himself, ready for action.

But then, something seemed to change. The water shifted, churned and rumbled, becoming more violent as the waves turned baleful and menacing. Clutching the tinnie to steady himself, Manolis took a moment to register what had come into view. It was a second ominous triangular fin.

"Look," he told Noah. "There. See it? It's a second shark. Christ, they really are hunting in packs. We're toast now."

"Second shark?" Noah replied. He checked where Manolis was pointing. "Wait, hang on a sec . . . look again."

Manolis squinted for a better view. On closer inspection, he saw the new fin was actually different – it was much taller, with a rounded tip, and black in colour. The great white turned a tight circle, its movements suddenly erratic and out of character from before. It passed by the boat one more time before it swam out to sea at speed.

"What the fucking fuck is going on?" Manolis muttered.

And then he saw it, recognising the distinctive white patches near the newcomer's eyes. Breaching like an acrobat and chasing the shark away – the glossy, black-and-white body of a magnificent orca. Intense and powerful, the ocean's largest species of dolphin appeared almost animatronic in its angular movements. Meanwhile, the shark was trying to avoid the orca's deadly intent using the same method that seals and turtles used to dodge sharks – jutting left and right – before it gave up on its would-be prey altogether and beat a hasty retreat further out to sea.

"Hallelujah for killer whales," breathed Noah with relief. "The only known predator of a great white."

Chapter 34

Sparrow stood patiently on a pier alongside his relieved colleagues. With the aid of the Nankervises, he had helped tow the tinnie back to shore. Both Manolis and Noah were sitting slumped over, huddled in towels and blankets and wearing a spare set of someone else's dry clothes. They were exhausted, the adrenaline having drained from their systems to leave only an overwhelming fatigue.

"You blokes are bloody lucky I got that message," Sparrow told them. "Not to mention the orca."

Noah said he'd heard many stories of wild orcas attacking great whites, holding them upside down to induce a state called immobility, which made them helpless and vulnerable. In that position, the orcas could then surgically eviscerate the shark's enormous peach-coloured liver, which was the fatty organ richest in stored energy.

"We've found maimed shark carcasses washed up missing their liver, digestive and reproductive organs," Noah said. "Orcas are the wolves of the sea."

But there had never been any reported instances of orcas killing people.

"Although orcas do seem to attack boats and try to disable their rudders," he added. "Apparently, they're trying to reclaim the ocean from humans. The oceans are noisy, overfished and overheated. Orcas aren't interested in us – they're interested in what we do in their territory."

"Communist orcas," said Sparrow. "Attacking superyachts, trying to sink the billionaires. Doing more for the working class than our elected politicians ever have."

"Now we just need to get them onto the golf courses," said Manolis.

"Some Indigenous peoples believe that killer whales are reincarnations of their ancestors, that they carry the souls of humans, often people who drowned," said Sparrow. "Explains why they prey on almost everything but people."

The pier's pylons were brittle and cracking, riddled with rusting steel and concrete cancer. The police were now waiting for the arrival of another boat from the ocean. Manolis and Noah had already shared their shark survival story. Meanwhile, Sparrow had shared his new theory on Marlowe.

"The idea came to me when I saw the lobster traps," he told them.

"Fucking hell," Manolis said. "You may be right . . ."

What Sparrow had described was aligned with Manolis's thinking, and it also tallied with the activity data.

"Let's just hope you're right," the detective said. "But excellent work, mate."

Manolis stared at the empty sea, a chill edging through his bones. Reflecting on all he'd just endured, he made a snap decision.

"Constable," he said. "Can I have a quiet word? Excuse us a moment, Noah . . ."

"No problem."

Noah made himself scarce, leaving the two mainland cops to square off. The Indigenous constable looked at his senior officer with grave eyes wondering what else he could've done wrong. Or was he about to finally pay the price for what he'd done earlier . . .?

"Sarge, look, whatever it is, I'm bloody sorry," said Sparrow, taking the initiative.

"Andrew, mate, just shut up a minute," Manolis snapped. "Let me speak."

Sparrow didn't like his first name being used – like when a parent pulled up an unruly child. Manolis never called him that. Sparrow pretended to close his mouth with an invisible zipper.

"Mate," Manolis said. He turned away, speaking to the ocean. "Now listen, this isn't easy for me to say . . ."

Sparrow expected further mention of Elvis, of unprofessionalism, of some kind of workplace sanction or even official termination. Instead, he heard Manolis cast him back to his hometown, to Cobb, to the stoning investigation that first brought them together, and then even further back to the memory of the murdered Jimmy Dingo. He was once the town's brightest young Indigenous footballer until he was stabbed in the thigh, with the death pinned on the local blackfellas as some kind of tribal punishment.

"Except it wasn't your mob," said Manolis. "You always claimed the police blamed your People, framed them. And what I'm trying to say is that you were right all along."

"Well, yair," said Sparrow. "My People already know that. Whitefellas just refused to bloody listen to us, to believe us. But why are you making such a big deal about it now, and out here of all places?"

"Because I almost just carked it," said Manolis. "And because I found out who really killed Jimmy Dingo."

"You what? Fuck me," said Sparrow. The words fell out of his mouth like dead weights. "Who?"

Manolis needed to compose himself. Should he just blurt it out? This was something he'd mentally prepared for but not fully rehearsed.

"It turns out that Jimmy had been secretly seeing a white woman in Cobb and accidentally got her pregnant. That was considered shameful, an insult to her family, so he was killed in retaliation. It was made to look like a tribal killing. The reasons are complicated and very old-fashioned but suffice to say, it was cold-blooded murder and . . . *my father* should've been convicted."

Sparrow took a moment to take in the wall of information, and the shock at the end.

"Your who? Your dad?"

Manolis turned back to face his colleague. "Yeah," he said. "My dad, Con."

"How'd you learn all this?"

"A confession, I won't reveal who, which I later confirmed by locating the murder weapon, which had been buried for decades."

Sparrow sat listening, letting the words sink in, taking a moment to process the new world. Manolis shivered in his clothes, feeling both cold and vulnerable.

And then, a slender arm shot out; it made Manolis flinch instinctively until Sparrow held it a moment before laying it reassuringly across the detective's shoulders.

"Mate," said Sparrow, tone soft. "Go easy. Like I said, my mob knew it was a whitefella all along. Which whitefella is almost irrelevant. That it was your bloody dad is more upsetting for you than for me. You were just a kid back then, you weren't to know or understand, let alone be able to stop it. I appreciate your honesty, and I'm really sorry to hear this – for you, I mean."

Manolis's pupils flicked between the lurching water and Sparrow's calm face, finally settling on the latter.

"The world's a different place now," said Sparrow. "Yair, it's still five hundred shades of fucked up but at least there's been progress."

Manolis's shoulders relaxed, his relief evident. He returned Sparrow's gesture with his own supportive arm.

"Thanks for understanding, mate," he said. "I still feel awful about it, and I'm sorry, too."

Noah wandered over. "Fellas, I hate to interrupt . . . but look there."

The boat chugged into view. The police approached as a unified front, with Manolis a small step ahead of the others. Conway appeared on the deck, gathering the long ropes needed to moor to the pier, and altogether confused by the reception that greeted him.

"What's going on here?" he asked innocently. "You blokes expecting someone?"

Manolis gestured to Conway's fishing boat. "We need to inspect your vessel," he said, voice firm.

Conway smiled. "Certainly, gentlemen," he said. "I'll just need to see your warrant . . ."

The police stared at each other blankly before Conway laughed out loud.

"I'm kidding," he added. "Right this way, knock yourselves out."

They boarded with Manolis heading straight for the stern, his focus on only one thing – the shark cage. He'd never seen one up close before, and was fascinated to see its design and structure, especially after his recent chilling encounter. Conway was understandably proud of it, having built it from scratch in his garage.

"Took me months to put together but she's a beaut," he said. "And of course, fully submersible."

"What's the material?" Manolis asked. "It's not steel, is it?"

"Aluminium," he said. "It's lighter, non-corrosive and stronger. A steel cage would weigh hundreds of kilos and need a crane just to get it into the boat. It'd also cost a bomb in diesel fuel to lug around."

Manolis tested the cage's stability with a non-scientific shake and rattle. It certainly felt infinitely more secure than the papier mâché tinnie. The cage had vertically oriented bars securely welded together in a similar arrangement to a jail cell. The bottom mesh fit snugly into the frame to give occupants a stable base on which to stand without needing to grasp the bars and put their hands at risk.

"Planning the bars' overall size and spacing was really important," Conway said. "There's a direct trade-off between retaining safety and providing a minimally obstructed view."

"View?" asked Manolis.

"To allow the cage to be repurposed and used for tourism," Conway said. "Shark selfies and shit."

"Is it made to industry standard?" Manolis asked. "Does it satisfy government safety regulations? Has it been tested for fracture toughness?"

Conway let rip a loud, incredulous laugh.

"What, are you going to slug me with a fine if it's not?" he chortled. "Report me to the regulator? Mate, go right ahead."

"How much she set you back?" Sparrow asked.

"More than I had hoped," Conway replied. "All up, about twenty grand."

Noah approached the cage, inspected it more closely. "What's this?" he asked.

He was indicating a hefty and conspicuous U-bolt bike lock hanging around one of the bars.

"I didn't realise shark fins were dexterous enough to be able to open latches," said Manolis.

"They're sneaky buggers, I put nothing past them," Conway said, smiling. "It's an insurance policy to keep the cage secure. Can't be too careful down there, you don't want the door accidentally slipping open during a dive."

Manolis looked at Conway for some time, scrutinising his full but weathered face. The fisherman casually blew the fringe out of his eyes.

"Search the boat," Manolis told his men. "And you," he told Conway, "wait on the pier."

Silently, Conway took an unceremonious seat on a discarded milk crate while the police scoured the vessel. Manolis wasn't quite sure what they were looking for, but he knew that he would know when he saw it.

The three officers came together after a few minutes to compare notes and consult each other. Returning to the pier, to Conway, now bored and restless and nettled, the detective composed himself and summed up the situation.

"We have reason to believe that this boat, and the shark cage in particular, were used in the commission of a serious crime," Manolis said. "We currently have two individuals detained in relation to the crime and this is part of our investigation into their culpability or otherwise."

He was careful not to mention any specifics, knowing that Conway would try to fill in the blanks. Not that that would be difficult given the nature of the island.

"I only bought this boat a short while ago, and then purchased it second-hand," Conway said. "Are you referring to something that happened before then?"

Manolis fixed him with a glare. "You know what I'm referring to."

"We have it in our power to seize any property to conduct a thorough police forensic examination," Noah chimed in.

Conway's eyes darted at the realisation. "Seize my boat . . .? But that would ruin my business. Look, if this is about Marlowe's disappearance, I had nothing to do with it, don't drag me into this. I was on the mainland that morning with my wholesaler, you're welcome to check."

Manolis nodded. "I'm aware of that, yes. But does anyone else have access to your boat?"

Conway stared out to sea, taking a second to gather his thoughts.

"I use it every day for my business," he said. "Right now, there's no scope to lend it out."

"You mentioned tourism," Sparrow said.

A smile broke across Conway's swollen lips. "Well, not right now. But maybe one day to earn some extra cash."

"Could someone have used it on the morning in question without your knowledge?" Manolis asked.

"You mean, stolen it?" Conway replied. "Doubt it, I had the keys with me. Fingerprint and search it if you doubt me."

Manolis said there'd be no point. "There's nothing credible that could be recovered from a boat at sea being drenched by salt water every day."

The detective looked back to the vessel, considering his next move. The ubiquity of salty ocean water and its expunging nature had made this an investigation like no other.

"Take photographs," Manolis told his colleagues. "Boat and cage. That'll do us for today."

As they filed back onto the pier after another ten minutes, Conway directed a parting salvo their way:

"I'll let you know if anything else occurs to me but I can assure you blokes, you're barking up the wrong bloody tree."

The police officers took stock nearby, reconvening at their cars in a secluded scrubby area near the main coastal road. Sparrow leaned on the bonnet and rubbed his eyes as if he were just waking up.

"Argh," he groaned. "Sorry, you blokes. I dunno if that was the right approach."

Manolis put a reassuring arm around Sparrow's bony shoulder. "Mate, don't stress it. I'm not sure what else we could've done."

"We could've bloody examined his boat without asking him," Sparrow replied.

"I'm not sure what that would've achieved," said Manolis. "There's been ample time for any evidence to be destroyed, so no wonder the boat is so clean. Our only hope was that he might've been cooperative with information, but it sounds like he's happy to keep protecting Elvis and Nails. And I just can't understand why."

"They're all old mates," said Noah. "Bonds like that are hard to break."

"But this is still a criminal investigation," said Manolis. "A man died." He quietly cursed the island's insular nature for the umpteenth time.

As they were talking, the hard rev of a speeding car grew in intensity before blasting past. Manolis jogged out to the road to see it disappearing into the distance in a nebulous cloud of dust, headed east.

"Now then," he told his team. "That *is* something."

"What's that?" Sparrow asked.

"That was Conway going past at light speed. And it's not insignificant."

Manolis went on to detail experiences of guilty parties who had inadvertently led police to their accomplices when a police investigation began to close in.

"Whether it's a corporate high-flyer or deadbeat druggie on the street, people start to panic when the noose tightens," he said. "They go looking for other parties, either for protection or to take them down with them."

"Makes our job a bit easier," said Noah.

"It'd be funny if it wasn't so true," Manolis replied.

"Criminals are criminals for a reason – they're not necessarily the smartest mob," said Sparrow.

"That Conway is heading out now, right now after our visit, and driving like a maniac is no coincidence," Manolis said. "Tail him, but keep your distance. I'll head back to the station to check on our two friends there."

Sparrow and Noah looked at each other, nodding their understanding. They drove away, tyres spinning in the dirt.

At the station, Manolis found Elvis and Nails napping in their cells like two newborns. He let them be and turned his attention to the important task of drying his dead phone, removing the battery and SIM card from its insides, dabbing it with a paper towel, and vacuuming its nooks and crannies. He then put it on to charge and remarkably heard it ring within seconds. It was Noah.

"Guess where we are? Parked outside Murden's house. Conway's gone inside."

"Oh," said Manolis, noting the time on the wall clock. "Oh, right."

His brain immediately kicked into gear – how could Murden possibly be involved?

"He's always come across as Marlowe's biggest fan," Manolis said, rubbing his prickly jaw. "Good work. Stay on him."

"Yep," Noah said. "And one other thing – I got a call from the freight company at the port. Turns out Elvis and Nails were there the morning Marlowe disappeared. So, I hate to say it, but their alibis check out."

Manolis thrust his neck back as if avoiding an invisible jab. "Is that right? Are you sure?" he asked.

"There's documentation, signatures, et cetera."

Manolis creased his brow and exhaled. "Well then," he said. "Bugger me."

The detective hung up with a look of bewilderment. This new information meant he had to release the two sleeping beauties and send them on their way. But halfway down the corridor to the cells, Manolis stopped to think a moment. There was still something he was certain he was missing, a single detail or clue or connection that would allow everything else to fall into place like the tumblers in a combination lock.

Just then, his phone beeped with a message. Manolis had to look twice to make sure his eyes weren't deceiving him. It was from Emily, who had received Manolis's peace offering.

"Thank you," she'd written. "Take care, come home soon, x."

It was seven-and-a-half simple words that instantly buoyed Manolis's spirits. But gazing at his phone, as if drawing sustenance, also helped shape his meditations. A moment later, he slapped a palm to his forehead with the realisation, and changed his course back to the office.

"Shit," he said. "The CDRs. Where the hell are they?"

The numbers were tucked away in the second filing cabinet drawer that Manolis checked. He scanned the ream of digits until his finger came to rest at the bottom of the third page. He then retrieved his phone and dialled.

The call was to a ministerial office – Manolis wanted to find out about the meeting that Marlowe had missed the morning he disappeared. He was obliged to suffer some tedious hold music and an automated, multi-layered phone menu while his call was transferred between relevant government offices. At last, he reached a real human voice, which turned out to belong to a strait-laced ministerial adviser.

"My name is Detective Sergeant George Manolis and I'm conducting an investigation into a possible homicide . . ."

"Oh," said the adviser with minor shock. "Well then, certainly. How can I be of assistance?"

Manolis listened carefully as the adviser provided details on what would have otherwise been a confidential meeting.

"Because of Mister Marlowe's influence and investment, he was able to secure the ear of the minister for a private meeting, one-on-one," said the adviser.

"What was the subject of this meeting?" Manolis asked.

"It was about a mining licence granted for offshore drilling. There were some questions in the public eye over how the licence had been secured, speculation over bribery, corruption, and so on, all of which the minister and his office vehemently deny. But irrespective of that unpleasantness, it turned out that Mister Marlowe had had a change of heart and wanted to hand back his share of the licence."

"Do you know why?" Manolis asked.

"I wouldn't normally reveal this, but it turns out Mister Marlowe was seeking to have the same stretch of ocean potentially declared a protected area," the adviser said. "Such a marine park would be a globally significant contribution to conservation and prevent anyone else conducting future mining and exploration. I believe Mister Marlowe was hoping to convince the minister, he would need his support for such an initiative. There would still need to be a public consultation, of course, but the minister was open to the conversation, aware that there's more to government than pure economics. And after all, this is an election year."

Manolis thanked the adviser for their time and invaluable insight and hung up. His phone showed a missed call from Sparrow. Manolis immediately rang back.

"Now Conway and Murden are both on the move," Sparrow said. "Heading west. We're following."

Manolis grabbed his car keys. "Fantastic. I'm releasing our two friends here and coming now. I think I've cracked it."

Chapter 35

"Step on it, mate . . ."

"Steady on, mate. I don't wanna kill us."

"Yeah, but we don't wanna lose sight of 'em . . ."

"Don't worry, we won't."

Sparrow was trying to keep their distance but also ensure they didn't lose sight of the vehicle in front as it wound along the remote rural road. Noah kept his eyes fixed on the variable surface like he was driving himself, riding every curve and bend. Late afternoon had now bled into early evening, the light in the day all but gone.

Without warning, the car ahead unexpectedly accelerated, driving and veering recklessly.

"Looks like they're on to us," Sparrow said.

"Gun it," Noah replied.

Sparrow pushed his foot to the floor, forcing them back into their seats. His steering became erratic, loose, as he struggled to maintain control of the vehicle on the slippy rural road. Fearing an accident, he gradually eased his foot off the accelerator.

"What's up?" Noah asked him. "Keep going."

"Can't," Sparrow said. "There's rules about police pursuits."

"I know," Noah said. "But there's hardly any public at risk here. The rules don't really apply."

Sparrow nodded his understanding, more to himself than anyone else. Though extra conscious of his behaviour following recent trans-gressions, he pressed down hard a second time. They returned to pursuit speed and soon to within sight of the leading vehicle. With headlights on, there was no longer any concealing the unmarked police vehicle and, given the white-knuckle way the two cars were driving, no denying what was going on.

A series of loud bangs pierced the air. It sounded like the car in front was backfiring.

"That's not the exhaust," said Sparrow, engaging his fast-twitch reflexes to jerk the wheel left and right.

"Gunshots," said Noah. "Those fucking idiots."

"They might not know we're police," Sparrow said.

Just as he finished his sentence, a bullet zipped through the wind-screen, making Noah duck and Sparrow swerve. More shots were fired, careering into the car's front grille.

"They'll blow our fucking engine up," said Noah.

"Which is one way to end the chase," Sparrow said. His forehead prickled with fresh sweat.

Sparrow kept gunning the accelerator, redlining the internal combustion engine and risking it stalling. The car ahead moved like a phantom in and out of his vision. The constable turned the steering wheel left and right, hugging the turns and dodging the shots. None of his police training had adequately prepared him for this – a headlong pursuit into a hail of invisible bullets through the veil of twilight. Noah slumped down low, avoiding the firing line and gripping his armrest tight as he slid around in his seat. Sparrow cursed the lack of a police siren, although that may have made no difference. He kept watching for brake lights, the flashes of diode red indicating the position of his target and where he needed to slow down and speed up. With the road curving like a cat's tail, he kept losing the leading car around corners. That the tarmac was strewn with fallen branches and newly caved potholes only added to the hazards he needed to avoid and underscored the slim margin of error at his disposal. There was being shot, and potentially murdered, and then there was losing control, and probably getting killed.

"Fuck me," Sparrow gritted.

The vehicle continued to slither and slide across the dubious, unsealed surface, deeper into the dark depths of the national park. Sparrow's arms tensed as he fought to maintain the car's path and integrity. At that speed, he didn't expect them to turn off and go hiding in the scrub.

"Any idea where they might be headed?" he asked.

"Dunno," Noah replied. "At the speed they're travelling, they're more likely to launch themselves off the western end of the island."

Another round of shots, continued swerving; Sparrow was reacting instinctively to the noises, completely unaware if he was evading the oncoming slugs or turning into them, and always a half-second too late. Their lives hung on pure, dumb luck. And with Noah having already called upon considerable fortune in the ocean earlier that day, sooner or later, he was going to use all his up. It was more activity than Noah had seen in the field for some time, and certainly too much jeopardy for a father with young children.

"Shit!"

Sparrow's exclamation was combined with a hard reef of the steering wheel that threatened to send the car skidding into the surrounding scrub. It was a roo, a bushfire-blistered boomer, all of two metres in height and rippling with muscle, standing doe-eyed in the middle of the road like an impromptu roundabout. Once upon a time, Sparrow would've thought to clatter straight through such a marsupial knowing their tiny brains and sturdy shape were more dangerous to passing traffic than the other way around. But it seemed Manolis's love for animals had washed off on his younger colleague, even during a police pursuit. The kangaroo blurred past Sparrow's window like an apparition, the cop's trail of expletives resounding into the night.

"Great driving, mate," Noah panted. "Keep going."

The pursuit continued with the gap between the cars closing and widening depending on the contours of the road. Sparrow felt infused with a sudden confidence as if the path was becoming clearer, the task easier, a new video game level unlocked. That was, until the next bullet cannoned into the car's front left tyre, causing it to blow into gnarly rubber tendrils. And no matter how hard he steered and braked or how assured and competent he felt, even Sparrow couldn't save the situation now. The vehicle ran off the road, skidding and fishtailing into the scrub, where it eventually rolled, executing three soul-removing somersaults before coming to rest on its punctured tyres. And then, the only sound in the air was of an escaping car accelerating into the distance and the squawking of the startled sulphur-crested cockatoos who'd settled down for the night in the mantle of surrounding gum trees.

The wrecked car lay silent, injuries undetermined, signs of life uncertain.

At that time of day, in that location, there were no guarantees that a passing vehicle might come by any time soon. Or, if it did, that the driver would see the crashed car in the darkness of the scrub and stop to assist. The likelihood was they would take it for just another abandoned vehicle and drive on without stopping.

The silence continued, valuable seconds expiring, vital fluids and organs and tissues being stretched and tested. The car had crashed somewhere between the middle of nowhere and the end of the world – on a remote island off an island continent that was thousands of miles from most of humanity's consciousness. Tiny animals crawled across the land, insects and rodents and reptiles, curious at the new arrival, the heavy and concerning smell of petrol engulfing the air.

A sharp intake of breath finally punctured the silence; a gasp and a series of rapid breaths announcing the return of life. But of what quality? And by whom?

It was the driver. Sparrow undid his seatbelt and forced his misshapen, damaged door open. With an agonising groan and painstaking effort, he dragged himself free of the battered vehicle. But it was a very different story for his passenger – Constable Volavola remained seated, unconscious, blood trickling down his face from a deep head wound.

"Noah! Hey, Noah!"

Sparrow implored his island colleague but he remained unresponsive, still securely strapped into his seatbelt.

The next concern was Sparrow's own welfare – he felt dizzy and shaken and his body ached in multiple places, especially his neck and shoulders, clear trauma from the rollover. But he was otherwise miraculously unharmed. It was a similar diagnosis for his lifeline, his phone, which had a fresh crack in its screen but remained operational. Reception was the problem – there was none. Sparrow knew he couldn't move Noah on his own and didn't want to risk it for fear of further injury. Treading carefully, crunching his ankle-high safety boots across broken window glass and scattered chassis parts, Sparrow stumbled through the newly flatted grass, following the trail back to the road. His only grain of hope was to wave down a passing motorist who was willing to stop for a draggled-tailed individual who looked like death.

With stressed tears in his eyes and choking dust in his nostrils, Sparrow engaged his phone's flashlight and began walking. He noticed a slight limp after a few steps, which became worse the further he hobbled. It was the same for his emotional state, his feeling of responsibility to Noah's family. The high-speed pursuit in those conditions had felt like a bad idea, no matter what Noah had said to reassure him. And now, Sparrow could only think about what it might be like to explain to Tessa all that had happened. After Holly, the island didn't need another young widow so soon.

Sparrow stumbled on through the darkness. The light appeared before the sound – a pair of high beams on a long stretch of straight road, followed by the drone of an accompanying engine. Blinded by the glare, Sparrow held up a hand to shield his eyes and waved his other arm in the air, signalling for assistance. But the car failed to slow and either didn't see him or didn't care, continuing to accelerate past. Sparrow felt its cold slipstream as it flew by, leaving him with only a lingering sense of failure and hopelessness.

He shambled on, unsteady in his own stride but resolute in his task.

Through his scratched windscreen, the road appeared hazy to Manolis, the surrounding darkness suffocating in its intensity. He followed it west, driving with determination, hands at ten and two, headlights slicing through the growing darkness. He'd already slowed several times for local wildlife, their influence on the roads becoming more pronounced after sunset. Manolis had full confidence in his colleagues, trusted they had the situation well in hand, but knew his presence would be needed to bring things to a peaceful and lawful conclusion.

But whereas Manolis could swerve or slow for animals on the remote country road, he was forced to slam on the brakes when a human specimen appeared in the middle of his illuminated lane. He was shocked to see someone in distress, and then staggered to recognise the individual.

"Sarge, thank fuck." Sparrow coughed through the resultant cloud of bulldust. "It's Noah."

"Where?" said Manolis urgently. "What's wrong? Is he okay? Are you?"

Sparrow guided Manolis to the relevant spot, a few hundred metres further down the road. Manolis could readily identify it as an accident scene from the markings left on the surface. Parking the car by the roadside, they speedily walked the rest of the way.

Manolis clasped Noah's wrist and felt a dull throb in his radial artery.

"Thank fuck, he's got a pulse," said Manolis. But they were unable to rouse him, which wasn't a good sign.

"He may have spinal injuries," said Sparrow.

"Christ," muttered Manolis. "His family, his kids."

He briefly reflected on how Emily must've felt every time he was on the late shift, her concerns for her husband and their son's father. It wasn't him at home worrying if the door would rattle open in the middle of the night, or if the bell would mournfully ring.

Fortunately, Manolis had phone reception. He summoned an ambulance.

"We can't do much more now," Sparrow said. "And to make matters worse, we let those fuckers get away."

Manolis smiled. "I know where they're going," he said.

"Then what the bloody hell are you waiting for?" Sparrow said. "Keep going, bring them in, make this all worth it. I'll stay here."

Manolis glared at him for some time, considering his options, before nodding his understanding.

"Just be careful," Sparrow added. "Those fuckers are armed."

The sight of Conway's dirt-spattered vehicle parked in the driveway told Manolis that he was in the right location. He killed the parking lights and exited his car silently, sneaking around the outside of the building. He was grateful for the white noise of the rolling ocean nearby – it offered him a level of cover as he searched for a way inside. And one soon presented itself in the form of an unlocked door.

Entering the residence, Manolis heard loud voices, the heat of an argument underway. He smiled to himself at the prospect of an investigative jackpot. As predicted, with the noose tightening around their collective necks, the culprits were turning on each other. In the current situation, it was Conway and Murden united in their criticism of their third accomplice. Manolis crouched down low against a wall, secreting himself away in a corner. He made sure he was within earshot to overhear the entire criminal enterprise recounted in angry, resentful detail.

"You absolute fucker," Conway spat. "First, you make us do your dirty work for you—"

"And now, you wanna just walk away?" Murden added.

The two men paced the spacious living room, stress and hostility leaching from their bodies. Meanwhile, Lavender sat comfortably in a modern armchair listening to their complaints with a contemptuous air like an esteemed judge considering arguments. There was a distinct power imbalance: the rich blow-in versus the poor Islanders, the have versus the have-nots.

"This was all your bloody idea," said Murden. "Drugging Marlowe, stealing the boat, dragging him out to sea."

"The shark cage, the watch," added Conway.

"You can't just let us now take the blame for it," said Murden.

"I didn't even wanna have anything to do with this," Conway said. "I only got dragged into it after you took my boat."

Lavender looked confused. "But I bought your silence," he said calmly. "I wiped your debt to Murden for the shark cage, twenty grand doesn't grow on trees. That's a pretty generous deal when all you have to do is keep your trap shut."

Lavender turned to the island's mayor. "And you're going to benefit from this drilling project, too," he continued. "The local economy will go gangbusters."

Murden shook his head. "But what's the fucking point if we're behind bars?"

"You've got the money, you can afford a great lawyer who'll save your rich arse," Conway said. "We've got nothing, just our word. And our word is worth shit."

Murden smiled. "But it's still our word against yours," he told Lavender. "Two versus one. Personally, I like those odds."

Lavender chuckled to himself. "I see," he said. "Yes, I see your little game. So, what is it you want now? How can we work this out? Name your price."

Conway and Murden said they didn't want any money – instead, they wanted to be absolved from any involvement in the death of Richard Marlowe, and for Lavender to accept sole responsibility.

"Next option," Lavender replied swiftly. "Sorry, but I've got too much to lose if I'm incarcerated for any extended period of time. This mining permit is going to be a licence to print money. Ergo, name your price."

The locals tried again. "Then we want your expensive legal counsel to defend us," Murden said.

Lavender scratched his chin in thought. "Okay," he said. "How about this then. I won't give you my lawyers, who are highly respected and only take on certain clients. But I'll give you the money to buy yourselves the best legal protection you can find. And lawyers aren't cheap, I can assure you. There's only one condition – that you plead guilty and leave me out of it. You'll get five years, max. And on top of that, I'll give you each a million dollars. Surely, all that is more than enough."

A tempting offer, perhaps, but it still came at the price of their freedom.

"Last option," said Murden. "We want safe passage to the mainland on your chopper. Help us escape, and then help us find sanctuary."

Lavender laughed. "What, and then I stay behind and face the music, cop the heat? No thanks. No assistance, no chopper."

The air was tense. Neither party was willing to shift their position, leaving the culprits at loggerheads over how to proceed. The living room went quiet as the sea grumbled its evening song. Manolis knew there was at least one firearm in the room, which may or may not have had any remaining ammunition, but he couldn't be sure there weren't others. Imagining the worst, he reached down and prepared his own weapon for action. But suddenly, he saw Murden looming over him with his shooter drawn. Looking around, Manolis spied his darkened reflection in a nearby window and realised how he'd been sprung.

"Well then," said Murden. "And now we have another problem on our hands."

Chapter 36

Under a full moon, its face lit up like a fiery demon, Conway's boat chugged out into increasingly deeper and colder depths. The owner was comfortably at the wheel, safely navigating the breakers, which gleamed with phosphorescence and were even more violent at night due to the moon's force of gravity. Lavender and Murden were out the back on deck, each with a firearm pointed squarely at Manolis who sat cross-legged, hands clasped together in his lap like a condemned prisoner. His likely fate had quickly dawned on him as soon as Lavender told him they were "going for a little drive". The prospect was even more terrifying at night with so little visual information. Whereas the offenders had once turned on each other, they had now unified against a common foe. It was an elegant solution – at least, for the time being.

"Do you honestly think you'll get away with this?" Manolis asked them abruptly.

Lavender replied coolly, in his own time, staring at Manolis like they were doing a boardroom deal. "Oh, I think we will. After all, it worked so well the first time. In business, you stick to what works."

"But I am a senior officer of the law," Manolis said. "Do you even fathom what that means? I'm not just another corporate rival."

"You're an adversary," said Lavender. "Mentally, strategically, it's the same process."

On this occasion, they at least had the forethought to successfully confiscate Manolis's phone and ensure any tracking devices were disabled. But the detective's stainless-steel watch remained on his wrist. It came from a city department store and only told the time and date, and more often than not, unreliably.

"The others know what you've done," said Manolis.

"But they could be dead by now," said Lavender.

"We saw their car run off the road," said Murden. "It looked nasty."

They laughed, long and heartily, jaws and guts shuddering. It made Manolis question whether they were gaining some kind of sick satisfaction from their execution method – nefarious, but ingenious. Their eyes seem to harbour some kind of borderline mania. It was a criminal mindset Manolis recognised from other investigations but that always unsettled him, the strange, cold universe from where such sinister motivations and reactions were dredged.

"From the days of the very first sealers and smugglers, this island has always been different, a place of savagery and decadence," Lavender said. "And savagery and criminality go hand in hand. A criminal's just a savage in better clothes. We're simply following in a rich tradition."

"That's ridiculous," said Manolis. "You may as well argue that you should bring back slavery or Indigenous massacres and call it a rich tradition."

The night air wrapped its chill around them. Spray pelted the deck. Manolis started to shiver, his reserves running on empty, mental and physical, drained by the prospect of what lay ahead.

Without warning, the boat was plunged into darkness as the lights went out and it lurched to a sudden halt. Confusion and panic took over, raised voices, barked instructions, doubt and questioning.

"Power failure!" Conway called. He was heard clattering around the bridge. "Everyone just relax, this has happened before, I know what to do . . ."

Manolis felt even more anxious and vulnerable now that he was immersed in blackness so many miles from shore, his brain foggy and disorientated from the lack of spatial awareness in an unfamiliar environment. But his police impulses also sensed an opportunity. He knew he would need to act fast and hope that his instincts were on the money.

But before he could move, the lights flared back to life and the boat restarted with a loud mechanical squeal. Manolis tried to hide the disappointment as his eyes refocused in the glare and the weapons recommenced their positions. His heart returned squarely to their crosshairs as the boat's engine grumbled, picking up speed, making up for lost time.

Reaching an arbitrary position in the oily black ocean, Conway killed the boat's ignition and navigation light. Powerful flashlights now appeared, cutting through the darkness like sharp swords as a light drizzle began falling. Manolis knew he was running out of time and considered the few options he had left. He could do something rash and jump overboard but knew he'd be unable to swim the distance back to shore, let alone through shark-infested waters, even more replete with the apex predators at night. He could try and overpower one of his adversaries, but that would still leave two others. And as for a third option . . . well, there was no third option.

Operating the controls, Conway moved the shark cage into position using a noisy electrical winch and opened the door with a hefty clank. Manolis gazed at the cage, a modern-day iron maiden. Lavender approached, his blue eyes aflame like gas burners.

"Any last words?" he asked.

Manolis stood with a steely expression, communicating with his eyes alone, like a cornered animal.

"Nothing to say?" Lavender continued. "No plea bargain, or plea for your life?"

Manolis gritted his teeth. "I wouldn't give you the satisfaction."

Lavender laughed out loud. "You're a better man than Marlowe ever was," he said. "He grovelled like a common beggar, offering me the world. He was almost unrecognisable, and in the end, it was all in vain."

Manolis shook his head in disbelief. "All this, and for what, more money?" he asked.

Lavender nodded seriously. "Money is transformational, generational," he said. "If you've never had it, you have no idea."

It was an intentionally condescending remark taken from yet another world that Manolis didn't recognise – a world that had always been on the doorstep of Kangaroo Island but that had recently arrived in force.

"And if you don't transform, if you don't change, then you wither and die," Lavender went on. "In business, you embrace change and innovation, you make quick decisions or get left behind in the dust."

"The activism seeking to protect the oceans is an eco-grab with no basis in science," said Murden. "It's supposed to send shockwaves through Australian communities who rely on marine estates for employment, tourism and recreation. It's all bullshit."

Lavender motioned to the dripping shark cage with the barrel of his firearm. "Inside," he told Manolis.

The detective stood resolute, refusing to move.

"You deaf, mate?" Murden asked. He pressed his firearm firmly into Manolis's forehead. "*Move, now.*"

He eventually had to shove Manolis into the cage, which Conway closed and secured with the solid U-bolt bike lock. Manolis grasped the bars like an inmate on death row, with no chance of a last-minute pardon.

With grim, expressionless faces, the three accomplices watched from the afterdeck as the mechanism engaged and the cage was slowly lowered into the ocean. It was the coldest water Manolis had ever felt, shocking his entire system as it pooled around his ankles and knees, before reaching his waist. As it rose, Manolis's thoughts retreated to his family, his declining mother and long-suffering wife, and especially his young son and what life would be like for them. Manolis hadn't properly moved on from his own father's death, it was a trauma that continually re-emerged, and he feared it might be the same for Christos – only much worse given his age. He had desperately wanted to be there for his son, but would now forever be remembered as a selfish rather than selfless father. It had continually tortured him to be labelled as such, but no matter what he tried, Manolis seemed to always screw things up and his efforts only created more chaos.

The cage continued to lower, and the ocean to rise. Manolis hoped for another operational failure, but the machine's mechanical gremlins now lay silent.

As his neck and chin went under, Manolis opened his mouth wider than ever and filled his lungs with as much air as possible, his cheeks and chest expanding and abdomen contracting. The water continued to climb until it found Manolis's nostrils and ears and eyes, rushing into his head like an unstoppable, endless force. Moments later, he was fully submerged, plunging to a depth of several metres, with everything around him going deathly quiet.

A second later, an unprecedented panic gripped Manolis. It was the combination of cold and darkness and no oxygen as he held his single life-giving breath and frantically started to work away at his metal tomb. He operated by feel, trying to find a weakness in either the bike lock or the cage, bashing and pushing and pulling. Manolis felt his pulse rate and blood pressure skyrocket, he knew he only had a minute, maybe two, before he would have no choice but to open his mouth and fill his lungs with toxic water. But nothing was working, the bars and lock remained steadfast. Manolis flailed, he thrashed about, fight-or-flight, caught like a rat in a trap. With the freedom of water all around him yet restricted in his movements, it felt like a cruel deception, unnatural to the human spirit. Unable to hold his breath any longer and about to black out, Manolis realised he'd reached his breaking point. Involuntarily, he gasped and finally inhaled, feeling the icy liquid smash the larynx at the back of his throat. Briny sea water rushed into his lungs as an overwhelming shadow and strangle swiftly enveloped him, straining his pulmonary pressure.

But then, a few moments later, the tension in Manolis's chest instantly cleared and he again felt like he was breathing fresh, clean air. There was a deep burning sensation at first but because the water was so cold, Manolis felt soothed. He let his eyes slip shut as if it was the most natural thing in the world. With the feeling of panic leaving him, Manolis felt like he was entering another space, a strange but pleasant peace taking over. It was absolute calmness and tranquillity, a kaleidoscope of colours, his body weightless, floating, like a feather . . .

"How much longer?" Lavender asked, staring overboard into the murky depths.

Conway consulted his thick diving watch. "Not much," he replied. "No man could survive such a—"

His sentence was cut short by the blinding glare of an unfamiliar light.

"Hands up, drop your weapons!" said the gruff voice, pointing a firearm in silhouette.

The voice was Sparrow's. Alongside him were the Nankervises on their lobster boat, with Elvis and Nails as crew, their own firearms fixed squarely on the culprits, who dropped theirs in surrender. The rescue party had used their radar to track the location of Conway's boat out to sea and then killed their engine on final approach to the bow, silently storming the vessel and swiftly seizing control.

Sparrow looked to the water. "Get him up, quick," he demanded. "Get him out now!"

Operating the control unit under the influence of a drawn firearm, Conway returned the dripping shark cage to the surface. It took longer to ascend against the force of gravity and with the weight inside. Slumped at its bottom on the wire mesh was Sparrow's superior officer, unmoving.

Sparrow climbed into the cage and took a limp, unconscious Manolis into his arms.

"The docs are with Noah, he's gonna be okay," he told him desperately. "And so are you, mate. So are you."

Acknowledgements

Sincere thanks to Paul Engles for incredible publishing, editing and support; to Martin Shaw for being an agent extraordinaire; to Rita Winter for meticulous proofreading; to Christine Walker and Vivienne Greenshields of the Ramindjeri people for manuscript consultation and comments; to Sarah Court for careful reading and feedback; to the Kangaroo Islanders for their friendliness and knowledge; and to my family for their enduring love and belief in my books and writing.

In conducting research for material contained in this book, I consulted numerous texts by authors who are deeply experienced in this fascinating region and its rich history. I acknowledge works by Rebe Taylor in *Unearthed: The Aboriginal Tasmanians of Kangaroo Island* (2019), *The Crow Eaters: A Journey through South Australia* by Ben Stubbs (2019), *The 99th Koala: Rescue and Resilience on Kangaroo Island* by Kailas Wild (2020), *The Kangaroo Islanders: A Story of South Australia before Colonisation 1823* by W. A. Cawthorne and Rick Hosking (2020), *Humans of Kangaroo Island: People Make a Place* by Sabrina Davis (2021), *This Southern Land: A Social History of Kangaroo Island, 1800-1890* by Jean M. Nunn (1989), and *The Forgotten Islands* by Michael Veitch (2011). I recommend all these excellent books if readers are curious to learn more about this unique part of southern Australia.

I acknowledge the complex history of Indigenous Australians in this region and have tried to represent this as accurately and sensitively as possible in this work of fiction. People of the Ramindjeri, Ngarrindjeri, Kaurna and Barngalla nations were believed to inhabit this area approximately 16,000 years ago, before rising sea levels later caused Kangaroo Island to become separated from the mainland of South Australia. I acknowledge the region has understandable sensitivities, which I have tried to capture in the spirit of equity and inclusiveness. If I have underrepresented or misrepresented anyone from the region with the material portrayed in this novel, I apologise; I know I cannot do them full justice here. I acknowledge the Traditional Owners and Custodians of the lands, waters and skies where this story is set, and pay my respects to Elders past, present and future, and honour those who continue to share their wisdom and learning with new generations. I also acknowledge all Australian Aboriginal and Torres Strait Islander peoples as the first inhabitants of the nation of Australia and the traditional custodians of the lands where we live, learn and create. Sovereignty has never been ceded. This always was, and always will be, Aboriginal land.

PETER PAPATHANASIOU was born in northern Greece in 1974 and adopted as a baby by an Australian family. His first book, a memoir entitled *Son of Mine* (Salt), was published in 2019. Peter's writing has otherwise been published by *The New York Times, Chicago Tribune, The Seattle Times*, the *Guardian, The Sydney Morning Herald, The Age, Good Weekend, The Australian Financial Review*, ABC and SBS. He holds a Master of Arts in Creative Writing from City St George's, University of London; a Doctor of Philosophy in Biomedical Sciences from the Australian National University (ANU); and a Bachelor of Laws from ANU specialising in criminal law. *The Bolthole* is the fourth novel in the series that began with *The Stoning* (2021) and continued with *The Invisible* (2022) and *The Pit* (2023).